lardland

lardland

a new book of waste
part 1

richard eccles

First published in 2021 by

Red Hand Books
Kemp House, 152 - 160 City Road,
London
EC1V 2NX

www.redhandbooks.co.uk

ISBN 978-1-910346-43-3

A CIP catalogue record for this book is
available from the British Library

Prepared for publication by Red Hand Books
Cover design © Red Hand Books
Illustrations © Bethany Poolman

It’s fucked, mate, it’s all fucked

Adil of Casnewydd

About Georg Lichtenberg

He is not a character in this novel, but he is the inspiration behind a *New Book of Waste*. This is the sort of waste that he wrote over a thirty-five year period:

> *However did men arrive at the concept of freedom? It was a great idea.*
>
> *We cannot truly know whether we are not at this moment sitting in a madhouse.*
>
> *The prospect of mankind's progress towards greater perfection seems a dismal one when we consult the analogue of all that lives.*

He was born in 1742 and died in 1799, and began writing a series of *Notebooks* from 1765 onwards. These notebooks are collections of the writings of a man enjoying expressing honest thought, freed of dogma and restraint. For much of his life he was extremely popular as a writer and speaker.

He visited England and the court of George III where he enjoyed conversing in German with the Hanoverian monarch, who was so taken with him that he turned up unannounced at his lodgings. Lichtenberg visited the world's first production line in Birmingham and Margate, a popular bathing resort. Two things that did not exist in Germany at that time.

Many things he wrote would make ideal epigrams for books.

Prologue

Send me your story. You won't win a fiver, but fair's fair, if you get through these stories of fantasy and violence told to me, why shouldn't you want to let me read yours? No matter what I hear from people I meet, I always want more. I want to know what their quiet, grim, beautiful truth is, in all its shitty detail.

About You

Imagine the opposite of you. Think about it. Loads to go at. Write it down.

1

About Hope

A nice cup of tea. Teabag in a cup and add hot water. I sit back on the sofa, have a minute to myself. Stir it around a bit, maybe – just maybe – leave it to stand, if I have time. We try to keep it calm. No rush, no clocks, no limits. It's sometime around 10.30, I think. Had two in today. One by one. Before they get to talk to us in this room, they get a cup of tea and can sit in the warm, over in the Clubhouse. If they're asking for money they get referred, like a patient seeing a doctor. We get genuine people as well. I've left the bag in till now and now I feel I can take it out. Used bag goes in a glass ashtray for recycling. I add the milk. The eleven rules for serving tea seem as ancient as the *Rigveda*. Tea, like a lot of things, has gone down the pan.

Chow Mein takes a biscuit from the tin and passes me the tin. I'm not having one, even though they're Authentic Biscuits from just down the road. I don't take hold of the tin, so he has to get up and put it on the shelf behind me. He crunches a brandy snap loudly to annoy me. He says nothing. I stare out of the window.

We get regulars and we get one-offs, we get mad ones and we get the lost and distraught and we get the ones that fall into every category of human unhappiness and there's a few of them we can help. Invisible cities of despair pressed ever closer together, packaged in a bundle of skin and bones with squeaky voices and dignity ebbing away to where it never comes back. I look down the narrow road past the circle of trees at a woman who comes up here often, pushing a buggy, with a jaw set into the wind and two kids struggling to keep up. She comes in the morning, says nothing to any of us, sits the kids at a table in the Clubhouse where she gets the food. She never asks what it is. She hardly speaks to the kids. She never says thank you. Then, she's off, back to where she came from, the kids becoming like her, slowly descending into a fierce silence. 'Same long coat,' I say to Chow Mein, 'every day same clothes.' He turns his head to look out of the window. He's been there, chasing his mother as a child, I suddenly realise, and gave up speaking almost before he started. He just looks at me.

First guy who came in was a witness in a court case. He'd stumbled on them, ripping the hell out of a family of badgers with their dogs. He's a bit of a twitcher, takes photos. He's being threatened, been attacked, had his car damaged by the gang of lads he testified against. He's been to the Police. He's having sleepless nights, panics, *he's going into himself*, in his own words. He describes what he saw in detail, but without the emotion. It's like a witness statement. He doesn't want to be alone in knowing that sort of horror. That sort of cruelty and inhumanity.

'What's the opposite of badger baiting?' I ask him.

He looks at me, lost for a moment. 'Not sure what you mean?'

'Find something that is the opposite of what you saw. Think about ways of getting control of these good things and allow the bad to be. And about the threats to you – are they serious, do you think?'

'They feel serious when you're on the end of them.'

'Are they online, on the phone or in your face?'

'Some online, somethings shouted at me – but the damage to my car and the attack outside my house were very real.'

'Yeah, that is nasty.' I paused. 'Do you think they'll stop

bothering you after a while? Maybe doing nothing's the answer.'

He looked away. 'You can't help either, can you? There's just nothing to be done, is there? Just let myself be bullied and intimidated until they get fed up or I end up in hospital.'

He had his head in his hands and he sat silently like that for more than five minutes. When he raised his head, he looked like he'd aged ten years. 'Thanks for your time.'

'Come back in a week, please. We'll do something. We will help.' He didn't look at me, but turned away and walked out.

The next person was a woman. 'I've come for my friend. She's a very good friend, and she's going through a lot of problems after what happened to her. She's asking me to help her, but I don't know what to do.' She takes a breath and looks straight at me, seems to be reliving earlier versions of this conversation. 'Don't tell me what to do, ok, or to get more help or anything like that. I've tried everything for her. I've already asked everyone you could think of asking. I just came here because –' she looks down, then away from me, but I just let the silence hang... 'I came here because, if I do stop looking, stop thinking there might be some justice, it's as if I've run out of hope because I've run out of people and then that's it, isn't it, it's just gone, evaporated, like it was never there. It really never happened. So, I've come here because someone said that they knew someone who, ages ago, you helped them...' She stops and looks straight at me. She doesn't move a muscle.

'Can you tell me what happened?'

'She was raped.' She is definite and prepared for the questions.

'That's terrible.'

'Don't you want to know how or why, or what else happened?'

'How can we help you and your friend? If you say you've spoken to everyone already, we'll do everything we can, but how can we help you?' The sunlight pours in the window and I shade my eyes. 'I'm thinking you – she – has been to the Police?'

'It *was* the Police. It was a policeman. 'Not enough evidence,' said the CPS, even though she knows him.' She looks at me, then turns away, as if disgusted by me, as well. 'She thought he was a friend.' Then she gets up to go.

'Leave your number and we'll put together a list of the options, everybody we know and every organisation who can help you and your friend. There are ways with these things. Whatever you do, for as long as you and your friend have the strength, do what you have to do so it doesn't destroy you.' She nods and leaves.

We discuss what we can do about both cases. Chow Mein wants to ride out and seek retribution for the weak and the mistreated and for all else who need it. He's seething with the injustice of it all, but doesn't release the words and the anger, just uses sign language to describe which bits he would cut off first. Then, we make a list for our second visitor and prepare a series of strategies for our first.

He quietly makes notes and sends out some instructions to Smoothie, who runs the database and everything else technical.

Then, I'm greeted by Dotty, who makes me feel like I'm the guest, as she hands over some baking as a present for doing something she says we did, but I don't really remember us doing it.

'By 'eck, this place needs tidying up,' she says, 'them cars 'n all that, down't road wants scrappin, young man. There's nowt fancy 'baht havin wrecks litterin' the place up 'n mekin' it all clarty. Somun's set fire to 'em. I have a good mind t'ring Polis an' do it me'sen if thee's too busy...'

'Very lovely to see you, Dotty, don't worry about the mess, it's all getting sorted in the proper channels –'

'You're chelping na,' an' ya drinkin' that flippin' type o' tea, ah'v told thee 'afore, they're all liars, every man jack on' em...'

'Dotty, what you on about?' I meant it.

'Believe nowt yer read an' only half of what yer see, is what I say.' I must have looked puzzled. 'You keep drinkin' this bloody tea, yer big lump, and sit here chuffed as Father Christmas an' supportin' half the criminals in't world.'

'Oh, I see, we're drinking the wrong sort of tea? But it's got Rainforest Alliance all over it, it's passed everything it could pass. And it actually tastes all right. You must know, you drink it as well.'

'I do not,' she says, 'I'd say their bloody Fairtrade wan't even fair-to-middlin' trade. Them folks have to pick twenty bloody kilos of the stuff, which in old money is more than three stone – think of it, yer big lummux, that's more than three stone of tea leaves in a day. While you 'ave to get someone to put yer bag in't cup.' She laughs at her own joke, then slurps from her cup.

'Yer knows what we says – where there's brass there's a fiddle – think abaht it, us all livin' t'life of Riley an' them uns barely on a dollar a day, so we can sit callin' over a brew. Na' yer flummoxed. If we dun do nowt, who the 'eck'll do it? Wha' yer 'av to say to tha' then, sittin' here all grand, like a Pasha at a weddin'.'

'You're right, Dotty, we have to do summat –'

'Well, frame thi'sen then. Ooh, my Frank'd put you lot dahn as a bunch o' saps. I'll go t'foot of ahr stairs if yer do owt useful or got any sense to it, I will as well. Yer know how old I am? Ah'm past 84 year old an' there's summat I wish'd ah'd known that there's bloomin politics and power-mongering and controlin' us an' settin' t'world up jus' as theys likes it, an' them that's runnin' t'country hav more brass than brains an' ah'm jus' bloody vexed by them poor lasses in India an' where hav yer, gettin' raped, an' HIV an' what have yer, an' livin' worse than beasts in t'fields an' now they's tryin' to do't same 'ere...'

Then, she looks up at me with red-rimmed eyes and her voice all wobbly, 'An' I'm jus' so bloody angry I din't fight, fight an' bloody fight 'em all me life, an' stop 'em jus' one bit, jus' one little bit o' summat ahd dun agens them what's throwin' us workin' folk in the shit, time after time...'

And she grasps me with her veiny hand. 'Do summat, all o' yers, do summat decent for all oursen's sakes.'

She pulls her hand back and takes a white lacy handkerchief out of her pocket and dabs her eyes. 'Start wi' tha' bloody tea you serve...' she says.

'We will, Dotty, we will make sure, we won't believe anything we read until we see it with our own eyes.'

'Ooh, ah forgot why ah came...' and she stands up. 'Don' tek no notice of owt I say, it's jus' a silly old woman cleckin'.'

'Dotty, do you want a lift somewhere?' She shakes her head.

I watch her walk off down the drive onto the road in her busy, wobbly way, till she disappears out of sight.

Chow Mein shakes his head. Wonder why she came? He looks the question at me. Chow Mein signs till he needs to speak, then he speaks.

'Not sure,' I say, 'I know she's been here before, but I can't remember why. I need to remind myself what she wanted or said last time. Do you remember her?'

He shakes his head.

'She's certainly a character. We need to sort the bloody tea out and check if what she's saying is right.'

It's right, he signs, *100%, I checked while she was talking.*

'What she was saying really got to me, I tell you, man, I was nearly blubbing with her and when she touched my hand, it felt like someone's message from a deathbed, regret and failure and despair.' I looked at him. 'This thing we're doing here is getting more and more difficult, you know? We're listening to this stuff coming at us and I'm floundering.'

Chow Mein nodded. Yeah. Then, he stood up and reached for the Authentic Biscuits biscuit tin.

‘No, thanks,’ I said. ‘I’m not in the mood. I can’t drink this tea and I can’t eat anything.’

Then he spoke out loud. ‘I’m not offering you a biscuit, I’m showing you the tin. Look at the tin, you big lummox,’ he said, laughing.

I took hold of the tin. ‘Yeah?’

He showed me the piece of paper he’d been writing notes on. It was a list of words and phrases.

‘Everything she said came off that tin, yer sap. I started writing down the phrases she used.’ He was laughing as he spoke.

Authentic Biscuits in an authentic tin. The tin’s got loads of funny, old-fashioned phrases from Yorkshire on it. I looked at them. More than twenty phrases that she’d cleverly linked together and delivered like a method actress who could have convinced my devout, tubby grandma to give up food and religion.

I shake my head. I’m looking at Chow Mein who’s searching in the tin for another biscuit.

‘Silly old cow, what was the point of that?’

He shrugs and goes back to his computer with another brandy snap to annoy me.

About Grit and Silt

People are rocks, aren't they, but in miniature? Laid down, fired up, dumped and deposited, burnt, squashed, crushed and exploited. Millenia happens in threescore and ten. Shunted, pushed around, other people overlaid in layers, moved from here to there and then flipped and folded and bent into ludicrous shapes so the thing that emerged at birth is barely recognisable at the end of the allotted time. Dust to dust. Cambrian to Silurian to Jurassic. Just look in the faces of some folk.

The River Aire flows between Malham and Airmyn for more than 140 kilometres. Rises on rocks that are more than 300 million years old then, falling into a hole to play cat and mouse, re-emerges unconvincingly, then passes Skipton to meet the Coal Measures, where the grit ends and the carboniferous softness of the newer rocks begin. Here, the waters begin to shape, scar and dictate the difference. And Leeds is halfway down. In the softness.

The rocks make the place and the rocks bear the river that scours the rocks that makes the place. And the silt fills the river that makes the crossing place.

The river was the source of drinking water until the 17th century for the folk of Leeds. After this the softness becomes the slow dying of the river. Where before, salmon were fished and noted men came to try their luck, by the early 1800s the river was devoid of life and the space around it was drowning in the industrialisation of human lives. A reservoir of poison, kept for the breeding of pestilence for its residents. Into it flowed all the debris of slaughterhouses, dye works, mills, gas works, privies, sewers, drains, infirmaries and mines. And more.

As the consequences of all this industry began to be felt, legislation was passed to limit pollution of air and water and as the smoke of the First World War cleared, so councils were moved to build homes for heroes. Public housing appeared, built according to strict guidelines. And at some point, on a slope above the river and the railway line on the one hand, and the empty green spaces rising to the valley divides on the other, a small-scale development was envisaged, houses with gardens and curving streets, greenery and trees. To seem like a village.

Then, the main road was widened, and a supply of clay was discovered in the widening of the road, so they moved the main road, knocked down some of the houses, and suddenly the 'village estate' had the sewage works on one side, steep land above the river and canal blocking in the other, and a clay mining site that ate into the land around them, literally, every year.

The stone Victorian factories making nails and rims and piping and other metal things along the canal shut down, and they put up a steel fence to keep people out of the disused works. Then, the clayworks became unviable and the workers made redundant. And the people kept getting fewer. The council didn't know what to do. They tried re-developing it, but that didn't work. A housing estate between a sewage works, an old claypit, disused factories, a railway line and a dirty river is not winning hearts and minds.

When the gangs moved in, the place was boarded up and sealed off so many times that slowly, with time, the place sank out of sight. The broken-down people deposited like silt.

2

Milton

I went and found a packet of teabags and read the statement on the side that Dotty had referred to. Was it true? Dollar a day, exploitation, no rights? I looked over my shoulder, Chow Mein is doing the same on his computer. For more than twenty minutes we read the reports on the web from *The Ecologist* and other sites: land grabs, sexual abuse, poor pay, exploitation. Of course the companies denied it. I picked up the packet again and read the words on the side of the packet for the third time. Chow Mein reached for another Authentic Biscuit.

'How can you do that?' I asked.

'What?' he said.

'Eat those biscuits.'

'Biscuits are fine, man.' Then, he switched to signing, *It's you who's letting it get to you...*

When everything changes forever, you have no idea at the time. Who can ever know that from any particular moment onwards, from here on in, everything will be different?

This one fidgeted as he walked across to sit on the sofa.

You can tell a lot about someone from what they choose to tell you and what they choose to leave out. His name was Milton. He said it wasn't his real name. But a real lie.

'If you tell me your name is Milton. It's real,' I said. I ask him what he wants to talk about.

He tells me about his days. Sounds bored of it all, the job and the journey to work. He goes to the gym but hates it, same routine in everything. He stops several times and stares and asks me why would I want to listen to this. I tell him to just talk, so he does, about his lunchtimes and how he's already eaten the stuff he brings for lunch before lunch, and how he sometimes goes out and buys himself a whole piece, just for himself.

'Piece?' I ask, 'that's a strange word. Why that word?'

'You know, a piece that the wife buys for the whole family.'

'What do you eat that you bring with you?' I ask

He pauses, starts to frame in his face the questions. *What do you want to know this for? What's this all about?* But stops himself. 'I usually get a crappy tomato, sandwiches, bag of crisps.'

'What sort of 'crappy' tomato?' I ask.

'Red one,' he says.

I wait for him to answer. He's reluctant to speak, as if he's working out who's taking the piss of who.

'Usually smallish, tasteless, sort of sweet...watery. The sort you have to put in your mouth completely, otherwise the fuckin' thing spurts everywhere if you bite into it.' He goes quiet and cloudy. 'I notice that I never get one of those tomatoes attached to the green viney-thing that I see in the fridge. Wife must be doing something else with them.'

'What else could she be doing with them?' This question takes even longer to answer. Half a minute maybe. I'm thinking he's holding back.

'Doesn't she like the small, watery, tasteless ones that she gives you? Have you ever asked her?'

He fidgets with his ear, he's not looking at me.

'You asked me about what I do on my drive home. You asked me, remember, to tell you about going home, from work, like, the journey. The whole routine thing.'

I nod. I'm wondering what he wants, and why he's talking about what his wife makes him for lunch. It feels like he's only half telling me the truth. I want to tell him to get on with it, thinking about the poor guy being terrorised by the badger gang, or the woman whose friend has been raped. I don't know why I'm wasting time on this one. But I don't say anything. For my sake, not his. Just keep listening and asking.

He speaks quickly, as if he hadn't let himself admit he has been waiting to tell someone for a long time, 'I don't hate the job, but sometimes I do. I could be much higher up, but I open my mouth and I haven't always made myself popular. I want to tell them like it is, that's all. Nothing uppity or clever arse, just what's wrong, why the track doesn't always work, and the ordering system is too heavy-handed and how some of the guys are working the system and I could make it so they can't. So, by the end of the day I've had enough. By the end of the day, I walk out the door and I'm pretty pissed off. That's typical. That's very typical. Can't always tell you why, and sometimes I'm not.

'First time, a while ago now, maybe four or five months ago, I drove to a part of town that I didn't know. Didn't want to go home. She's often out anyway, the wife, so she didn't notice or say anything at first. Bingo or sick relatives or something. Ann Summers, maybe. Always something. Anyway, this part of town, full of empty little streets and old boozers on a corner, always seemed deserted. Felt right to stop, park the car, get out and just drift into one of these little corner pubs. I find out it's called 'Sid's' from the guys in there. It became my stopover. It's become my little game. It's not a game, though, is it? I don't know. I park somewhere different every time I go there. Outwit them, you see.'

All the time he talks, I'm watching him as closely as I can, but I don't look at him. I try to feel his words, coming from a small-framed body, once wiry like a terrier, in that English squaddie way. His breathing is shallow, coming from what were once a fit pair of lungs but now gone to seed. Once upon a time, he smoked, but hasn't for a long while. He's losing his hair. He doesn't sound like he eats well. At some point as an adult he lived in Derby, but he wasn't born there. There are layers to his accent and he maybe be able to switch easily between Birmingham and North Midlands and other places off the M1. There's a tremor in his voice that could mean he's lying. But, more often than not, there's a tremor in people when they tell the truth. There's more to fear in the truth.

'When did you give up smoking?'

He's taken aback. 'I dunno.' He shakes his head and moves his mouth and chin, almost ready to accept the fagbutt. 'Five years ago, maybe less.'

'Why?'

'Why what?'

'Why did you give up smoking?'

'I dunno. Just did. Didn't want to do it anymore, I suppose.'

'Cost? Health? Hygiene? A woman? People like you don't have the power to just give up like that.'

I liked the reaction. 'Fuck off,' he said. Then he shrank back down again.

DON'T PUT YOUR HEAD ABOVE THE PARAPET.

'Sorry,' he said, 'it just came out. You see what I mean?'

'Did you mean it?'

He didn't answer. He's looking round the room. Curious, but trying not to seem as if he's taking too much of it in. Accepting without comfort. There's a microphone on the table that he can see but it isn't attached to anything that works. There's a camera hidden behind me, pointing at him, that's filming his every move. And there are at least two microphones in this shitty little council house front room with a shabby e-Bay suite, where the Friedbreads like Milton sit and explain their situation.

He won't know about any of them. On my right, against the window is Chow Mein looking bored, playing with a pencil and paper, as if he's making notes. He does make notes but they aren't words, because he hates writing. He got a pencil and compass through the neck at school. He got lead poisoning, excluded and school phobia from then on, but not in that order. He doesn't have to write because he remembers everything he ever hears. It's his hobby.

'If you meant it, then it's true.'

'But I came here for you to help me.'

I didn't answer. I wanted to look straight at his eyes at that very moment and find something to work with. Lined and puffy, supported by one or two soft folds of skin, tiny little veins apparent just under the surface of the skin, dry and lacking the oily liquid, easing movement, small, a little too close together, too round, too beady, too eager but brown and vulnerable. And tagged onto these mirrors of the soul, two patches of lilac-grey around the outer corners, the one on the right bigger than the other one. I wonder what he really is.

In Australia, people squint because of the sun so their eyes are distinctively lined and marked. Probably not a place for white people, at their present state of evolution. In Lardland, eyes are damaged by other things.

He shifts in his seat and would light up if he could. His arms and hands move between reaching for his pockets, clenching his fists, and trying to fold them.

'Milton, can I ask – do you do work that strains your eyes?'

He hesitates. 'My eyes aren't your problem. You aren't a bloody doctor, are you, why are you going on about my eyes? I came here so that you can help me. Can you help me?' He backs off again. 'I know my eyes are all right. I can see just what I want to see.'

This time, he doesn't apologise. If it were in a pub or down the club and he was this agitated, he'd pick a fight. If he'd had a drink or two, then he'd be up for it. *Don't push me*, he smells of it. *Not here.*

'Take your right shoe off.'

'No way.'

'Take your shoe off. I want to show you something. It won't hurt, I promise.'

I nod to Chow Mein to get up close and personal. Milton bends to remove his shoe and sock and comes up puffing with them in his hand. Chow Mein goes right up to him, eyeball to eyeball. Milton looks worried. Chow Mein has to bend down quite a bit.

'Eh, steady up, feller...'

'Chow Mein won't bite, but he sometimes likes to sniff.'

'What?' Milton's looking at me but finding it hard to catch my eye 'cos Chow Mein is so big. 'What's going on? I ain't done nothing. What's happening?'

'Steady. Relax.'

I like the theatre, so I take it very steady myself. Chow Mein is a mean actor and instinctive and fierce. We call him Chow Mein because he's got red, sticky-up hair and he's big. He actually feels like the size of a council house porch. He doesn't speak much on account of what has happened to him, but when he does, it often leaves me unable to speak.

He can also be mean as fuck. He sits out of the way when people come round to see me. They stop noticing him after a while. They are right to ignore him because he ignores them. He loves just sitting, imagining he's on the palace steps or the courtyard of a Buddhist temple, wagging his tail at the monks as they pass by or growling viciously at a visiting dignitary from a faraway province. He's fanatical vegetarian. He'd put garlic up every orifice of every punter if I let him.

'Breathe out slowly.'

Milton doesn't quite get it.

'Milton, breathe slowly into Chow Mein's face.'

Milton has never breathed into a man's face like this before. He turns. Chow Mein is as impassive as a trained dog. He blows. Chow Mein doesn't budge.

'No, relax. Take a deep breath. Then breathe out slowly. Enjoy it. It's a lot worse for him than you.'

Milton tries but it's still too blowy. He tries again. Chow Mein remains utterly unmoved. Then Milton smiles. He isn't going to be beaten. He takes a breath and breathes slowly into another man's face. With impunity.

'What do you smell, Chow Mein?'

'Instant coffee. Greasy meat. Processed stuff. Floury bread. Tooth decay.'

'Milton, that sounds like the last thing you ate was a kebab. Is that true? Milton, it's half-ten in the morning? When did you eat the kebab? Last night?'

Milton looks uncomfortable again. 'No.'

'When then?'

'This morning. I stop off for one on the way to work. There's a takeaway that's open 24 hours a day near us. I can't tell the wife, but if I'm feeling a bit down, I stop off for a quick one. How did you know, anyway? How did he know? What you lot on?'

'Milton, rub this on your foot. The one without the sock. Don't argue. Remember – Chow Mein found greasy processed meat, instant coffee and floury bread on your breath. Is that fair to say?' I hand him a clove of garlic.

Milton shakes his head but does as he is told. As he's doing it, I ask him again about his visits to Sid's.

'You said 'outwit' a minute ago. What did you mean?'

Milton is still rubbing. Whatever else you might say about Milton, he's a good worker and probably does what you want most of the time, very obediently.

'Outwit them, yeah. Look at it. A man can't go to the boozer without being on camera. There's CCTV everywhere nowadays. How many times a day is every bastard one of us caught on camera? Ten? Twenty? Thirty? I bet some people are on camera more often than Bruce Forsyth. You look up and they're there, everywhere. Sinister-looking, grey and silent. Some of 'em even move. Someone is sitting somewhere with a joystick, getting off on making 'em twitch and turn and pointing 'em at whoever they fancy or whoever they hate. For that moment, they just pick on people 'cos they're bored and why? If someone does something bad, it doesn't help at all. All you see are some vague figures, usually in hoodies or crappy, chavvy clothes, not that they need them anyway, them hoodies, 'cos you can't see nothing with them CCTV cameras, anyway. Just a joke, all them cop shows where they're looking through the footage and get the proof they need and find the murderer or some bloke having a wank in the flowerbeds. It just so pisses me off 'cos we're letting 'em spend millions of our money on stupid cameras and monitors and people who are doing nothing but spying on us. Don't they know it's our country as well?'

'Yeah, but if you ain't doing nothing wrong then what have you got to worry about?' I said, hoping for a reaction.

'What about freedom? Civil liberties, all that stuff? If we're going about our normal business, then why do they have to film us? I don't want to be on film. I ain't doing nothing wrong when I go to the boozer for an after-work drink, so why am I on film twenty times? Why ain't they pointing the cameras in a different direction?'

'What do you mean?'

He looks red-faced and he's still got one sock on and one sock off. He's peering at me and then at Chow Mein and then back at me, but only half-looking, like a dog, for something more than he's getting.

'Look, I don't know what I mean, really. I'm an ordinary bloke, right? A proper Englishman and I go to the boozer in secret 'cos it's about all I can think of to do. We were brought up to do what was right and that we lived in a decent country and Dunkirk and all that. My Grandad was at Dunkirk and his dad was in the trenches. It ain't special.'

He had more to say but he went very quiet. He was looking away and then, when I looked away, he looked at me. There was the tremor again that I'd heard before in his voice.

DON'T PUT YOUR HEAD ABOVE THE PARAPET.

'What's the point?' He was suddenly deflated and slumped back into the couch. He seemed tiny against the worn, red draylon and shrank into the corner, against the big arm.

THINK THE SAME. BETTER STILL, DON'T THINK.

'What am I telling you this for? Outwit them, hahaha. Outwit them? What a joke. I can't even outwit my wife and I don't know who *them* is. I come here to you and I try to tell you what's going on and all I'm telling you is this shit about tomatoes and cameras and shit...and end up sitting here like a wanker, with my trouser leg rolled up and no shoes or socks, rubbing something into my foot while a big ginger bruiser smells my breath. Get real, will you. Fuck's sake.'

He goes to put his sock on, full of angry energy again. He's really fighting his own sock and scratches his leg as he struggles getting the heel and the toe to line up comfortably. 'Fuck'.

I feel I have to give him something.

'I need people like you.' He cocks his head at me, like a retriever waiting for the shoot. He stops everything to listen.

'What?

'I listen to people everyday, whenever they come to me for help, I try to help. I listen to a lot of people who feel really down, in despair or frightened. Two days ago, a guy comes to me. Reminds me of you. Nice guy. Maybe he'd call himself ordinary. He ain't an idiot either. Huge hands, I remember he had huge hands that he holds out to me. He doesn't speak for ages. Sits where you're sitting. I don't know if he's committed murder, robbed a bank or wants to borrow a fifty. He comes in, sits down. Looks me in the eye just the once, and nods. Then, he sits and slowly, before my eyes, he crumples. Huge hands laid out and upwards as if he is asking for something, begging, and all the while, his head slumps further and deeper into his chest and his shoulders shrivel and I watch a man on this same seat unravel, wordlessly, in front of me. I watch the only things that aren't unravelling: his huge, great, calloused, dry, twitching hands. I never thought I'd ever see a person drown. Not on dry land, anyway. Not in this house. You know what I heard, Milton?' I paused as I remembered the sounds. 'The slow, faraway, choking, dry retching of a huge man with huge hands.'

I can see his hands again in front of me, even though he is long gone.

'He held out his hands for a very long time and I watched as they seemed to disconnect themselves from his body, take on a life of their own. And I'll tell you, I was scared, I was really very scared. Of all the shit and nonsense and stupidity and violence I've seen in my life, I've never faced my own self like I did in those long moments. What he was feeling, God only knows, in those moments, in that seat where you're sitting. But, I'll tell you that I regret every moment that I didn't reach out and put my hands into the twitching, reaching hands of a drowning man. I could pass him in the street and not know his face, but those cold, huge hands have changed everything.'

Milton had stopped everything, but once I stopped speaking, he tried again to shift his sock around, so that foot and form were aligned.

'Tell me how you'll outwit them. Then, we'll deal with them.'

He looks at me like he's changing his mind, and makes one

last adjustment to the alignment of sock and toe and foot and slips his shoes back on. Tan slip-ons.

'My wife's called Sandra, everyone calls her San. I call her, San the Man. She can press triggers I didn't know I had. We've discussed marriage guidance, but I think I really need something different – an effin' hitman might help. One day, she's on to me about a letter we got off a credit card company about an unpaid bill. I said I didn't use that card. I didn't think we had it anymore. She said that we did have it and I used it as much as she did. Usual shit. I found out later that it was the card with my name on it, that we hadn't used for ages which I'd presumed was dead, so I cancelled the direct debit on it. Only, she went and used it without telling me. Dinner out in some famous chef's place in Leeds for £124. *That's a lot of eating when you're on your own*, I said to her. I remember it well, the argument that is, 'cos it was the first time I put my fist up to her. I didn't even ask her who she was with. I think she was drunk and paid with the wrong card, and then forgot about it, and that's when we got charged loads more charges. So, *I* ended up owing them nearly £250 for a meal that my wife had had with some other geezer.'

Milton stops. Then, he looks uncomfortable and pulls his shoe off and inspects the inside, as if he had a stone in there, then slips it back on.

'I can't remember what I came here for. Why I'm talking to you. I feel like that drowning man who was here where I am now...and what's all this bloody bollux about rubbin' garlic on my feet.? What's all that about?'

'No rush,' I said, ignoring the garlic remark, for now.

He leans forward a moment, his head hanging down almost to his hands on his knees, then rises up like he's just surfaced.

'Have you ever put your fist in your wife's face? Could you imagine what that makes you feel like? Shit, I tell you. Like the low-lifers and the perverts you read about in *The Sun*. I'll never forget that. I didn't sleep all night, slept in the spare room, going over and over what was wrong, not just between me and the wife, but in everything. I didn't want it to be like this, all anger and rowing and feeling churned up all time, not knowing if I'm going to get home from work without punching someone, not knowing if I'm going to get through an evening without punching the wife, not doing anything except prowling...I'm lying in my bed...' Milton is struggling now, '...lying in my bed feeling angry with everything and everybody. Asking myself why my life is so shit. How the fuck did I end up like this? A piece of crap threatening his own wife. No one to come home to. Job, money, marriage...all of it...what? Floating in the shit? Sinking in the shit...?'

He takes a tissue from the box on the coffee-table. *Do you mind?* he asks with his eyes. *Of course not*. He takes a breath.

'So, I got up in the middle of the night. I was still very angry, and I'd planned to go down and show her what it was like living with her, by wrecking her precious kitchen, smashing it up like some stupid kids had been there, who just get pleasure out of ruining something that doesn't belong to them. But, as soon as I got down there, I knew I couldn't do it. That would've been the end. The final straw. So, I left her a note and stuck it in the fridge. You do some daft stuff when you're all over the place.'

I AM SORRY
BUT THIS FRIDGE IS HALF MINE

'I felt like I had staked my claim to something. At work the next day I was on time, kept myself busy and stayed the full course of the day. At the end of the day, I was finishing off when the boss bent over my desk and asked me to come to his office. I thought he was going to ask me for a drink or my opinion about a new project.

'There's been a complaint,' he says.

'About what?' Not getting his drift straightaway.

'About you.'

'About me?'

'Yeah, I'm afraid so.'

'From who?'

'Can't tell you that, at the moment.'

'Someone had seen me repeatedly pocketing stock in an unsavoury way, apparently. What that was supposed to mean I don't know. They said they had CCTV footage, and it was going to be handed over the to the Police.'

'Where are the cameras in this building?'

'In places you might not expect', he said, as if it was funny. 'Would I sign a piece of paper to say that I was resigning with immediate effect? Or did I want the *ignominy of going through a police investigation?*

'To be honest. I was so churned up I couldn't think straight. I couldn't for the life of me remember if there were any CCTV cameras in the building. They just wanted me out. But my mind is racing. Who wants me out? Why? What's going on? All the questions you ask yourself when you get...I don't know... cornered.'

'What happened then?'

'As usual I was angry. I threatened him a bit, told him he was a liar, told him what I thought of him and the company, told him he could call security, they were my mates. Turned out, of course, that they weren't really my mates and had jobs to do, and I was thrown out by all three of them. Never was allowed back. The one thing that was on CCTV was me being manhandled out the door, but not the punch to the chest, in the car park, by a guy who I used to think was a mate.'

I watch his mouth move as his tongue rubs itself all over his teeth, as if he's looking for something hidden in his mouth. And he's clenching his fists, then releasing them, then clenching them again.

I let him take his time.

'I get in my car, take some deep breaths. They've ripped some buttons off my shirt and my jacket is scuffed. I didn't want to go home. I don't feel angry, I just feel crap, crap about myself, and crap 'cos I can't do anything about anything at all. I needed a beer, but now I'm in no rush. I've got away early, haha...so, I do the usual route and start to spot the cameras and count them. They're everywhere: at traffic lights, on streetlamps, on the sides of buildings, at entrances to shopping centres, businesses, car parks, banks, even churches have got them. I've never noticed them, but I've lived with them all these years. How long have they been there? When did they first start to come in? Why? Who pays for them? I'm getting angry again. I'm punching the steering wheel. I'm shouting up through the windscreen at these vampires, these eyes, these fucking school prefects telling on us all. And as I shout up these soundless words, somewhere faraway, but not too faraway – maybe these guys are faraway, like in Scunthorpe or somewhere with cheap labour – I'm sure there's some twat looking back at me, focusing in on me, shouting soundless words as well – 'Get a life, tosser. Get real, tosser. Go away, tosser. Loser. You're a loser.' And then, just as suddenly, he switches to another camera where there's something more interesting to perv at, like a group of ten-year-olds with sticks, teasing a little girl of six with special needs.'

He looks taut and slumped all at once. 'You look tired.'

'No, it's just beginning. I want to start the fight-back. But I need a drink to think about it. My chest is wheezing. I'm gagging for a fag, even though I can't breathe and feel bruised and shaken. For the first time since I started my little drinking outings, I park somewhere else. Sid's is two streets down from a main road, with a flyover. Sometimes I park down this little dead-end street about a hundred yards away. It's always dark down there, even on a sunny evening. But this time, I park about ten minutes' walk away. I need time to think. It's really strange down there. Loads of little terraced houses, redbrick, poor, rundown. A little triangle between the motorway going north out of the city, the old gasworks, the flyover and the old sauce and pickle factory. Funny thing is, there ain't never any people around. Never hardly ever seen a soul. Is there anyone in those houses, I'm thinking? Just immigrants, illegals and poor old bastards stuck there, waiting for an intruder. People who remember what it was like when decent people lived there, and everyone knew everyone else. The sound of your shoes echoes down there. For the first time in my life, I heard my own footsteps, like I was the only one left alive. It was so weird. Everything's feeling weird though. I'm shivering in the sun. Desperate for some people, some real noise, not just the sound of cars somewhere in the distance. I cross a road and turn right, past a plot of land with those spiky grey railings that split into two lethal points at the top. There's weeds growing three foot high between the big slabs of concrete. I stop and stare in. Out of nowhere, this mental alsation comes running at me, barking insanely, and I pull back, instinctively. It stops and doesn't jump at me 'cos it knows it'll hurt itself more than me. Then, I hear a voice shouting at me from across the plot. Some goon in a peaked cap on the steps of a portakabin telling me to fuck off and stop upsetting his dog, or he'll set it on me. We can't see one another too well 'cos of the distance, but I step back and coo at the dog and take the scene in. A man in a uniform with a dog in a portakabin guarding a completely empty plot of land that's fenced in. Nothing to steal, nothing to vandalise, no walls to graffiti, just crappy, rutted, worn slabs of concrete on a corner plot of a dead place. Put a fat twat in there with a peaked cap and a sad dog and pay him the minimum wage. The dog follows me barking all the way to the end of the fence. So does the cormorant in the cap.'

'Cormorant?'

'I used to be into birds, before I was married. Everyone's got the characteristics of a bird in them, somewhere. Struck me since I was a kid how people look more like birds than humans.'

There's a silence again. No rush. A crowd of faces comes swarming in. The people who've come and talked. They swarm in and leave, and all I feel is empty. Sometimes, they come just to talk, sometimes they come to listen and for help. Most of the time they know the answers and most of the time they can't face the action. I make a note of their names and when they come to see me and what they tell me, only I write down maybe five words, sometimes ten. Sometimes, I help them, most of the time, I don't need to. Listening is enough. To feel the tides and currents under the surface of their words is not a gift. But the people need the theatre, so the people think it's a gift.

My father used to say, 'Talking is enough. All you need to do is to talk. All the issues of the world could be solved by talking.' And so, he would talk, like a man with a list waiting for someone with an empty tablet of stone:

The greatest leader who ever lived
The three nations of the world who have taught the others how to live
The finest batsman to swing a bat
The songwriter par excellence
Why I nailed 'If' to a kitchen unit
The failures of Labour governments
What's lacking amongst today's youth is National Service
The Princess: British Leyland's onto a winner
Take the tellies off lazy coal miners
Why they can't cook fish and chips south of Sheffield

Including South Yorkshire was his version of being magnanimous. Not mentioning his half-brother, Jack, a shop steward at a Barnsley pit, was part of a much bigger series of issues. There was no end to the great thinker's explanations of how exceptional his radical ideas were:

How to dig a garden pond in a weekend
Why Wales and Norway are the same place
How to put an LP on a record player
Using B roads is better
Most inventions were British
Why would I want go to to see friends, relatives, children or old people, or go to the supermarket or the library or put the bins out or even visit my wife in hospital?
Or why go to your best friend's funeral whose wife rang you specially?
Mostly everything was British if you looked
Why would you want to go to Wimbledon/Glastonbury/Church/Disneyland/the dentist/Shakespeare's house/the Bingo/Fleetwood/parents' evening/the Council tip?
The Royal British Legion snooker room is the Colosseum where modern gladiators fight and the only place worth putting trousers on for
Certain pie manufacturers of his youth
The sanctity of motherhood & the Queen
Personal hygiene, fastidiousness, the washing of hands, cleaning nails, nail files, filing nails, regular shapes of finger nails, cleaning nail files, washing feet, clipping & filing toenails, placing a towel where clipping is to be done, not leaving scraggly ends, hoovering around the chair
Why using B roads is killing Britain

I did nothing but listen. I listened for as long as I can

remember. In fact, I got so obsessed with listening that I started to study the use of silence in language and reading about communities where *not* speaking is the general rule and the complex and fascinating rules of silence in politeness and status strategies and protocols. The language of silence.

REDUCE EVERYTHING TO NOUGHT.

Milton starts talking again. 'And I can't get this cormorant out of my mind, like he's the same cormorant as the boss at work who just sacked me and, you know, I keep seeing these strange connections and it's really shaking me up...'

He pauses again, like things are taking shape, but cloudily, a long way away, that he can't quite touch. His hands are clenching and unclenching into fists, and his foot is twitching as if there's a stone still irritating the flesh.

'I see what I haven't noticed before. When I drive, I don't take anything in, but now, I can see these little houses are neat, not spacious, but safe and neat. And between them, at regular intervals, are little alleys for people to get round the back and into little courtyards. In one little alley are two lads, maybe fifteen, hanging out. One's white, pale, skinny in a baseball cap, the other's mixed race, shorter, healthier looking. They're smoking and talking. 'Hey, mate, need any gear?' says the white kid. I don't get what he means at first, I'm still feeling the punch to the stomach from the security guard, and the bruising is settling into my ribs and throbbing.

'The other one speaks quickly to his mate, 'Look at the fuckin' state of him. Like a pikey, man.' I'm still too slow. Who does he mean? Me? Why is he speaking like that? Then, just 'cos I look easy meat, the white kid does a sort of kung-fu side kick at me, right-footed, balanced neatly on his left. It catches me a glancing blow on the right side, but I'm knocked off balance. I hear them laugh. I'm thinking, What is this? Why am I being kicked by these two lads who I don't know and have no quarrel with? I go down. They stick the boot in. I haven't got a chance. I don't know how long I was down. I curled up, like you do, but when I rolled over to try to get up, I looked up at the white kid, full on in the eye, I saw something so frightening in there that I shiver when I think about it.

'He was shouting abuse, of course, swearing and all that, effing and blinding, as if I'd murdered his mother, holding his cap, so that it wouldn't get in his way or block his view of his kicking. I looked in his eyes and I saw glee. The only word for it. You don't often see it. Not proper, childish, innocent glee. Glee in his eyes and anger on his face and violence and hate in his voice.

'They stop kicking and the mixed race one starts to run off. I hear why, rather than see why. A voice with a foreign accent has opened an upstairs window. 'Stop it,' she's shouting, 'stop it now. I'm going to call the Police.'

'The white boy comes back for one last kick and I manage to put my hands up to deflect it. When I pull myself up, they've run off down the street. I look round. All the windows are closed. I couldn't tell you from which one the voice had come. It was the soft voice of someone from the West Indies.

'I get up. No cars. No people. Nobody. No sound. Nothing. My shirt's ripped, my body aches, my face is bleeding, my jaw aches and one eye is shutting. I want a drink. In my own town, all I want to do is to walk to the pub for a drink. Stupid, ain't it? I'm so thirsty. I get across the road, walk to the flyover, fall over under the flyover. Pull myself up. All the while checking, touching, moving exaggeratedly, making sure nothing's broken. Nothing is broken. Means I can have a beer. Open the door at Sid's. They don't know me too well, but some of them usually nod. It's very quiet today, but when I walk in, it goes even quieter. Barman is a fat geezer, sullen type, sixties, seen all the shit in the world, or so he thinks. 'Beer, please.' He looks at me like I'm gonna be trouble. 'Not sure it's a beer you need.' 'Just a beer,' I say. He lets me stand at the bar while I drink it. My mouth feels like it's already been wired, and I can hardly move it. I never realised you could feel as if your mouth was made up of a hundred pieces that wouldn't work together. I know the beer is cold 'cos I spill a lot of it down my front. After three attempts at drinking it, my legs go, and I go down again, collapse at the bar. No one moves or someone moves. Some arms get me up and help me and park me on the seating. Five minutes later, I find myself being lifted up and half dragged, half-carried out of the pub. Two guys, perhaps a third hovering. They take me to the main road by the flyover. They leave me there, propped against a wall. I'm feeling totally out of it and can't quite make sense of time or what's happening. I hear an ambulance. Feel the lights and am asked questions I don't know the answers to. Then, they put me into the ambulance. Next day, I'm discharged from hospital, patched up, bruised, aching worse than ever.'

He stopped there. He was different now, but so am I. What happens to the listening mind and the expectant body and the suffering space around the soul as the tale chases *The Next Thing*, like following a swallow in summer gathering food on the wing. I wince when I hear of a wincing body on the stone of a deserted street. I feel the air bashed out of my body when I hear a body being kicked by the booted feet of angry men. I ache and am dazed as the events happen too quickly and the mind doesn't catch up with the flailing, running, shouting, swirling demons pulling me along. I have to stand up to speak. The room changes during the *information* – the word for what we hear when people come and tell us what they want us to know, for whatever reason they want us to know it.

'Milton, are you ok?' I pause, trying to weigh him up and work out where this was going. 'You need a walk round outside, take a breath. Sounds like you've had a tough time. Take it easy for a moment, we'll get you something to drink.'

And he looks up. 'Ok.'

I think it was me who needed the break. 'Just give me a minute...' and I walk out into the kitchen. I'll put the kettle on, take my time. I'll take him a cup of tea in, won't ask him. Outside, I have a moment to recollect.

This is a very ordinary house, at the head of an ordinary street. Except, there are no 'ordinary' streets, with 'ordinary' houses full of 'ordinary' people, not really. Was your house like everyone else's house? Isn't every house a kingdom, lived in by a series of dynasties, each with people playing for power and caught up in tales, as valid and as powerful as the House of Lear or the House of David? No house can be an island but belongs instead to the mainland, with neighbours as wild as Cyclops or as peaceable as San, forming regions in unknowable cities, as large as continents.

For the dweller in Leeds cannot honestly say that in London they don't do things differently there. And to come from London to Leeds is to cross invisible boundaries. Imagine arriving at the mouth of the Amazon, landing you on Platform 8 at the Railway Station, and as the swimming tides of people come against you, miss nothing of the overhead paths through the steel trees, the swirl of comings and goings on boats on rails, the clothes of the people who all look different, the colours and tones of the melting pot of human skins and shapes and bones and brains. In the air at the station taxi rank, listen to the dialects of the people in the brewer's air and the stoops of the sullen or the briskness of the busy. From the street pavements, look at how they sell their wares or what they buy or who they're with and how they leave their houses. Find me here in this magic house.

Follow the main river of traffic due west for nearly a mile. Go north, where the watery stream is hidden underground in pipes and concrete conduits. From here, you will see how everything changes. Fewer cars, fewer people, long distances hard to describe. At the stone marked with cup and ring and formerly a place for dancing, which is the highest point and flattest point, you will have walked far more than an hour. Fifty yards due north is the quiet tributary of tarmac, the only way into our world. In this treeless jungle, every comer-in is seen by the eyes that are everywhere and we move as one. You will not believe me if you do not believe me. But walk on, follow the turns of the paved streams and the banks of verges and always aim higher, keep the sun behind you and as it goes down, to the left of you. We have removed the names of the streets. You will come, by and by, to a pair of rowan trees. This marks the main entrance to the way to this house. Go between them, and see how we have planted the street with our own trees, still sacred and powerful, oak around yew and alder and elder around oak and hazel and apple around alder and ash, until a circle of land opens up, wide enough for the whole people to stand and be. A sacred circle. No plaque, no sign, no monuments. But to the people this is sacred land. At the head of this circle is a house, with a covered stone at the head of the driveway. In this house is where we are.

I find Milton is odd again when I get back in. 'I'm taking up your time. I'm...I'm –' He gets up to go, but doesn't want to go.

Chow Mein has a blank face, nothing's happened.

'I've made you a brew. Only go when you're ready. Here.'

I pass it to him without asking and sit down. He accepts it and then puts it down on the table.

I sit back, look as if I have the time to sit back. Don't need to speak. I'm not sure I know where this is going. I'm not feeling sure that I believe him, but I'm not sure why I shouldn't. I'm nearly half-way down my brew when he starts speaking again.

'Listen, I read the papers, watch the news. Reading about the scroungers, the foreigners, the fuckwits freeloading, whoever they are. It makes me so fucking angry.' Pause. 'People come here just so they can have their teeth done or grandad's heart bypass or I don't know, 'cos they've got bad wind and a soggy arse. I dunno. That's what they tell us. I believe it. Then, I don't want to believe it, I want to know it's just lies. Then, I want to scream at the bastards robbing and thieving off of other people with nothing or off the old people. What are you supposed to do with this stuff when you read it? Current affairs or whatever they call it. Bollux. It's sickos and psychos doing what comes naturally, more like. Then, when they catch them, they give 'em a colour telly and a right good listening to. 'Why exactly did you insert your penis into the barely developed vagina of your girlfriend's eighteen-month-old baby girl? You must be very traumatised. Would you like a couple of DVDs and some blow to calm your shattered nerves?' Bollux, man, total bollux. Then, when they don't have the real bitchy, spoilt Diana anymore they give us the dead Diana, the saintly Diana, the new Diana, the unreleased Diana, the confessions of Diana, the Butler's Diana, the naked Diana, Big Brother Diana or Lezzie Diana in all-girl three-in-a-bed romp. Or the next Diana, Princess of Pouts and ten grand frocks. I can't stand it. I'm your next Drowning Man. I'm just so...fucked, man. Wife. Job. Everything. Fucked.' He bows his head before me. 'They even had to shave half my head to sew me up properly. It won't grow back.' I can see the bald patch on the right-hand side of the back of his neck.

He nurses his cup of tea, turning the cup round and round in his hand whilst looking at the floor, not drinking.

'That's why I've come here to see you. 'Cos it's all bollux and I need someone to help me. Before I do something really stupid.'

He looks up at me without swerving away, for the first time.

'You aren't going to do anything stupid, Milton.' I look at him trying to work out what's coming. 'What happened after you got out of hospital? How did you feel?'

He pauses. The phone rings in his pocket. He ignores it.

'Answer it, no worries,' I say. He gets it out and presses a button and the call goes away. His face switches into a grimace and then back again to lost.

'After the hospital, I felt I had an excuse to pretend I didn't have to go to work, 'cos I was off sick, wasn't I? She fussed a bit at first, 'cos it gave her something to talk about to her friends. But I don't remember her asking me how it happened or where or why or anything like that. She patted my head a couple of times, pulled a face when I started to tell her what happened as if to make me stop, so I stopped telling her any more of it.'

He puts the tea down, untouched.

'She told me she thought we ought to sleep in separate bedrooms. She didn't want to upset me after my 'fright'. And she'd made up the spare room. I lay around the house, hardly saw her for days on end. Once, when she did come back, she asked me if I had been to the Police. You know what, I never once thought of going to the Police. Last time I went to the Police to report my car stolen, I was cautioned, and they wanted to take my DNA 'cos they said I was being aggressive to the bitch behind the counter. She wasn't a real copper, just a completely up-her-own-arse admin bitch, so I didn't want to go there again. But I was feeling better, so I thought I ought to do something.' He looks around. 'I need a drink. Can I have a drink?'

I nod. People don't drink enough water. We filter it here and we analyse it every now and again to see what they're putting in it. We find all sorts of things in it: chlorine, fluoride, lead, pesticides, bugs, bacteria, fertilizers, drugs and estrogen from all those pills and powders being flushed through systems. So, we filter it a few more times, see if we can make it safer.

'Would you like some homegrown?'

Chow Mein brings in a jug of water, two glasses and an unlabelled bottle full of cloudy, pale yellowy-green liquid with a scum of tiny, white-petalled froth around the narrow part of the neck. I pour one glass of water and wait for him to respond.

'Do you have it neat? he asks. He needs a drink again.

'You can, but I wouldn't, not at this time of the day.'

He thinks we're hard-drinking gangsters. He pours himself a shot without water. He lifts it to his lips and swigs it back in one. His face goes very flushed as if he has an oyster stuck. He gargles and coughs and pulls faces.

'What the hell was that? It's like decorator's glue.'

'Don't you like elderflower cordial?'

'Whatever that is, no. It's like drinking my grandmother's flower water that she's had in her vase for two months. Disgusting.'

'It's better with water.' I pause again and mix some cordial with some water and pass it to him. 'Please. So, you were feeling better?'

He still pulls a face as he sips gingerly from the watered-down version and feels the particles of petals with his tongue and teeth, gnaws on them as if they are bones to be wary of. He's still swilling the liquid around as he puts the glass down.

'Tell me what you did when you felt better. Bring me to why we're here.'

He looks dry again, almost withered. 'I'm just an ordinary, practical bloke. I like to fix up the house. I sometimes think that's why she married me. If ever the washing machine broke, she could save herself the callout charge. With me around she didn't have to pay a gardener. I'd had enough of sitting and brooding and thinking and going over what happened. I'd had enough of being on my own in the house. I've got to face the thought of not having a job, so I went and tried to sign on. I got to about page twenty-four of the forms and stood queuing for about thirty minutes for help with some questions I didn't understand, when I got pissed off again. I went to the desk and was told from behind the screens to wait my turn. I said I've waited my turn long enough. She starts getting uppity with me, and so I start getting uppity with her and I look round me and there's like loads of people from everywhere – Poles, Asians and Africans and some losers from round here, and all sorts dressed in funny clothes and material wrapped round their heads and there's one gang of about twelve of them, not including the kids and wives, and half of them are getting translators and personal help and get shown into nice little fucking cubicles where they can shut the door so no-one can hear their sad, fucking sob story but when I've been stuck in this fucking place for an hour and no one gives a shit, even though I'm almost the only knob in there who's ever paid any taxes or done a day's work in this country...don't get me started again...just don't get me started. Fucking country we live in.'

SHOW AN EMOTION, SHOW ANGER.

He gulps down a whole glass of the elderflower cordial without pulling a face, other than the rigid, angry one he's got fixed at the moment.

'So, she calls security and he's a big, lanky, pasty git, with a foreign accent and a deathwish haircut, and I asked him how much he weighs. She's talking over me and telling me I can't be seen at the moment 'cos they're really overstretched and there's procedures and that I will be seen, if I wait. She doesn't like it when I start pointing out that other people are getting preferential treatment and starts to tell me that she will get the Police in 'cos I am being racist and that she has her rights, too. 'And no, I can't take the papers out of the office and do them at home 'cos they'll need to be checked by someone in the office and that they've got procedures and that the papers belong to the Government.' Then, some other jumped-up cow with a massively fat face joins in and says that she's the Manager and waves some paper at me saying that according to this document everyone was seen in this office within five minutes of arriving and that this office was third in the national league tables for service and fourth for client satisfaction. 'Think about it,' she says, 'you're in one of the top five Job Centres in the country. Top four, really. You're one of the lucky ones. I can prove it. This document proves it.' She's got big, round glasses and a posh scarf that probably cost a hundred quid wrapped round her fat neck. 'Pissing fat capon,' I say to her and grab hold of her lying report and rip it up into as many pieces as I can. Deathwish lunges for me, but he's too gangly and full of crap with his flailing hands and pipe-cleaner ribcage so I elbow him as he goes down and throw what's left of the report in the air. I don't run out either, I just walk out. *Easy easy*. They can all go to hell.'

It's fascinating watching him take on the world. He's like the tide, he comes in as he tells his story all puffed up and swollen breaking his waves against everything loudly, crashing against the jagged, granite rocks or the soft sand in equal measure and then just as soon falls back, almost soundlessly, draws back into himself, almost apologetically withdraws, a wordless, invisible retreating.

'I go to Sid's. I've got the last fifty quid I can get my hands on and put it behind the bar. I wouldn't know if the same people who were in there when I was beaten up are there or not. I tell the same sludgy barman to not let me out the place until all the money's gone. And to buy everyone in there a drink. 'That's twenty-five quid gone,' he says. 'Why do you care?' I say. I stay at the bar till I need a piss. I stare straight ahead, don't want company. Every drink I order is different. Get there much quicker if you do that. But drinks start coming to me, as people buy me one back. There's a never-ending supply of shorts. Soon, I'm going round again through his whiskies. I feel a presence at my right shoulder. For some reason, I feel spooked and get a wave of goose pimples down my right arm.

“Looks like it’s all going down the pan for you, mate,’ says this geezer. I sway a bit, but he makes me feel really dodgy. He’s heavy, swarthy, got a round head, too small for his body, hair too black for his age, bit sweaty. He sees right through me. You’re the second, he was the first. Two people looking straight at me and seeing what a piece of piss I am, all in the space of a week. And I felt it after all those shots. I felt like I’d aged ten years, sobered up, and was fifteen again, all in about ten seconds.

“Come through, I want to talk to you,’ he says to me. He walked off through into a little snug, off the main lounge. I hadn’t really clocked it before. I couldn’t not follow him. ‘You were in here not so long ago, bit worse for wear,’ he says, as I sit down at one of only three tables in this tiny room. The door closes behind me and someone locks it from the outside. All I can see through the carefully opaqued and crafted glass of the door is a dark figure stood as black as a rook against it.

“In fact, every time you’re in here you’re a bit worse for wear, aint you? Don’t worry about him,’ he says, nodding at the guy behind the door, ‘we’re all looking after you. Like we did when you was in here last time. Cheers, by the way,’ he says, lifting his glass. I’ve left mine on the bar, so I just nod. I’m feeling sick, for all sorts of reasons.

“It’s a shit world,’ he carries on, ‘when you come to think of it, innit? I mean, you’re walking along minding your own business when suddenly two little wankers attack you and next thing you know you’re in hospital and everything goes, how do they say, pear-shaped? Nothing wrong with pear-shaped though, is there? Gives you something to aim at.’ He’s got this vile smirk in his eye now. ‘So, you just gonna let them little shits get away with it? Turning you over like that. You looked a right mess when you fetched up here. They’ve done a good job patching you up. Pity about the scar on the back of the head. Ain’t you very angry? Is that why you back here? Not just to buy your old mates a nice drink, is it? You wanna get even, don't you?'

'Then he reaches at me with these hug bear paws, and I can tell you, I nearly shit myself. I could feel the panic surge through me stomach in an instance. He grabs my shirt front. I thought he was gonna lift me up and just mercifully strangle me, like a farmer doing a chicken. Nothing has ever frightened me as much as that man did then. I wouldn't have resisted. I was just the proverbial caught in the headlights. Jesus Christ, he felt like a beast of a monster. And he had hold of me shirt front.

"Don't you feel angry?' he asks.'

"Of course, I do. Fucking could kill 'em,' I said, but I hadn't thought that until I said it, and I certainly didn't want to kill 'em before I said it. I didn't even want to kill 'em after I said it.

'He relaxes his grip. 'Good,' he says, but he won't let go either. My arms are helpless by my side. I can't feel my arms, they've disappeared. As he relaxes his grip, he reaches down from under the table and lifts up a Tesco's bag. 'Little pressie.' He smiles as he lets go of my shirt. He puts the bag on the little, round, red formica-topped table. The table wobbles again very slightly. I open the crinkled bag. *Oh, for fuck's sake.* I think I said it aloud. 'Erm...' I definitely said erm, 'cos I remember it made him laugh.

"Erm. Erm. Erm,' he said, taking the piss of me and laughing a dry little laugh. 'Have it for free,' he said, 'give it me back when you've finished with it and I won't charge you.' He stands up at this point. I don't want him to stand up. I want to be the one to stand up and I want to be the one about to run away. Only the door is locked, and there's a huge black rook on the other side with the key. 'What do they say? One good turn deserves another. Do us all a favour.'

'He knocks on the door. The key turns. The door opens. 'Help this gentleman get dressed,' he says to the rook. I don't get it at first, and try to walk through the door. The rook stops me, simply by being huge between the woodwork. I can't believe this. I just can't believe this. I came here to drink away my sorrows, buy some nameless guys who once helped me a drink or two, and here I am, trapped in a tiny back room of a crappy, old, backstreet boozer with this psycho and his enormous corvid mate.

'I'm just an ordinary guy. Please,' I say, 'please understand that I'm not what you think I am.' The rook doesn't speak, he just shepherds me back to the table, just two or three steps backwards, picks up the bag. I notice he has leather gloves, of course. He opens my coat pocket and slides it into the satin lining of the breast pocket, muzzle first. I watch it, as if it isn't really happening to me. I see the glimpse of grey metal where the bag has ripped, as it lands very uncomfortably into my possession.

The rook looks so pleased 'cos the handle sticks out comically over my left lapel. I have to hold it to stop it unbalancing out of the pocket and onto the floor and so, of course, touch the handle through the bag. 'Don't be too long with it,' he says as he pushes me out of the door of the pub, 'imagine it's a library book'. The door shuts. I'm alone on the street again, wishing I was back in time, being carried to the corner for the ambulancemen to pick up and I could start all over again.'

Milton stops, reliving it, intensely. He reaches for more water and mixes cordial. He drinks and as he does, he shrinks again.

This is not an easy one. I look at Chow Mein, his face is creased, and I can tell he thinks what I am thinking, only ten times worse. This isn't really what we do. I'm going to find it hard to tell him. We definitely don't take on gangsters. Well, we do, but not the ones with guns, not the ones who use them in an open, honest way.

Milton starts again, unannounced. 'I'm just as dazed. I can't think straight. Got to walk into town, got to get home. All I can think of is getting home. I want to sleep. I walk into town 'cos I don't know the buses around here. Why would they send buses into a place where no-one lives? The weight of this thing is just frightening. I feel like I'm being watched all the time. In fact, I spend every waking hour imagining I'm being watched. I've stopped sleeping, 'cos I feel I'm being watched. I tried to get a taxi, but there isn't one in sight. I can't tell you what it feels like getting on a bus with a gun in a Tesco's bag. Everyone stares at you, 'cos they know you're carrying a gun. It's in my left hand, casually in its bag, but tucked under my coat, like it's a book or something. He told me to think of it like a library book, so he wants it back. It ain't mine, is it? I think about having to go there again and face him and I felt utterly sick. I never carry a book, but particularly never one with a muzzle. At one point, the driver brakes and swerves and swears out loud, and it unbalances out of my hand and lands on the floor with a strange, heavy thud. I want to die. Shrink. Just shrivel up. My mind is whirring, I can't think straight, can't work out what it is they want me to do.'

He stops but doesn't drink. He has withered again.

'So, you came to see us.'

He doesn't answer.

'Have you done anything else between then and now? I need to know.'

He shakes his head and doesn't speak.

'Then, I need to know how you found us. But not now. We have to meet and talk again, and I have to tell you, Milton, that this isn't what we normally do. It's outside of our remit.'

I'm struggling finding the right words again, words that might offer comfort, a little hope and leeway for us to get out. Remit is such a wanky word.

'Leave it with us, ok, and go home. But, for goodness sake, don't do anything at all, ok? Don't leave the house. Don't ring anyone, don't do anything.'

'Yeah, but don't just dump me, please. I don't know what to do. I can't take these guys on. These are serious. Hooligans with guns. Gangsters. Please don't just make me go away.'

I let him subside. 'Do you think you were followed here?'

'No.'

'Ok. Wait here a minute.'

We leave him and go to the back room. I ask Chow Mein if he thinks he's genuine.

'If he isn't genuine, he's a very good actor. This could be very dangerous for everyone if we get this one wrong.'

'But this isn't why we are here, is it? What goes on within the Circle is what we do. We aren't the rubbish collectors for every Friedbread who comes in 'cos Slut or the Council or whoever don't do their job out there and everything else is falling apart.'

'What about The Drowning Man?' says Chow Mein.

'What do you mean?'

'Look at who's coming to us. We run the Circle now, yeah, we do it quietly, we've fought our battles. But we didn't know Drowning Man. Who was he? We don't even know how he heard about us, never mind what his problem was. We don't know this Milton. Last week, we had the woman come to us who thinks her son is dead in Iraq but can't get an answer and was threatening everything, including setting fire to things, including herself. Then the woman whose father had committed suicide two months ago and she thinks it was all about money and losing his job and finding out there wasn't a pension fund and he couldn't cope with his sick wife and then, the two young lads so frightened of their dad but sick of the dog fighting he was organising – B-man, look at it, look at what's happening.'

'Don't say it.'

'I don't want to say it, either. But we have to listen properly to every whisper of every leaf. You said that. I am not sure if it's possible, but we got a proper big whisper going at the moment and it's all about us. Look at all the people who come here. We don't know them anymore. We watch them come up the drive and they're just little packets of eaten-up Friedbreads. We sit them here, treat them like proper people for five minutes, tell them they aren't just forgotten turds floating away down the river. But they come here with a bit of hope and they come here because Lardland is frying. And we listen for as long as they got. Most of them talk too much and we listen, and we do what we can, but it isn't enough. They're getting more and more demanding because they think we're more than what we are. They go away with a bit more hope. And we don't do much more than listen. We don't even tell them about the Circle. Christ, we'd have the opposite of Armageddon if we did. What is it we're doing, brother? Do you want more of this, flooding us, leaving us as helpless as them? I'm just losing the idea of where this is gonna end.'

'No way, but where do we stop?'

Chow Mein is staring out the window. He leapt about in his thoughts for a time, till he got to the right rock.

'What about the reason this all started: would you want to change places with them?'

'You're absolutely right.'

We need pauses to settle this between us.

'Milton is in a mess, carrying a gun. He drinks too much, and he gets very angry. But that doesn't mean he should get disposed of 'cos of some midden-boy gangsters. Take him home, see where he lives. Get him to talk if you can about himself, check him out, see if it all adds up and that he's telling the truth. If he's good, tell him we'll be in touch, but do all the usual checks to see if anyone's tailing him. If they are, take him out to Huddersfield and come back on a narrow boat.'

Chow Mein paused again. 'Ok, ok, I can handle him, but what about what's happening? The bigger picture?'

He pauses.

'Why did you tell him about the Drowning Man? You know the rule about not talking about the other punters to anyone.'

He stares at me as if nothing's falling into place.

'I must be losing my grip,' I say.

'He was the first one who came here to die.'

'We don't know he came here to die.'

I go back into the room where Milton is playing with his ear and staring very blankly, straight ahead. He has such a plain face it's difficult to focus on anything in particular.

'Milton, thank you for coming to see us. We'll work things out and talk again about what you've told us. Go with my friend here. Do as he says, Milton.'

'Can I ask a question?'

'Of course.'

'What happened to The Drowning Man?'

'It all ended happily for him.'

'How do you mean?'

'That's two questions. Milton,' I smile.

'What's this shit with the garlic? It's bollux, isn't it, just for show, huh?

'We can smell garlic on your breath, not 'cos you've eaten it, but because we rubbed it on the furthest bit away from your mouth, your feet.' I smile at him, not knowing how far to take the next bit.

'So?"

'So, it's all connected, isn't it? You come here with a problem – a plastic bag full of problems – we rub garlic on your foot, which is the furthest bit away from your mouth and within minutes we can tell what you've been eating and we can see connections where before there didn't seem to be any. It's all connected, isn't it?'

He doesn't look much happier. As we escort him to the door, he asks, casually, 'Who's Burgerman?'

'We'll be in touch, Milton, and till then, take it steady.'

I stand up, go to the window, watch the flutter of the new leaves in the trees. If there's anyone else waiting to talk today they'll have to find someone else, I can't do any more. They'll have to come back tomorrow. I'm going over the things Milton described, trying to picture Sid's, the cormorant, Milton's wife, San the Man, the kid's doing kung-fu kicks, at the same time as I absent-mindedly make a cup of tea which I don't really want.

I lift the tea-bag still steaming out of the cup and try to imagine its journey. Planted, picked, packed, transported, sold how many times? packaged, bagged and put through the checkouts. The hands picking the leaves working so quickly fix me to the spot. The tea goes cold.

3

Smoothie

I walk over to Smoothie's office, still on edge after that conversation with Milton. Chow Mein is going to see Milton home and make sure he's ok and find out what he can from him. Smoothie will do the same, but online, using all the secrets he's garnered staring at screens and going deep into the online world, with fellow remote warriors of the digital age. Smoothie is our tech man. He's wired the place so we can listen to anything, watch anything and access anything on our own patch. He's working on the rest of the world.

When I get to his office he's already working his way through *Milton-formation*, as he calls it. Not much. No face match, no job match, no car match, although we haven't seen his car yet. I ask Smoothie to make sure that Chow Mein gets his car details, if he has one.

'Try to find Sid's,' I ask him, 'and where he worked.'

'You missed that one, B-man. I almost radioed it in, but I was lost in the story, as much as you,' he said.

He calls me B-man. Burgerman. My name. Smoothie's story is locked in my mind, I can almost tell it word for word. But he tells it better.

'When I went in the army, I thought I was a white guy and listened to the usual white shit, like the BeeGees and that. I was only sixteen, judge didn't give me much choice really. 'Army, sonny or prison for minors.' I didn't want to go, and I didn't not want to go.

'First, it was good. Got slapped a couple of times, 'cos I gave the Sergeant a bit of verbal, but I settled down. One night, I'm on the train, had a few beers in the next town along the track from the barracks. Group of Paras get on who I thought I knew a bit. Four big white guys, a lot older than me. Told me I was a black cunt. I told them to piss off. Took a beating on the train, they broke my nose, damaged my wrist and caused so much pain down my arm it felt like I was getting electric shocks repeatedly. They were all laughing. Tears of pain streaming down my face, man. Everyone on the carriage was turning away. I ain't gonna get involved, if I was one of them. I don't blame 'em. These guys are trained to fight and there's four of them, they're hard together, but they're hard apart. This was just a bit of fun for them. Me, I'm crying and my arm wilting and hurt like shit and I'm hurting and I can't see very good out of one eye and I'm so bruised breathing hurts.

'I get off at my stop and I know something for the first time in my life, I ain't confused anymore. They told me very clearly, I's a *black* man and I been a black man ever since. When I get back to barracks, I get to jump through the Sarge's hoops and get the worst jobs for a month, for being a mess. Even with an arm in a sling and wrist in plaster and a nose in a splint and packed, I still got to mop and clean and do shit. Everyone take the piss of the plastic on my nose. I get so angry I get into a fight and they're just trying to hit my plastic nose for fun. In the end I take it off.

'But I got a little plan. I'm going to find these guys and tell them I'm real happy that they stopped my confusion. Takes me a while to get the plan right. I want to be sure they're the ones who did it, want to make sure they're clear I'm truly thankful.

‘First, I get some Hendrix and some Marvin and then Curtis and then dozens more till I found my love, Brenda Holloway, with her hair in a cut I never seen before, and while I’m reading about her and dancing to this different sort of music, I’m discoverin’ a roomful more of these beauties, Mary Wells, Aretha Franklin, all of the Supremes, Cindy Scott and Barbara Lewis. Then no need to ever go further than Nina. Nothing no one can do to you when you got music like this, written for you, personally.

‘And the music sort of learns me to fit my body and change my mind. I grow my hair, they tell me to get it cut, I grow my hair and they don’t give me a second chance – they cut my hair – four of them hold me down in the showers while I get the worst haircut that any black man or white man has ever seen, and I seen some horror stories on the head variety. They’re trying to break me, making me clean up with a comb. They’re almost winning. No one cares that I got a broken wrist and nerve damage to my arm. It’s one of those things that happen on an army camp and my parents, who aren’t my parents, are glad that I’m here doing something useful for the community, as my Dad says. They probably think I deserve it, after doing all those stupid things that got me here in the first place. Kicking off in the pub and smackin’ the DJ, the gaffer’s son, getting thrown out of college for having a go at the teacher dissing my attitude.

‘I keep my head down, get on with it. Do as I am told. Pull back. With guys like these, they constantly looking for little weaknesses and ways in to get at you. It’s part of the army thinking, if people don’t fit in, then we don’t want you, ‘cos if you ain’t thinking about everyone else’s backs in the unit, then your unit is a weaker force and you’re a liability. Simple. I am the weakest link, and I don’t know how I got there. I don’t even know I’m the weakest link, but I once heard someone say that every group needs someone to hate and that one is me.

‘Then, I hear the news – the Paras are leaving for Afghanistan, for a sixth month tour. Next week. Some of our guys are really angry ‘cos they want to go and have a go at the camel-fuckers. Me, I want out and before I want out, I want to say thank you to these guys for making me understand what I am. I’m thinking just where and how? I’m going mad thinking where and how. It’s all I think about. I got less than a week and I got to think all this shit out and I’m scared, ‘cos I know I’m goin’ to get more than a beating if I get it wrong. Even I get it right, I’m probably going to end up in deeper shit than I can imagine.

‘Worse thing is, I don’t even know who they were. I’m jus’ thinking – ok, where did I see them? What can I remember? I begin to put it all down on paper. Draw them, do a photofit from memory, think of what was special about them – hair, eyes, shape, size, the way they talked and what they said. It’s coming back, but it’s hard, a lot of blur. After the drink. Everything happen’ so fast, and I was on the end of eight fists and eight boots, on a train, at half eleven after five Stellas.

‘I haven’t had a drink since, but I’m shaking again. I’m so angry, angry with all the shits here. Not just the shits who beat me up, but the shits who cut my hair, the shits who trip me up in the showers, the shits who call me *cocoa* and stupid names, so stupid, the shits who do as they’re told without thinking, the shits who do the shouting. Shits in ranks and rows. Now I don’t care how I leave or if I have to leave. One thank you, and then I’m outta here, down the hole. The bigger and shittier the hole the better, ‘cos no one’ll wanna follow.

‘What day is it? It’s Wednesday. Three months ago tomorrow I was on a train back from Staniforth, last train that night. Think about it, idiot, I says to myself. Thursday night out, last Thursday before Afghan, last chance for a few beers and let off some steam. Same thing every time. Same patterns, same rules, same discipline, same pals, same fucking jokes, same stupid angry boy shit looking for some little kid who happens to have a black dad and a white mother who he ain't ever met. Sort it, boy, I tell myself. Think. Plan. Act. Simple. Man, I'm shaking, the shit they tell us in the Army has got to work for me as well.

'I get off early on Thursday afternoon. I have gone into stores with a little requisition and forged a signature. Then, I have to get the train to Staniforth and catch the shops. It's only a small town, but it's got everything I need. I get a bag and a few things for the journey and a few little things for the journey home. I buy a cheap motorbike and drive it out to a tiny place below the railway on a forestry track and park it there. I walk the half-mile to Cragside station, about halfway between Staniforth and the nearest station to the Army Camp and get the train to town.

'Some early-doors squaddies are already coming into town on this train. I get off and plan the timing of the rest of the evening. There are about four or five bars which are popular with the grunts. I trawl them all and find a vantage point in each. Then, I disappear to get dressed. I discovered how much I like dressing up since I left the army. I always liked dressing up as a kid, but my father wouldn't let me do it. He wouldn't let me do almost nothing. I haven't seen him since the day he agreed with the judge. I've dressed up a lot since then. Can do a very good sixty-year-old Jamaican woman with a bit of paddin' and a bit of lippie. This is a bit of a gamble. They might not come, I might not recognise them, or worse they might recognise me. Except they probably never saw a black girl like me.

'I sit with my phone, like some girls do in towns with bars near army camps. I play with my phone and look sullen. Some guys leer and shout a bit, but I turn my back and get back to my texting. I like being a girl like this. I'm small and slender enough to be a girl and definitely like camping it up a bit. I got a black-girl-with-straightened-hair wig, I got tight ass-gripping jeans and a baggie top that hides everything, but promises a lot.

And I got a nice big bag, hidden down behind the seat, full of goodies. I have to wait. I have to move bars. I have to do lots of looking down at the pavement and lots of furtive eyes up. Even for a black girl, in a town full of testosterone on the last Thursday before Afghanistan, this town is buzzing, and I seen two or three fights before ten o'clock.

'I'm panicking I ain't going to see my dates. I really want them honeys now. I had one small drink, just to take the edge off and if any guy gets close enough to smell my breath, I don't just smell of fear and cheap perfume, but I smell like I should smell. I walk the bars. Flick my eyes up, but mainly down. Listen to the shit and ignore all of it, except one moose who slaps my arse in a bar that's so crowded when I turn round, I can't tell who did it. There's about eight of them sniggering into their beers. I have to walk on and ignore it. Is this how we treat women? Is this what they come for, all this caveman shit? I make a big serious vow to go somewhere a long way away from the crappiness of the world when I have done this.

'To make myself feel better, I go to the ladies. I remember her so well, the lady in there talking to her friend with the cubicle door open.

"I'm sure some arse has spiked my drink,' she says, spitting into a bit of toilet roll a few times. 'It tastes really weird.'

"Throw it away, then', says her friend, putting on the next centimetre of filler.

'There's only one cubicle and there's only one sink and mirror and I stand, awkwardly.

"What you doing in here?' says the lady in the cubicle with the door open. Then she stands up and wipes herself in full view. There aren't any knickers around the ankles to be pulled up. Her spray on tan stops at her crotch, I notice, and find it fascinating.

"What you staring at? Look at her, she's staring at me. You

queer or something? You won't get much tonight, they don't like darkies here. You should be down in town doing the streets.'

'Both girls cackle like muppets, and I slip into the cubicle and lock the door.

"Got no fuckin tits either...' More stupid laughter, as they leave the toilet.

'I slump on the seat. I feel stupid and ridiculous and scared like I've never been so fuckin' scared before in my life. This could go in any direction and I won't be able to cope. What am I thinking, dude? What am I doing? Just get out now, while you can. Ditch the getup, get into your civvies and walk away from this. Walk to the train and back to camp or walk to the train and never come back. Either way, it won't be as bad as the shit you're about to walk into. Come on, man, do it. Get out now. It ain't too late. Just pull yourself together one last time. Walk out of here like you came in. Sorted. Decided. So, I open the door of cubicle, adjust my hair one last time, like any girl would and walk out the door.

'It's loud, crowded and banging and some wankers are twitching and itching to dance but still not drunk enough. It's funny in a way, 'cos it's Michael Jackson. I can't see the two witches who sensed something earlier in the toilets. All I have to do is get to the table where I left my stuff and then I'm out that door. I push through the crowds, ease my way through like no one noticing me, between the shoulders and the arses, and find my table. I pick up my stuff. No worries. Everything's where it should be. Turn to cross the little bit of the bar to get to the door. Eyes down, really don't want any contact with anyone. Someone's coming through the door, but I don't want to know.

"Hey, look where you're going, sweetheart.' He moves out the way politely. I don't know him, or his voice, and I don't look up.

"Make room for the lady,' says his mate, holding open the door for me. I shiver. It's a voice I know, and I have to look up at him. He's a big guy, and last time I saw him I was looking up at him from the floor of a railway carriage, and he wasn't holding the door open then, he was trying to shove my head through it, without opening it. This time I smiled, without speaking.

'Where you going then, gorgeous?'

'I mimicked the sign language of a woman going for a fag outside of a bar.

"Let me get you a drink. What do you want?'

"No, no,' I mutter with a pout and a flick of the head.

"I insist, it'll be my pleasure. What do you want? Go on. Something to come back in for,' he said grinning.

"Rum 'n' coke,' I said, mainly mouthing it, breathing it, thinking I'm going all Nina Simone, and walked off sultrily, to get my breath.

'When I go back in a few minutes later, I go via my bag and go the long way to the toilets. Get out what I need and back in to find my drink. I have my story ready of having a really bad cough so I couldn't speak much. They're still getting drinks when I get to them. Tonight, there's four. I make a note of what they drink and think I'll start with the one who bought me a drink. Listen to his shit for a bit and let him get a couple of drinks in him. Cough a bit when it seems like he's going to ask me something but otherwise I smile and agree and laugh a lot in a coughy way. I catch him looking at me in that way boys do and so I stick my arse out a bit more and play with my hair. He loves it. He has a big, bad grey mole below his nose, and it looks a bit malignant. I hope it's really serious and they won't be able to save his face. When it's my turn I get him a drink and have worked out that three of them are drinking lager and one's on bitter. I get the names: Wayne's my mole-baby, with his eyes on me, then there's the lovely Dylan, who's got no brain whatsoever, not even the size of a piece of shrapnel lodged in his head, and magnificent Kev is small, but strutty like a big cock, but a bit wilier, and Smithy was on bitter. I knew it was my turn to get the drinks. How do you spike someone's drink in a busy bar with loads of people at the bar and loads of people between you, the bar and the people who are about to be rammed. Easy. You don't. You take your little, girly glass of shit to the toilets, act like a drunken arse and push your way in and make up the cocktail of whatever evil gear you want to inflict on someone and then buy three vodka chasers and *whoay ho, doopety dee*...throw all the glasses in with the pints of lager and make sure everyone gets a bit of a vodka and a lot of evil. I did it. I hadn't done it before and I ain't ever done it since, but it fuckin' worked.

'A girl has to make it work for her in anyway a girl has to make it work for her. Talk about listening to shit for the next twenty minutes. Talk about toasts and cheering and swearing undying love to one another. My gaydar is popping off the scale, brother. Is this what these guys are really like? Why have I never noticed before?

'Then, it kicks in. Wayne has put his wallet, keys and phone on the table. He's the first one to start to feel bad. He looks terrible. He doesn't look anywhere near as bad as I looked halfway through what they did to me, but he looks bad. I almost feel sorry for him, but then stop myself. Smithy is holding the fort and trying to work out why his mates are acting a bit strange. I told him I put a double vodka in there, as we'd agreed, and he shook his head.

"That shouldn't bother these canny lads,' he says.

"Poor guys,' I say. 'Can I help?'

"No, they'll be fine.' Wayne starts to stand up, but he falls over, and he starts laughing, really badly.

"Listen, I might have to go in a minute,' I tell him, my baby-sitter and all that.'

"Yeah, yeah, no worries, luv,' says the sweet cock, Kev. Except, I remember the Geordie git was the one who held my arm for the others to stamp on. I remember him laughing with a Geordie accent, but I don't remember anything he said. Except how funny they thought he was.

'As I stand up, Wayne makes another attempt to stand up and as Kev tries to catch him, I slip Wayne's phone into my hand and disappear into the crowd. I slip out past the toilets to a long passage and at the end I push a door and find myself in a little outdoor courtyard with a door leading into another passage leading to a backstreet. No one around.

'I start at the top of Wayne's contacts. Each one gets a different aspect to Wayne's character. If it's a woman answering I tell them about Wayne's long list of infidelities, his peccadilloes, his recent sexual exploits on top of me, his ability to fuck three women and still pay for it every Thursday night. That one's aimed at either his Aunty Joyce or someone else very old. If it's a guy who answers, I tell them about the way he's seeing a schoolie, shopping his mates to the MPs, crying about going to Afghan and considering leaving the Army and about his gay reputation, which is undermining his ability to do his job as a sergeant.

'I didn't know I had so many accents or so much bitchiness in me. There wasn't a person I hadn't rung about Wayne in those twenty minutes. Except one person. The CO at the base. I put on my best South Walian accent, refuse to give my name but tell him that I have information that Sgt. Wayne Jennings is actually a paedophile, and that I'm about to ring the police. Such fuckin' fun as I had that night. Then, I turn the phone off, put it in my bag and go to watch the party unfold.

'By now the boys have vomited and are being thrown out of the bar by the guys on the door. They could hardly walk. The doormen aren't very sympathetic. Kev's doing his best. It's the last Thursday before the boys go to war. Everyone's seen it all before in this town. I slip away. I see him try to get a taxi but all the taxi drivers refuse. Three guys like that and in that state. *No way, Jose!*

'I go the back way to the train station. I really need them to get the 10.05. There would be hardly anyone on it. Another two trains before the last one and then we could finish this, and I'd be away. I get to the station and wait for them to come round the corner. They stumble and retch and fall together onto the platform. Kev is really concerned. He knows that he has to keep this out of the way of the Military Fuzz, and out of the way of everyone, 'cos it could affect them getting off to the big fight. I hide around the corner of the steps leading to the Park and Ride area below the station. No one else around. Everyone's partying. The train comes. I watch them get on. I get on at the very last minute.

'In my carriage there's only two other people. I discreetly let off a stink bomb, right in the middle of the carriage. They look at me as it drifts down the carriage, but I look completely innocent. 'What is that shit?' says one.

'I cover my face as well. 'Disgusting,' we all chime. They get up to go to the next carriage. I watch them settle in their new seats, safe in the much fresher air.

'I saunter through looking for Kev and the boys. I can't disguise my joy at seeing them again on this very train and ask how they doin'.

"They ain't fucking well at all,' says Kev, looking green himself.

'The big meatheads are taking up a lot of room, spreading out over the train carriage benches. 'Poor things,' I say. 'What can we do? I have some stuff in my bag that I use with the kids, but you might have to come with me and see if it'll be of any use. When you're a mum you have to deal with this stuff all the time. My two are always ill. Come and see what I've got that might help them, I'm just in the next carriage.'

'Kev gets up reluctantly. Wiry and more cautious than

the others. And vicious and racist as well. I wiggle down the carriage, try to take his mind off his troubles. I get him into the stinky carriage.

"Jesus, luv, what's been happening here?" he says, covering his face.

"That's why I wanted you to come with me 'cos there were a couple of yobs in here, and they were messing around, and I felt a bit uncomfortable. Is that ok? And I've still got some drink left if you want some,'

"No, I shouldn't,' he says.

'Come on, the night's become a stinker, literally like. Come on, Kev, darling.' I need him sitting down. I get the wine bottle out and open it and as I pour him one the train rocks over some points and the red wine goes all over his shirt.

"For fucks sake,' he says, 'what was that?' and he takes his eyes off me for a few seconds as he's wiping his shirt, and I get the handcuffs out the bag and get one around his wrist before he notices, and then the other one is around the vertical handrail before he can say, *You bitch, you planned this*, I've attached him to a piece of metal in the middle of a deserted, stinking, late-night train carriage, on the same line where they beat me up so badly, I lost all my confusion. He looks utterly incredulous and shouts the inevitable, 'Fuckin 'ell, what's all this about.?' but it's all lost, 'cos I smash the side of his jaw so hard with the bottle of Hungarian Bull's Blood, that it leaves shards in his face and the last of the wine spills down his front. Just for good measure, I stick the broken end into his ear.

'He reacts, but he's slower than me and only just gets my blouse, but he's stretched now and attached to the rail and can only reach so far. I get to my bag. In it is the small baseball bat that I smash repeatedly against his hand, attached by a handcuff to the vertical handrail. Luckily, it's his right one, so he'll probably have to re-learn how to use it all over again. He shouts and screams and lunges for me and swears he'll kill me when he gets hold of me. I walk into the next carriage.

'The three stooges are lying prone in pools of crap and looking like they're sleeping uneasily. I look out the window and check where I am roughly. This'll have to do, and yank the emergency cord.

'The train shudders to a stop. I open the door with the emergency lever. Dylan is first. I pick him up and take a small run with him, even though he's very heavy, and manage to get him out at reasonable speed and he immediately falls down the steps of the train and lands face down three feet below on the rocky overgrown embankment and rolls into the undergrowth out of sight.

'Wayne is easy. I tattoo RACIST with a razor blade on his forehead. Quite deeply. A bit too deeply. The other one, I just leave to wonder when he wakes up, why I didn't do him like the other two. I'll leave him feeling crap 'cos he got away with it, wondering if I'll come for him at some point real soon. Or when they'll come for me.

'I can see the driver coming through the next carriage, so I jump off the train carefully, down the embankment and run off into the woods. I head off in the opposite direction to where I've parked the motorbike, then double back on myself and after about forty-five minutes I'm sat in leathers on my bike, with a bag of ladies clothing on my back and as free as any man can be.'

Complicity Competition!!

Extraordinary, the extent to which people are complicit in their own repression.

It's back, our most popular competition!!
Send us your tale of when you shat on someone else to make the bosses happy – it could be any arse of any boss of any sort across the country, as long as you can prove you've cacked and licked, in the right order, in the right arsehole, then you'll be put into the mix.
Come on, join in the fun!!!!
It can involve someone you don't know very well, or someone really close to you. It could be spragging on your boss to your boss's boss or dobbing in the lowest ranked volunteer to the Chief Constable of your local boys in blue, it's all about complicity, at the end of the day.
Was it at work? Or was it at home or just out and about in your neighbourhood?
Remember, to have a chance of winning, your story does need to include how you shat on someone else (or it could have been *lots* of losers) in order to maintain an organisation or institution that you think you believe in. Or for your self-promotion. Or just out of spite or for the benefit of the bosses.

Fill in the coupon below and send it to:
The Media Newsstand, London SWI NDL
We promise to read every entry. Come on, you could win five lucky coins of your choice, from our
Coppers of Complicity Lucky Dip Bag!!

Here's the story of Matty B., former teacher and now highly esteemed educationalist and consultant:

'I was a young bloke surround by loads of really horny teenage girls and although there were rumours about me, they were never proved. But I did shit on a couple of other blokes who were trying to be clever and take the piss of me in front of others, even though I was always mocking their accents and that, and the way they were trying to impress the women in the staff room annoyed me. Well, one day, one of them went too far, mocking my re-structuring presentation in front of the whole school – which I thought was excellent, but which he was saying was going to increase the workload by 25% – so I fitted him up with some of these young lasses and although they didn't like him really I gave them a few hundred quid to follow him round town to a few of the night clubs and then spike his drinks a bit, nothing too serious, but get him pissed, and then take some photos of him with his arms around these girls, obviously the worst for wear. Then, as if by magic, these photos appeared in the Principal's (a good mate – we played squash together) inbox and the Vice-Principal's (a very attractive (older) lady) inbox and, lo and behold he's resigning. I went to his disciplinary hearing to support him and provide a character witness, but it didn't seem to help. Now, he can never work with children or young people again. Shame. Great loss to education.'

This is an absolute belter, THANK YOU, Matty B.
You're the Shitter of the Week. Ruining someone's career, when you're the real shit, is hugely popular with the readers.
Keep 'Em Coming!
Better still, can anyone shit on Matty? Now that would be a Scheisse-Sturm of a story. Come on guys, get to work.

Shit on the Shitters and you Double your Money!!!!!!

4

About the Lady

I tell Smoothie I've got some jobs to do and to keep in touch, let me know what's happening. He loves his office. He loved stealing the kit as well. He never does the front doors of shops, says that's for playboys. The weakness is before it gets on the shelves. PC World have lost half a shop to Smoothie.

I have to visit the Lady. She's dying. I always go alone. She lives alone. It's one of the few journeys when I take a car. The rich don't need buses in quite the same way. And if I cycle, I appear before her dishevelled and sweaty and if I were to shower it would appear too familiar. On the way there, across town, I always assess the weather as if it's different for the rich. Today, the sky is grey like aluminium, a shiny, uniform grey.

The house is on a small ridge overlooking the city but screened by trees and unseen. It's situated at the junction of four roads that meet at a large, three-quarter roundabout, of which the fourth quarter is the fencing at the front of the Lady's house.

I should call before I set off, but I don't. I can' face the wait for her, or someone looking after her, to get to the phone. There's no point, since it's a long while since she wasn't in. I park the car half a mile away and walk the rest. I walk very slowly to the first corner of the fencing and gawp in like a foreigner at a funeral, hoping to catch a glimpse of life-as-it's-lived and to look at the two-storey, high-windowed, late Georgian residence and try to imagine wanting to get closer to it. Sometimes, a car passes and the lost driver and passenger stare out in surprise that something like this should be here, or a couple with a pram having a Sunday walk stop and sit, or a group of lads on bikes will do wheelies on the paving in front of the fencing before they get bored and spot the more inviting tracks into the woods opposite. So, the Lady lives unseen.

There are rumours about her. Some people claim outlandish things that they know are true about her: she was married to a foreigner, a super-rich Muslim playboy; she's extraordinarily wealthy in cash, lands and the costly jewels; she has no heirs; she changed her name after the war; she still has real servants; or ever more factual stories: she has seven children but they never come to see her and are waiting in the wings for her to die; she had bucketloads of money but the family fortune has disappeared and she's only living in the house because of a secret pact with someone important; she still has gentlemen callers; she suffers from periodic madness and has to be sedated and locked in a special room, and so on, to ever more wonderful, speculative and imaginative mythologies: she has special powers and can hypnotise; she wields amazing control over huge numbers of people; she's a witch and can steal dreams and can fly and can heal with her hands and through her tokens and she commands armies and can wither you to the spot.

I press the bell on the keypad of the gate. A voice trained to be hostile will answer, and haughtily demand to know Who? Only one degree of softening when I tell them it's me. Sometimes new staff don't know me and have to check who I am.

The gate miraculously opens. The CCTV cameras follows my entrance. The gravel crunches and I count my steps. I always try to make it in less than fifty. Everything about the exterior is immaculate, the paintwork, the weeds, the lawn edges, the old-fashioned, hand-made wooden guttering, the worn stone steps. The doors swing open and a man in gloves greets me. He assures me that the Lady is expecting me.

The stink of the house hits me full on. It always catches me off-guard. The butler must have neither lungs nor sensitive nasal hairs. I cough spontaneously. 'Visible administering' it should be called, because the 'visible cleaning' is lacking power. More than thirty rooms, each smelling of medications and the decay of a single human, more violent and pernicious than whole hospitals. All this for one old lady to die in hyper-comfort.

I pass someone on their hands and knees scrubbing a floor and two people cleaning, polishing and rubbing opposite ends of the main staircase. In the near distance, two vacuum cleaners are competing. No babble of voices filters through.

I am led up the stairs, through the main corridor and a dining room, a sitting room, a lounge, turn a corner and lose the daylight past more anonymous, shut and empty rooms with panelled doors. The air is thick with air fresheners and dried scented flowers to disguise the power of the sewage work's stench. Poor cow. The Lady will receive me.

The fantastical Lady of such speculation is not in bed, as would be usual, but is being made up, *at her toilet*, she calls it, by an assistant, at the opposite end of the room in front of an enormous glass mirror. As I walk in, I can see the reflection of my legs from mid-thigh downwards.

She cannot speak because the assistant is applying facial makeup and to do so would mean a disruption to the routine. Her eyes acknowledge me with a blink. There is no speaking from anyone in the room. No one acknowledges my arrival. I have to rest my eyes. I hear one of the assistants open the Lady's mouth to pop in a spoonful of liquid medicine. I can hear her close it again and begin to massage her jowls to encourage her to swallow. Someone else adjusts a fan, perhaps to include me in its arc. A sash window is lifted and then lowered again to within millimetres of the same spot. There are three visible tubes and a catheter bag going attached to tubes going in and out of her.

I haven't spent even a minute in her company but I'm already weary and exhausted. This succession of pointless adjustments and silent attempts at achieving micro-perfection, in the hope of the blink of approval, is nerve-searingly and agonisingly unbearable and humiliating. To even open my eyes in the presence of these acts may be seen as complicity, as if I, too, need her approval, but I have to make it very clear.

'Is there any way we could be alone for a moment?'

She doesn't blink and no one else responds.

'Have you seen a proper doctor?'

The makeup artist is painting on eyebrows as I speak. The Lady's head has to be held because the wasting disease has devoured most of her own musculature. The wheelchair she's sitting in is large and specially made, like a small couch, big and comfortable enough for two normal-sized adults, and I see that she's strapped into it, so that she doesn't slither out. She is grossly overweight and swollen, but her painted-on face has not swollen to quite the same degree and looks tiny on top of the body. The most striking thing is how pink she is. Her makeup artist is struggling to disguise the flaming, virulent pink.

A silent assistant comes forward to me and whispers, 'The Lady will soon be dressed for dinner. It may be that Sir would absent himself for these preparations.'

I know that she is dressed three or four times a day in different outfits and see that my chance may soon pass. Then, the door opens, and a man with a tripod is ushered in and busies himself finding the right position ready for the camera to take its truth.

It is the ritual.

In all this time, I don't remember having seen any signs of the Lady's chest heaving underneath her heavy breasts. I may be too late. I am in a room with about ten silent people going about their operations and tasks and none of them is checking to see if she's alive. I need to speak to her before I go.

'Auntie, Auntie Annie' I hiss at her. No blink, except from me.

'Please, Sir,' one of the chief flunkeys grabs my arm, '*Ma'am* or *My Lady*. This is the proper form of address.'

I look at him and nod. 'Not to me,' and smile, politely.

She has always been Auntie Annie, who looked after my mother when my mother was supposed to be looking after her, when I was still at infant school on the other side of town. The one thing my mother asked me to promise was to look after Auntie Annie, because she had looked after my mother. More than that I didn't know. Over the years we had just let it go unsaid. And now, here she is, a grotesque version of something that was once human and real. I'm surprised they still let me in to see her. For my mother's memory I suppose.

'Auntie Annie, you must listen. Can you hear me? Remember me, Eileen's son? What are they doing to you? I hope you can hear me, and I'm sorry for all the things that have happened and we haven't had time to sort it out. I can't talk to you in front of these shadows, you know that. You are very ill. I am going to try to get the doctors to get you proper treatment, this is cruelty.'

The photographer calls everyone over. 'Look at this,' he says, 'I've really captured her inner spirit. They are going to love this.'

He was beaming as if he'd caught a prize salmon. I turned to see what he had produced. 'The wonders of modern technology. It's beautiful.' He looks so pleased.

He hands me a picture. It was a fabulous picture, literally. I looked at him to see if there was any hint of irony.

'What is this a picture of, exactly?' I asked him.

'The camera cannot lie.'

Was it simply malice, or a particularly black sense of humour testing the waters to wind up the gullible?

The picture showed a woman, who could have been the Lady,

Auntie Annie, as she may have been, just, when she was in her early forties. The other assistants gather round to gaze.

'Fabulous...adorable...exquisite...perfect shape of the lips... gorgeous...they are going to go potty over this...oooh, the presence, the style...so lovely.' Nearly all join in, some of them without even looking at the picture.

I notice the photo has today's date on it, which is the only thing resembling what I am looking at. The Lady weighs over twenty-four stone, is excessively pink, has a degenerative wasting disease that no-one will name – a mix of gout, excessive consumption of rich food, force feeding, type-2 diabetes, colonic diseases and a type of muscular atrophy affecting several parts of her body and speaks with difficulty, but is surrounded by an expensive range of medical equipment, has been operated on over fifty times and has over a dozen monitors fixed to her body.

'That creature over there is a woman on the far side of death, but your picture shows her nearly forty years ago, as if she's just stepping into a soiree with Coco Chanel,' I say to the photographer.

'Ridiculous, absolutely ridiculous,' he says to everyone but me. He takes the picture and waltzes off with his equipment under his arm, to a door that miraculously opens.

The makeup artist is tinkering with some brown ridges. The dressing assistant reminds me again that she is about to be dressed. Within the hour they will have the latest 'pictures' of her wired out to the press agencies and will be writing a story about the latest outfits she was spotted in today that within weeks will be available in dress shops. Then, there'll be calls for celebrations of her contributions to the community and subtle reminders towards the civic pride that seems so lacking these days. She's a reminder of what made our country great.

I leave feeling helpless. I have failed Auntie Annie and not delivered on the promise to my mother to look after her.

I try to remember the way out but always get lost and end up on the back steps. I can hear two voices the other side of the back door.

'She's amazing for her age, isn't she?'

'She is, but you know what I been thinking – what would I get if I sold my story to the papers about what goes on here?'

'Ooooh, you wouldn't, would you? Might make a bomb.'

When I push through the door, the conversation stops, and they stub their cigarettes out and disappear inside.

5

Loidis

I hit the traffic very soon after getting out of the estate, from the woodland-lined lane descending to the tree-lined avenue, down to the tatty concrete and steel fences and windblown, litter-wracked, deserted, scrubby beachhead of the ring road.

Underneath the strange grassy mounds dividing off arterial roads from kiddies' play areas, there must be treasure. Dragons in dens lurk here, the death goods of the mighty for the final journey, stolen from the grave and hoarded by the Most Evil of Beasts. At the top of the tower blocks of the poor are the Halls of the Kings and maps of the secret routes laid out of the invisible city below the visible city. Only from the sixteenth floor can the patterns and the planning of the layers and subtleties be traced. Look at the letters formed by the interlacing of the streets. The light and dark shading of the low and the high ground contrasting with one another, worked by the long-gone artists and ghost workers of our people, to spell out the message of man, material and spirit.

The lights change but we haven't moved. I want to walk my streets. I turn off the engine. I flick up my hood, put the dark glasses on and open the bag that we all carry when we leave the Circle. In it, there's a small dressing-up box of fun. Today, I put on my hipster beard and open the door. Don't forget the cane, the white one. That always works. Except mine is titanium meant to look like wood. I get out, go to the rear of the car, lift off the plate. Always take the rear one first. We always attach them loosely. If you take the front ones first, the busybody behind you, bored without limit, has more chance of clocking what you're doing. Some people can't help but shit on everyone around them. They can't help it because they're born like that. So, very quickly, unclick the rear plates, turn them round, make them invisible and go round the front of the car and do the same.

Don't look back. Stare straight ahead. Limit what you show of your face. The car is unlocked, the key is in the ignition. May the next user enjoy it as much as I did. Easy. Duck into the first side road. Walk briskly, don't run, plates hidden away under the jacket. You'd think I'd done a bank heist, not given away a car, the way they sometimes stare. Or shout, like the Fourteenth tribe of the Lost Shouters of Arabia.

Some people leave books in telephone boxes. Read and forgotten, or boring, or unwanted pressies or full of hope with a message for the willing and open-hearted that need to be passed on. There is nothing we have, or nothing we own, that we wouldn't leave in a telephone box. Full English came to live with us so long ago I can't remember when he wasn't there. He used to live down south in one of those maisonettes they put up in the seventies. They look like electricity sub-stations, but they're two-storey dwellings. The top half is clad in bits of wood from B&Q, the bottom half has one window the size of a small serving-hatch. They come in rows built diagonally up embankments with tiny gardens and little wicker fences. Next door had moved out, and some squatters moved in, so the Council got them out and boarded it up. But in all the confusion, the roof started leaking and it got damp. He told the Council. Nothing happened. It got worse. He got fed up so, he started to repair it. The Council came and told him that he didn't have the jurisdiction to repair it, so he asked them nicely to come and stop the leaking.

Nothing happened. It rained and got damper. The wood started rotting. Amazing how quickly wood will rot, even painted wood, when exposed to rain on the plain. He rang the Council, visited the Council, wrote to the Council but nothing happened. So, he started to leave bits of the dwelling in telephone boxes. Nicely packaged, with a label on them, so that whoever found them knew what was in them. Luckily, he lived on the end of the terrace because very soon he'd got rid of the porch, the upstairs flooring, a nice chest of drawers, three hundredweight of topsoil and a low-quality set of kitchen units, all nicely labelled and left in public telephone boxes within wheelbarrowing distance for a man with the time to deliver.

One fateful day, he had to stop as he was coming round the corner with his wheelbarrow, having just delivered a few loads of bricks from his rear wall to a fellow who'd offered him a hundred quid for the whole of his breeze block brickwork. Unfortunately, he was only halfway through redistributing his rear wall when he saw Fat Slut and two guys with folders and paperwork marching purposefully out of their parked cars. Like they weren't coming to repair anything that needed repairing but rather to begin the paperwork trail concerning his charitable works. Or bang him up for it.

Anyway, it appeared to him, like a miraculous vision, that he'd come to the end of this useful work with the useful reassignment of potentially rotting building materials and walked into a different drive and leapt over their back gate. He left the keys to his house of a door he never locked on their back steps. She was Irish Catholic, and he was black Jamaican, and her parents hadn't spoken to her since before she gave birth to the first of her handsome children.

'If you've got something another fellow needs, it might as well go to a good home', he always says, when he tells me the story. When he speaks, he sings in the thrawn glory of his Scottish tong.

When we met, he still had the wheelbarrow. On the inside was a worn, chipped face of Margaret Thatcher, that he'd painted there. The bottom of the tray was her face, but the chin and both eyes had been a little bit extended to take up a part of the sides. 'But I barely had rroom for herr hairr,' he said. I thought he had real talent. 'Trying to do a runner on a train with a full wheelbarrow is not easy, parrrticularrrly from one platform to another when you have to gerr up the fekkin' sterrs and there's two wee wankerrs from Trransport Police afterr ye, who'v din fekk all fer two weeks...'

EVEN THE GIVING WILL COME BACK TO HAUNT YOU.

STEALING IS THE EASY BIT.

And as I walk, I want to sing the praises of our civic living: legion are the types of paving in our Leeds. The corsie, the pavement and the boardwalk, the cobbles, the setts and the blocks, the sandstones, the limestones and the conglomerates, the kerbing, the verges and the safety stones. Feet clatter and chip the hard surface, the rain washes and wears, tyres and weight find the weaknesses and heavier than the air, the particles of soot and carbon and dust from the Sahara leave marks and grind away. In the way of the world, liquid and solid and gas and friction combine to stain and wear in equal measure. What is lost is restored and what is left is evidence. At the root of all things is the eternal grinding of one thing against another.

And what manner of miracles is beheld in our Loidis! The cleanliness and the godliness of our chequerboard centre on the inclining slope of commerce. Goods there, the like of which cannot be described in a book the length and depth of the Good Book. A man could go half-mad in comprehending all the wonders of fabrics and goods and machines and toys in the halls of our businesses and shops, our emporia, markets and outlets, our retailers, businesses, counters and vendors, merchants and dealers, purveyors, traders, peddlers and hawkers. In the doors of the hallways of the owners and the Unknown Rich sleep the poor and the wretched, still. God bless 'em. And black men, brown men and sickly white men sweep the streets of the chequerboard centre where the people walk of our commercial town.

Everyone's doing their best.

It would be easy to say that the world is one place. That one place is simply one place, but you know it isn't true.

Here are some verses from the *Apocryphal Loidian Gospels*:

Take the Cyclops out of the cave and put in a candle and a statue of Mary and it's no longer a cave, it's a shrine.

Put the squatter in the Manor and it's no longer a Country House, it's a nest of hairies.

Empty the slums and put up tower blocks and you've got streets in the sky and failed social housing.

Knock them down and put up glass tower blocks and you've got gentrification, great views and pieds à terre. And displaced refugees without communities in windblown avenues.

Redevelop the docks and you've got swish offices and apartments. And scores of unemployed men.

Shut down the shops and open up chains and you've got customers in droves from the soulless plains.

Shut the mines and the factories and the libraries and the hospitals and the pubs and the railway stations and the schools and the workshops and the foundries and the buses and the Working Men's Clubs and the dance halls and the churches and the Community Centres and the post offices and the local butchers and the parks and the greenbelt and let them take to their cars to the out-of-town Shopping Heavens and you have got Lardland.

Lardland, I taste the word, like forbidden fruit, whetting the anger of my tongue, knowing in moments like this how Habbakuk felt,

'Behold, I raise up the Lardlanders, that bitter and hasty nation, that march through the breadth of the earth, to possess dwelling places that are not theirs and let them sing as they push their trolleys as they are much puffed up to seize all the goods of the world, at a price that is smitten down, whilst the aisles overflow and they can rejoice in the queuing.

Oh, how they tolerate those who deal treacherously, and keep silent when the wicked swallows up the man who is more righteous than most Lardlanders. Let there be Lardland!'

And I can hear them singing in loud voices,

'Let us be in ones and twos together down the aisles behind the Lord's trolleys and walk to the places of discount promise where we can buy freely.'

I am cast into the wilderness with the wild beasts. I will be dashed to pieces in the storms of heaven and struck by lightning in the lowest valley. But a man has to do what a man has to do. I am shaking. This is not planned. I do not know what will happen. I have thought about it in an unclear way for a long time. I have my bag, drift off down a little alley where the skips are for the restaurants, into a doorway, take off the beard and the dark glasses and extend the cane. I hobble out the other side. I know there is a camera up there on the right, pointing towards the people coming to the railway station.

Practice what you preach. Sometimes you have to preach.

It's after lunchtime, it's pint-time. Leeds breathes out. A man in a coat sits on a bench by Brewery Wharf and for a moment, considers leaving his marriage in a canoe, pushing away from it all, pushing out to sea, and almost lobs his mobile phone into the canal before putting it down again on the bench, under the dull, calm paperlight of Loidis.

Women in ones and twos with shopping bags, mothers and daughters or just old friends and office workers going for a snack. Scally kids, angular and thin as straws, taking up all the pavement. Uprooted, temporary bus stops and small crowds of tired people, not daring to seem too hopeful. Dudes in suits and totty shared between them, being polite. Human wreckage in doorways with navy blue collections of tied-up rubbish, or one step up, the smelly shits who are still getting benefits, propped up against a parapet in trainers, worn like fighting dogs, breathing through a nasty fag. Everyone stares so no eyes meet.

KEEP YOUR FUCKING HEAD DOWN.

Between the railway station and the Corn Exchange is a pub. Everyone passes it and ignores it, or steps round the swelling men as they emerge. It's a Leeds pub. That's LUFC Unquestioned Loyalties. No prisoners. You're not welcome. Fuck off. I've never been in before. They smoke in there as if there's no law against it. This is a Business Centre for Gents with Tats, Geezers with Stainless Toys and Shaven heads. Bruiser fuckin' meathead animal Dogmunchers.

I have to speak to order a drink. The barman is foreign, he's Polish. He either doesn't realise where he is, or he's madder than any of them in here. At the far end of the bar are a comedy couple, arguing about something. He pulls her hair and her head back and spits something aggressive into her face and she responds with a spiky knee into his balls and he reels back and sinks to the floor, taken aback. He's got phlegm in his matted beard and her glasses are on the floor. When she finds them, she stands back at the bar to finish her drink. No one except me bats an eyelid. I'm conscious that there are more people looking at me before I even order my drink than the two functioning mentalists having a domestic. Nothing obvious, just a glance or two. The sort of glance that the hairs on the back of your neck pick up 'cos your eyes are too busy sweating with fear.

'Half a lager, please.'

Please was a mistake. Two guys three feet away are talking quietly. I don't tune in straight away. One's got three gold earrings in one ear, tall and fit. He drinks half his pint in one down. Orders another one with a thrust of his glass into the barman's chest. Just below his throat. 'That cunt can wait,' he says, meaning me. 'Schnell, schnell, you fuckin' Nazi' he says, and the others laugh. 'I can speak fuckin' Polish better than you.'

The barman puts my nearly full glass down and puts Mr. Personable's glass into the stream of lager. Since he's East European, therefore he's not really fucking human, he has no face to lose, except maybe literally. He doesn't smile, and he isn't looking at anybody or anything, just staring like a blind man at the telly. He might not even be breathing. I'm suddenly aware that he does know exactly where he is. I'm not sure why this worries me more than the thought that he is actually a naïve twat. Not sure what that makes me.

I'm lucky. I'm nearly always lucky. There's a big mirror behind the bar. Mr. Personable is looking at me, and I know that if he turns before he has properly squared up to me, I will go down with one of his punches. So, I have no choice. Either I do nothing and wait for a smack or I step out the way. I look at him with absolute steel and drag his gaze to the mirror. Even as I'm shouting with my eyes, *Look* and pointing at the mirror with my gaze, voice and left hand, so that his head turns away to look at himself, even though he doesn't want to, I'm tensing, flexing and vaulting directly over his head with my left hand gently using his shaved bonce as a guide. He watches it all in the mirror against his better judgement. To look me in the eye again he has to turn around completely. Meanwhile, I have landed upright on the marked, sticky, wooden floor, four or five feet away. Before he can speak, I have sprung another three or four feet and landed on an empty table.

‘Gentlemen,’ I say.

Mr. Personable is bristling. He’s has been made a fool of, but not quite in a way that has touched him. He feels like he’s the centre of attention and has to act like he’s bothered. He only has one reaction and moves towards me, puffed up. I have nowhere to go and don’t try to escape. There’s an old man on a chair between him and me and that gives me time to pull out of my mouth a paper chain of coloured loops that I can extend as far as I can reach, but the chain just keeps coming out my mouth so I have to throw it to the old man from my outstretched arm and I can feel it sail through the air to his lap, where he grabs it and holds it up, laughing. It’s like a magic trick.

The pub stops. Mr. Personable stops, then starts. The old man won’t move easily. I pretend I’m gagging and that he’s shaking me like a dog on a lead, and I reel towards him like a fish on a line, but the fish is in charge. He’s so sodden in his lifetime of inactivity that he’s the dead fish holding the fishing line. All that is filling my mind’s eye is Mr. Personable and his reaction. Everyone laughs, even the two warring tavern-patch dolls, who for a moment take their eyes off one another. Mr. Personable steps forward and wants to rip the paperchain out of the watermelon’s soggy grasp, annoyed. Even when he stands absolutely still, he looks like he’s doing something horrendous. Someone claps and then it dies down.

‘Mash, leave it,’ a voice from the back of the pub. A deep, lowing voice that’s tired as well. ‘Leave it, Mash. Touch him and you’re dead meat.’ A tubby man steps forward in a waistcoat. I hadn’t noticed him at all.

‘Very good,’ he says to me. ‘Like *The* bloody *Matrix*. Mash, go back into your kennel. Come on down, now. Show time’s over.’

He’s leaning on a low railing that divides the pub in two.

‘My good friend, Mr. Godfather, a moment of your time, I have to speak to you.’ I eye him, and then straight at Mash. ‘All of you. I found these words written on this piece of paper and I want to share them with you.'

'If you're a religious nutter I'll fucking set him on yer, so you can fuck off right now,' says The Godfather, gesturing at Mr. Personable.

The way in. There's always a way in, there's not so easily a way out. I pretend to read from my regurgitated slither of paper that appeared to have come out of my mouth. The pencil marks are just acronyms for the sections of my text.

'Exactly,' I began looking at him from my tabletop. 'The Vicar's Thong', I began to declaim as if I were a religious nutter with a lisp:

'Trapped in the pulpit between the bride and the vergers
It's thongs of praise in the wedding thervith
But the listhping vicar's got his thongth mikthed up
And his thongue-thied thermon's getting in knots
The bride's father is doing his nuts
At the vicar's stream of conthiouthneth.'

'That was fucking terrible', shouted someone.

'He doesn't think so,' I said, nodding at the old man who clearly has no idea why he's laughing his head off.

The Godfather is smiling. 'Next one's gotta be better than that,' he said.

I perused my slithery strip. I started on my next piece, with a cockney-geezer-wartime-Tommy's-hammed up thirties voice:

'Hitler's Thong. Have any of you seen Hitler's thong? Imagine him wearing it on the Eastern Front rushing to do a *Heil Hitle*r after a heavy meal. Here goes:

'Wat wiv oanh jackboot in Rahssia
and de aver shtretchd aou' aver norff africah,
it aint any wander
De Furred Reik went to cock in tha bankhar.'

The mentalist with the beard had snorted his lager through

his nose when he heard the title, 'Hitler's Thong', and it had unfortunately landed on his lady partner's chest, so she stamped on his foot and as he bent down, she poured her lager over his head, and went off to the toilets to clean up.

'That was worse', shouted the same whinger. The old man was chuckling. The Godfather had an amused look. Mr. Personable did a salute. I was wondering if it might have been a mistake to attempt this.

'It rhymed. More or less,' I replied

'You've got some balls coming in here with this fuckin' shit,' said the small guy with the metal teeth, next to my main man.

But deep, *deep* down, they are loving it. Spectacle, carnage, human humiliation, the theatre of undisguised disbelief. This is an unexpected episode of *Britain's Got Knobrot Talent* right in their own backyards, on their doorsteps, over a beer with their mates. They're laughing. The tension's gone.

'I love shit like this,' shouts Mr. Personable. 'Got any more?'

I tease him slowly with the opening to 'The Fishfryer's Thong' which is dirty, smutty and laden like an illegal trailer with innuendo, worked on a variation of that most singalong tune, 'Living Next Door To Alice' and he loves it. It's got a bit of a chorus and I get them all to join in,

'You wanna bit of fish before your batter?'

and they're listening to each line and then shouting back in answer, like a finely conducted choir on an Alabama prison day out. I string it out, add some movements and then some sounds and slapping of arses and moving of hands and hips and eyes and then some tongue-wagging, hakka-style lewdness where they stand in pairs, facing one another and shout in unison,

'We've run out of roll for wiping up the dripping trap' and by the end of the poem they're living the poem, body and soul, and I clap them. Everyone's laughing and still they won't stop.

Even the tavern-patch dolls have joined in with the bits they can manage, including the full hakka-face-on-face tongue-stretch that turns into a massive snog when he grabs her hair again. This time, she just grabs his hair in return, but he won't stop snogging her so hard, so she just pulls out of the embrace and nuts him firmly just above the bridge of his nose. He goes down once more, with a silent wince.

I'm still on my little stage of tables. I can walk on tables. The Godfather's got the look of a successful impresario on his face and is looking round at his customers, who look like they've just had their tombs opened.

'Is this what you fuckin' came here for?' he says, with a smile.

'*Britain's Got Talent*,' I say, and he thinks he knows what I mean and smiles in agreement. 'Time to turn up the volume, as they say.'

This time, I get them into two teams, a full face off. Mr. Personable heads his team and Metal Teeth, a thin-faced guy whose sneer could open a can of tuna, has a stocky guy as his right-hand man, in a singlet and tats from his finger ends up to his neck-end, and a couple of young lads who've got the look of having been banged up abroad. I want it to end in a fight, I think. Maybe. The Godfather waves a beer at me. I wave it away, I haven't come for fun.

I get four fivers from each team and slip most of them in my pocket. I keep one fiver out and I hand it to the team that doesn't have Mr. Personable in it. He wants that fiver. He can see the play.

'*Britain's Got Talent*,' I say, and tell them the rules. 'Start off with four lines max, got to try to rhyme, got to show the other team who's boss, wind 'em up, then when you've had your go, you gotta listen to what they say and then your team responds. You can't just shout out or I'll keep giving out the fivers to the team that plays by the rules.'

Personable looks less personable when he hears them.

'Fuckin bollux,' he says, but loves a chance for a row.

I start with the slow opening of 'Britain's Got Talent', one of my classier poems. It's got a nice rhythm, like a pop song and Metal Teeth's team pick up the words easily and taunt the other team:

'You lookin' for the money,
We're lookin' for the looters,
You looking at me funny,
'Cos we got all the rulers...'

and they don't let that drop, but continue repeating it in a low humming way, like they are waiting for the line of the opposing army to appear on the ridge above them.

I knew they'd be good at this 'cos it's what they do every Saturday afternoon on the Kop of Elland Road, making one another laugh and winding everyone up with ragged and clever bits of poetry.

While I set Mr. Personable's team off with their little starter,

'We got all the graftin',
we got all the tools,
you…'

and tell them to continue.

They look at one another as if they don't quite get it.

'What do we do now? Fuckin' stupid this…'

No, I don't want to stop this, that's the point.

'Look at them, look at what they are doing – don't let them get away with it – they're mashing you into the ground. You want that wad of fivers, don't you?' and inch my little wad out my pocket. I help them out again,

'We are Leeds, we are proud,
Standing up, singing loud,
And there's nothing you can do,
Against the yellow, white and blue...'

'That's it, imagine these twats are Scum fans,' I say to Mr.

Personable, who actually looks round looking for anyone who looks vaguely like they are ManU.

That gets 'em going, they love that. And they launch into a rousing chorus of the Leeds clap, that stomach-churning, single-word, Viking chant of *Leeds* with four beats of clapping. It's awe-inspiring what sound ten blokes can make. Metal Teeth's team joins in, but then he shushes them and he puts them in a huddle, with some muttering and whisperings. After a moment, he turns round triumphantly. He wants to play this for real. They start chanting again, in complete, full-throated, football-fan passion:

'You're just a load o' scroungers lookin' in the trash,
You dirty fucking dolies hanging round the scrap,
You're looking for the fag ends,
'cos we've got all o' the cash…'

at which point they pull out fivers and tenners out of their pockets and carry on taunting the other team and dancing and shouting out their little verse.

Mr. Personable is not happy, and he's looking at me like I'm to blame.

'You trying to make me look like a cunt?' he says.

'No way,' I say, 'but we're all cunts at the end of the day.'

He doesn't like that remark, so he lifts me up by my throat. He's taller than me and I feel my feet leave the ground. I dangle for a moment, having known at the back of my mind it would reach this point. Strangely enough, the volume increases from Metal Teeth's team. They walk towards Mr. Personable, teasing him with the money-waving and further variations on the lyrics of their previous inventive verse, suggesting this time that he and his boys are signing on in a number of DHS offices across the north of England. When they mention Scunthorpe and Grimsby he starts to laugh, and puts me down, with Metal Teeth waving what looks like £250 in loose notes in his face.

'What you fuckin' doing here, you fuckin' nonce?' he says, shaking his head, very unsure.

'You lookin for the money?

We got all the money…

you lookin' for the money,

we got all the money…'

chants Metal Teeth, taunting his mates.

'You angry with me or him?' I ask him, but shuffle back in case he lashes out. 'Or yourself?'

'He's angry 'cos he's lookin' for the money and he ain't got the money,' says Metal Teeth, waving money around and drinking from his pint.

'I think he's right. You do all the grafting, you don't see all the money.'

'And what the fuck do you do?' he says.

'That's a good question,' I say.

'Fucking dolie or a scrounger,' and turns back to his pint on the bar.

The place has gone all tumbleweedy. Good. The Godfather is leaning on his little railing enjoying the show.

'Just imagine if it wasn't just a joke,' I said, to him. 'In a place like this.'

'What you mean?' said Metal Teeth, stepping across and furrowing his brow, like homo sapiens meeting a Neanderthal for the first time.

To my right, I can see the mixed martial arts lovebirds have got bored now the entertainment we were providing has gone back to just words and the threat of violence, so he's trying to wrestle the bar stool she's sitting on from under her, while she has a fag in one hand and her pint in the other, necessitating her to grip the stool tightly with her thighs, whilst he lifts all four legs of the stool off the floor and then, lifts the stool level with the bar, so that she is, in fact, now almost horizontal but steadfastly refusing to let go of anything. They do it almost soundlessly, like some bizarre footage from a silent film of the early twenties.

'What if one of you asks one question each, and I can ask you one question each.' I didn't wait for their response.

To the stocky guy behind Metal Teeth, 'Why does your man here,' pointing at Metal Teeth, 'enjoy that little thing we just did with two teams making up shit to sing at the other team?'

''Cos he's good at it, he can fuckin' mek songs up anytime, always got new ones for every match,' he says.

'So, he's a poet. Fair do's.'

And to Sneery I ask, 'You a fuckin' dolie?'

'Fuck off, won't you. No way am I a fuckin' dolie. You fuckin' look like one.'

'So, you work?'

'Fuckin' non o' yer bizness.'

'So, if you work you must have a house, a car, money in the bank. Nice.'

'No fuckin' way. Get fuckin' lost, no fuckin' way 'ave I got fuckin' any o' tha."

'And what the fuck do you do, comin' here with this shit?' said Mr. Personable.

I looked at them. 'Cos I'm as angry as you.'

'We ain't fuckin' angry, cunt, except with you,' says Mr. Personable.

'It matters what you think. It matters what you do,' I say.

'What?' says Metal Teeth.

'Fuckin' gobshite, that's all,' says Personable.

The Godfather speaks. 'Shut the fuck up a minute. He's got some balls coming in here talking like you wankers matter...' and he starts laughing. 'You some religious nutter or what? I can't see what you're doing here. Do you just go around doing this stunt for a laugh or what? You like getting beaten up? You some pervert type?' He starts laughing again. 'I think you're funny. But a fuckin' nutter.'

'There's more rules to the game we started,' I said, 'where one set of people get more and more things they can't say, like they can't mention money, or guns or power or can't do anything like, can't dance, can't sing, can't move from the spot and the other team start getting more of the money, more freedom, more chance to speak more often, more lines and then in the last bit of the game, people from one team can have a chance to join the other team and guess what, no one ever wants to join your team,' pointing at Personable's team again, 'and eventually, the other team have got everything and only the stubborn and the angry and the weak, and the stupid are stuck together.'

'Just a fuckin' stupid game, then,' says Mr P.

Not sure he got the reference to being called stupid.

But Metal Teeth pipes up, pointing at Mr. Personable.

'If it's just a fuckin' stupid game, why you gettin' so angry about it?' Then switches again to waving some fivers around and doing a little jig to the tune of his last winning verse. No one else is laughing.

'Cos of him, he fuckin' winds me up,' he says, pointing at me.

'Not him you should be angry with,' says Metal Teeth.

'Mash, you're always getting so fuckin' angry. Stop gettin' angry so much,' says The Godfather.

Mr. P turns back to the bar with his pint.

'If just one of you here asked one question about the game we played and that one question from one of you turned into one more question from just one more person you know and they made just one more person they know start to ask questions and that went on throughout the whole country, just imagine then what would happen. That's why I'm here.'

Just at that point, there was the sound of a smashing glass from the loving wrestlers at the bar where she had rammed his head hard enough against one of the little glass partitions, set at a right angle to the bar to create an intimate space, that it caused him to flail with his arms and knock both pints of beer over the other side of the bar and smash. The bartender was bending down almost immediately and apologetically, to sweep up the glass and liquid. Everyone else registered the scene for a long moment before resuming their previous stances.

'I don't know why we give so much fuckin' money to foreign aid,' said Metal Teeth, 'when nothing hardly fuckin' works here.'

'That's a start,' I said.

'And I fuckin' hate cunts like you from private schools, fuckin' wankers,' says Mr P.

'I agree,' I said. 'What you gonna do about it?'

'We could privatise them,' said Metal Teeth, laughing.

That was funny, I thought.

'We could kick the bastard Brewery company out of this pub, for a start so I could sell decent beer. Not that these beasts of the field would know any better,' said The Godfather.

'Wish we could kick you out,' said Metal Teeth, 'and fuckin' nationalise your house. You've got the biggest house I've ever seen, so brewery must be doing something right,' and everyone laughs.

'He's rippin' em off, innee?' said Sneery.

'All we need to do is work out who the enemy is, then?' I said.

'Every other cunt in this town, by my reckoning,' says Mr P.

'Are you sure? Fifty thousand Leeds fans? These blokes? Your family? Guys like you? Are you sure? Are they the enemy?'

'Most of 'em are cunts,' says Mr P.

'That's 'cos you're a cunt,' says Metal Teeth, and everyone's laughing.

'I don't think he's a cunt,' I said.

'Fuckin' faggot,' he says and everyone laughs.

I thought about this. 'Work out why you're angry,' I said,

'then you could become the fuckin' Prime Minister.'

Metal Teeth is straight in there, 'Order, order...order order...' and they're all shouting with him and raising their beers and it's all over.

They turn their backs on me and I watch them, for some reason, clambering over the trenches on the first day of the Somme and other hellholes, with their names inscribed later on war memorials in Calverley, Farsley, Horsforth, Armley, The Headrow, the list goes on and on. There's fifty-eight of them in Leeds.

One last thing to do: Milton. I go over to The Godfather. He'll know. I'm thinking about Milton's story and how I might get a little nugget of information, without mentioning any names or guns or details. Except one. I reckon he might give me a clue.

'I need your help. There's a pub that you might know, little old corner boozer, what with being in the trade and being a businessman in a prestigious establishment yourself, I thought you might perhaps know of these people. Referred to, locally, as *Sid's*.' I wondered if I was making a mistake involving him in our business, but I needed to know what we were dealing with.

'Sid's,' he considered, 'well, if it's the place I'm thinking of, just off the old flyover way out the other side of town...'

'Think so, yeah.'

'Why you asking?' He looked suspicious.

'What sort of a guy is he? Is he a friend of yours? He's giving a friend of a friend some bother, need to sort it out in a nice, steady way. Nothing dramatic.'

He took me through to the back of the pub, to his little office with a too-big desk. He looked at me and sucked in a deep breath through his nose.

'I don't know what you are up to, brother, but,' again he spoke slowly, 'stick to the day job, whatever the fuck that is. My advice to you – don't go down there throwing some tricks like a fuckin' prize clown. You seem an all right bloke.'

He stares out through the little window, which is glazed to let in the gray from outside.

'Don't say you haven't been told. What's your name?' he asks.

'John,' I say instinctively, 'John Hampden, nice to meet you.'

'And what's yours? 'I ask.

'Marlon,' he says, 'Marlon-Brando.'

I laugh.

'It's not a fucking joke,' he says, 'Marlon-Brando Jones. Dad was obsessed. You know what I did when I was about twenty? I fuckin' punched him on his nose for wha' he did to me, calling me that name, an' what I had to fuckin' put up wi' 'cos of it.'

'They know not what they do, do they?' I said.

At the door, he stops me again. 'Come back for a drink. Don't come back with any more tricks or any mates, ok? Keep it friendly. And if you go and visit your friends at Sid's, the only way you'll be leaving Leeds is in the boot of a car. No, beg your pardon, there was that guy who was found strapped under a barge over in Stalybridge when his body kept getting the boat jammed through the locks. Still don't know who he is, no face an' all that.'

'Thank you for your time, Mr. Jones,' I say.

As I'm walking back through the bar, I see Mr. Personable turn and look at me with his hooded, sad eyes and further down the bar the lady tavern-patch doll is stroking the hair of her beloved, as tenderly as any Zelda with her Scott. I put all the fivers on the bar and tell the barman to get them all a drink.

By the time I reach the door I'm back in the groove, limping. I want to leave the right impression.

About Hippos and Hagfish

For a brief moment can we consider the hagfish. They are the only known living animals to have a skull but no vertebral column. They are extraordinary creatures in many ways, with eyespots rather than eyes with lenses that can focus, skin that is described as *fitting like a loose sock* since it's only attached to the body along the ridge of their 'backs'. They are also capable of releasing copious quantities of mucous from upwards of 100 glands called *invaginations,* which they use as a means of, literally, slithering out of a predator's grasp or choking it to death. Politicians, lawyers and corporate folk come to mind.

Like hagfish, lampreys are also jawless and therefore, chinless. They have a toothed, funnel-mouth that sucks. Their name may be Latin for 'stone-licker'. In many ways, they are the sister of the hagfish and were found in the Thames and other rivers of England till pollution got the better of them. I don't know if I can trust anything with only a single nostril. What makes both species interesting is that they are classed as *Agnathans*, without jaws. Everything else with a skull and something like a backbone has got a jaw.

The oldest rocks of Leeds are upwards of 300 million years old. The millstone grits that have stood the test of time, when much of the North was a huge river delta pointing south, and more or less all the landmasses in the world were connected to one another. Half the time, Britain was underwater, trapped in the middle of countries that are now thousands of miles away. Enough climate change to drown a continent. The Carboniferous Rainforest Collapse saw the reduction of species of all types and the creation of little islands that couldn't support the previous diversity. It got very cold. And dry. Then, warmed up and what was left of the rainforests shrank and collapsed.

If you want a glimpse of life as it was all those million years ago, find a hagfish. Or a lamprey will do. They've barely changed since Leeds was a rainforest on the equator.

Permian. Triassic. Jurassic. Cretaceous. Palaeocene. Neogene and Quaternary. Leeds was there if you look for it, making its slow way northwards. Like it was just last week, as the North Sea is formed in the Palaeocene period by a series of uplifts rising miles away, so erosion wears down the Pennines. Later, huge floods break through the land bridge linking Britain to Europe. And there's always ice, somewhere in the story.

If Armley Gyratory is shut, Leeds is brought to its knees. 100,000 cars are estimated to pass through this busy roundabout every day. But one day, the cars might be gone and the hippos come back. In one warm period between two frozen ones, Leeds was as warm and as lovely as the African savannah and European hippos grazed where the traffic shudders round the roundabout. Parts of the ones that were found there are around 130,000 years old, discovered when they were digging in the clay soil that preserved the beast; the clay itself a side effect of an ice age and the eternal processes of erosion, deposition and change. In the same death spot were the elephants. And no people.

But out on the beach at Happisbrough are some human footprints that are 900,000 years old, of a family group wading through the shallow waters of the river that we would come to call the Thames. They probably had no words for anything.

6

About Tanya

Out in the light, people are walking where other people were walking before them, on the same hard surfaces of 1970s paving slabs, recent tarmac or patterns of pinkish purple artificial stone. Remember the first time you had sex. Afterwards, meeting a friend, they show no interest in your world-changing experience because you don't know how to talk about it. For them, nothing is any different. But my clothes smell of smoke. My shirt is sticky with sweat. I'm sticky in every depression and I'm always hungry after these things.

There's a set of road works just outside Subway. It's a guy with a pneumatic drill and three blokes poking around in fluorescent hi-vis and hard hats. The generator is blowing more compressed air out of the coupling than it is down his pipe.

I walk down the high street in the opposite direction and just before I stop to check the phone for Chow Mein's message, the drill stops. There are no messages or calls. I wonder why not. I wonder where he is with Milton. I walk on. The sound of drilling starts again but it's from a different direction and, at first, I'm confused. I step round the corner and there's another set of roadworks cutting off the whole pavement and half the road with the same set up – one guy with a pneumatic drill and three guys in hard hats and yellow fluorescent hi-vis poking around with a brush or leaning on shovels. He drills like he's found gold in 1849. Then he stops. As soon as the other guy hears he's stopped, he picks up the tune. It goes on like that for fifteen minutes. I'm looking for the telepathic communication because they can't see one another, and wonder how they can coordinate this sympho-cacophony. Not only that, but this second set have just laid waste a wonderful section of proper Yorkshire stone paving – those great big, creamy pieces of limestone that must have been a source of civic pride for a hundred years, and now just a ripped up thirty yard section of paving, transformed into a pile of rubble, to be replaced by soulless tarmac.

I walk between the two sets of roadworks in a valley of Victorian architectural style and sensibility, while the slum-clearing city fathers, who built the Town Hall and the Corn Exchange or the astonishing, terracotta Hotel Metropole that belongs in Paris or Barcelona, will be thumping on the ceilings of their family vaults. I can count more than twenty changes in the paving surface – darkling gritstone, tarmac like sponge, slabs of eastern bloc uniformity, concrete blocks, delicate tiles meant for other climes, another sandstone, more tarmac of a different hue and quality, chipped flagging of Chinese slate, original pavement with a beautiful, rounded corner allowing entrance to a side street and on the opposite side, only a few feet away, some kerbing of pre-fabricated concrete at a different height, and so it goes on; no wonder nothing makes sense, the very fabric under our feet was composited by some hyper-blind subterranean symposium of officers and bureaucracies all giving permission to anything except quality and aesthetics.

I have been at the queue for the 3Beard for a small period of depression, however long that could take to get a grip. While I've been there, the queue has got longer. I arrived in the rising of the moon before the setting of the sun, in the second quarter of the year. My fear is which moon I will leave in. Now, the shadows are long and the quiet amongst the people at the stop is as soft as water barely moving. A dozen people either side of me lean like old trees on the hillside, accustomed to the prevailing wind, here, the Wind of Waiting, in this place of silence, swamped by rackets and dins.

From behind me, I follow a shift of weight from hip to hip, a woman's snuffle and the rustle of soft, chubby fingers on plastic wrapping. I warm to the delicious expectation of the deft, one-handed grasp of packet and search for the tiny golden clit of cellophane strip to jerk and pull and twist to unwrap the first layer of pressie-packaging for the pleasure, the gorgeous, wicked, desperate pleasure of casting aside the wrapping and flicking the crispy carton-top wide open – nearly there, nearly there, *oh, yeah* – only the silver-embossed underwear of final layer of covering, before the experienced press upwards on the soft, giving belly of the packet pushing, thrusting a fresh pair out of the packet – and, all in one hand, remember – moist, dry mouth to hand-held, silver-wearing, protruding, filter-bearing, condoms-for-smoke-attachments and the beautiful life-or-death cigarettes. The scratch of matches and the match of light to tobacco and the tension eases, almost audibly, and as the drift of greyish-blue curls goes up and around the line, no-one complains. Perfect. We are wound together in the waft of tobacco burning.

No-one coughs. No-one complains. No 3Beard. It's Adlestrop without the birds. Only the duhdudhdudhddh dudhhdduuddhh of Road Work Station #1 in the far distance and then a tiny break before the dudhdhh dudhdudhdudhdhdddd of Road Work Station #2 to kill the monotony.

The cars come past. The girls in high heels and the ones in suits signal the start of something else. There are several ways to get to the Circle by so-called public transport, one of them is Charon's skiff, the 3Beard, the bus. All of them involve some walking. And always the waiting. We waiters in this queue are just travellers lost on a highway, at a crossroads, high in the limestone hills and night will come down, as it does, on the road to Thebes. Offstage, there is murder, rape, incest and hubris. Onstage there is a chorus waiting for a play. But these glorious raggedy people at this noshow could fill Homer's eyes to bursting.

'Excuse me,' I said to the man in front, 'does this bus go to Whiteside?' There is a bus coming out of the shadows, with evil intent. Will it be carrying Satan or the Saviour, the Dardanians or the Myceneans?

There are no seats at this noshow. Partly because the pavement is narrow. Or because it's cheaper without them. Or they'd just get stolen or vandalised. Or sat on.

He didn't hear me at first. 'Excuse me, is this bus going to Whiteside?'

He's leaning very heavily on a stick and is panting softly, even as he didn't move. The bus swooped past this bus stop.

'Dunno.'

His feet are forced into big, heavy trainers with a protruding tongue and no laces.

'Would you like a seat?'

'Uh.'

Neither a question, nor an answer. Mental effort and mouth fallen into indifference. He has a belly, swollen, covered in black trousers, looking like a tower ready to topple. He smells delicately of piss and he pulls his eyes away as I speak again, desperate to be left alone in his unspeaking, uncomfortable wheezing.

'Wouldn't a seat be more comfortable?'

This time he didn't even grunt.

The woman behind joins in.

'There should be seats for people at these bus stops. For the old folks and that.'

She has a blue chiffon headscarf on and looks older than him.

'There were seats at other bus stops, but they don't want us waiting around on them, here,' said the woman behind her.

'He don't look well,' said the woman in the chiffon headscarf. 'He shouldn't be here.'

'None of us should be here,' I said to her.

'Poor bugger,' she said, 'only comes out 'cos the Social mek him look for a job.'

The Queue pricks up its ears in a low, doggy way at the exchange, as if there might be a morsel of aggro of sorts that they could partake in. At the thought of having to act, it begins to shift a little and feel aroused, like a dog around the right tree. Someone in front of me turns away with music in their ears. Behind me, the smoker stubs out the ciggie and puts his hands back in his baggy pockets. Everyone is not looking anywhere much but glancing furtively to look without looking. Not even in the direction of the traffic anymore.

I look up the street and down the street and across the street. No seats in sight. No cars even. It felt like a blip in time, just one long, elongated stretch of existence without the ticking of a single watch or the step of a single human or the up and down of a single piston. Barely a breath. Even the duhhhduhduuuu of the Jackhammer Orchestra were having an interval.

No moveable things to make a seat. No benches to move nearer, no refuge for the frail or gathering place for coming together.

'Why aren't there any seats?' I said to no-one. 'There doesn't seem to be anywhere to sit for half a mile.'

Annoyed. But why do I care? Why not just leave the old git to pant to his death? I look at him so hard, to make him look back and say something, but he wasn't with us here, in this place, at this time. He has good hair, like they always do, but greasy, unwashed, in an Alzheimer-cut, half-finished in the past. His beaky face is positioned in an unreal way, like an abandoned forward post in Belgium, because of his terrible posture, but had he been more military he would have had the chin line to make a fabulous Tory MP.

'We should do something,' I said.

It felt like the loneliness of the bad bit in a Greek myth.

'We should write to the Council,' said the other woman, 'that's what we should do. It's a bloody disgrace.'

She turns round to continue her theme to the woman behind her, and it all goes very quiet, like a Mexican wave, down The Queue. The Queue knew what that meant when anyone said those words. The Queue surfed momentarily on the anti-ecstasy of the thought of writing to the Council. They all had known the inevitable drowning that it brings and that deeply-known knowledge swept them in an instant away from the woman's suggestions and each was led into a private reverie, as far away from the Council as could be reached in thought. Even the child at the back of The Queue slumped in its buggie over a burger that it kept holding out in front of it, as if to say, *Someone, please take it away*, looked bored. Like the staffie, attached by a lead, that was curled up and breathing heavily until it made a half-hearted attempt to lick its balls, but was thwarted by the lead and slumped instead, meekly.

'Y'are funny, mekin' me larff,' says a voice from in front, 'always wantin' it upfront 'n' ready-made, aint it?' And laughs and laughs.

Everyone's looking now. At me, not him.

'I cud larff all day an' night at wat yu doin' an' not doin', an' fussin' an' goin' on wi' yuself,' and laughs again, without even seeming to look at me.

'Look at it. Yu wanna seat, yu mek a seat. Yu wanna change it, start wi' your own eye.'

His black eyes have gone from soft to mad and back to soft

again. He's stopped looking at me with dipped eyes and turned to the noshow bin, still softly muttering and murmuring.

'Ooh,' said the lady in the chiffon scarf. 'I wonder what he's doing.'

The other woman said to me, pointing at the sick man, 'He looks worse than my Derek did when he died. You better hurry up.'

From the bin, the black man with the white stubble produces two handfuls of stuff. He hands me two or three used plastic bags.

'Mek two really strong loops like dis. No messin'. An' I need a nice shoppin' bag an' whatever else dey got to give away.' With that he walks away from me and the noshow and The Queue.

'What's he doing?' said the dying man.

My turn to say, 'Dunno.'

He's speaking without breathing, like a miracle.

I have to speak to everyone in The Queue. 'Does anyone have anything to give away?' I realise that is a stupid question. 'We need a nice shopping bag.'

'What we doing this for?' says a short, round man towards the end of The Queue. 'Bus'll be here in a minute.'

I don't know what to say.

'My Derek never had a minute,' says the chiffon scarf lady, 'when he was left in the street 'cos no-one could be bothered. Here you are, luv, here's my bag. It's a bit old, but you can have it. I want a new one anyway.'

That's all it takes, often. One single act and something good follows, as if for a moment, people are freed from being hostile and can act as they really are, without thinking. In return for her large, old, navy-blue, cotton-mix shopping bag I give her a thin plastic supermarket one for her bits of shopping.

'Thanks, luv.'

I go down The Queue, collecting whatever people can

give, but I'm not sure what I'm collecting for. They look very confused.

The black man with the white stubble has moved up the street to the islands of trees, shrubs and flowers, there to decorate the streets. They are neatly protected in big concrete boxes, but they are flourishing enough. He seems to be picking some of the leaves and stems.

I knot the plastic into two strong loops. They're talking a little bit now, in The Queue. The man with the woman and the child in the buggie and the staffie offers me a cigarette, silently. The dog sniffs my shoes and trouser bottoms, and I stroke behind his ears. He tells me he spent three hours at the dentist, but the dentist couldn't see him for free 'cos she's gone private since he was last there. The young woman grips the buggie handles, curling her fingers repeatedly, just finishing off a burger and licking the tomato sauce off her fingers. Then, she tosses the paper on the floor. The kid is still holding out the burger as far away from itself as its little arms will reach.

Out of nowhere she speaks. ''Ad toofache free daze.'

'Yeah,' says her bloke.

He offers me another cigarette, seeming to forget I had declined just three minutes ago.

'You got any money?' she asks.

'Yeah,' I say.

'Gi' us a fiver. Please.'

'Tanya,' says her bloke, 'don't ask, will ya.'

'Shurrup. Hav yer got a tenner, mate? We need it.'

'Tanya, for fuck's sake, I fuckin' sed don't ask.'

'You should be asking, not me. You don't bring nuthin' in aar 'ouse. Always me askin', so if you dahn't like it, ger a fuckin' job, won't you?'

'Tanya, fuckin' ell.'

'Have you got that tenner or not?'

'Yeah,' I say. 'No worries, my friend.' I reach for my wallet and find two fivers.

'Tanya, you fuckin' gorra stop doin' this.'

'Shurrup,' she says. 'Have another ciggie. You're the only knob I kno' what pays for 'em.'

Then, quiet for a moment.

"An' shurrup, 'for yer start,' she says.

He does as he's told. He turns away to light another one. I don't remember seeing what she did with the two notes.

'She gorinta a bit of a row at the Dole Office just nah. Fanks, mate, I owe you one. She's allus fuckin' gerrin inta a row dahn there. Fuckin' hate goin' wi' her.' He's whispering into my ear, in between drags on his fag and facing away from Tanya, so she doesn't hear.

'Take it easy,' I say.

He goes off to pick up the burger papers which are lying there, looking tomato-saucy and used. I smile at him. In another world, I think, what could he be?

Down The Queue, the rummaging has stopped and a voice speaks to me. 'You shouldn't give them money, you know. Charity begins at home. They sit at home on their arses and cadge the benefits and never work.'

She's tall, in a wool cardigan and trouser-suit trousers and hasn't looked in her bag.

'Are you getting a pension?' I ask her.

'Yes. What's that got to do with anything?'

'It's a state benefit, isn't it?'

'Yes, but I worked all my life for it, and I have a right to it.'

'Indeed.'

My phone goes. It's Full English. It must be serious, he hates phones. 'Ya need to get up here. Smoothie says to rring ya. There's a car we don't know come in through Gibraltar.'

'I'm just in the middle of something here. Get the lads out to play footer at Thetford. If you can, find out who they are. Plain clothes Slut or what?'

'Don't think so. Will do.'

'Oh, by the way, you heard from Chow Mein? Not heard anything for ages.'

'Not sure, will let ya know.'

'I'm on my way.'

Shut my phone. At that exact moment, seven things happen all at the very same time. You have to understand that this bus stop is at a busy intersection of three roads going in five directions, and of buses stopping to drop off and pick up in a concentration of space, and of pedestrians walking singly and intently, or loitering, hand in hand, in threes and fours, talking ahead and behind, walking without looking and drinking whilst moving.

The black man with white stubble has appeared at the front of The Queue. The woman from the back of The Queue has begun to address the woman in the white cardigan, loudly and with intent. The dying man is leaning on the little Asian man standing behind him with lots of shopping. Tanya's boy tries to intervene to get Tanya to calm down, but the kid in the buggie starts shouting and he goes back to it. The black man asks me for the shopping bag and the plastic bags. The woman in the blue, chiffon scarf is shouting at Tanya, who looks like she is winding up to smack the woman in the woollen, trouser-suit trousers. Tanya's bloke stiffens, as round the corner, past the entrance from the public toilets, come two lads in white trackie bottoms. He grabs hold of the dog lead and the buggie handle. The black man pulls the shopping bag out of my hand, roughly. The little Asian man is staggering backwards with the weight of the heavy, last-gasp-fattie dying man.

Seven times seven, or is it nine times nine? Each act breeds another similar act. One of the trackie-bottie boys takes a swing at Tanya's boy from behind and catches him. The dog is going mental and tying itself in knots round the buggie. The kid is screaming, the dog baying, scratching the hell out of the paving slabs and barking mentally. Tanya is so used to noise she reacts slowly to the threat to her bloke, but when she sees the perfect moment, she is straight in with a massive crack to the back of the head of one of the trackie-bottie boys with her knuckles. He stumbles, wondering where the hell that came from. His mate bends down to pick him up and Tanya's boy kicks him really hard in the front of the face. The noise is unique and lives long in the memory of boot on mouth and nose.

The two trackie-bottie boys scuttle off in a pretty cloud of expletives and blood. The black man with white stubble works on undisturbed, and has looped two hand-made, palm leaf ropes around a metal bar on the overhead section of the bus stop and attached my knotted plastic bags to the cotton-mix bag to the two palm-leaf ropes to make a comfortable seat, like a swing, for the dying man.

'We di' dis all de time in Jamaica, took me back, hehehee.'

I'll never forget his laugh. Holy, and beyond all concerns with human folly. He pushes the swing, just like a parent would push a child on a park swing. It swings easy, but untried.

'Yu aks me for it...now look at 'im...'

The dying man is now resting on the collapsed Asian man on the floor. My phone vibrates in my pocket. It has always been a mistake to not answer the phone.

Someone is bent over the dying man. 'He's really struggling breathing.'

The woman in half a trouser suit comes to me, flushed.

'You started this whole,' she's white, with sincere put-outness, 'nonsense here, you stupid, stupid man. It's all your fault.'

'She's right,' says the woman in the light blue, chiffon scarf.

What I didn't expect was the slap across my face.

'Don't you fuckin' do that, yer daft bitch.' Tanya comes running to my defence and slaps her just as hard. The woman takes the slap better than you might have expected.

'You'll like tha, won't you, bein' slapped. Your bloke used ta slap yer like tha', din' he, dirty bitch?'

My phone goes again. The black man with white stubble has retreated into silence at the front of The Queue, staring into the middle distance. The dying man pants. The short man helps up the Asian man, who has ripped the knees in his trousers. My phone goes again. Tanya's bloke with the bruised eye and the bleeding cheek pulls Tanya off the woman in the half-trouser suit.

'Sorry, mate,' he says instinctively.

He pulls her back to the relative safety of the back of The Queue, but she resists him, shouting, 'Everyone's always having a go at someone in this effin' dump,' and goes back to quieten the spinning dog and the shouting child.

'We need to get 'im to a 'ospital' says the nursing woman, 'and 'im as well,' pointing at the little, shaken Asian man. 'He looks worse 'n 'im.'

'It was your fault' she pipes up again.

Without anyone noticing, the 3Beard has come. The doors open, and the driver is in no mood for charitable acts.

The black man with white stubble doesn't trouble to look behind as he speaks to me, 'I know who you are...' and skips lightly onto the bus.

I don't quite catch the whole phrase.

The little Asian man struggles on, too, but forgets a shopping bag and the lady in the blue chiffon helps him, like she does her grandchildren. She looks at me with another type of pity as she does so. The nurse gets up and struggles in her bag for the money for the pissed-off driver.

'I have to go, sorry.'

I know who you are...I know who you are...

Did he really say that? Am I going mad? I rush down the side of the bus and see him sitting on the other side of the gangway, on the far side. I run round the back of the bus. It sets off, and I have to speed up to try to catch his eye and look at him full in the face. When I do, he stares straight ahead and won't look at me. I knock on the glass. But he won't look.

The bus goes off. The cars toot for me to move out of the road. I go back to the noshow. Both roadworks are at it, back to full, ramped-up, concert pitch thrust.

I bend over the panting, dying man. Tanya's bloke comes rushing back to the stop, speaks whilst I'm kneeling.

'Tanya needs a drink to calm down. But thanks for the money, mate, like...' as Tanya pushes the buggie off down the road, and jerks the lead of the staffie repeatedly, till it does as it's told. And as he goes, Tanya's bloke turns more than once, but then has to run to catch his lady and child.

So, just me and the panting man and the hand-made, natural fibres, bus stop swing and the sudden silence. I look at my phone. Two missed calls. Chow Mein.

I ask the panting man, 'How you doing, buddy?' as I kneel over him. I can't help but be amazed at the size of the man's trousers. From the mid-thigh down, they are more or less wearable by any man, but the size at the top of the opening is quite extraordinary. I can't help but stretch the waistband to see how far it will go, now that his sagging stomach has spread flatter on the floor. It lifts right up. It's the size of a burial pithos. It's the size of a pithos cut in half. It's not what I should be doing.

Maybe, he said, 'Dunno' again, I don't know.

I decide it's time to ring 999. There's a phone box just thirty yards away.

'There's a guy down. Pretty urgent. He's struggling breathing'

'Can I have your name?'

They always want your name. Why do they want my name, when I'm not the one lying at a noshow barely able to breathe?

'Sure,' I say, 'Milton Brown.' That'll do.

'Is this your number, Mr. Brown?'

'No, it's a phone box.'

'Can we ring you back on this number?'

'No.'

'Can we have a contact number?'

'I don't have one.'

'Well, I need one.'

'Ok, have this one as my contact number, it's my office number.'

'What's the nature of the problem?'

My phone is vibrating in my pocket. And from across the road and down the street, I can see two Plastics running to see what the commotion is. I can't be here any longer.

One question leads to another.

'Ok. Big guy, at the bus stop, number 254, Kirkgate, Leeds City Centre. Needs help.'

And put the phone down. And don't look at the fat, gasping dying man.

And keep my back to the Community Safety Officers.

And keep walking away.

7

About Rowena

I walk away. I think of a little dream I keep on having. Maybe walking away from the scene at the bus stop, with all its chaotic and uncontrollable elements, makes me think of my dream of my notebooks. I've lost it, or left it somewhere. My current one, that is. My memory is thinning. I have to record everything, so I write it down as it comes to me, in my notebooks. In my mind's eye, all the notebooks are going to be the same, so that they would match one another and be seamless on the shelf. The idea of shelves of thin, elegant, black moleskin books melting together into a consistent record of the glories of my minnowing time, in the effortless rush to deposit something more substantial out of the passing of the days of the people passing them with me, has become another of my failed realities: huge piles of papers, thigh-high towers in rough order, made up of cuttings, scraps of papers, jottings, cheap jotters in pink or light blue in hundreds of different bindings, cheap, ring-bound, plastic-covered, pages ripped from books, letters, print-outs, stolen sheets of music, or things that I knew I would never come across again rise from the carpet of my room. The latest notebook's gone in the mess of things that are supposed to record this passing. I'm heartbroken in the dream, so heartbroken, I wake up with a pain in my chest.

I slip into the Victorian market that is beautiful. The artistry of the red brickwork and the imagination of the design is intricate and lovely in a mix of utilitarian and delicate, with its myriad of small-paned windows. The windowsills have curved bricks that encourage the raindrops to gather and amalgamate under the sills which are set off the walls, so the raindrops fall as closely as possible to the walls without touching the walls. The delicacy and artistry must have contrasted ferociously back in the 1890s when it was being built with the stench and sounds of animals about to be slaughtered in the abattoirs and the hurly burly of the slums that surrounded it. Two brothers from London and a family of engineers from Batley built it.

I pass two security guys on the door who nod as I pass. I nod back and ask without words, *Any grief?* with a look. They know the look. *There is no grief*, is their reply. Good. These guys stand behind me in the Don Revie stand. Two or three rows behind me. Safe as houses. It's not an easy job watching all the stuff that goes on here, and then knowing what to tell to who, and what not to tell to who, and why you're doing either, or neither.

Reminds me of the story of a guy who was on security here a couple of years ago. A decent guy. He'd come up from the Midlands a couple of months earlier and started work and was keen. When he spotted a bit of petty thieving and intervened, which then turned a bit ugly, which led to this lad being arrested, who turned out to be a runner for some pushers, he told the police his story. Which was fine. Everybody happy. Except, three days later, he was parking his car for another shift and found someone shutting the door on his leg as he was trying to get out, who then followed through with a sledgehammer. Six months later the doctors were still trying to work out how to treat him.

These guys are ok. They ain't ever seen anything until they've checked with everyone who might need to know what they ain't never seen. Don't need good eyes to see that much.

I slip down the first aisle, first right after a haberdasher's, then left, then right again past a Chinese material shop, then left around the stalls, not hurried or busy, but like I've got business in the market. If anyone's following me, I'm ok 'cos I've doubled back on myself and am slipping into a discreet booth selling ladies goth clothing. You can't see inside and you can't tell what it sells, unless you're inside.

Right behind the till, is the Mistress of the place. *Market trader* does not do her justice. She's got dyed grey hair, cut short, with the cutest little curly points at the temples. She doesn't speak, she just blows me a tiny kiss across, like she's blowing a feather. I blow one back. She's wearing a tight, black, half-lace dress that trails slightly along the floor and long, black, velvet gloves that go beyond her elbows. And librarian's glasses. I'm drawn to her red painted lips, particularly the uneven cupid's bow of her upper lip.

I'm coming through to the changing room, I sign, *any possibility of closing the shop?*

She signs coolly and fluently back. There's the elegance of her hands gyrating through the words and then there's her mouth modelling the material of sound, like a potter, but, what she's making doesn't fit the expectations, like the most avant-garde artist leaving the gallery speechless.

I'm just looking at her face and lips, bewitched. I'm so far behind her because I'm back where I always am when I see her. She's got me pinned in an instant, like an insect in a museum. I wonder if this is what love is like. Or just a fantasy, wriggling under the gaze of unspeakable beauty, and all power removed? I can't go there. I can hardly speak either, and my fingers feel clumsy, 'cos my banging chest is taking all my mental energy.

I don't ever remember learning to sign, it's just something I could always do and as soon as I met her, years ago, she brought it out of me, from wherever it had come from. She looks at me like she did then, and I'm superglued. I avoid her ninety-nine per cent of the time. That's how I know what I feel. Today's different. Today, more than any other day, I don't want to be here, doing this.

Rowena can't say anything that isn't poetic. I ask her to close the shop, just for two minutes. When she responds, she's not just shutting her shop, she's become Seithenyn and holding back the sea before he overdoes it and initiates the drowning of the *Cantre'r Gwaelod*. She smiles and goes to turn the sign. I tell her I have to make a phone call, but I do it to her back, because I'm not myself. I will tell you Rowena's story, but not now. I would let her tell you, but she makes me say her words, and in between my mouth and her words are her sounds on the tape: full of laughter and full of sounds that are throaty and nasal and grunts of textures and tones, remote, and from a time when we could read the talk of birds and animals and mimic the murmurs and groans and spaces of the wilderness around us and the whispers of trees and sounds of loneliness and soughing. All made by a human who is deaf and dumb. It was the first tape I ever did. And she reads minds.

When she turns away, I'm calling Chow Mein. I'm safe to talk at last. I hear the phone ring and ring. He's not answering. I look at the time, it's 3.53. Three missed calls. No voicemail. We don't like voicemails. We change phones every few weeks, but not like the Friedbreads. We do it for other reasons. We don't do contracts. Not that they'd give us one. Not that we'd want one. One day, they'll start making everyone give an address for a new phone, like they do for the TVs, so they can check up on us. Till then, we'll keep on getting new phones with new numbers that don't lead back anywhere. Nothing can lead back anywhere.

After a minute I cut the call, then, ring him again.

'Hello.' Only Friedbread crap on the phone.

'Yes, sir, how can I help?' he says. I'm relieved to hear him.

'I placed an order, and I haven't heard anything. Milton's *Paradise Lost*. All good?'

'Thanks for your call, just checking a few things out. There's an issue with this order, so am just looking at the details, the delivery address isn't showing on our system.'

'OK, thanks, I'll ring you back,' I say, ending the call.

She tilts her head at me. There's nothing I wouldn't tell her. The phone goes again. I don't look at who it is, thinking it's Chow Mein again. 'What?'

It's Smoothie. 'Good afternoon,' he says, then he says it again, 'Good afternoon. The company's come with a steel delivery. Two guys, want a signature. Want to speak to the owner.'

He just waits for me to say, 'Yeah, OK.' Then, he's gone.

You good? asks Rowena, when I put my phone away. *You feel...* and she does a shudder from top to toe, but smiles. *Like that?*

Not exactly, but near enough, I sign back, and smile.

She's got her hand on her hip, and I'm wondering how all the choices I've ever made in my life could beach me up here. Now. With her. Like this. Then, I'm wondering what the next set of choices will mean.

That first call was Chow Mein. He says we've got some problems with a guy who came to see us. I don't know what 'cos he can't tell me over the phone, I tell her.

She tilts her head the other way. *I knew it was the Chinese one, because you always talk to him in a particular way.*

He's not Chinese.

I can never get his name.

So, I sign it for her, each letter, each sound. She signs it back to me, then I try to make her produce the sounds: the unvoiced, post-alveolar affricate of *ch,* followed by the rounded diphthong, *ow* but she gets frustrated. So, I show her the first sound with my mouth, and then I put my fingers on each side of her mouth and gently squeeze to get just the right amount of lip-rounding to form the diphthong of *ow* and she lets me. She wants to get it right. *Ow* I say, softly, and I put her fingers on my lips to feel the shaping and the tensing and the release of breath. She shuts her eyes. I sign in the tactile way on her neck, *WOW*, then *WOW* and *WOW* again. She opens her eyes, startled, and without thinking utters the sound, *wow* perfectly.

I have to break this magick or everything's going down the toilet. I pull back.

The second call was Smoothie. He said 'Good afternoon' twice, which is the sign for danger. Then, he said 'steel delivery' which is code for gun. I have to go, Rowena. I don't want to go. But there's a car come into the Circle, two guys in it and we don't know who's in it or what they want. And they've got guns.

'Hmmmm,' she says, gently mocking the sounds non-deaf people make, and signs in baby signing, *Gun very bad. Stay away from gun,* and smiles. Then, she moves towards me and touches my hands, so we are standing face to face.

I need something from you, making the signs on my hands, not in the air. She does not rush, she never rushes. I have all that time to remind myself of the smoky, dark blue eyes that can cloud over to dark grey in an instant, and the most delicious white neck, encircled by an elegant, dark platinum choker that flares out gently in the middle, etched with intricate animal designs of dragons flowing into snakes and ships prows. And from her right ear an amber bead hangs below a metal figurine in a single earring. She pulls her hand away and brings out her phone and she shows me a video on Youtube of a woman playing a Welsh harp, interspersed with images of water flowing over a stream and the lyrics of the folk song appearing and disappearing on the stream.

What is that? she asks.

A harp.

After a few goes at practicing the aspiration and holding her hand over my mouth to feel the air being expelled, and pressing her fingers to my Adam's apple and my lips, she can make the sound of the word.

'Haaarp, hhhaaarp, haaarp,' she says, over and over again. Then, her eyes cloud to black.

What does it sound like? she signs, and puts the video to her ear, and then to mine. *You can make it sound for me,* she signs, then laughs her oddly ethereal laugh.

Of course, I will. But...

I know.

There it was again. That nagging, gnawing feeling that this is torment beyond bearing and all I want to do was to seize her in that very second and to run away with her from what's coming, and take her somewhere desolate and soundless, except for waves on the beach and the wind and the birds, and spend the rest of my lifetime telling her exactly how each wave sounds, till we've stopped hearing anything else.

She touches my hands again and rolls up my shirt sleeves. With her fingers she writes something on my skin, so softly I want to scratch the itch.

What is this? she writes.

'Harp,' I say.

What do you have to do?

I have to show you it.

Yes, she giggles.

And I write on her hand, *I have a question for you.*

Anything, she writes.

Are you ready? I write.

She nods. My hand goes to her neck, and below her left ear I write my question, *Why only one?* and just for a moment she tilts her head again, and then she squeals and writes on my neck,

I only have the one amber. You know why.

Oh, I write on her neck.

I broke the spell that I will always regret.

Tomorrow, I need you to do something else. Will you help me? I will come for you after you shut the shop. There's a few little things I need you to do for me, ok?

She pulls away and flicks her eyes to say, *Go. Come back soon.*

Notebook VIII.3

24.05

Why waste our time teaching the badness of Stalin or Napoleon when the goodness of Octavia Hill goes unnoticed? She is one amongst many of the great ignored. She's not in favour of women voting. Not in favour of much government intervention because it leads to demolition, re-housing and destruction of communities.
There is almost nothing to be done about education here. Knowing anything is the least valued thing you could imagine. It has become a sort of best of all bad world's childcare system where those who know least shout loudest at those who've forgotten what they thought.

25.05
People just want to get on with their own lives. Do they? At what cost to everyone else? The smell behind the thought is fear of engaging with the other. Idiot is from the Greek root associated with self, private. Namely Me, Me, Me....

30.05
Celebrity culture is the truest reflection of just how shit most non-celeb life is. Imagine caring about someone who puts different lipsticks on, and takes photos of it for you to like. This is at the heart of death. Death by emptiness.

Young love is like arriving in the car park of B&Q, the dream of walking down the aisles and getting the tools and screws you need, so that all the unmoving things are in their right place.

01.06
There just aren't enough laws about what to wear when reading poetry.

8

About Malcolm

Rush hour traffic means I can't use a car or take a noshow at this point. Take too long. Could take a bike, but that has complications as well. From here in the middle of town to the Circle I could do it in about thirty mins, maybe less. Running. A few little things I need to tell you. Here goes.

You probably don't run. I once saw this movie with di Caprio, set in Africa, about diamonds. He sets off running like an eleven year old on school sports days who's discovered that he's better at sports than his classmates, doing a dramatic version of something he's seen on telly – big use of the arms, puffing and panting exaggeratedly, head back as if about to cry and stamp feet. Bad running is very bad. Bad running also gets the attention of the guys sat in offices, watching the CCTV on banks of screens. They're so bored, they follow people around, depending on their sexual persuasion, but often looking for trouble. A man running means trouble. Running in not-running-gear needs a reason.

So, I compute a route west out of the city, walking absolutely normally, where I know the BingoBins are pointing their cameras at me, and then running when I know they're not. There's a lot to know and I don't have much time. Slow out the market. Take a baseball cap off Jock on the Bling stall, as I go out. He wants a pint in return. *Anything for you, mate.* The callers running the BingoBins hate baseball caps, they hate anything that covers faces or indistinct clothes or shapeless shapes or bad light or shadows or distance or too many people or backs to the cameras or broken cameras. Or the wrong sort of light. These guys make traffic wardens look like softie parents of a spoilt two-year old. We know 'cos one of us works there. Malcolm. I'm going to tell you Malcolm's story. I can remember it word for word. Not too long. One more thing before I begin.

Walk out the market from the far door where I came in. Cap on. Coat turned inside out. Plum-coloured, looks like chav shit, but although it's light, it looks like it's done a bit of a gap year through the charity shops. Get the hipster beard back on. I get the cane out and tune into the limp. I think 'Elegy in a Country Churchyard', start to mouth it silently. By the time I'm up to,

'Some village-Hampden, that with dauntless breast

The little Tyrant of his fields withstood...'

I have the rhythm of the stressed and unstressed alternating syllables in my head, and feel the uneven, but balanced, lilting limp flow through my lower body. There's nothing that distracts the coppers like a limp.

Turn right out the far door down into a little side street. Pick up my speed, right at the bottom, round the back of the Market and in a few seconds I'm only a hundred or so yards from where I went in, then cross over the main road, shuffling like de Niro and getting across quicker than the fleet of foot, with valid use of the walking stick. All good.

Malcolm came to see us three years or so ago. His lop-sided 'tache caught my attention. His hair was matted, and he was shivering. One of those little guys who look like they missed out on bits of puberty, so they grow a bad 'tache asap. Chow Mein found him wandering by the canal and brings him home. Afterwards, I was left wondering why he trusted Chow Mein enough to just follow him around.

'What's up, feller?' I ask him.

'Huh?'

'You ok? Need anything? Food? Place to stay?'

'Huh?'

'What's up?' I say again. He wasn't really getting it.

'Put him in a dorm and we can take him back tomorrow. What you think?' I said to Chow Mein.

'He hasn't spoken ever since we found him,' he says. 'We've tried everything and got nowhere. Doesn't seem to want anything. Won't tell us what's up. Hasn't said a word since we found him.'

So, off he goes to the dorms. They aren't really dorms, more like little rooms, where people who are passing through can find some peace. We're all passing through and we don't all find peace, so I suppose it's the least we can do. He's meek as a lamb, doesn't look at anything, doesn't focus, doesn't seem to care, doesn't resist, doesn't struggle. Nothing left. Pure Friedbread.

Once across the street, I can duck into the dark of the little alleyway and speed up, there's no BingoBins there. Pull in my stick and run. I run past a guy putting rubbish out for the restaurant, who's laughing with his mate smoking in the doorway, and am ignored. A guy in a car, on the phone, looks businessy and the car is too sleek for Slut. It feels ok, but I clock the reg just in case. At the end of the alley, I have to slow again and walk into a small, open place below the Corn Exchange. It's been repaved and the kids love it for skateboarding and it's out of the way of adults and shoppers, so they get left alone. I scoot down a little street with closed-down restaurants where once the yuppies used to hang out and spend. Under the railway line, into some of the arches. Clip-clopping of office wallahs between meetings. Everyone's got their eyes lowered, except the kids sat on the walls, laughing and flirting and impressing on the boards, with new flicks and turns and balancing on imaginary runs and picking up imaginary speed. Most of their parents have given up with their kids' daft dyed hair and trousers that don't fit and sloppy, easy-going vagueness that is aimed at the removal of words like 'career' and 'ambition' from the English language. Malcolm was never one of them.

Next morning, Malcolm is brought to me again. We hadn't figured everything out in those days, so we're a bit cagey about people coming into the Circle like this. People who we don't know.

'What's your name, feller?'

Nothing.

'Where've you come from?'

Nothing at all. He looks neither happy nor unhappy. I can't tell what he's seeing when he looks forward. He hasn't washed and his hair is stuck up at the back. I carry on for a few minutes with questions, but nothing comes back.

I talk to Chow Mein in the back room. 'This could be like a serious depression or something seriously affecting his mental health – we can't keep guys like this here – they might need proper medical attention.'

'Yeah, I'm beginning to get that impression. He didn't choose to come here. We've done what we can for him. Shall I take him back where I found him?' he asks, in that way he has, where everything is pre-ordained and to be accepted.

I love his Dudley accent. Everything sounded so caring and concerned with its soft, uncertain, rising twang and particular stress pattern and peculiar vowel and diphthong lengthening. I couldn't ever tell him these things.

'Take him to the hospital and pass him to Bo on the gates. That way Bo can take him in, and you don't have to answer any questions.'

We went back into the main room. I sat down in my Ikea seat. It cost about £4 and spins.

'We're going to take you into town and ask the hospital to see if they can help you,' I said to him. 'We can't help you here, not really.'

He didn't respond any differently than before. Smoothie makes sure we tape every conversation in this room. No matter who's in it, we tape it. If you don't want to be taped, don't speak in this room. Our code.

As I took a little turn on my chair and fiddled with the remote, planning my next move, a noise came from him.

'What? What's wrong?' I asked, very surprised.

'You've got it –' then he stopped as if he didn't have the energy for this speaking effort. 'You give it me –' he spoke as if through gauze, and it wasn't clear. Then, he stood up quickly and went for the remote in my hand. My instinct was to pull back and not let him have it.

He grabbed my hand in an icy grip that was enormously strong for such a small man, so retreated from the world. He wouldn't let go. Chow Mein grabbed both our hands and the remote, in his enormous bear grip and tried to prise his hand away, but he couldn't. Malcolm looked like he was clutching at a lifebelt and I shouted at Chow Mein,

'Let go, let go...LET GOOOO...' and as he let go, I let go and let Malcolm have the remote.

'I know this,' he said, as if he was six.

'What is it?' I ask him.

'I love this,' he laughed. 'I love it,' and was smiling and laughing and pointing it all round the room, oblivious to the fact nothing seemed to be reacting to the pointing and pressing.

I motioned to Chow Mein to turn off the gear, so we didn't lose the recordings, but before that happened, Malcolm had got the player to rewind and we were listening to Malcolm's silence again. All the words that Malcolm hadn't spoken came flooding back and we all three sat listening to my voice and the space and the silence, and then Malcolm did something that shocked me to my core, and that I still carry with me to this day.

Then, cross High St, bear right and left and into The Calls, same word as *calle* in Spanish, the path to the old ford and the present Leeds Bridge. Cross Centenary Bridge, pedestrians only. No cameras. No cars. A guy running, so what? The air stinks of brewing, the river sullen, grey, full of metals and chemicals. Like canal water, going nowhere. It's forgotten, like everything else, just a thing that's in the way. Not sure most people want to see anything at all as landscape, now.

Along the riverside are all the new offices and units housing the replacement for work, whatever the replacement for work is. 'Mekkin' things' is not what is done anymore. The industries of Leeds are almost gone – the wool and textile industries, and the forgotten men with them, who could invent machines for spinning flax, or the ghosts of the mining and engineering industries when they could count one hundred and eleven pits in 1880, or the small armies of people in the chemical and leather industries. All this labouring to 'mek' that filled the coffers of the Treasury and propped up our armies across the world, done by the people who worked in these 'mekkin' things' industries, whose descendants are now shoved out of the cities and into inaccessible estates where they can be contained again and ignored again and used again and blamed again, are gone, their knowledge and skills gone, their secrets, trades, humours, language, morals and values are as gone as the peoples of the Nile, who built the Pyramids.

The bridge moves slightly under my feet as it rises to meet me, and the gritty surface shifts even more as I stretch for the downside. In the sun, on the southern bank of the river, the sunglasses are out and the chatter and the clink of glasses and ice cubes and jugs is king. I jump the three steps and adjust my stride and weight to the cobbles of Dock Street. No cameras here, but cameras at the end of this street on the main arterial road from the south into the city centre, and just up to the right there are traffic lights.

I go in the pub at the end of the street, a lovely, old Victorian place that's still got the room dividers and fireplace and original tiling. If I go in this door, the north door, and then discreetly slip round the back of the bar and out the other door, the south door, I don't appear on any cameras. So far, three minutes.

Down Hunslet Road and across into Hunslet Lane. Old roads to an old place that now houses the old and the washed-up and the poor and the slumdog millionaire dreamers, and cheap units for guys who are on the edge of the city and the law and a long way from the edge of the money, but can 'mek things'. I'm getting out of the city centre. One more sweep south of the river and I need to be where the canal begins. The Leeds Liverpool canal that splits the Aire, emasculates it, and was meant to be a pathway to riches. Built on the backs of the labouring navvies it brought gangs of Irish into the area, leaving behind wild, dark-haired children and rented houses and cellars, crammed with young children toiling in a dismalness that is hard to imagine in these empty lost streets, only three or four minutes sprint from Harvey Nics. It was the Irish that Engels disliked, with their pigs in their houses, in his grand survey of 1842. Past the brewery, along Salem Rd and across the dual carriageway and squeeze in between Asda HQ and the road, then walk across the pedestrian crossing and keep it steady.

Water Lane. Across the river I can see Leeds Railway Station, which actually covers the Aire in a very Victorian way. Straddling the river in a section between two bends, it's a feat of engineering which is not at all apparent when you're in the station. Hundreds of thousands of gallons of water off the Pennines roll down under the station on stilts every day, every hour, without anyone taking a blind bit of notice. Being

Victorian and redbrick, there are properly built walkways, tunnels, access points and paths, dealing with the demands of the water on the one hand, and man on the other. No-one goes there. Big metal gates, surrounded by barbed wire, to keep out the amateur and the nosey, but we have a purpose. We are the rats of the city who they don't want to see. If we swim, die and feed, all quietly and quick, we'll be left alone, until one of us begins to stink under their noses, and then it's different.

So, walk calmly with the stick, cross the road, walk along it south of the river and then, skip, sweep and jump and I'm in another world. Unless you were looking over the parapet into the dark, dirty depth below, you wouldn't expect to see a man running at full tilt along the beautifully built Victorian red-bricked and elegantly-edged footpath of the magnificently unknown beck that gives Holbeck its name. It's fast flowing and narrow and channelled to perfection. I run along it unseen. Down there I can only see the sky and hear nothing. I am in another Leeds.

Malcolm's action was shocking for more than one reason. He was the meekest person who'd ever come to us, thus far. He was one of the most slender men I've ever met, who wasn't a druggie, an alcoholic or terminally ill. He was one also of the most vacant people I'd ever met, but when he rose and grabbed the remote, and I let him have it and he sat and listened to his own absence, something in him simply snapped and from the hidden depths of the collective spirit that must have first motivated the first apes to do more than just stand, came a force and an energy that still makes me breathless to this day. Not out of fear, but out of awe.

He let go of the remote where he sat, at the same time as he stood up, and, as if catapulted to life by a powerful electric shock, he screamed with his head back and arms thrown out wide, with all his rage and unsaid, abysmal silence, while we put our hands to our ears and felt the ringing pain of shrieking sound waves hit our eardrums, time and time and time again, in an instant. It was truly appalling, more than truly deafening, and truly piercing, more than truly loud.

Then, after the battle cry of *The 300*, he launched himself with terrifying speed at the wall behind me. The room is not very big, and almost all of the furniture has been removed. At first, I thought he was coming for me, but he didn't see me at all. He ran head-first at the wall, which is made of brick. Something cracked. Me and Chow Mein were reeling – this wasn't the usual day at the office. I could see from where I'd thrown myself onto the couch, to avoid standing between him and the wall, Chow Mein stood with his hands still covering his ears, bent double and on the other side of the room, in some pain himself. Out of the window, I could see someone running up to the house. Malcolm turned round, and in an instant, we were looking straight at one another, his face was streaming with blood and his head tilted strangely to one side, but he smiled, and out of old, old habit, he stroked his moustache and discovered that the blood was catching in the hair. Then, without one instant of thought, he knew what he was going to do next, and I half-guessed and went to grab him.

I love running like this. Definite and without obstruction, at pace, but not rushed. How I have rushed in my life and how little it has achieved and how much it has hindered. My steps echo in the narrow channel and relax my thinking, and the surge of making an effort gives me the energy to make more effort. I have to plan the next part of the route carefully, and don't want to take chances, but want to minimise distance and get there quickly and unnoticed. As I get to the turn, the air changes and the sound of the water changes, so I feel what's coming next. I listen for voices as I emerge out of the safe little conduit, expect the looks as I slide over the parapet and then limp off to cross the road, disappear round the warehouses and past Whitechapel Junction, where the railway lines bundle and then unravel. Get to the Roundhouse and I'm going to hit the groove.

Up above, the interchange is the prison of cars and commuters, trapped in boxes of convenience, but down here, here I'm in a subway, underneath the trains and the roads out to Pudsey, full of pissyness and graffiti and glass and unimagination, and free to float as I will. Not everyone dislikes subways. Malcolm likes subways, although you won't always get him to admit it, but I've seen him do it more than once. His canvas is the arched or curved tube of the tiled subway. He needs the grip, so if he judges they're the wrong sort of tiles he won't do it, and the bane of his life are the big lights in metal cages in the roofs.

Once, after they put his neck back together and the glass shards pressed themselves out of his skin, more or less, and he got back his energy, the most extraordinary energy I have every witnessed, I saw him *screw the subway*, as he put it. We're walking into town, late one afternoon. Kids on bikes coming the other way at high speed, nothing doing, just daft, taking the piss of the small guys in the world, like Malcolm, and sort of coming for him half-way down the tube. I sense he's going to do something and know what he is capable of and instinctively step back and behind him, because I can feel the focus of his energy and am glad it isn't me. As they come riding towards him, he starts running towards them – almost a standing start and he's within a few feet of setting off at some speed – they're just big kids and aren't looking enough at what's happening, thinking he's easy meat for a laugh – they're at full pelt, he's at full pelt, and they can't move 'cos they're coming together and start to break and shout and he, well, he does something beautiful, and steps up the walls of the tube just in time to miss them, they lose their bearings and crash into one another and he goes all the way over the top of them both, completely upside down, and runs down the other side and ends up some distance away. One of the kids has his foot caught in the bike frame of the other lad's bike and is crying out. The other one is shocked and lying a few feet away, having been thrown by the force of the other boy's impact. He's got a badly twisted knee and is in tears and shouting the odds at me. Malcolm doesn't look back, but carries on walking away, as if nothing's happened.

'Don't, lads, just don't' and I leave them with those words.

At the end of the subway, we split up and arrange to meet five mins later. Can't ever be too sure. It was then I knew that Malcolm was mended.

If I pick up the real canal, I can save time avoiding the cameras, but I'll take a slightly longer route. I need to tell you a couple of things. At Whitechapel Junction two lines go south, one of which carries on due south and one splits into another southern line and a line out west. But one line goes west-north-west and just before it goes back into the flat of the valley, a line splits off and takes the trains off in a northerly direction. That's where I join the line and drop down onto the track, that's where I begin to feel safer, but, it's a risk, but it's another sort of risk. If I keep my head down, I'll be off it in a few hundred metres.

Think, as well, of the railway lines you know. Where the wildlife flourishes and you tell your kids not to go. Where the fences and the overgrown embankments and the bridges and the suicides are. This is our motorway. Wide, forgotten, ugly and easy. But, there are guards and employees and sometimes trains and blokes sitting with something to do, but not in the mood for doing it. All depends on fate. I need to follow this through the maze of industrial estates and dead-end roads and high security fences and unleashed rottweilers and the guys sitting in the flash cars, parked up for no good reason, in a road that goes nowhere, that's almost impossible to find, unless you don't want to find it. Where men meet women other than their wives, and the girls on the street get taken to streets like this for a turn, and the pimps sit waiting for the calls. Or the holes that men like Milton, who haven't got anywhere else in our whole beautiful realm, go down.

Milton, the guns and the gangs, me engaging with the dudes in the pub today, the phone call, the car we don't know coming up our home fairway, the way the whole world seems to be lifting the curtains and looking at us, when for years it didn't give a shit. I know there's a connection.

The wind is off the Pennines coming at me, as I settle into my stride. Without interruption, I can take the sleepers in threes. In a matter of minute or two, I'll be at the viaduct and can drop down to the street below and pick up the canal.

Malcolm had burst, and there was no dam holding his breaking waters. Courage is often mind-bogglingly stupid. Ask Socrates. Malcolm had it in spades and buckets and open-cast-mining-mega-digger size. He's still holding the remote. He's looking at me, intently. He stood for a milli-second, saw that I was going to grab him and thus reduce his speed and impact, and so spurted in that incredible standing-start-of-his-way and ran full-face at the window I had just been looking through. Most people would have at least covered their heads, protected themselves with their arms in some way, hunched their shoulders, minimised the point of impact but maximised their force, but not Malcolm. In fact, Malcolm never did what would have been expected when it came to him dealing with the essence of matter – his matter – in relation to the matter of the universe around him. My lunge from my prone position on the couch, to at least catch his ankle, was comically too late, and I just watched as he stuck his little pointy chin out and pushed his tiny frame through the window, at some considerable force. I haven't told you too much about the Circle, or what we do, or how we live or the homes we live in. Suffice to say, at this point, that these are solidly built houses, built mainly between the wars, and meant to last. Malcolm hadn't noticed, in any sense, the wooden cross-pieces of the windows that would offer more resistance, and possibly more harm, than the glass of the windows. It was a Viking-warrior, bone-crunching thwack of a cleaving when his forehead hit the horizontal cross-piece. Very, very surprisingly it gave way too, in the same, easy manner as the three feet square sheet of glass.

What Malcolm had completely failed to measure, in his insistence at self-harm, was that the whole window was mounted on a brick wall that reached somewhere between most adult's knee and crotch. He saw that the wall was low and so, sprang from the arm of the couch, but because he used his forehead to break the wood, even he wasn't small enough to avoid tripping over the low brick wall of the house. Otherwise, he would have been away to attempt to bring down the pillars around Leeds Town Hall with gay abandon. So, he tripped over into the space below the wall on the outside. I had, by then, managed to stand up and get to the window to watch him scramble to his feet again, with a comically large piece of glass sticking out of the back of his head, which suddenly made me laugh out loud.

The guy who had been running to the house, when I looked out the window, was now in the house from the side door, and I sent him after Malcolm.

'Be careful of the glass sticking out of his head.' I shouted. 'Take him down easy.'

I watched as Malcolm thought he could run where he wanted. Of course, it isn't running away as we would normally think of it. Malcolm wasn't running for freedom and open space, Malcolm was running at anything very large and very solid which would help him finish his existence. Even cars could help him on his way, not that we have many of those.

It was difficult, at that point in time, to watch Malcolm running round like a mental, quite big chicken with a head and a piece of glass sticking out of it, and imagine that one day he would become one of the people I would most trust and most admire. But all I could do was collapse onto the floor in a flood of laughter and watch through the broken window frame and shattered glass fronds the trail of wretched silliness that Malcolm was weaving behind him. The lads chasing him were trying to work out why he wasn't trying to make a run for it and what exactly he was making a run for. Chow Mein was not laughing, but still rubbing his ears.

'Man, you got rubber ears or something. I hurt...oo...ooof.'

He's rubbing his tiny ears, but that just makes me laugh even more, and as I roll over, I get tiny bits of glass in my hands.

The air is heavy with the smell of hawthorn blossoming all around me. It's such a peculiar smell from one of our sacred trees. It fills my head and lungs, like fumes in a dodgy nightclub. This air, that we breathe in, in the monotony of our own personal machinery, is bringing inside of us all the volatile, scent-bearing molecules, the esters, unfiltered without me, the owner of the machine, having any control of all this chemistry. From the tiny hairs on the neurons at the top of my nose, these unseen molecules, fragments of trees and flowers and the vast range of vegetation all around us, are converted by this chemistry into the taste and smell of this sickliness. Not for death of course, but for making new life.

I hear the traffic now and feel the smoke of engines and the energy of motors pulling up the hill to my left. I'm over the viaduct, which is over the canal and the road and the river. An extraordinary place. The viaduct is placed on the bit of land left between the south bank of the river and the north side of the canal. Halfway there. Twelve minutes to get here.

I need to be on the north side of the river, but if I go north of it now, at this point, the way is busy, difficult and easy to get noticed, and there are no short cuts. The Council and the Police have installed cameras all along the way and I'm more known there. I don't want to get noticed by anyone. If I stay south of the river it's a bit longer, a lot quieter and I won't get noticed, but there's only a couple of bridges and the river splits and creates little islands.

Need to get down to the canal. First, I go north onto the north bank. It's a long drop to the little road behind the bowling alley, then across the car park and round the recycling centre, and the little bridge they call Gott's Bridge. Into the nature reserve at Kirkstall, keep the river on the right-hand side to where the river meets the railway. On the other side of the water is Kirkstall Abbey and under the railway line and up to Bradford Road. Under the road, along the canal and into Toad's Hole Wood and across the lock gates, up the bank of the railway and cross the river and another hundred or so feet along the railway and we cross the river again and are back on the south side, slide down off the railway line, take the little service road and now, you must trust me, this and no further, I have more to do, more running, but until you come to see us because you need us, this is the end of the journey for you. Trust me, it is better for us all if I bring the journey to a close well before the point where I enter between the sacred rowans and whisper my greeting to our sweet roots in this our earth, in the old language of our people. We all do it in our own way.

Everything in your Lardland is your choice.
Everything from now on, in our way, is our choice.

I want so much to tell you about the rowans, and why they are there, and what they tell us, and how we respect them, but for now the story takes the turn of the intruders. I want to tell you as well about the burnt-out wrecks of cars and the piles of fly-tipped waste and the uncut grass that you will see as the sign that you are to come no further. If you come past these signs then you must be looking for something. You must be prepared to look further than the obvious.

Less than half an hour.

No farther seek his merits to disclose
Or draw his frailties from their dread abode.

Nearly there.

9

About Visitors

The problems are plenty. I don't know who they are, or where they are, or what they've done, or what they want. I don't want them to see me run into the Circle appearing like this. I don't want to ring anyone in case that puts anyone in danger. I have to get to see them before they see me and then, I have to present myself to them in a way that allows me the upper hand.

I can't hear any engines, so I know they aren't cruising looking at what they can see, which may mean that they know what they want. If Full English or Smoothie hasn't rung me again, which they haven't, then it might mean everything is being dealt with and they are controlling the situation. I'm running again. The Circle isn't big, by any means, but it's spread out and once again, I need to not be seen, even by my own people. And I mustn't be seen by these people until I'm ready. There are no cars in the Circle, so if I do hear a car, it'll be a stranger's. I hit the perimeter road on the inside, hoping to get up to the place that we call Thetford, the centre of our community. I'm sure that they'll have found their way there, eventually.

On my right, from a high window, a hand gestures. I step through the hedge behind me and see Smoothie signing.

I'm good, all good so far. 2 people, 1 car. Been here nearly an hour. Staying in car. Want Burgerman. Shotgun between front seats. Malcolm is watching. Got the kids off the street.

Brilliant, I sign back, *thank you. Facing up or downwards?*

Down.

Ok. Wait a minute, Smoothie. I'm thinking.

You always say that. I'm laughing, he says back.

I do stop and think. I need to get out of this get up. I need to get into my normal gear, my old man's gear. My stickman gear, the wasted, drunken-old-git-made-a-bit-better gear that is gentle and offers advice. That's who they're waiting for. That might do it.

Two minutes later, I've sneaked into Smoothie's house.

'What's going on, do you think? Who are they? Where's Chow Mein? We want them out asap. Are the microphones on?'

'Don't know what's going on or who they are. Chow Mein's not here. Mics on, yeah.'

He fits me up with a mic and headphones. The sexy ones you can hardly see and wear close to your ear and pin on your shirt.

'Let's see if this shit works, man, yeah, yeaaaaah', and Smoothie does the world's quietest whoop as he sets to work.

We can listen to anything in the Circle. The mics are in the trees and in the lamps and flowerpots and hedges and everywhere. They're even in the street furniture and the bins and the benches and the road signs, although we don't like signs, so we've taken most of them down. The whole place is an electronic expert's wet dream come true and add a bit. We ain't used it for ages, but we put it in way back at the beginning, and we've been glad of it. The sorts of folk that have taken up residence here, you wouldn't believe.

'Yeah. Listen, have you checked the car reg? Have we got a good view of what they look like, any photos? And if you can, get Chow Mein to stop what he's doing and get back here. And turn the external electricity off so we can hear everything.'

'No pics of them yet, can't find the car reg on the database but I'll have a look when I've got a moment.'

Smoothie is working away, switching on his little generator, turning on his amps and his trackers and his recording devices and his mike network and adjusting it all till he gets it right. He's one of those wiry guys who make good sportsmen. He got his nickname from his shaved head and his warm, brown eyes get him nice girls.

I dress quickly in my padded green shirt, stained black trousers with a broken zip and the navy jacket that hangs slackly and used to belong to a coach driver I knew, who swapped it in return for me spending ten minutes on the phone with his wife. I pretended to be a doctor and explain why he was being kept in for observation with bleeding from the anus and some serious stomach pains. I felt bad lying to his wife, so that he could shag a couple of desperate pensioners on a Turkey 'n' Tinsel weekend. It was a low water mark moment, but the jacket is a classic. I always wonder what he told the coach company. I pick up one of my walking sticks with a proper handle.

Out of the back of Smoothie's house, down the short garden and into the little snicket behind the houses, I run on the edge of the Circle and take the perimeter walkway. I want to meet Picnic before I take a look at them. Within a minute, all the lights that were on have gone off. There is total silence, except the late afternoon wind through the trees. Not for a long time has the Circle had to be silent, but now the trees rule again, and the wind is the mouth singing, and you can hear the creak of an electric car window being opened tens of meters away. Five minutes later, and I'm behind the Hall, talking to Picnic.

'Good to see you,' I say.

He nods. 'You look tired. What's going on?'

'Smoothie tells me that these two haven't moved since they got here and are polishing their shotgun. Just be around if anything happens but stay out of sight.'

'You gonna be ok? This is like the old days,' and laughed.

‘I think if they wanted a fight, we’d know about it already, but I don’t want to be getting in that car with a gun in my face.’

‘I’ll get Smoothie to get the exit road blocked. We haven’t done this in a while. I’ve missed it.’

I shook my head. ‘I haven’t. Give me five and I should be engaging them in polite conversation, ok?’

He nodded again. I walked from behind the Hall, round the corner and a couple of hundred metres down the main drive.

None of this was planned, I tell you, none of this was planned. I didn’t plan taking over the Circle, I didn’t even know it existed, even back then it didn’t exist like it does now, and from today, well, anything could happen. I should tell you about how it started on the eve of how it may all fall apart. No matter. Nothing matters. This will spring up again in another time and another place maybe. Maybe not. But for now, there’s these guys, sitting in the middle of our square causing me to run across the city, to have to begin the closedown and tackle them and their noisy electric windows and their shotgun between the front seats. That means that somebody wants something from us. But we ain’t got nothing anyone could possibly want. We don’t have money, we don’t do drugs, we ain’t got weapons, we don’t pose a threat. The only thing we got you can’t buy, and most people are too stupid to know they’ve not got it, and too frightened to think about what that might be.

Our main square is on a slight slope. Smoothie tells me that their car is facing upwards and is a black BMW, one of the older models that look like they were designed by children of seven. I get in the mood with some of my favourite lines, my face remembering the grief, hobbling as fast as old men can hobble:

‘*Yr aelwyd hon neu’s cudd dynad*
Tra vu vyw ei gwarseidwad
Mwy gorddyvnafai eirsiad...’

‘This hearth, ah, will it not be covered with nettles?

Whilst its defender lived
More congenial to it was the foot of the needy petitioner...'

I don't want to allow myself to be frightened, but I'm more troubled by these men coming here than I can explain. We have planted some trees, some rowans densely together, but in the midst of them is a space hidden away, three elder trees planted together to make an enclosed space. I sit and listen to the birds sing and imagine what may be about to happen. I think of all the times that people work so hard to find a small space for peace, and one day they're working away in the fields when a group of horsemen appear on the horizon, soldiers on the low ridge above the barley field, or the official car driving up the dusty road bringing papers proving falsehood. I think of the hearth covered in nettles. The circle of greed against which I can do nothing but push my flesh to fill the crumples of my clothes and shape the wrinkles of my face and neck to play the part of the man they want to meet.

I switch on Smoothie's mic and come out of our Sacred Grove. He will see me walk into the Circle. I can feel him watching me silently and unseen through the cameras on the trees and on the houses. The car appears to my left across the space of grass and trees. I can see them watching me strain slowly down the hill. They will see the hurried, limping, ageing man, the overweight, out-of-breath leaning on a stick, smoker's cough-blighted old fool with years of bad diet behind him. They have asked for me. They have heard of me from wherever they have come from. They fiddle with the shotgun, they adjust the rear-view mirror, they stare at me in between staring for clues at everything else. The late spring sunshine makes me sweat, as I finally come around to the bonnet of the car. I rest on it briefly and press down on the metal with my tired heavy body. I want to feel it – how old it really is, is there any extra weight anywhere, what it might sound like, in its own individual way. There's something extra in the boot, it's too heavy. They don't get out. I'm hoping they will get out of the car and get angry, tell me off, but they just stare. I walk round to the passenger door and look the future in the face. It isn't pretty.

'We want to speak to Burgerman,' says the driver. The passenger lazily swings the shotgun round, so it's not quite pointing out of the door at me. He talks like he's trying to disguise his West Country accent with acceptable Essex.

'Who's he?' says I.

The gun spins into my stomach. I pull back, instinctively.

'Hey, steady,' I say, 'this isn't what you think. It's just a few folks living here temporarily, before the Council claim it back. We don't do guns or drugs or anything like that.'

The shotgunner starts to speak, but I'm overcome with such a coughing fit, that he has to stop and puts the gun down to wipe off stray spittle that has landed on his jacket. Now, it's pointing at the Driver.

'Disgusting piece of shit,' he shouts, 'you've coughed your guts up all over me. Fuckin' hell.'

He's going to get out of the car, and I think that he's bound to swing for me. So, I put my hand on the lock button in the side of the door, so it's nicely locked, and then proceed to buckle under the weight of my triple emphysemic explosion in my chest. He's really easy. All I do is reach in, desperately flailing for breath, using anything for support, and my hands wrap around the shotgun. The Driver instinctively pushes the barrels away from his face and the Passenger tries to grab the handle from me. What is really loud for me is probably extraordinarily loud, and possibly painful and damaging, for the two in the car. First, one shot and then the other. The recoil is powerful and smashes downwards into the Passenger's thigh, then his crotch. I pull my body and arms out of the car to see what the damage is. The first shot passed harmlessly out of the Driver's window, but the second went very near the Passenger's face and out through the roof by his head. It was very close. The hole in the Beamer roof is not quite a sunroof, but it's letting some light in.

I hope Smoothie didn't catch too much of this through his headphones. In the car, there are shards of metal and glass all over the both of them, and the smell of smoke and sheared metal.

'Oh, my goodness, what happened there?' I said, and started with another violent coughing fit, again, which seemed to annoy them as much as the accident with the gun.

The Driver rubbed his left ear, from which emerged a tiny trickle of blood. He looked dazed and shocked and didn't speak, just stared at his hand with the trace of blood while he traces the outline of the holes in the roof, still too shocked to understand how it got there. The gun, meanwhile, is still pointing upwards between them, although the Passenger has begun screaming and shouting and rubbing the tender areas of the shotgun recoil. When he sees me coughing again through the window, he desperately tries to point it at me again, but it's just too big in that small space to get the right end aimed at me, without having to hold it above his head.

'It's not loaded,' I said.

'You've just fucking destroyed our car,' shouts the Passenger. 'What did you do that for? What the hell is wrong with you, you old wanker? You've shitted up our car shooting our gun at us. You're bloody disgusting, you smelly old piece of shit. Get out of our car.'

'Look, I'm very sorry, really, it was an accident, I didn't know it was loaded. I was frightened. I really am very sorry. We could get your car repaired if you like.'

I start coughing again.

I reach for the cigarettes in my pocket. 'Sorry, have one.' I proffer the packet. They both take one. I study them both. The

Driver still looks dazed and hasn't really spoken. He has about three earrings in his ear, and hair with a shaved pattern on the side of his head that is beginning to grow back. His tattoo is a zigzag stripe down his neck that must carry on all down his arm, because the same pattern comes out of his left cuff onto the top of his hand. He keeps scratching his ear and staring at the blood on his finger, then shaking his head like he has got some wax in there. The Passenger is a different kettle of fish. He's lean and nervous with a thin face and poppy-dry skin. He's got the confidence of a salesman and manners gone rough. I wonder what he did in a former life.

'You ok, pal?' I say, 'I am so sorry about this. Do you need a cloth or something for your bleeding ear? Can you hear ok?'

'Listen, you old fucking twat, we don't want anything from you. His ear's fine. He was a deaf twat anyway. If you don't want to get your head blown off, just tell us where Burgerman is.'

'Have you got some more bullets for that thing?' I asked.

He couldn't help but point the shotgun at me, to help him make the next point. 'I've got plenty more bullets for this thing, you stupid wanker, and I'll use them if you don't find me this fucking arsehole, Burgerman.'

'Why so much swearing?' I asked. 'Is it just something you copy from young people?'

He prodded my stomach with it, as if to prove it didn't really need reloading. 'Where the fuck is he?'

'Eh, steady, old chap. Just calm down. We don't know who you are or why you're here. It seems like a fair question, given the circumstances. Don't you think?' I smile. He's weighing me up. I can't tell if he is buying the old-fashioned-gent persona. 'Oh, and he really doesn't like weapons,' I added.

'We'll decide about that. Find him for us. Bring him here.'

'Sort out the fucking glass in here. Don't want to drive all the way home wondering if I'm gonna cut me arse every time I fart.'

‘Sorry to have to ask again, but who shall I say is calling? We don’t get many visitors these days.’

‘Tell him two gentlemen are here for his opinion.’ He was catching the game a little better now.

‘About what?’

‘About mind your fucking business.’

‘Are you Police?’ I asked.

‘Listen, he knows we’re fuckin sat here. We’ll just wait here till he decides to come and see us. And if we don’t get home in time for supper, then there’ll be about thirty people like me coming to pay him a call, only they won’t be so fucking polite.’ He added with a shout and wave of his shotgun – ‘Get a fuckin move on, you stinky piece of fishbreath.’

I hobble away, back in the direction I’ve come from. After turning right at the corner at the bottom of the square and when I’m sure that they can no longer see me, I speak to Smoothie, softly, over the mic.

‘Hope you got all that, Smoothie boy?’ I can hear him laugh at the other end. ‘Find out what you can get on the reg? I’m coming in now. They want to see Burgerman. Is Chow Mein back yet? If he is, get him to come round to yours. If he isn’t back, I’ll need someone else, quick time. I’ll be there in a minute.’

Smoothie hums ‘Takin’ It to the Streets’. He can almost catch the harmony singing on his own.

The singing of the spring trees ripples through our air. It’s not time for the nettles to take our courtyards and hearths. We’ve got to get rid of these jokers, satisfy them that there’s nothing here to know. That there’s nothing to take or takeover. Nothing to fight for, nothing to see. Nothing to come back for.

The sky is turning to evening now, and I shiver with how little time we’ve got. They must leave before sunset. I round the last corner of the snicket to slip into the back garden of Smoothie’s office. The curtains are closed. Inside, Chow Mein is sat at a computer screen monitoring the CCTV footage. Smoothie is sat at the screen next to him, watching both screens.

'Brother, where have you been?'

I say to Chow Mein. 'Very glad to see you.'

He's still got his big earphones on, so he hasn't heard me. I prod him. 'Where you been?' I repeat.

He shakes his head. 'Tell you afterwards. Not good. Listening to this from these two comedians.'

'They've been here nearly an hour,' Smoothie says. 'I had the audio on all this time. Soon as we got these dudes in our piece, I got everyone off the streets. When I ringin' you, we was all gettin' worried 'cos they were jus' drivin' slowly, round and round. Very slowly, like they were lookin' for something. And so, I sent two of the kids, Dog and Hot Dog, on bikes, to give them some lip. They did well. We got both of 'em out the car, and when they out dealin' with the kids, we manage to get one of the boys to slip in a little bit of Smoothie's listening equipment, so we been listening to everything they been saying, even their little, lovin whisperins...'

'Good boys,' I said. 'I'm wondering if this is connected with Milton. I'm wondering why they're so fidgety and so intent on pointing that gun? I'm wondering how they know they want to speak to Burgerman? They know something, but what and how?' I talk out loud.

'I don't think it's got Milton on it,' says Smoothie, 'they've not mention any names we know or anyone that's come here before. They don't know what the hell going on here, so my guess is, it's jus' co-in-ci-dental.'

'OK, and the gun?'

'Look at it from their PoV. They don't know us, 'cos if they did, they'd know they don't need to bring no guns. They're just geezers, ain't they?'

'OK. And Burgerman?'

'Everyone wants a piece of the Burgerman, man,' he says, laughing. 'You know that.'

'Long way to come for a piece,' I say. 'What about the reg? Can you find the car anywhere? What about the faces? We don't know the faces, do we? Does the Driver speak?'

'I don't know, but I have rung Gerry's to sort out their new sun-roof before they go home,' says Chow Mein.

'Nothing on the reg. It's not registered anywhere I can find.'

'Meaning?

'It's home-made. Or scrap, stolen an' drop off the records. Or...' Smoothie goes uncharacteristic on me.

'Or?'

'Never thought about this being like this, but like the Feds they use dead children's IDs, this could be secret service like, secret plates.'

'Are you sure that's possible? That's really not what we want.'

'Well, anything's possible.'

'Those two clowns aren't MI5, otherwise there must be real recruitment issues down at James Bond Towers.'

'Jus' a thought,' he added. 'Law of probability say that eventually the shit comes down to them. But listening to them makes me think not these two ballers,' he says.

'So, we don't know who they are, we don't know where they're from, but we know they want to speak to Burgerman,' I said.

'Not all doom-laden gloom-laden,' says Smoothie, ''cos I've been runnin' their speech through my machine and they have some interestin' characteristics. You wanna hear some stuff?'

'Just tell me, Smoothie, bit pressed for time at the mo.'

He laughs. 'OK. They smoke like power station chimney. The Driver big style. The Driver don't speak much, but he has an accent, like he's lived in a Spanish-speaking country. Can't tell if he's Spanish, but maybe his mama was English or maybe he's English but live in Central America since he was a teenager...'

'Is it important?'

'Dunno. He don't say much, but always laughing a lot. I guess they're doin' weed, something intoxicatin', maybe Cuba...'

'Maybe Columbia? Maybe cocaine? And the little, ferrety passenger?'

'Low-level. Very low-level in everythin'. Been talkin' up hisself exploits. He foul-mouthed and think he's a gangster. More he talk, the more the Driver don't.'

'What are they doing here?' I ask him, needing him to say out loud what I was already thinking.

'They wan' to link up in some way and need to find the Man they call the Burgerman. See if he real or not.'

'You keep askin' tha' one question in more than one way, you know it turn my dial,' said Smoothie, 'but I can't tell you more in this momento.'

'You're right. Did they say anything else important?'

'I can't say if it's important, but maybe is. They might belong to a group on the edge in Sheffield, somewhere there, and these two is jus' the messengers. They into low-level direct action, internet hacking, disrupting meetings, Animal Rights, bit of demo-ing, Occupy, this sort of people, but they haven't done detail. Maybe they been train' better than they look..'

'And what do they want with us?'

'They've heard something about us. They've heard about the beautiful Burgerman and they want to make friends?'

'You laughing again, Smoothie, even though they brought a shotgun...and two shots were discharged –'

'–Yep, I heard them. Both of them, very clearly. Better than the two losers in the car. But because I know you, I expect you to do it, so I pull off the cans all the way and put it on speaker. One day, you gonna do something I don' expect, then I won't have my ears or eardrums or anything between my ears left...'

'You way ahead of me, Smoothus. So, this set of hairies and

loonies have heard a name on the grapevine and want to meet the Man and make some links? Any suggestions?'

'Listen to what they have to say. Deny nothing, tell 'em nothing. Send 'em away. Tone it down for a bit.' Chow Mein spoke.

'Yep, I agree – we need to get them out of here as quick as we can, before they pull any stunts, give them the dull-up till they don't want to know. Find out what we can about them,' said Smoothie.

'OK. Send someone out on a bike to get them to follow them down to Australia House and we'll meet them there. Smoothie, set up the house so we can listen and watch. I can't be seen by them again, that won't be good. Chow Mein, you go and front it. Is there anyone else around we can put in?' I ask.

'I think Picnic would be good and his lady friend. They look the part,' suggested Smoothie.

'You right. Chow Mein, play it low and slow. Ask them lots. Tell them we want to help everyone, but we're just ordinary folk. The most anarchic thing we do is work hard in the allotments. You know what to say. Picnic is good fun but keep him on a leash. Tell them it's all safe and they can put the gun in the boot and lock it there. Good?'

I thought of the horsemen on the hill. Always some twat coming to spoil your party. Even when you aren't having a party.

We leave Smoothie's office by the back door and go out of the back garden. Chow Mein rings Picnic to get down to Australia house with his girlfriend and explains what they need to do.

Australia house is right on the outer ring of the Circle, on its own, in a little redbrick terrace of two. We call it that 'cos it's a paradise for squatters. The garden is overgrown and is dressed with an over-turned, rusty, old pram, broken, plastic kids toys and dug-up paving slabs, stacked neatly. Looks like everything getting ready to be sold for a few quid when the inhabitants plan on getting stoned. The original gate has gone but the new one is home-made of chicken wire and some sawn-off bits of rotten wood. There's a mattress propping up the fence and a dog kennel with a door hanging off and some dried-up turds in there. Looks just like the dogs escaped only yesterday. What works really well is the bare, baked earth, trodden down by kids and bikes and dogs and beery barbecuers. The bare, baked earth theme goes through into the house itself, where the carpets have long gone. Mother Courage's own set.

When we get inside, we work really quickly. Smoothie has wired this house so he can plug in really easily. In the kitchen, he's got some kit hidden in the cupboards next to the boiler with no pipes. In the hallway I have a much-needed piss. The stain and the smell of fresh piss from people who can't remember what a toilet is for. I hate doing it to well-built (ex)council property but it's like Jane Austen said, all about providing entertainment to our contemporaries.

The plan is to get these two chaps into place in the front room, where they can interview Chow Mein and Picnic and his girlfriend. We can watch and listen to everything that's said. The massive broken 56 inch TV screen is connected to a little camera, so we can sit and watch what goes on, and the room's wired so we can listen to every word. No one lives in this house, it's one we keep just nice for guests like this. And Picnic is a dream. You're going to love Picnic. Picnic arrives in silence through the back door with his girlfriend. We don't speak. I point him through to the front room. Girlfriend looks a peach.

I sign, *Give me one minute.*

Back in the square, a motorbike arrives out of one of the side streets and pulls up next to the black BMW. The rider stares through her blackened glass visor and beckons to them to follow her. She takes the long route to give us more time to set up, driving via the unmade back alleys, making sure they notice the woman hanging out her washing, the kids playing with the dog, the old man emptying his bins. *Everything here is so normal, lads, if you will just look.* She makes sure they don't have much to do, as they drive round part of the eastern side of the Circle. The ordinariness is everywhere. There's even a family having a row on a settee in the garden, shouting at one another over the Tennent's Super Strong fine lager.

Back in the house, I sit Picnic and Peach down with a nice can or two of cider with vodka. I explain: Two guys on a mission looking for The Burgerman, Chow Mein will head them off, but convince them that we're just another set of no-hopers, taking the state for every £26.85 a week we can get. We want them to go home thinking that it's all bullshit and they don't ever want to come back. Bit of piss, bit of spillage. but don't wind them up 'cos they've got a shotgun in the boot of the car. Play the Dane. And the Danette. They nod and spill some cider on the settee where the boys will sit, right opposite the telly.

Picnic is of course completely bonkers, like all good actors. In one of his former lives, he was a classically trained actor who was going really well in rep and then got a big part in a company touring South Africa. He can mimic any native African from Cape Town to Cairo speaking English and makes us laugh with his characters at the drop of a hat, despite being beaten for 'acting gay' by South African security. They didn't like him taking Shakespeare to the townships. In the townships, of course, they loved him. The second time he was attacked by the security forces, they burnt his hand, after he played Othello with a Boer accent and did Nazi salutes to the whited-up actors playing the Venetians. They only released him after five days of unlawful detention. When he came back to England, his family didn't recognise him after he'd got a home-made tattoo covering his whole face and neck of a black man with a metal neck-collar. He struggled getting work in rep after that. And now he's here, in scrott gear, like a washed-up, loser-druggie, blaming all the world, like a goodun. I look at him and see the warmest eyes, but I wonder what goes through them. I wonder, when he watches the telly, what he sees.

We have this game where we sit for a given time period – twenty minutes or an hour, or however long – and we focus on one another's minds, like mental hide and seek, except you want to be found. We always start off with a thing one of us has brought in, like a stone, or a coat or a picture of something we can both access. I speak as much as possible to Picnic in as few words as possible. Like now. I tell him my fears, my real ones. I tell him about the smoking hearth and the nettles and what I fear is coming. He nods. We don't speak. He lifts Peachy onto his lap and messes her huge hair, black like a cowl.

Chow Mein comes in and parks himself in the doorway.

'Where's the piss?' he says.

They point to the only two spare seats.

'Hospitality at all times,' he says.

We lock ourselves away in the kitchen, put on the cans and settle down into our silence. Outside, the motorbike pulls up, followed by the Beamer. She gets off and opens their door. The Passenger is no less nervous. He has his shotgun hidden like a joke, under a jacket. She points to the boot with the gun. At first, they refuse. She signs that if they refuse there is no meeting. They eventually put the gun in the boot and lock it. She walks them to Australia House, then disappears. They walk nervously up the drive watching where they tread. Their faces say it all.

Good.

Inside, we watch Chow Mein lead them into the front room where Picnic and Peach are snogging, oozily.

'It fuckin stinks in here,' says the Passenger.

'Welcome,' says Chow Mein 'What can we do for you? This is Alan and his wife, Lynn. The Council let them stay here whilst they're undergoing rehab. Would you like a cup of tea or something?'

'No,' he says.

'Well, have a seat, please.'

They sit down.

'Where's this fuckin' Burgerman? We don't want any more bullshit. We've been sent to make contact with Burgerman.'

'Who by? Who sent you?' he asks.

'Look, mate, I don't want to be funny or anything, but you don't seem like the bloke we want to talk to.'

Chow Mein pauses. 'I should have introduced myself. I am Paul, Area Manager for this estate, and if anyone can help you here, it's me. I know everyone here and I have a very good relationship with all the residents. Who do you mean is the Burgerman?'

'Look, Paul, it could be that we've made a mistake. It could be that you're not telling us everything, but our friends want to speak to Burgerman. The message has got to our people that there's a guy up here running a setup that's interesting to us. People are talking about what he can do.'

Almost unnoticed, the Driver speaks, 'The situation in this country is moving very quickly. Everywhere is discontent. If you're the man we want, we can tell you somethings and if you know him, you'll tell him yourself. If you don't know anything then you won't have anything to say to anyone when we're gone, so, we'll be honest.'

He paused. I heard what Smoothie had mentioned earlier, the distinct crispness to his vowels, just the slight jarring of register. The style of someone who didn't belong with the loser with the gun.

'Why the gun?' asked Chow Mein, beautifully.

'Something unexpected, unknown. The Burgerman isn't alone, is he?' He sweeps the room, not taken in at all by any of it.

'You've fuckin set us up here, haven't you, Paul, or whatever your name is?' shouts Passenger. 'I knew there was something wrong – this seat stinks and it's got piss on it or something –' He stands up and gets ready to slap someone.

'Calm down, calm down, mate,' says Chow Mein. 'This is what I mean, this is how people live here. Normally this house is in a better state, but we have to let these people stay here.'

'You can stay here as well, my friend,' says Picnic, turning his head away from Peachy for a moment and giving it his best Tanzanian accent.

'Jesus, who are you?' says Passenger, as if he has just taken in the full features of Picnic's face. 'This is a freak show, man' he says to Driver, 'got to get out of here. It's just piss city here... come on, these set of wankers couldn't organise a piss up in a brewery.'

'Aw, come on, mate,' says Chow Mein, 'have a little respect for people. They're trying to turn their lives around and I'm working with them. These guys have had a hard time, show some respect.'

'Yeah, well, revolution ain't gonna start here, is it, with a bunch of low-lifers and crackheads?' He's still rubbing his trousers as if it will make the smell go away.

'What do you mean, mate?'

'Nothing. No point with yous, is there?'

'Well, you've come here with a gun, asking for someone we don't know and we let you into our homes. Are you coming clean with us?' says Chow Mein.

'My friend gets a bit touchy, Paul,' says Driver, 'he's ok when you get to know him.'

'Well, that's good, 'cos all we want to do is help, but I am not sure us at the Council could help him with a revolution,' says Chow Mein, smiling nicely, to Driver. 'Is that what you do?'

He pauses again before he responds.

'As I said, there are a few groups who are beginning to work together towards clear goals, if you like.'

'And you think this Burgerman could work with you?'

'We'll never know. But if you do see him, perhaps you could tell him,' also smiling nicely.

'And what are these clear –'

'Goals? And what are the Council's goals, Paul? Perhaps they're the same. If only we all worked towards the same goals, eh, Paul?'

'We only work for the benefit of the community,' he said, 'not very fashionable anymore, but we give it a go. Share what little we have, and all that.'

'Yes. Well, it's been a pleasure,' he says. 'Sorry about my friend's behaviour.'

'I've told you to stop friggin' apologising on my behalf. They're the ones who should apologise for living like shit.'

Driver ushers his colleague out of the front door but in the pissy hallway he turns to Chow Mein and grabs him by the throat at lightning speed. We can't see it, but we can hear it. We can't go to help him either but listen to him speak. I can feel Chow Mein offer no resistance, acting like any Council helper would, choking and panicking. 'If you speak about this to anyone except him, we shall be back to put you at the bottom of the Council tip. Do you understand? Speak, so everyone can hear!'

Chow Mein chokes out a yes and a cry to let him go.

'This is so near to happening, this is so dangerous for us all that I have to tell you to trust me and to fear what they will do. It's not personal. You understand?' He relaxes his grip. Chow Mein coughs and splutters. 'You could be him, anyone we have met here could fuckin' be him. But I know we're near him, so I won't kill you.'

The Driver looks at him as if he's memorising every feature

at microscopic level. Then, he does an unexpected thing and grabs his hand in a handshake, raising their clasped hands to his chest. 'Trust me. If what they're saying is only half true, then we need him and you and all of you here, like you will need us. You will need us.' And he raises his finger to his lips and puts his ear to the wall. Then goes.

Chow Mein shuts the door quietly and locks it. He goes back into the front room. 'I need a glass of water. The bastard has a grip like iron.'

They all come into the kitchen. Chow Mein gurgling glasses of water. Smoothie examining his throat. Picnic waits and sweats and Peachy squeezes his hand, reading his mind.

'Just for a moment, I don't want anyone to say anything. We have to talk, but first, let me and Smoothie gather all the recordings and we can all meet in an hour or so when we've calmed down and we'll go through what's just happened. Let's meet in Soho and grab a drink.'

They all file out, except Smoothie.

'We need to know who these boys are. I don't want thirty of them camped here till we all get throttled.'

He doesn't respond. He's downloading the footage and he's preparing the sound recordings. In between, he picks out screen grabs of Driver and Passenger and looks for a match with anyone out there in the world that might ever have existed on a database.

Soho is the name of a little complex of screening rooms and mini-cinemas and projection rooms that we created from a building no one wanted from the Sixties. It's hidden away behind lots of trees and shrubs. We've grown ivy up it, made the balconies into verandas that completely encircle the first floor and boxed the rest in with shutters. From what was a squat, concrete, two-storey block of leaky, sweaty, unlit, four-box-room dwellings for the trapped urban poor, we've turned it into a Palace of Culture that, even from close-up, looks, for all the world, like a timeless classic of the English countryside. We've even put a false roof on it, so that when the Feds come scooting over with their sneaky drones or their big choppers with Oświęczim-style search lamp attached, chasing some teenage ASBO-ridden Friedbread, who's nicked his mate's pushbike, it looks like all the other shitty, asbestos low-risers to Mr. Toad behind the joystick.

Strangely enough, that was the hardest bit, the bad roof that wasn't a roof. One of the few times that we had to go and nick some real roofing off a project that was going to be demolished. We nearly got nicked ourselves by the security firm guarding it from the people who used to live in it. We had to spend more money on paying them off to *not* go to the cops, than it would have cost from the scrappy. Although, as we pointed out to them, the scrapyard wouldn't buy this off them. 'Well, why do you want it then?' said the Brains with no upper teeth in the un-ironed uniform. 'Model railways,' we said. He took his sixty quid, pushed back his peaked cap and went back to his *Sun* in his portakabin and his noisy generator and a few silver cartons of his breakfast curry.

There's a heartbeat in the Circle in the way so many of us are connected and tonight, it's beating slowly like the cool-down after hard exercise. This is our poem to the world we love, and these are the people who love. If you don't love, you need the constant oiling of words to make it all work with people you don't love. We try here to use the right words. That's not easy, but it's better. So, when I stand here and look through the trees, as the sun sits on the big mound behind the last houses below me, I want to say the right things to you and to the people who walk into the Circle, in goodness or in anger, in fear or in unhappiness, and to those like Smoothie and Picnic and Chow Mein, who have stepped aside and melted into our lovely, thin air, right here amongst you. But I lean back and am tired as well. Immensely tired of the fight. Just five minutes more to listen to the birds' wings cutting the air above the treetops and the blackbird scratting and his brother singing a few treetops away and the quiet descent into night.

We've all forgotten about Uncle Kevin. Tonight, it's Uncle Kevin's night. We'll turn off the streetlights to honour the night and to pull tighter the cloak of un-seeness and let Leeds and all the other cities hum and splutter and shudder into hopeless sleep. I lean forward on my stick and breathe out all my breath for as long as possible to see if I'm prompted to draw in the next one. I wait and hover and wait and finally let the impulse and instinct to carry on fill me up for the next inevitability. An hour later, I will have listened to the trees, remembered the occasion of planting, and studied the uniqueness of each of the trees, the sound it makes, the texture of the bark, the shape and colour of the leaves and how it has changed while I have known it.

But for now, we're all inside Soho, watching the footage. Smoothie is narrating what he knows as the images flicker in front of us. I study the car, the faces, the movements. I watch again how the Passenger reacted instinctively to shrink back when the tussle began with the shotgun, but the Driver kept his eye on me and the gun, at all times. He let the Passenger do all the talking until he took over at the meeting in Australia House. Then, in the final meeting, we watch again how he dealt with what he saw of our set-up. The last of the footage of them leaving the Circle tails off.

Burgerman: We did ok. Thank you. Let's go through it again. Tell us again what happened.

Smoothie: BMW comes into the Circle from the South. It's black, classic, maybe twenty year old. Two guys. I ring you. No answer. They drive in nice an' slow.

Burgerman: So, they want us to see it. They want us to take notice. They aren't just cruising looking for bother. Let's take it that they know where they want to get to.

Smoothie: Then I ring you. We make it look normal, like we always do when we get visitors like these we don't know. They drive roun' the square twice, but we put the word out, so apart from someone gardenin', the Proff and his family on the settee having a family chat, there's no one. They park up. I'm trying to get everything on the mics.

Burgerman: So, they're sat in their car, not doing door-to-door. Why would they just come here and park up?

Smoothie: Well, when I'm listenin' to them, there's no dates, times or places but plenty of talk from the Passenger. Nothing we can fix on, nothing we can check. Lot o' names – Beano, Doug, Cameron, just names, then 'Dog's Mob' and a few references to another group who seem similar to them. They have something going on with 'the plan' though, but it so vague, an' they talk about if it will happen, if it will cause any problem but nothing fix – no detail, nothing you could pin on them – trained to talk about things without being able to pin anything on them.

Chow Mein: They're doing as they're told. I can imagine someone has sent them up here with a specific job – check us out, check the place out and find the Burgerman, that's it. These guys are just foot soldiers.

Burgerman: OK. So, maybe they're a bit more professional than we think. Let's assume that they have some training, that there's some organisation and that they have a greater purpose than at first seems obvious. Picnic, your professional opinion on them, please: who was acting and who was covering what?

Picnic: I may well be wrong, but my instinct says that they weren't acting. There was a good deal of fear, but they weren't afraid of us exactly, but they're afraid.

Burgerman: Of what?

Picnic: Difficult to say. Of us passing on info. Of what might happen if they get it wrong, or someone finds out who they are. Maybe the same things we're frightened of.

Burgerman: So, it's conspiracy. It's trust, it's information. Cooperation. They want confirmation that maybe we're the same as them? That we're up to the same things as them?

Picnic: I would say that the Driver is used to action, maybe he's one of the dogs who does the dirty work and has previous. The way he spoke was calm, extremely threatening and not panicked. The other one was different. At first, I was thinking he was a small-timer, a crook or a dealer who's turned. But now I am thinking that he's got more of the brains.

Burgerman: Something political? Which one of them mentioned revolution?

Chow Mein: Driver mentioned discontent, changing situation. Passenger mentioned revolution, but only when he was pushed to it.

Burgerman: So, one is your thinker and the other is your doer. It might be that the one doesn't know who the other is.

Smoothie: Might be that one of them is an underwear model. Or both of them.

Picnic: I don't think that the Driver is underwear.

Peachy: Underwear?

Picnic: Cop pretending to be one of the boys, undercover.

Burgerman: Apologies to you, Picnic, for using your phrase but – but I don't think either of them are undercover.

Picnic: Why not?

Burgerman: 'Cos they didn't seem interested in us. They didn't ask anything at all, except where the Burgerman was. They didn't want to stay and talk. They didn't nose. They didn't ask enough. All they wanted to do was to make contact with The Burgerman. That's what messengers do – bring a message, take a message. I'm not saying that the Feds aren't in on this somewhere and I'm not saying that everything is at it seems.

Chow Mein: One thing's for sure. If they've gone home, then they've heard about the Burgerman from a way away.

Burgerman: Why? What do you mean?

Chow Mein: I've got the lads to drop a tracer in the boot. They're tootling down the M1 as we speak. Probably won't stop for a coffee with a gunshot hole in the roof.

I wanted to laugh but I couldn't, 'cos I felt that I had in some ways endangered everything that was the Circle. I had wanted to see if the shotgun was loaded. I didn't want them riding around with a loaded shotgun, so I made sure the gun got fired. I had made some decisions that had maybe *backfired* – meeting them in Australia House, sending in Chow Mein when I should maybe have dealt with it. I should have told them about the Burgerman. Dispelled the myth or admitted to the myth but dealt with it.

Burgerman: Have we tried to be too clever? I need us to be really clear if we could have handled this better?

It went quiet. I watched the green and red LEDs registering all the communication in the Circle. I watched as the streetlights on the CCTV dimmed to nil as if by magic, and the screens we watched slowly fade to grey.

Burgerman: What do we do now?

Smoothie: Keep going, change nothin'. Changin' things bring more attention than changin' nothin'.

Chow Mein: I agree. People are still gonna come for help. These dudes with their guns and threats might just be a flash in the pan. Might never turn up again. Feds might get them. Might just fade away. Probably just losers looking for some fun.

Burgerman: Picnic?

Picnic: You could go and find them. Find out what they're up to. Distract them from what's happening here by going there. Then, they won't have to come here again.

Burgerman: Peachy?

Peachy: Tone it down. Kill off the Burgerman. Explain it's all a mistake. Mistaken identity, crossed wires, Chinese whispers. Diffuse it bigstyle.

Burgerman: Yep. That's just what I was thinking. All those things. Let's see if anything changes without us for today and tomorrow. Then, let's talk again. We need to do a few things before then. Find the car. Find anything about who these guys are. And then there's Milton. We've forgotten about Milton.

Chow Mein: Let's just have five minutes nursing a beer, man. My neck's still so dry.'

He rubbed it gingerly and pulls a face. The others get up to leave.

'You know where we are,' says Picnic, 'don't dawdle, showtime in twenty minutes.'

'Oh, yes, sorry, forgot all about the show,' I said. 'We're coming. Five minutes.'

Chow Mein rocks back in his chair. 'That was bad. I can't remember a time when we had that sort of visit. Even though the ones who come with briefcases do more damage than those who come with shotguns.'

'Wise words, comrade.' I paused, knowing I was tired, and so he. 'How many years of this have we done now? Ten, twelve, more...? Just a little place to find some peace, that's all we started doing and you look at us now and it's like we're still fighting for survival against mammoths and lunatics. No matter what you say, you can't argue with John Donne, can you? No man is an island. We'd get less attention if we went on Air-fucking-BnB.'

He laughed. 'Might all just blow over.' His turn to pause. 'We haven't got long, Uncle Kevin won't want you to miss his spring special,' he said, 'so I'll just tell you, ok? I took Milton home after we spoke today, he lives the other side of town. He got really cagey about where he lived, but I said we had to know 'cos he was our main concern at the moment, and we needed to check he was for real. I think he was taking me the long way round and about five or six times he made a few excuses about having to do this or that. I told him that he was making me real nervous and that all I wanted to see was where he lived. If he wanted us to put ourselves out there for him, the very least he could do was prove who he was and where he lived. Eventually, after about an hour longer than we needed, we pulled into an estate, nice trees, private houses, cars in the drives. Took a couple of turns and we end up in a little cul-de-sac of maybe twelve houses. 'That was all I needed to know,' I said, 'thank you, we'll be in touch."

He seemed mighty glad to disappear into his side door. I turned around and made sure he saw me. I made a note of the reg of his Škoda Fabia in his drive and left.'

'And?'

'Well, apart from wondering why he hadn't come to visit us in his nice little Fabia, I was also surprised to see him appear in his car so quickly and in such a hurry.'

'What happened?'

'That guy has worried me since the moment he walked in. I think we're putting ourselves out for him more than we should, and I don't want to walk into any sort of trap – just want to know exactly what we're dealing with. So, I sat down behind a fence in one of the gardens, facing the opening to his road, and I only had to wait twenty minutes and he's driving out of there, with a very worried look.'

'He could be going back to work. He could have somewhere to go. We don't know everything about him. He might have an ill relative. Could be a million reasons.'

'Granted,' he said, 'so, I went back to the house opposite his and knocked on the door. A lady answered, a pensioner, I thought, always at home. 'I am so sorry to bother you,' I said to her, 'I'm looking for the owner of a blue Škoda with this registration. He was a lovely man who helped my wife when she was involved in an accident in town about a week ago, and without his help my wife would never have got to hospital in time. I got his address, but I didn't get the house number and I have come to give him a present and say a big thank you.' I described Milton for her. At first, she was slightly sceptical, but she was old school and trusted people till they did something bad.

"Ooooh, that must be Mr. Hubbard, he lives over there. Martin Hubbard is his name. He's not there now, I'm sure he was there a minute ago.'

"Perhaps his wife is in, I can leave it with her?'

"Mr Hubbard, oooh, he's not married, no, he's never had a wife, not even sure he has a girlfriend.'

"Has he been here long, maybe I have the wrong guy?'

"No, he's been here for years. Often come and goes though. Between you and me, I have no idea how he makes his money, never seems to go to work. Not what you'd call nine-to-five, anyway. Would you like a cup of tea?'

'I wish I'd taken her up on her offer.'

'Well, you might still be there, if you had, and missed all the fun here,' I said. 'So, you reckon our new friend, Milton – Martin – Mr. Hubbard, is lying?'

'Seems like it. Doesn't have a 'normal' job, doesn't have a wife or a girlfriend, is always coming and going...'

'This isn't good, is it? Did she say anything else?'

"He's very polite and helpful. And he has a friend who comes round to help him do the garden.'

'Nice.'

'Nearly eight o'clock, it's showtime. Come on.'

He grabs my arm. 'This is the first time we done this. If we get it wrong, I dunno, maybe we should just leave it.'

'You're right. Tomorrow we go to Sid's, find out how real the rest of his story is. Then, we find him, make it clear to him what we know. Then, we kill Burgerman.'

Chow Mein looked at me and nodded, like he did when he wasn't sure he agreed.

WE DON'T WANT TO KNOW ABOUT YOU OR YOUR FUCKING SHITTY LARDLAND.
WE ARE ATTACHED BUT WE AREN'T PART OF IT.

WE DON'T WANT ANYTHING FROM YOU AND WE DON'T TAKE ANYTHING FROM YOU.
YOU'RE IN LARDLAND AND YOU DON'T EVEN KNOW IT.

BUY SOME SHIT YOU DON'T NEED.
WATCH THE SHIT THAT ISN'T TRUE.
HATE THE PEOPLE THEY TELL YOU TO.
WORK HOW AND WHERE AND FOR AS LONG AS YOU ARE ABLE IN THE WAYS THAT YOU DON'T CONTROL.

PAY YOUR TAXES.
PUT YOUR FACE IN THE TROUGH AND EAT THEIR SHIT.

WELCOME TO LARDLAND.
MY JOB IS TO KEEP YOU OUT.

AND MY PEOPLE SAFE.

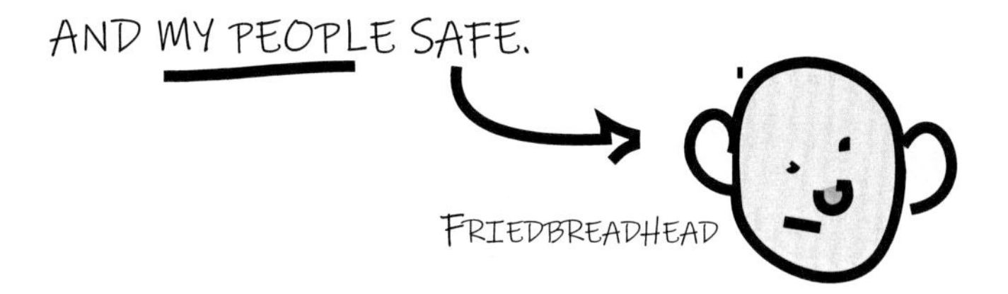

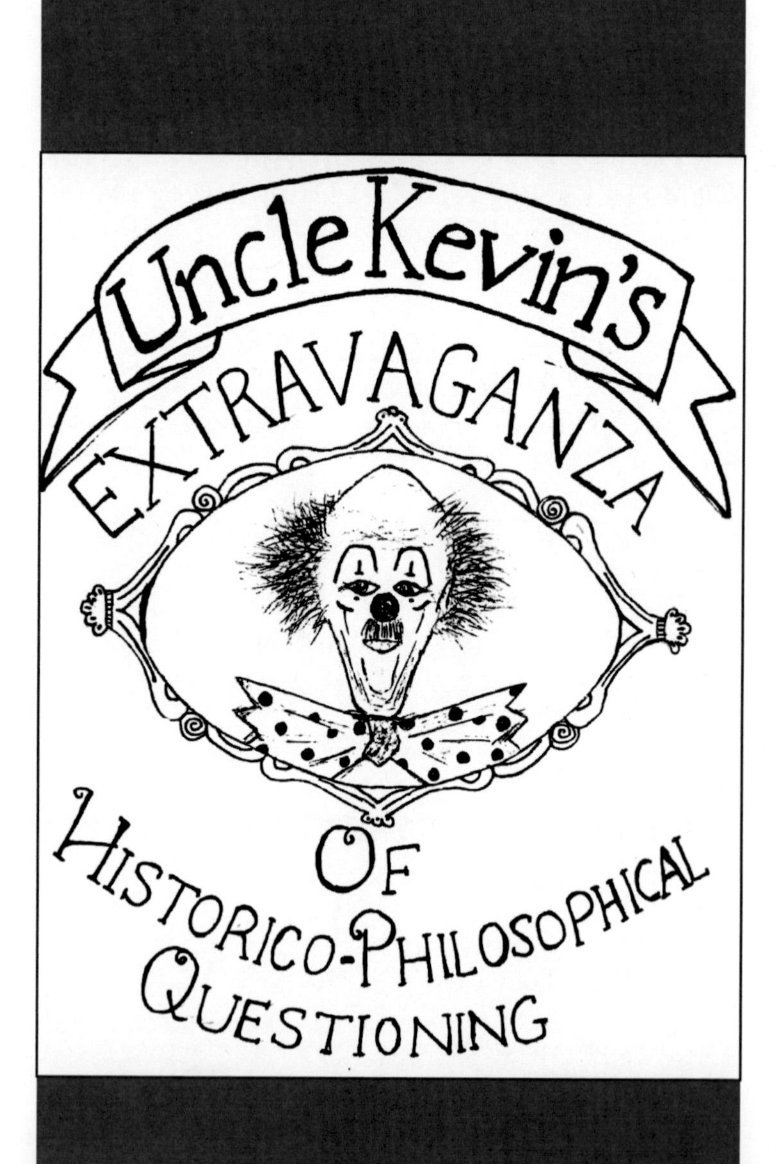
Uncle Kevin's
EXTRAVAGANZA
OF
HISTORICO-PHILOSOPHICAL
QUESTIONING

10

Uncle Kevin's Extravaganza of Historico-Philosophical Questioning

I'm amazed at how quickly the space is transformed: one minute it's the scene of a face-off involving a shotgun and a misunderstanding leading to a blasted sun-roof and the next, there's a flood of lights in the late spring evening and the aromas of food served on tables and the sound of piped Victorian fairground music sitting on top of a chilled Ibiza beat.

There are people chatting on rows of unfolded wooden chairs, holding plates, and laughing between mouthfuls. People you haven't met, like Linda, Heather and Sami who share the same house with their kids, all four of them, who just like hanging out together. And the Prof and his wife, Dr. Forager, who do the guerrilla gardening around the Circle and further afield and can identify at least six types of edible things in any given square metre, and Tomos, who collects anything and breaks it down into its component parts, to such an extent that we had to stop him going through the rubbish (which is where we found him) and promised him his own rubbish tip, which he's cultivated, flourishingly. Now, we have zero waste, on paper. There must be a balance to the equation which says that, just because it isn't thrown away but stored, it hasn't somehow become waste in a different form. When Tomos talks he's eyeing up your things, which will only be redeemed when you're naked of everything.

And all the lovely others: Tommy Knockers, Jim Gammon,

Stainless, Bigboy, Pistol, Eggbox, Brown Stout Isiah, Dishdash, Hooli and Gin Min and all the rest whose stories, if you're willing, are there to be heard.

But the lights flash and the music changes.

'The highlight of the evening, the week, the month...' there's a voice on the mic that's stoking the fires of expectations, and with each addition of superlatives there are wows and shrieks and whistles from the audience, 'and once again, that magical time has come, when we're being loudly entreated to enjoy one of Uncle Kevin's extemporaneous and confounding challenges to the erroneous factationary counter-theories, in a once-in-a-lifetime re-evaluation of the human perspective that will leave you questioning the very denial of your pre-existence... Laaaaaaadddies and Gentlemennnnnnn, Uncle Kevin's Uuuuultimate Extravagaaaaanza of Historicoooooo-Philosophphphphphical Questioninggggggg!!!'

Huge, wild cheers, flashing lights being flicked on and off (by Smoothie) and exhortatory cries from all across the Square. This is how we'd do the Olympics, if we ever let them come here.

When Kevin comes on the little stage, the audience go bonkers. There would be stage diving, but the stage is only about a foot off the ground, consisting of eight pallets nailed together. He has two helpers holding up cards.

Holder No.1's got:

CLAP, IT'S KEVIN!!!!!

Holder No.2's got:

GET FACT!!

and when the Great Man points at this card, the audience know what to do, 'GET FACT' they shout, like they're about to win the school swimming gala that's being filmed for Netflix.

No.1 is not going to be outdone and she turns a card:

WHAT'S BEHIND THE FACT?

No need for a card, they know the script, 'ANOTHER FACT'

they shout back, and No.2 raises up her next card:

DO WE KNOW THE FACTS?

'Of course, we do,' they shout back, and then No.1 moves just to the left of No.2 with her new card,

HOW DO WE KNOW?

'Cos Uncle Kevin tells us...' they shout back, as loudly as they can.

Then the voice on the mic tells us, just as the spotlight reveals 'The Factotum of Facts' himself, Uncle Kevin, who's here to raise the tempo of discussions to superheated level of miscellaneous and hitherto unconnected diaphanous ideas that, once exposed, turn the listener into the naked man in the courtroom, embarrassed and shrivelled, in the hitherto infant-like state of his unprotected intellect, while the cruel spotlight of the factification exposes his blushing and mortified pride into a snivelling worm of a thing scurrying into the long grass...'

And so, Mighty K begins, amidst cries of 'Worms don't snivel' and 'Worms can't scurry,' and such banter, engendered to sugar the pill of Uncle Kevin's non-factitious lecture.

The day ebbed into a warm, dark place and the now of these moments ran forward like a playful child. We watched as he reached out to us with his probing questions, carefully planned to eventually connect and fit together, glued with thoughts, ideas, quotes and facts and figures that zoomed off into space and then came clattering back, like your father's fireworks on Bonfire Night. He had developed such a following amongst us that we knew we could rely at some points during the show on some classic lines that would bring out the repartee and the shouting. It was the politics of release.

'What did the Romans ever do for us?'

'Nothing' (crowd in unison)

'What did the Romano-British ever do for us?'

'Even less'

'What did the Anglo-Saxons ever do for us?'

'Nothing, they're all dead' Laughter.

'What did the Normans ever do for us?'

'Absolutely nothing'

But tonight, like every night, he would shift us, move us, along and surprise us.

'What did the Hwicce ever do for us?'

'Who are they?'

'What did the Jutes ever do for us?'

'No-one knows'

'What did the Normans ever do for us?'

'Absolutely nothing'

'Of course,' he said, 'but nothing's good. Lovely King Bill, William the Conqueror, the bastard son of a waitress in a pub... nothing wrong with that *Cheers* who landed here with a gang of thugs *Groans* and Madame, (looking at Sami in the front row, nursing a bottle of home-made wine) you look like you've peeled some mushrooms in your time, *Ooooooh* What's good about thugs? '

'Nothing'

'Where were the Anglo-Saxons? Fighting Vikings and one another. Were they all fighting Vikings and one another? You telling me that the entire country was empty between Pevensey and Stamford Bridge at that exact moment in time? In October, 1066? But does it matter?'

'Yes, it does'

'Does it matter more than beans on toast?'

'Yes, it does Why? Tell us why'

'Because we're still suffering from what they did. But before we do that, why is nothing good? Imagine two thousand years ago, the invincible Roman army is peering across the River Rhine in the middle of Germany and they are sooooooo happy that there is a dirty great river between them and what they can see on the opposite bank. If they get high enough up, they can see quite a long way onto the land behind the opposite bank, and all they can see are...?'

'GERMANS'

'Well, yes, but they can't see the Germans for the trees. The Hercyginian forest was one of the few things that defeated the Romans. They were terrified of what was lurking in there. Were they right?'

'MAYBE'

'Did Bad King Bill the Conk visit Elland Road?'

'NOOOOO...'

'Why not?'

'SHIT-SCARED...' *laughter*

'No, well, yes, he couldn't see Leeds for the trees. He didn't come anywhere near it, which meant that he left it alone and he didn't do what Normans always do – which is?

'HARRY...' l*ots of laughter*

'Harry, yes, so much harrying on that in most of Yorkshire there wasn't a house, farm or cow left standing and every man, woman and child they found was killed. His own biographer said it. And also said that God would punish him for it. By the time of the Domesday Book, nearly every landowner in our shire has a Norman name. Nearly a thousand years later, tell me, who owns our land?'

'THEY DO...' *groans*

'Who writes the laws?'

'THEY DO'

'Who keeps the law?'

'THEY DO'

'Who writes the rules?'

'THEY DO'

'Who polices the rules?'

'Exactly, this is the best joke ever *Hahaha...wild thigh-slapping laughter* This land has never been ours. This land has NEVER been ours, not for a thousand years or more. Ask the rent-payers, the ground-rent payers, the tenant farmers, the evicted, the dispossessed, the homeless, the mortgaged and the un-landed...the *we* who have nothing and never will. *Silence* This England was the first colony. The land that was seized a thousand years ago by unspeakable violence and where everyone in it was dispossessed and stripped of all rights and then set to work to maintain a system that kept them enslaved.'

Pause.

'Tell me one thing that the ruling classes have ever done for us?'

Silence.

'Exactly, they have kept us mute.'

Out of the darkness, an illuminated screen appeared with pictures of castles and country houses, pretty gardens and fountains, interspersed with black and white photos that lingered longer than the others so we could take in the detail.

Then, a picture of a row of backyards and three children playing in the mud and a date of 1927 in the bottom corner. Sami on the front row shouts out, 'That's my Granny in Bradford,' and everyone claps and whistles.

Then, more pictures of the Bradford Pals and the Leeds Pals going off to war in 1915 and Kevin stops, 'And that's my Grandad, one of only 15 who came back from the whole of that company.' Respectful claps.

The names and genealogies follow of the Beauforts, the Talbots, the de Montforts, the Howards, the de Lascelles and Kevin asks, 'And who owns the land your Granny's playing on?' and he shows a map from the 1920s of the middle of Bradford, 'where Sami's grandma lived, in't that right, Sami?'

Sami laughs, 'How the bloody hell did you know that?' and the cries of 'UNCLE KEVIN, UNCLE KEVIN' ring out in riotous cheering.

'And who owns that land that house sits on, that your granny's mam paid ground rent to?' he asks, sweetly. *Silence* 'Oooh, I thought you'd know...' *Laughter* 'One set of the ruling elite, the landed gentry.'

'NOOOO...' *groans*

'And what have they ever done for us?'

'NOTHING'

'And where are they?'

'THEY'RE BEHIND YOU...' *loud hoots of derision,* because the screen is full of flushed faces straight out of Debrett's Peerage.

'Yeah, they're behind me, the port-filled visages of the retiring aristocracy. Some of them MPs, some of them dead, but most of them alive and quietly running the country and keeping huge herds of cattle, horses and people busy, and in their place making sure that nothing whatsoever disturbs their extensive estates, apart from the vexatious problem of who their children are going to marry. Some of them, of course, run extensive estates they hardly ever visit, in foreign countries, like Wales, Scotland and Ireland. And why do we care when they get married?'

'WE DON'T...' *laughing and mock waving of flags*

'And just before we launch into the highlight of tonight's show, 'Uncle Kevin's Metaphysical Pub Quizzingo', *Shouts of anticipation* where, with a little bit of cunning knowing, total factual recall and the luck of the balls as they come out of the machine, (he waves his £1 bingo machine from Poundland) we're going to elucidate the contribution of these people to our lives: three faces, three photos of well-fed men, all with a similar parting on the right-hand side which is then swept across, in an attempt at Cavalry officer swagger, perhaps. Names withheld, but available on request, all landowners within thirty miles of our seat of learning, here in the Circle, upon which we are tonight uniting in our seeking spirits.

'But let's, firstly, look at Lord B, this one, remember these are all real, their pictures are real, their power and inherited wealth is real *Groans* This Lord B. owns approximately 35,000 acres...'

'Good man, good show...'

'7 complete villages...'

'Good man, hey ho'... *hoots*

'Over 20 farms...'

'Good show...' *and laughter*

'And sits on the board of over 35 businesses...'

'Very busy...very, very busy...' *hoots and laughter*

'One of which is responsible for the cutting down of the yew trees that are over there, about two miles, or rather were there...'

'Good show...' *hoots of derision*

'Because, although they were over a thousand years old, they were in the way of his new housing development...'

'In the way...' *hoots*

'...that was opposed, sorry, *is* opposed, by fifty three thousand people in that part of our city (points over the hill) and luckily enough for Sami, he is the great-grandson of the man who evicted your Grandma from her house in 1927 (photo of Sami's grandma appears in close-up as a child, on the screen) because your great-grandfather was a striking miner.'

'Good show, bloody workers, three cheers for Lord B...' *hoots of derision and whistles*

'The other two are his sons and heirs, one was an MEP for the Party that wants to pull out of Europe...'

'No irony...' *hahahaa...*

The laughter dies, then the applause and the night falls quiet and Kevin fills the space with a conductor's instinct for drama.

'Thank you for your continued support, people, you can

settle down now for the award-winning, Transformational Pub Quiz with Bingo Wings, but, before we stop, one last piece of Factation Nation Contemplation before you go.' He looks at us and turns to look at Lord B. and holds our gaze intently. 'This man's lovely family go all the way back, yes, you've guessed it, Sami and family, all the way back to the ruling elite of mediaeval England...and would love to claim kinship with William the Lovely Conqueror....'

'Rule Britannia, Britannia rules the waves...' is sung in huge, ironic choruses, together with a standing ovation for the great man and his insightful, pantomine history lesson.

Kevin bumbles off stage, but then comes back on because he's forgotten a file.

In between choruses of 'For he's a jolly good fellow' and standing ovations, the card holders are back on stage providing various prompts to thank Uncle Kevin for his illuminating and philosophically motivational extravaganza of questioning.

He gets the slaps and the pats and the thanks and the smiles and I watch him as he retreats into the Kevin who I know better. The shy, retiring, man with the big, old-fashioned moustache and the trousers that continuously slip down a stomach that no belt can tame. When I go up to him, on his way for a pie and a pint, he pushes his glasses up his nose, three or four times.

'How was that, boss?' he says.

'As usual, transformational,' I say, 'you're a natural.'

He laughs and blows a bit of pork pie crust at me. 'As long as you think they were listening a bit...'

It sounds like he's not listening to himself anymore. I wonder if he sees me in the same light as his former wife, someone to be 'dealt with'?

'Kev, they love you. You should be on telly, do it for a living.'

'Hhhmm. This is better than't telly. They wun't let me do this on't telly...' and he flicks through his papers to get ready to call out the questions and the numbers in the game he invented, in which you can win a country house, become a Lord or Lady and even be awarded a whole county, with just a line, or be thrown out of your terraced house, thrown in prison or even be sent to Australia, if you're the last to shout House, '...still fuckin' hate people,' he added, before he walked away.

One day, I'll find out why he says that to me most weeks.

Kevin found this place before we did. He'd moved into the house he still lives in when the place was full of lunatics, pushers, criminals of several sorts, and used by passers-by who wanted a place for a party or a fight or a place to hide or fire up the veins or the mind with drugs or booze.

Kevin had a car and a job. He always carried a briefcase and one of those tape measures that is the size of a discus and can measure up to 100m, and he actually had a clipboard, which he always has on him, somewhere. I think the clipboard might have saved his life, because all the low-life thought he was doing something important and used to scurry off when he arrived.

He wouldn't have noticed them anyway, because of 'The Project'. He needed a distraction as part of his big plan, so he had a love affair. An intense, all-encompassing, torrid, love affair. And immensely well-documented. Pictures, texts, messages, the works. When his wife found out, he was very pleased. She was broken and threw him out the house with what he was wearing and his briefcase, his clipboard and his beige raincoat. Kevin was over the moon. He could focus on 'The Project'.

He kept all the photos, the messages, the texts, just in case he might ever need them. Anyway, since he'd written all of the texts and taken all of the photographs and posted all of the messages himself, he felt he owned them. He had fabricated the whole thing to free himself of his burdens and his wife and the constraints of his life. It had cost him over three hundred and fifty quid to get a friend of a girl in the office to be in the photos. The wig she demanded had cost nearly a hundred quid. It was perhaps the most creative thing he had ever done in his life and he was hugely grateful for his wife's uncompromising actions.

The wife got their house. He got a house on the Circle. She got their car. He got a company car and kept his job, which was brilliant, because it made his project so much easier. He had no idea what else she got out of it. He didn't even know if she was alive.

When I go to his house I marvel. There's no hall, so you are immediately into his front room and have to negotiate skyscrapers of paper that sway as you walk past them.

Kevin's a big guy and loves eating, so how his gut and the roofs of those skyscrapers in the narrow walkways between don't collide is a mystery. I often wonder if there's more of an act going on than I will ever know. I'm convinced that inside he's not clumsy at all, he's not vague and odd, he's not sartorially challenged, he can eat without firing it all over the place, he's not awkward with people or shy. He's just playing and expanding the things that create the barriers. I have come to the conclusion that he probably isn't even fat. But I don't know how to check.

In his back room, every wall is plastered with maps. Mainly maps of Leeds, north and south of the Aire, but the wall leading to the kitchen seems to be stretching to maps further afield, of Dewsbury and Heckmondwike and places like that. They are relatively new. And here is 'The Project'.

If you ask him about it, you might regret it, like a lot of people who have given up real life to pursue their passion, it's either crushingly dull or like entering Tutankhamun's tomb for the first time. Or maybe a mix of both. They say all history passes through everywhere eventually, but all history has entered Uncle Kevin's house and never found a way out.

I remember the first map he had on his wall, years ago, when

I first arrived. It wasn't like these large scale ones he has now, it was just a walker's OS map. There was a mauve wine stain over Morley and to the northwest of Bradford was a gaping hole, where the paper had been cut out of the map. I had to consult another map to work out that he had annihilated Wilsden for some reason. I found out later it was where he'd lived with his wife. Strangely, some groups of streets in Pudsey in the folds of the maps seem to have been nuked with big bomb drawings clouding out the street names. I never dared ask about those. It didn't seem to matter. What was left was a network of hieroglyphs etched into the whole map, in various colours. Some areas were heavily highlighted and circled and there were other marks around some roads and some houses and some areas. But no code, no key, no glossary. I stared at it for hours while he grunted in his kitchen and made a cup of tea and cut up a pork pie. To be fair, most of it had been eaten by the time he brought it through. I didn't speak for the next two hours after asking him, 'What are these...signs?' I was trying to think of another word, but it wasn't necessary.

For three hours he led me down the lanes and roads and streets and snickets and yards and cloughs and terraces and closes through the range of houses, types of builders, types of bricks, types of urban planning and the lack of urban planning where the modern age was born out of the slattern that was mistress of the earlier, rougher, organic Leeds. And no subject was left unturned: the geology, the sociology, the financial, the manufacturing, the Romans, the Nazis, the Tories and the warmongers, the colonialists, the immigrants, the pogroms, the weather and even all the lovely people who don't live on the Cayman Islands, they all got a mention whilst Uncle Kevin sang his song.

I was mesmerised. At no point did his glasses slide down his nose or one word appear on his tongue to falter or fade into insignificance, or any gap appear at all in the seamlessness of his connections, links and stories.

'Kevin,' I said, when he stopped to excuse himself to go to the toilet, 'that was amazing. Absolutely fascinating, and without doubt, *the* most comprehensive lecture connecting every aspect of our lives together in a wondrous web of extraordinary depth and experience. Thank you. Unique.'

'I really need to go to't toilet,' he said, and shuffled off, like an exhausted actor after performing all of Shakespeare's plays with Henry in the title, one after the other. On his own.

When he came back, I noticed he'd left his flies half open. 'Kev, mate,' I said, and nodded down there, 'that was very interesting, but I'm still not sure what exactly all these signs mean.' I was conscious what this could lead to in terms of the lecture, but he seemed like a man spent.

'Empty houses,' he said. 'Different sorts of empty houses. Age, type, ownership, reasons for being empty. And other signs. But basically – empty houses.'

'What, you're saying that all these houses here with signs around them are empty?'

'More or less.'

'That's a huge percentage. Look at them all.'

He nodded. 'I look at them every day.' He looked at me and pushed his glasses up his nose. Then, he turned and walked into his kitchen. I went back to the maps for a minute or two, trying to count the houses just in one street, but his signs made it very complicated. Just as I'd counted sixty-seven of the same sign, he appeared at the kitchen door, 'Bye' he said, and turned back to whatever he was doing in there, and the door swung quietly shut behind him.

From the moment I met him, Uncle Kevin was engaged on 'The Project' and he had a job. He lost the job a few years later when they found out what he was doing. Quite by accident about eight years after meeting him, I met a woman who had tried to buy a house from him. It was a big house and she was on her own. Uncle K decided that it wasn't suitable for her and wouldn't let her view it. She didn't need a big house, according to Kevin. It took her three months for her to get to put in an offer that was way above the asking price. She thought he was working on commission for one of the other purchasers.

Uncle Kevin was the worst estate agent I have ever met.

Uncle Kevin was the finest estate agent I have ever met.

Eventually, she admitted, she made sure he was sacked.

11

About the Circle

The dawn was maybe an hour away when I woke up. There was a hum of sound like radio waves from another planet, and that strange yellow blur of the streetlights of the city centre converging miles away just visible above the trees. I had that gnawing in my stomach that was dread, but it was the remembrance of dread and the dread caused by the rush of memories of things I had done in my life, not the dread of things to come. Before I had gone to bed, I had texted Rowena. I knew I shouldn't have, but I did. The violent longing to spend some time with her was squatting there and poking me. What would it be like, to give all this up – the Circle, the people, the way we do things – and just do what you do when you find someone to love, and that love takes over your being? We had exchanged light, flirty, funny texts. I imagined her in her bed, and her deft fingers flying over the screen, like buzzing midges dancing in the summer air. I tried to imagine what a lady running a goth clothes shop slept in. Then, I tried to forget how we met. That was a bad thing to go to sleep on.

In bed, on my own, I had lots of time to think, at four in the morning. Who's on duty to make sure we're safe tonight? CJD and his girlfriend, Jalapeña. She's Argentinian and seems to have spent twenty years demonstrating and protesting, which inevitably led to her moving continents. We put the bollards across the only road into the Circle at night, but I always worry they'll find a way in. There's always a 'they', lurking out there, in the back of your mind.

Milton has a gun. Why did that not bother me at the time? Why has he lied to us? What is he up to? Is he connected with the guys with the shotgun? What did they want? I wouldn't have handled it the way I did, now that I have time to think. No matter what you plan or practice or prepare for, you can bet there'll be something goes wrong. I think now that the losers-on-the-sink-estate act we pulled was wrong. We should simply have listened to what they had to say. And all these guns. Where did that come from? And how to move forward, keep us safe? Get them all to just fuck off and leave us alone.

I roll over, change position, try to sleep. I think of Rowena, imagining her here, now. I can't remember why she isn't here. I must ask her tomorrow, why she doesn't live with us here. That doesn't help at all. The moon cuts through the curtains and I get up to close the gap. It's a full moon. I feel wide awake. I know what might make me feel better.

Outside, the air is so fresh and soft, and the moon is like a spotlight, steered by a great, unknown lighting engineer, who is forever embracing the darkness behind. That is the closest to God I can get. I cut across from my house around the grove full of secrets, the island of trees, that are now more than twenty feet high. That's how long we have been here, time not measured in years, but by what we have planted, grown and made good. Time, like space and the material of our world is not only linear, it's also compounded by all the other things that touch it. Even language touches time and time changes languages and the material of our world changes us. You can now listen to what the voice of an Egyptian priest, Nesyamun, who was mummified more than three thousand years ago, would sound like, or you can record yourself and your voice, and tell yourself whatever lies or truth you want, and listen and broadcast your lies and truths for an audience you will never see.

I am in the house that is the façade of a house. The place that I keep all our recordings. The Speaking House. The House of Stories. The Caravan Depository. It's semi-secret. Sort of.

'Tomorrow everything might be different,' I begin, into the tape player. I correct myself, 'Today, everything might be different.'

'I will begin as if this is the beginning of the story, but, of course, it isn't *the* beginning, it is only *a* beginning. When I hear myself speak, I can hear my father, his words, his phrasing, even the same irritability I used to hear in his voice. It sounds like he's speaking through me. From his father, maybe he learnt to talk in the way that he had heard him speak, thus, what I'm hearing in myself may be not my father, but my grandfather. But I shall begin, not with the details of birth and family and such commonplaces, but with the details of the circumstances in which I found myself, which led directly to me sitting here, recording in this room. Now.

'It's February in a small northern town, nestled in the lee of the Pennines. Years ago. The clouds are blackening, and the threat is snow. I am the Exams Officer in a school full of wankers. The staff rooms are ablaze with discussions over what happened to one of the Science teachers last night at Parents' Evening. He was punched in the face by a parent. The Police were called. The Head intervened. We imagine it'll all be hushed up, like always. 'A misunderstanding,' was her word in briefing this morning. Not sure it would have been a 'misunderstanding' if it'd been the other way round. The kid's a 'KT'. A 'Known Twat'. So, is the father.

Today, like most days, I have three or four exams to organise. Doesn't sound much, does it? Sorting out 250 kids in a room with six versions of modular Biology GCSE retakes. I don't give a fuck, I just do it. I find it works best that way. Anyway, if they fail, or if they miss it, or if they don't turn up or if they get a crap mark, it really doesn't matter 'cos they can do a retake next week or next month. Today, I have the people doing Module 1 for the first time, the people doing Module 2 for the first time and the people doing Module 1 for the second time and the people doing Module 2 for the second time and the people doing Module 1 and Module 2 together for the first time and the people doing Module 3 for the second, third or fourth time and the people doing Module 4 for the nth fucking time.

Madame's in there, as usual, with her Three Horsemen of the Management Speedwagons. She has the lost the ability to speak and has gained the power to bark. She's urging me on to get the lists checked and done, so that she can send the Horsemen off round to the kids' houses who haven't turned up. The good kids get up and trudge through sleet and snow and rain and get barked at, while the fucking little shits, who we all hate, get a wake-up call from the Aged Senators of the Senior Management and words of soft encouragement to shower and ready themselves for the arduous journey to school, courtesy of one of the Mondeos of the Three Horsemen. One more of life's little jokes. Another one is that the kids have got no idea which exam they're doing. They're like me, most of them, they don't give a fuck either. Just a motion to be gone through.

I speak to the assembled hordes, about the seats, the exams, the modules, the rules and the times and wonder if I'll be able to slip out for a dump if the call comes, as I expect it might, during this taxing session of biological multiple choice ticking.

Oh, one more thing. I forgot about Stevie P. Just as I've got the kids who are here settled, and the Horsemen dispatched to the fourteen kids who aren't here, the coppers arrive at the back of the room and everyone turns round to see who it is. When some of the lads see it's Stevie P, they wave to him and he, in turn, waves back and does a big whooping, football-terrace cheer, 'Whhhhhayyy, all right.' And they shout back in like vein.

'Gerrim out, please,' I say, to the two young coppers. This upsets Stevie P, who refuses to leave the Examination Hall. Scuffle ensues. Stevie ejected. Me and Madame shouting for calm and pushing the lads back into their seats. After five minutes, we start the exam. Shouts can still be heard from the vestibule of the school, where presumably Stevie P. is being restrained from re-entering the Examination Room. She tells me to go and sort him out with a room. Before you start feeling sorry for Stevie P. – don't – he's on remand for raping of one of the girls who's currently in the Examination Hall, sitting an exam. He's nearly sixteen and comes from a 'good home', apparently.

Outside, he's refusing to go to the room we've prepared for him to do the exams in (Modules 1 and 2 for the first time) under police supervision. He wants to go into the hall where he can be with his mates. His case is next week. We try to persuade him to stay and do the exams in this room where he will not be disturbed (or be allowed to disturb others). He thinks this is against his human rights. Eventually, just before it's time for Module 1 takers and Module 2 takers, who are not retaking anything, to leave the room, and for those who've done one of these exams and are re-taking another exam, or the Module 1 re-takers or Module 2 re-takers who've more modules to take or re-take, to start the next exam, Stevie P. is finally back in the police van, without having taken or re-taken any exams.

'When you've finished in here, come and see me,' says Madame, when the second exam of the morning has been started, and walks out.

An hour later, I knock on her door. 'I'll be brief,' she says, 'there's been another complaint about you. Apparently, you were rude to a parent at the school gates this morning.'

'Yes,' I said, 'I was, but not half as rude as I should've been.

The man is a thug and a menace. I wish I'd said what I really wanted to say.'

'He is a parent, and we are a place of education for young people and we have to set an example. And, frankly, there are too many complaints about you.' This is at full bark.

'So, it's OK for a parent to punch a teacher at Parents' Evening but not ok to suggest he should actually be in custody for causing actual bodily harm? What is that teaching the kids? Punch anyone you like if you feel a bit annoyed?'

'That's not the point. We have a reputation to uphold and I will not have parents being heckled by members of staff on a public highway.'

'Well, I won't have perfectly innocent people being punched in the face at a school event and not face any consequences.'

'Well, I won't be spoken to like this and you'll be getting a written warning and I'm calling in the Education Department. I think you need to think carefully about your future in this school.'

As I walked back to my office, I noticed the snow had begun to fall and thought about the journey home. The last, steep hill up to my house was always a problem in my car in snow. I thought I'd set off early to beat the weather. Exams all done.

When I got to my car it wasn't surrounded by a beautiful carpet of untouched white snow, but rather a scuffle of footmarks where they'd stood when they slashed all four of the tyres, scratched the doors, all four of them, and smashed the headlights and rear lights. I didn't really believe they'd do this.

When I knocked on her door, there was no answer. I could hear voices from within, so I opened the door, and she was in a meeting with a Horseman and some other suits. 'I need to talk to you,' I said, 'it's urgent.'

'Tomorrow,' she said. Normally, she would have barked but today, in front of these people, she spoke normally.

‘It’s really urgent,’ I said, ‘I wouldn’t disturb you otherwise.’

‘Tomorrow. Because I’m in the middle of something. As you can see. Thank you,’ and she closed the door.

Through the door, I heard her say, ‘That is what I have to put up with every day. I cannot have him in my school.’

I sat in the reception area. There were no taxis, all busy because of the weather. And everyone at school had their own little world to sort out. No chance of a lift. I was still there an hour after the kids had left. The Police couldn’t say when they would be there to ‘assess the situation’, even though I said I knew who’d done it and wanted to press charges. ‘Do you have any witnesses?’ they asked.

Three hours later, I was in the pub about a mile from home. I was soaked, hadn’t brought a coat and was shaking with cold. At least they had a fire. Barman was concerned about me ruining the furniture and insisted I had to sit on a wooden stool, where the run-off from my clothes collected in a big puddle on the stone floor.

I set off into the soft, thick snow that was still falling, struck by the silence and the cold. It took me an hour to stagger the mile home. Seven or eight whiskies and chasers, maybe more, had helped warm me up a bit. When I got to my front door, for some reason, I couldn’t get the key in the door and it seemed quite funny. So, I sat on my front steps, in between efforts to unlock the door. I was laughing, with my head in my hands.

When I got into the cold, dark house I took all my clothes off immediately in the tiny hallway, because I had carpets in the rest of the house that might stain in my present sodden state. It felt good to get all my sodden clothes off and I dried myself with a tea towel. It was then that the overwhelming sense of being alone swamped me. Of really being alone in this big, unpleasant world where stupidity and injustice reign, except for brief, bright moments lasting no longer than the time it takes to strike a match and for it to burn your fingers. I remember turning on the gas fire. I remember being very cold and trying to find another tea towel.

At some point later, who knows how much later, I heard a banging in my head, from far away, which is where my head was. The room was swinging, floating and the whole of space was filled with big lights, flashing in several colours, and I wanted to make it all stop, the whirring, the noise, the lights, the smell, that awful smell. This was like death. It was very strange because coming from the back of my mind were the French and German exams for tomorrow morning. But I didn't know how to get to them, how to reconnect with what I'd known and knew was real and I felt the carpet still wet underneath me.

I remember the knocking grew louder and it seemed to be coming from outside. I crawled towards it and tried to have a conversation. I could hear voices on the other side. I was on the floor at the foot of my front door but wasn't sure what to do next. A pair of eyes appeared at the letterbox. 'Hello,' I said and laughed. Then I remembered how cold it was. 'What do you want?' I didn't really get what they were saying from the dark side of the door.

'Open the door, open the door...' she kept saying. Ten minutes later I got what she meant and stood up and opened the door. There was a Police Officer standing there and she said, 'Sir, I need to talk to you, OK? We're coming in,' and I felt the door being pushed out of my grip and she was pushing me into the front room. I suddenly realised I was naked. She pushed past me and turned off the unlit gas fire that had been gushing away since I arrived home.

'Sir, you need to put some clothes on, before we can go any further,' and she nodded to her colleague to go and find me some clothes from upstairs.

'There's been a complaint that you've been appearing naked

at the window and the neighbours have rung to come and see what's going on. Then, we smelled the gas. I think you're a bit worse for wear. All you had to do was shut your curtains but, apparently, you were standing in the window for ages. They've got young children.'

I couldn't really answer. Not with real words, only the ones that appeared and then, just as quickly, disappeared.

Down at the station, I was charged with a Public Indecency offence. But, not until I'd spent a night sobering up in the cell. Nothing I said seemed to matter, although they weren't unpleasant. I was told that, given the nature of my job, school would have to be informed and it was likely that this might lead to further action, but for now I would be charged and have to face the magistrate at some point.

After a few days, I finally left the house for an hour of fresh air. The snow had covered almost all the tracks. There were a few folk out doing erands and there were kids in gardens messing and having fun. After being in the cold of the police station for a night, the headache and the shaking had begun, and I'd fallen into bed with some tablets and a hot water bottle. I hadn't been able to get up for three days. I got a few phone calls but was too weak to answer. Eventually, school rang to say they were concerned about me, but more importantly, that I'd left my car in a very bad condition on the school premises and I was to sort it out at once.

The slide. This is how it begins. I'd heard about it. We're all just three, four or five events away from losing everything. I was lucky. I didn't have much to lose.

The snow had melted as if it had never been, and in its place came one of those blue, frosty late February days when I went to sort out the car. I waited till after school. It was nearly dark. The car park was almost empty. I could see the swathe of glass below the passenger door. The bastards had stolen three of the wheels and had propped it up on the nearest thing they could lay their hands on: tatty, battered copies of *Macbeth*. One push and the whole thing would fall over. The inside was a total mess. I called the AA, and they gave me the number of a scrapyard but advised getting the Police to give me a crime number before I got rid of it.

I waited three hours before the thing had been removed from the car park. I was thinking about what to do with the soggy, oily, ripped and strangely squashed *Macbeths*. Like cast copies from *Macbeth on the Estate*. School was still open, so I parked them in half a dozen neat piles in the English staff room. I even swept up the glass and put it in the bin. I didn't want Madame having a reason to ring. I cleared my office and put everything in a box: mug, t-bags, coffeemaker, LUFC key ring, diary, pack of condoms that I had only ever used to give to other people.

Walking down this familiar road, waiting at the bus stop in a freezing February evening, nursing a box of stuff from an office of a job that had just come to such an abrupt end suddenly felt strange and amplified and vivid, like in a dream you know you will never remember. The urge to walk just took over and I walked and walked and walked until I found myself at the bottom of the steep hill to my house. A couple of hundred yards behind me was a row of shops with old-fashioned doorways. One of them had the name of the shop owner from years ago, picked out in a black and white mosaic, *A. J Arkwright & Son*. I left the box there. Ripped out the pages of the diary that might refer to me and put the LUFC key ring into my pocket. Some things keep you going.

When I tried to get another job, I hit a brick wall. References, interviews, courses, qualifications, experience. That was just for a bit of van driving. Everything was accessed through a thirty-two page form to be filled out and checked. I even gave up with the social. I lost count of the days I sat at home. Or the days wandering around on stupid errands when I forgot why I had set off and found myself in a strange place but couldn't remember why. I did the trick with the gas fire again and sat for hours wondering why it wasn't getting warmer. This time, it wasn't the Police who came knocking at the front, but the next-door neighbour, who came straight in through the back door because he had a right of way round the back,

'What the heck you doing, sonny?' he said. And turned the unlit gas off straight away. 'I've got kids living with me, so you better sort yoursen out, anht you?' He kicked two chairs on his way out. 'Next time I won't be so pleasant, d'you hear me?' he said, just before he left.

When they sent someone to value the house, she told me what it was worth. 'But that's less than I paid for it,' I said.

'Not a good time to sell,' she said.

'Well, can I have some sort of extension?' I asked her.

'If you mean about money, not my job. We just sell houses. You need to go to speak to the mortgage company.' And walked off. Then she turned around on the front steps. 'Can I give you some advice?' she said, and didn't wait for an answer. 'If you want to sell it you need to sort out the...the smell. No one's gonna buy it if it smells like this.' She smiled and looked like she didn't know how much further to go, and with a hurried, 'Bye,' she turned away.

Within a week I'd cleaned everything three times, every surface, every wall, every window, every floor and every piece of furniture. Then, I started on myself. Cleared out bags of things that were redundant. Showered every hour. Every evening I ran. At first it was terrible. All the stress, the junk food, the lost days and hours meant after five minutes I had to stop with a stitch, with coughing and then after another ten, I'd be floundering with a headache and having coughing bouts producing handfuls of phlegm and gunk.

After a month I could do it. I could run to the hill on the far horizon, down to the old reservoir from the 1790s, round the far side, up through the steep-sided feeder valley and out onto a broad stretch of slowly rising moorland on a road that was potholed and unloved.

By the end of this week, I'd sold everything, except the bed and the bike and the fridge and the cooker and the big old, antique mirror. It was nearly six feet tall and I had no recollection how I got it. A lady rang to ask if she could come to see it. I said, 'Of course, before 6, please.' At 6, I had to run.

She was late. I was a few hundred yards up the road when I saw her car pull up outside the house and she got out. I remember thinking the mirror would never fit into her car. She was in a suit. The grey suit. Will never forget the grey suit. She bought the mirror. She also clocked everything in the house, or rather the lack of anything in the house. 'You going somewhere?' she said, like in an interview.

I laughed. 'You won't get that in your car,' I said.

'No, it's a very fine piece,' she said, 'where did you get it?'

I shook my head.

She passed me the money. And her business card. *Ssshh!* was the name of the business, in gold lettering on a grey card. 'Bring me the mirror to this address tomorrow, and I'll make it worth your while,' she said, with a business-like smile.

I watched her smooth the pencil skirt of her grey suit to sit on the cream leather seat of her BMW sportscar, and wondered how I would ever get the mirror to an apartment in the oldest quarter of Leeds.

It was a warm spring day and I had too many clothes on. Carrying the mirror seemed the cheapest way. Taxi would be a fortune, car long gone, so I walked it to the bus stop. I'd wrapped it in paper and cardboard and cling film, but still the bus driver managed to scrape some of the protective wrapping off the back as we manoeuvred it round the bars at the bus doors. When I changed buses the next driver was less helpful. In the end, an old lady stood up and held one end but kept letting it slip because it was too heavy. The driver just sat and stared with that way-beyond-my-pay-scale look. More scratches to the back.

'Hi,' she said, when I appeared at the doorway of her second-floor office. 'O, yeah, so sorry about the lift, sometimes it works, sometimes it doesn't. Come on in,' and opened the door so that I could carry it in. She clearly didn't do shifting. 'Put it anywhere,' she said and went through to her office. A deep red pencil skirt, this time.

'My name's Kate, have a seat, please. Ooh, you're all sweaty,' she said.

'Sorry, it's hotter than you think.' She made me feel very nervous, in a very odd way.

'Well done, for bringing the mirror. Clearly you are a very trustworthy person, which is good.' She smiled again. She had a pen in her hand and was holding it as if it wasn't just a pen.

Wow, I thought, I have never seen anyone hold a pen that stirred my loins. I shifted in my seat again.

'Good. Well, I have your contact details and I know where you live,' and smiled, 'just need to know a few more little things about you.' Pause. Steely gaze. This was Phillip Marlowe gone Politically Correct. 'I'm thinking you're in need of some income, perhaps, in a period of transition in your life, not feeling very attached to anything at the moment.' She stretched the word *attached* like she was pinning me for a museum exhibition in the entomology rooms. She stopped and held my gaze, simply for the pleasure of looking. She didn't seem to want a reply, and I don't think she was asking a question. I was looking at her lips.

'You don't speak very much, do you?' she asked, after a long pause. 'Which is good, but I hope you can speak a little bit, at any rate. When necessary.' She smiled again, and teased her lips with the pen. The pen was the same colour as the pencil skirt.

The way she said what she said made me laugh.

'Oh, good, you have a sense of humour as well. Excellent,' she continued, 'and as you can see from the name of our business, *Ssshh*! not speaking, but listening, is an absolute key element.'

She sat back in her chair and seemed to relax into the silence, like a cat when they tuck their paws into themselves and look seamless and sleek.

After another long pause, she asked, 'Any questions? You can ask me questions, if you like...'

I pulled my gaze off her and looked around the room. 'Where's the mirror going?' at which point it was her turn to laugh.

'Oh, I don't know. Somewhere.'

'Don't you live here? It looks like you live here,' I said.

'Thank you,' she said, 'I am glad you feel at home, but no, I don't live here. This is where I run my business.'

Then, the phone rang, and she stood up and mouthed, 'Excuse me,' and I'm almost certain she brushed past me as she swished out of the room. I heard the lining of her skirt rubbing as she moved. Without her presence I was able to breathe a little and take stock. Outside of the room, I could hear her voice but not her words. Inside the room, it was warm, and the big windows let in big slabs of light onto the leather and the wood and the wool of the surfaces, and I noticed she had real books on the shelf, not self-help books or IKEA books or pub books or coffee table books but books that someone would have had to choose to put together. This was not an office like Madame's from school, or with the chirruping of people busy doing office things, this was like walking into someone's life, but where you were only allowed to see the lounge of their lives and nothing else. Real, but with very definite walls. A compartment of a life that would always just be a compartment.

She strode back in and placed her phone down in her bag, by her chair. Nothing was out of place. As she sat down again, the waft of fresh perfume was visible, like motes of dust floating between us. I really didn't want to leave.

'I am assuming that you are interested in the income stream and in working for me. I do, though, have a couple of things that I'm going to have to ask you to do.'

I said, 'Yes, I am,' without knowing what on earth I was doing.

'Oh, good. One of the things I'm going to ask you to do is to do a medical. It's all very discreet and we pay, but it is absolutely necessary. I will need your bank details. I am assuming you still have a bank account? And I will need to see you here tomorrow same time and be free most of the day. Then we can – I don't like using the word work, really – I prefer the word, *engagement* – then, we can find suitable engagements.' She stood up and moved from around her desk, 'So, if you'll excuse me...' and set off towards the door.

My problem was that my erection was uncomfortably lodged since I had become more aroused, the longer I spent with her. I don't know if I had had just been through an interview or not or what exactly the job – the *engagement* – entailed, but the entire thing had been done with an aching, uncontrolled, un-wished for erection and it wasn't going down as she stood at the door.

'Are you coming?' she said, sweetly.

I stood up reluctantly, and walked towards her, trying to act as if there wasn't anything out of the ordinary.

'Good,' she said, 'very good,' and her eyes trailed from my crotch to my eyes and back.

I ran twice my usual route that evening. My sense of the dirty pragmatics of life, that no one does nothing for anyone except for themselves, was batting my thoughts around in a chaotic spin of excitement, fantasy, worry, fear and that overwhelming hooded crow of a thought that I was walking into a trap. I slept fitfully. Worked through in my mind every angle of taking up her offer, or never seeing her again. I walked around the abandoned house and thought about what I had: no job, no money, debt and no plan beyond handing back the keys to the house to the mortgage company as soon as the last of my belongings had gone. I watched the sun come up, saw the world start up again, like an old engine and all the little people, who I never normally saw, get in the groove that they were cast in. That was it. There was no real choice, was there? What did it matter? Nothing mattered. Fuck it.

It was a drizzly day, and she was waiting at the ground floor entrance for me with an umbrella. 'Don't be late,' she said. 'Being on time is being late. Be here early.' And she set off walking towards the town centre. We didn't speak until we reached the doorway of a large house in a row of Victorian terraces. 'Just do everything they ask, ok, it's nothing dubious or fishy, but without this we can't proceed.' She didn't wait for an answer.

There was no queue, no fuss, Instead, I found myself lying on a medical examination table, almost naked, being swept through a raft of tests: blood, blood pressure, temperature, urine and swabs and tests on every available orifice and someone clinical making notes, without one word of explanation. Then, the brisk, unsmiling nurse pulled down my underpants in one swift movement, which she had done thousands of times before, clearly. Everything genital and anal was examined, and swabs were taken from the urethra and placed ready for testing.

Come back in an hour, I was told. 'Thanks', I said. Great, I thought.

When I emerged into the swooping rain of a cold afternoon, she was not around. Instead, after five minutes a text arrived. *Get a coffee. Come back in an hour.* Everyone's done this before except me. Over a Café Nero cappuccino, I thought of yesterday's delicious eroticism. Today, I felt what I felt most other days. Nothing. Someone rang me about the fridge. Would I take forty quid? Yeah, I said, whatever. Five minutes later it was the same number but a different voice, a woman this time. 'Got a fridge for sale?' she said. 'Yeah.' 'Give you thirty for it.' 'Whatever.' Selling second-hand white goods is a strange type of hell. One guy, who came to buy the table, started haggling to buy my radiators. 'I know every radiator for sale for twenty miles,' he said, 'I know what they're worth.' Bully for you, wanker, I thought. 'Great' I said and made him leave. There was always someone mentally worse off than you, and it made me feel very uneasy. How the hell do you know you've reached the fucking bottom?

When I got back, three minutes early, Kate was emerging from the receptionist's office. She was clutching some paperwork. She set off walking briskly back towards her office and beckoned to me to follow, but after five minutes we turned into an unobtrusive, ethnic restaurant.

'Fancy a celebration?' she said, 'of your new-found career opportunity?' She was smiling. We clinked glasses. 'All good,' she smiled again, when she waved the envelope from the medical centre at me. 'I would normally go with you, but I'm really busy at the moment, so I've prepared a list of things for you to do today,' and passed me a piece of paper, folded neatly. 'Please do these in order. Any problems, let me know, and when you've finished them, let me know. I'll also send you an email with some final details which I would like you to read, sign and send back...ok?' I nodded.

Hairdressers, clothes shop, photographers. In that order. Places I didn't know about, in parts of town I wouldn't normally ever go to. Kate was running a very slick operation. All paid for, no fuss, no queues, no questions, except the ones about, *What size is Sir?* and *Which one does Sir prefer? I, myself, prefer the dark one...*

I didn't really read it, I just sent off an electronic signature from the internet café I found closer to home. I sent her a text to tell her it was all done. I got three hearts back.

By the time I reached the road that swung round the valley head, just below the high line of the moors, the rain had stopped, and the sun was setting slowly behind the ridge to the west, and the birds were singing. Up here, it was skylarks and moorland birds in West Yorkshire in spring. Hidden in the valley to the north was the unceasing, low-bellied thrum of the endless stream of cars on the M62 and I thought how easy it would be to jog up to the ridge above me now, and find some sheep trails through the heather and bracken and tufts of grass, gathering some pace and momentum on the downward trajectory towards the embankment supporting the three lanes of speeding vehicles driving into the setting sun, and seize the moment to run amongst them and find some end to this feeling of nothing. I could imagine the first impact that would smash my thighs and throw me high into the air, and even the sickening compression of hitting the ground. The rest is beyond me. The consequences would be horrendous. Not on me, but on the person who first hit me, and what would happen to him or her and the string of innocent people caught up in the horrific ripples of such an action, by someone simply seeking peace.

There was a knock at the door a few days later. I thought it was the fucker about the fridge. What I noticed this time was the lipstick. A purple that matched the shoes.

'I like coming out here,' Kate said, as she brushed against me again, to step into the house, 'it's so fresh, lots of sky. I won't stay, although I'm not sure if I am allowed to stay.' She smiled again, 'I have something for you.' She handed me an envelope. 'This one is just for starters, so you know we mean business. And this one is for your first *engagement*. I like it if you owe me, then you can't ever leave me.' She was looking at the cave painting I had recreated on my living room wall from Sinagua, Arizona. It was a hunting scene in reds and blacks, etched into the uneven surface of ancient rocks. I'd tried to recreate the mix of glyphs, signs and living things telling a story. She wrapped her lips around one another as she teased out in her mind why anyone would do this to the plastered walls of their living room in a terraced house. Her hands wrapped together over the straps of her matching handbag, which she was swinging, dreamily.

'Thank you, you're very kind.'

She smiled. Then, the smile slipped. She took one last look around the room and walked out of the door. I put the envelopes behind the few books I had left on a shelf in the pantry. I thought no one would ever check Thucydides or Xenophon. I didn't look what was in the envelopes.

Three days later a message arrived with a name, a time and a place. Then, an Instagram message with the list of rules. The same list I had seen before. I liked her title, 'Rules of Engagement'.

Melanie was a striking figure. Round, loud and with big hair piled up on her head. It was a media awards do, and she was hosting a table. I was her partner for the night. I made sure her glass was filled, her plate was filled and I smiled with interest at things she said to the people around us. Most of the time, the music or the 'entertainment' was so loud, I only heard every third word. No one else around the table cared because they were all talking at once.

Melanie, to be fair, was probably the best of them and since she'd been in the advertising business for nearly forty years, she could afford to throw her words of wisdom and her forthright wit around with some abandon, and if the youngsters around the table knew what was right, they were making sure she saw them laugh and agree. She put her hand on my knee and told me to take her to the dance floor. She was quite small, but she could rest her beehive against my shoulder comfortably enough as we waltzed around to a slow one and then to a faster one. She turned out to be quite a jiver. At the end of the next dance, she pressed herself against me and kissed me.

After another bottle of wine, the host, someone from Radio 4 apparently, who had been 'entertaining' the crowd all night, asked everyone for a moment of quiet, and for the first time that night, they actually stopped talking. A palpable sense that something was about to happen waved a wand. It was the awards part of the ceremony. A few cheers and lots of shouts, and a fair bit of running from the floor to the stage later, she nudged my arm, 'Might have a fuckin' chance with this one,' she whispered. The G-list celeb was now about to open another envelope, and she gripped my knee again and whispered in my ear, 'I hope for your sake we win.' We were then treated to the three nominated best advertising videos of the year. The first one appeared to be for some sort of country house hotel but was rounded off by a pitch from a bloke with a golf club, selling insurance. The second was what looked like a carjacking on drugs, with a car chase that was actually on a simulator and finished off where a JCB appeared to be surfing into the beach from a big wave, in what looked like Hawaii, that turned out to be for a groundwork company whose Chairman and owner did a thumbs up in a hi-vis jacket.

The third one was Melanie's. 'I think they hate me. They're jealous,' she hissed. It began in black and white, with a woman taking her clothes off in a field, and a rural type watching her in an arty way, that then faded into a Sixties drug-fuelled trip, seen through the eyes of a couple with backcombed hair, and then some footage of a war zone, which segued into a family playing outside a semi on a dull estate, who are visited by grandma and grandad, and then the next thing we're inside a plush old people's home. Whatever your parents did, they deserve the best, seemed to be the message, rounded off with the details of the very expensive care home.

'Wow,' I said, 'that's brilliant.'

'For best advertising video, this year's winner is...(drum roll)... *Sharp as Bricks*, with their innovative and ground-breaking use of...' His reasoning was drowned out, as the cheers and roars and ovations accompanied the rush to the stage of three bright young things and a tall, distinguished gentleman, who received the prize graciously to the sound of a big, spangly tune coming over the speakers.

'He's a twat,' she said pointing, at the Director of *Sharp as Bricks*. 'Thick as Pricks, more like. For fuck's sake. On yer feet, me laddo.'

In the hotel room, Melanie's first act was to ring down for more wine. 'Don't stop,' she says, 'if he knocks. And don't stop, if he comes in wi'it.' Her second act was to remove my clothes. For sixty-three, she still had some strength. She put me on my back and sat on my face. Then, she remembered she still had her knickers on and got off the bed, stepped out of them but fell over, and I had to try to catch her as she toppled away from me on the bed. She didn't seem perturbed and eventually, by resting on my shoulder, she got them off and then pushed me on to the bed again and climbed onto my face again. She still had her evening dress on, so I was pitched into a tight tent of fleshy, sweaty darkness and I did my best. I thought of Xenophon and Thucydides. I thought of Kate.

Melanie was rubbing so hard that I didn't hear the knock, but I was conscious that at some point she was speaking to the room service lad. 'Just purrit dahn, will ya? Tek a tenner or summat from me purse. Don't tek any more or I'll have you fuckin' sacked.'

After another ten minutes, I felt like I had been underwater in the dark seas off Blackpool and I got hold of the dress and threw her off me and sat up, gasping for air. 'Oh, you like it like that, do you?' So, she pulled the evening dress off to reveal her curves and her folds making appearances outside of her expensive, complicated underwear. She was determined, I will say that for Melanie, and with a drunken, practiced ease, she was sitting on my cock. At least I could breathe more easily, I thought, and once again did my best. It wasn't easy. I thought of Biology Modules and which retake they would be up to by now. I thought of the fat envelopes behind the books. I tried to think of Melanie as a young woman and what had happened in the meantime. I thought of Kate just to get through it. About two o'clock it stopped. To be honest, it had stopped earlier, when the Neanderthal in her had taken over, after she'd lost consciousness but was still upright.

I took refuge in the huge bathroom. I couldn't look in the mirror. I scrubbed in the shower. Checked my clothes for stains before I put them on. And walked all the way home. I set off in the dark and saw the sunrise as I reached the last stretch before home. Just a pale brightening from the eastern horizon, obscured by buildings and clouds melting into the grey clouds bringing rain from the west. By the time the roads were filling with workers, I was soaked, and the rain was already streaming down the gutter of the road, on the last hill before home.

Three days later. I had priced up flights to Buenos Aires. Emailed three charities in the Democratic Republic of Congo for a job. I had even gone on Facebook and fished around for the details of three women who I'd known years earlier and was now pining for – a nurse, a teacher and a PR exec. They were good people. I was the one who had ruined it. I also planned burning the house down and went through the minimum of twelve possible paths of possible consequences. Almost all of them seemed to involve the deaths of innocents.

One day, I set off walking due west over the moors and slept out in a hollow, out of the wind, fitfully and uncomfortably. It felt good to taste the dew of dawn and the dampness of peat and grass.

It annoyed Kate that I didn't take my phone with me everywhere. When I got back, there were several texts. Firstly, there was the sweetener, from Kate, with instructions to meet later that day. Then, because I hadn't reply to that message, she became more irritated asking questions about where I was and why I wasn't answering my phone, while she was organising *stuffing my little (pay) packet,* as she called it, wryly. I was already two days late. More followed: a stream of irritation swelling to over-boiling. By the time she had written the last ones, she had calmed down. *Call me when you're ready.*

I was in the bath when she rang.

'Don't you want the money?' she said. I didn't really know if I did, or not. She ignored the silence. 'Go to the Blue Dog Café Bar this evening at 6.15 and you'll get paid for your evening with Melanie. She thought you were very – what was the word she used? Oh, yes...thorough and unobtrusive.' She laughed. 'Not sure what that means, but that is high praise from her.'

She waited for a reaction. I didn't have one to give. I raised myself up to run the hot water tap, because the bathwater was getting cold.

'OK,' I said.

'And then at 7pm, go to the bar opposite where there is someone expecting you. Smart casual. It's called Sundowners. She's called Mariana. I'll send you the details.' She paused.

The only thing I could think of was a date with her, but I just said, 'Yeah. Thanks.'

She paused again. 'Take care. Keep your phone with you,

please. You might think you're on a zero hours contract, but you're not...'

For a moment, I could feel real words forming somewhere, wherever words form, but as I stretched to turn the tap off, the phone slid from my grip and I only just caught it before it hit the water. 'Better go,' I said.

The bar was lowkey and had that feeling of a room with a dangerous dog in it, that's sleeping. I sat down and a few minutes later, from out of nowhere, a woman stood above me, checked for a moment and then slid into the seat opposite. She passed me a magazine. 'There you go,' she said. Then she did what they all do and got her phone out. As if she really was there to meet me for a drink. It was 'Home & Garden'. 'Happy reading,' she said as she got up, and moved like a wisp of mist, out of the bar.

I got up to leave for the bar opposite, Sundowners, but before I got to the door, I felt guilty about the magazine and picked it up off the table to put it back in the rack. When I picked it up, an envelope fell out and crashed onto the floor. It had my initials on it. The barman looked at me as if I needed help. When I bent down, he was watching me with a curious smile. I smiled back. I thought for one moment about leaving it there for someone to find, but then I thought about what might happen if I did, and the effort of the do-gooder trying to repatriate the money might lead back to me with questions, whereas like this, it was just simpler. And I had to admit, I was disappointed. That feeling again that I was getting more and more often every time I dealt with her. I was disappointed, then annoyed and now the irritation was surging through me, that she had sent someone else to do her errands. She was pulling all the little strings. I found myself looking round the room to see from where she was enjoying this view of me. Then, it occurred to me that she might have a lot more to occupy herself with than me.

I had an idea. 'Hey, Mr. Barman, look, someone seems to have lost this...' and handed him the envelope.

His eyes narrowed. 'What?'

'I think someone has forgotten this envelope. I've just found it on the floor.'

'No, they haven't. That woman just passed it to you,' and he backed away and walked off down the inside of the bar, as if he'd not witnessed or spoken to anyone or anything. At the other end of the bar was the security in the suit, and they started talking. I took the side door out of the place.

I could have *not* crossed the road into Sundowners, but I had the envelope in my pocket. And I'd said yes to Kate. I could have turned away and walked away and thrown my phone away, but that isn't how we are made, is it? Not until the other choice makes more sense. As I walked through the door, I knew I'd already made the wrong decision. I doubted that old maxim that we always have a choice.

The greeter wanted to show me to a seat, but I said I was meeting someone who was already sat down. Couples mainly, squatting around small tables, trying to talk over the music, and some oddballs on their own pretending to do crosswords or banging away at their keyboards, ignoring their drinks or taking indignant slurps, in between letting rip about feeling lost and disappointed, with a megaphone in a virtual stadium the size of the world.

At the far end, near the toilets, was a group of girls dressed for a Mediterranean strip, talking over one another ,at the same time as typing with two thumbs on big blingy phones. I slid into the toilets, hoping Mariana had had some terrible news from her family and was on her way to a tearful gathering around a bedside in Barnsley, just in time to say goodbye. In the toilets was a guy at the sink, splashing his face with cold water whilst on a call on a phone, propped up against the mirror above. I went into a cubicle for peace. I stood listening to the conversation, proof that there sometimes is no choice. I could hear both sides vying for Stupidest Twat Ever competition, rendering speech into a series of howls, repetitive primal utterances elevating words like 'Na-Na-Na-Naaaagh-Haha-Yaaa-Yaaah' into passages of Shakespearean profundity. It had just turned 7. This is worse than what's coming. As I stepped out of the cubicle, the pitch was notched up, and the intensity of sound-making and the all-inclusive self-importance of shouting the word *long*, but like all the *longs* you have ever used, compressed into one very long *long*, accompanied by an all-inclusive arm wave, embracing all followers of every Twitterer in this great auditorium that is social media in a bloke's bogs, in downtown Leeds.

'For fuck's sake,' I said, as I dodged some massive sound waves and his wet water-throwing arms, not choosing my moment wisely to get out and make a run for the door.

I found Mariana by the brown glasses case on the table. I introduced myself, and she nodded. No smile, I noticed. Her dark hair hung around her face, and she looked unhappy and twisted her mouth as she read the menu. I asked her some questions, but I don't know if it was the music, the loud conversation around me, or the brash, hard surfaces of the place, but I was really struggling to hear her. After the third time I asked her what her job was, she shouted, 'You fuckin' deaf or what?' which seemed to make her smile. Briefly.

I smiled and went back to my menu, trying to indicate by signs that there was a lot of background noise in this place, when I saw her eyes looking up in an unexpected way. I followed her gaze. It was the guy from the toilets. He started speaking, but I really didn't understand what he was saying. I made a sign, pointing to my ear, 'Deaf, mate,' I mouthed. He didn't think this was funny, but I really didn't know what he was saying.

‘You fuckin’ deaf?’ said Mariana, looking angrily at me.

Now that was an awkward one, one that I was hoping she wasn’t going to ask.

I stood up, which is what the Shouter wanted. I moved out of my seat, which is what the Shouter wanted. His hands were getting ready. I made a mental note that for one so ready to make noise, he really spoke with his hands. I set off down the aisle, towards the door, and made a sign with my hands for him to follow me. Shouter very happy. Very. When we got to the *Wait to be Seated* sign, I stopped and pointed at it. This confused him, quite seriously. After a moment, the greeter came to me, and I smiled and pointed at my ear, and then demonstrated for her that this man was shouting a load of words that I didn’t understand, and that I had hearing issues when it came to him, and could you ask him not to disturb my night out. I left her with him, who passed him onto Security.

Mariana was sitting at the table on her phone. She barely looked up when I sat down. Then she looked up, ‘It don’t fuckin’ matter what I do, does it? It’s what you can fuckin’ do that matters,’ and smiled again with a smile that was the one below being spat at. The way she said ‘matters’ echoed repeatedly, all swallowed glottals and far removed from the ‘t’ sound of the unvoiced, alveolar stopped consonant you might expect in classical textbooks. She shut the menu and pushed her hair back behind her ear. ‘Not hungry.’ She looked at me, and her lips moved as if she was chewing two amoebas but struggling to control them. ‘You’ve put me off. Summat about your face that’s putting me off.’ Not sure what she wanted me to say to that. *Great, we can all go home, then*. Something like that is what I thought, but nothing came out. Her eyes narrowed and she sneered at me, needing a response. I couldn’t think of one thing I should say. She stared at me. Then, ‘Fucking dumb as well as deaf. For fuck’s sake.’

She looked away, which must have caught the waitress' eye, because she came to ask, 'What can I get you?'

'I'll have a new date, please, 'cos this one's a wanker.' She stood up and put her coat on. 'He's paying as well.' Then she went back to her phone. The waitress looked at me as if I should explain.

'If you get me the bill, I'll pay you.' I didn't move, just smiled at the waitress. I expected Mariana to walk off, but she was still standing there, still staring into her phone.

When she came back with the bill, Mariana was still there, looking even more annoyed. 'What you doing, sunshine, hurry up, I'm gonna get me money's worth. Come on, sort yersen out.' She had stopped chewing her lips and she pushed her hair back behind both ears. The smile was awkward, as if she had a mouth guard in there. She beckoned me to follow her.

'Got a car?' She waited for a reply, but not for long. 'Thought not.' She yanked me to follow her, and then to keep up with her, as we set off down a side street.

She walked briskly, fearlessly even, and had locked my arm into hers, so I had no choice but to keep up. She wove a way through little cobbled streets, over the river by a little pedestrian bridge and into that area of old warehouses, cheap, uncovered car parks and spaces slowly being reclaimed by weeds, where once stood workshops, little factories and the overcrowded housing for the desperately poor. She was walking quickly, but with too many steps, so it was difficult for me to match her speed and her short strides, and I could tell that even my gait was annoying her. She looked at me as if she had never met anyone she disliked more.

When we turned into a little walled yard, she got out her keys from her handbag and pressed them fiercely. A cute, dark blue sports car reacted with flashing lights and the click of the locks. A BMW, I think, very sleek. 'Fuck' she says and throws them back in her bag and picks out another set and presses them even more fiercely. 'What the fuck's wrong now?' she hisses and shouts, 'For fuuuck's sake.' Nothing reacts. More fierce rummaging in the bag, and then she checks her coat pockets and then her bag again, and finally, settles on another smaller set of keys, and when she presses it twice, the lights of an old Volvo estate flash weakly, and she tells me to get in.

'Where we going?' I ask.

'Wherever you want, darling,' and laughs for the first time.

She keeps looking at me and laughing. Past Elland Road, out along the motorway, swing left to go right towards Manchester, the sun just above the horizon, the traffic gone for another day. Then, while I'm staring out of the window, she takes a slip road, and we're off up a valley coming off the Pennines.

'Don't like the cameras,' she says and squeezes my knee, and smiles, almost indifferently. We go round past the old farms and down slow, single-track lanes, and the views eastwards are lovely, Leeds but a smudge on the horizon. 'Are you a bit deaf or a lot dumb?' she says. I don't think she really wants an answer.

'And what are you, Mariana? A librarian? The brown glasses case? The rudeness? Is it an act or is it just your unhappiness? Surely a girl like you doesn't need to pay a guy like me. Actually, don't answer any of that, it's not important, is it?'

Surprisingly, she said nothing. I was waiting for the torrent, but nothing came. She pulled over to look at her phone. 'Shit signal up here.' Then, pulled out again when she'd got her answer. I thought about asking her to stop and let me out. But I thought we might be going somewhere like a quiet pub for a chat. Or more likely an evening of gentle badger-baiting with a crowd of Jack Russells. I was getting very close to asking her to stop and let me out. There was nowhere to go up here. Strange to think there are parts of our industrialised island where you can still get to places where you can't see a house or a farm or a building and hey, ho! that was just where we were now.

‘Let me out, Mariana, please. Stop anywhere, just let me out.’

‘Not just yet, sweetie,’ she said, teasingly, with a smile, as she led the Volvo along the moorland road that must have crested the watershed, because before us, was the dying sun and views westwards to the mill towns of Lancashire. I thought about grabbing the steering wheel or the handbrake or her, but on either side of the narrow road were deep ditches, edged with barbed wire fences and not a house or help for miles. Suddenly, we turned off on our left onto a little dirt track and descended down behind some trees into a large, dirt car park and she pulled up in between two other cars. Between us and the road was a mature line of conifers providing the perfect screening. Unless you came down here, you'd never know what was going on. Unless you were looking for it, you'd never know it was there.

‘Fucking hell, Mariana, what we doing here?’

‘Ooooh, do you speak like that to all your customers? Naughty boy,’ she squealed, and she pinched my cheek.

Out of the car on the right-hand side, two blokes got out and out of the car on the left, three others got out and a woman. The one who got out the back was the biggest bastard I'd seen in a long time. I wondered how the hell he'd got in the back of a Ford Mondeo. They all seemed to know one another. I could hear the greetings and embraces and watch the kisses and handshakes. I opened the door but one of them shut it straightaway, and I heard the locks click as Mariana locked me in.

This can't be happening, this really can't be happening.

I got my phone out and thought about ringing Kate and telling her that I was trapped up on a moor with the lovely Mariana, whom Kate had described as ‘great fun, great to be with, salt of the earth but with a good heart – you'll love her.’ She'd clearly never spent any time with her. I dialled the number, hiding it inside my coat and waited for the dial tone. Nothing.

I looked down. No dial tone, no ringing, no Kate, no signal. When I looked up, Mariana was looking through the window, with the Brute looking at me over her shoulder. Mariana smiled and waved her finger, 'No, no, no, no noooooo...!'

I heard Brute shouting and laughing, and out of the mirrors, I could see men appearing from all of the cars ready to join in the fun. Next thing I knew, the car was being rocked up and down and a dozen faces were leering in and shouting at me, one of them even taking a video of me sitting trapped inside and adding a commentary to it, until I heard Mariana's voice shrilly rising up, 'Eh, you twats, leave it now, don't want you fucking up me Luvli-Vulvi, she's old and used and her suspension's going... don't you fuckin' say it, Mickey-Dickey, I can see your brain working...' and they all laughed, and the rocking stopped and they went off back to their cars. And for a moment, it was quiet, and I stared into the oncoming gloom, as the first drops of rain hit the windscreen, softly.

In the glove compartment was a map, and I turned on the vanity light and rifled through the pages to find where we might be. Working from our starting point in Leeds and trying to remember all the little signs and names of the places we'd passed through, I thought it can't be that difficult to work out where we were now. The motorway west, the first valley, the road running down to cross the railway line and then up behind that pub, then the sweep around the valley head and a series of swift lefts and rights as we followed the lines of the old fields, to join the only road over the hills into Lancashire. It's got to be there. Did I see a reservoir below us to the left? Got it. Nothing at all for several miles. I looked at my shoes, not ideal. I slid the map under my chair as the door clicked open, and Mariana slid into the driver's seat. She was wearing nothing but lacy underwear and a black masquerade mask of gold brocade, with a black feather at either side.

'Hold that,' she said and passed me a plastic bag. She made the last adjustments to her hair, which seemed to have got a lot shorter in the last five minutes and looked in the mirror. 'Nice, eh?' she said, with that smile. Then, she pulled the bag towards her and pulled out the big plastic tube and placed that by her feet. 'Might not be needing that tonight, the way I'm feeling,' she said, 'let me see...' She reached down between her legs, and for the first time, I forced myself to look: she had no knickers on, just suspenders attached to some stockings, stretched over her very ample thighs, which were spread over the brown plastic seating. When I looked up, there was already a couple of guys around the car, one leaning on the bonnet and the other one taking off his coat by Mariana's door.

'What's going on? What the fuck is going on, Mariana?'

She turned to me to reply, but as she held my gaze and moved closer as if to kiss me, she wiped her fingers all across my face before I pulled back. 'That's what's going on, luv, that's what they could all smell...my dirty pussy. Everyone wants my big, dirty pussy.' And laughed. 'And you've got first dibs.' Then, she lifted herself up and opened her legs around the steering wheel and started to play with herself in a very theatrical way. A couple more of the blokes gathered round, and a few yards away I could see a group of men around one of the other cars, presumably doing something similar. Then, her driver's window opened, and she reached through it to pull an erect penis into her hand and then into her mouth. A moment later, my window opened and I felt her hand against the back of my head push me towards the opening, at the exact moment that another erect penis appeared there, supposedly for me to deal with. I recoiled in horror. I fumbled with the range of switches in the console between us, trying to close the window, very quickly, but without squashing his manhood. That might make them all angry, but, whatever the cost, I had to seal off their way of getting in. Everything seemed either locked or didn't work. And every time I looked up, there it was, poking further and further in. All the while, Mariana was making a lot of noise and thrusting herself up into the air while she appeared to now have two willing members in her mouth.

While I was transfixed by the appallingness of the scene, I thought I could see one of them fumbling in his pocket with his free hand, and then I saw that he had hold of his phone. Oh, Jesus, oh, no, he's going to start filming and he's going to start filming me. I flailed around trying to open the door, shielding my face with the map and then pulling my jacket over my head. This all seemed to annoy Mariana, who didn't want to be distracted by my flapping, but I didn't care, even as her free hand (how many hands did she have?, they seemed to be controlling everything...) was punching the side of my head. As I ducked blows, my head went down as close to my lap as it had ever been in my life, almost into her plastic bag full of sex toys and gel. I grabbed it with my left hand, whilst holding onto my coat with my right, and emptied all the stuff onto the footwell, and in one smooth movement, had it over my head and my jacket back in its rightful place. I pulled it tightly into place, then realised I couldn't see or breathe, but also realised that I couldn't take it off. Oh, god, the scene of my asphyxiation came to mind, as I imagined the police officers who found my dead body, all pale and full of bodily fluids, like some failed Tory MP after a night of excessive sexual exploitation.

It was an old bag and smelled terribly, but I poked one eyehole through the plastic, just about where the first O of Coop was and another one in the other O. I poked a breathing hole through the Fairtrade branding. It was just then that something landed on the bag and made me flinch. Now that I could see, I looked over at the car window and saw a penis reducing in size, with a long trail of semen strung out from there to the

Coop bag. I reached up instinctively to pull it away, and when I caught the thin stringiness of it unexpectedly in my hand, I felt a surge of reflux coming up from my stomach and just in time I aimed it out of the car window, forgetting that someone else still had their cock in there. I saw the flash of surprise and anger in his eyes as he instinctively stepped back, while I wiped the last of the vomit from my lips. The bits that hadn't been propelled through the window were slowly making their way down my arm, jacket and the inside of the Luvli-Vulvi's passenger door window.

The shouting and the movements on my side of the car were driving Mariana to new levels of fury, but she was also caught up in the excesses of her pleasuring. She was absolutely raging, as she turned away from the two swollen members that were seconds ago in her mouth, and shouted, 'What the fuck are you doing now, you fuckin' moron?' Her mouth was drenched, in and around with slaver, and as she hissed at me, I was once again covered in male bodily fluids. Or rather the bag was.

'I'm not doing this,' I shouted, but the bag impeded the words, and she was forced to ask once again,

'What the fuck you sayin'? Fuckin' ruining my cum...'

And before I could think about it, I released the handbrake and the car started to sweep silently backwards into the darkness of the car park, whither I knew not where. Her face went white and at first, she couldn't quite believe what was happening. Her initial reaction, being in the driver's seat at this unexpected movement, was to press her right leg on the middle pedal, but because she had her legs up on the dashboard, she couldn't do anything but squirm as she tried to move her substantial form to get her legs down. She made a grab for the handbrake, but my hand was firmly on it, and no way on earth was I going to let her pull it up. Just as she started to dig her nails and draw blood in the fingers of my right hand, the car stopped with a bang, the impact throwing us both forwards, and then we recoiled backwards. At that moment, the big vibrator that had been buzzing away shot out of her vagina with such force that it marked the inside of the front window before coming to a rest, still whirring, on the dashboard. And very, very slowly an ancient airbag swelled up out of the steering wheel to trap her legs either side of it and pin her down in the seat.

I took my chance and flew out of the door, which had somehow been released on impact. I headed for the nearest edge of the layby and the trees, at full speed. As I hopped over a barbed wire fence onto boggy, tussocky ground, I looked back to see them crowding around, first, Mariana's Volvo, then the car of the person who had been rammed by it. When they saw me clambering over the fencing, they pointed and started running towards me.

I picked my way as carefully as I could through this stand of trees that ringed the car park, conscious that I cannot trip or fall or hurt myself. I just needed a path and then I would be safe. I took the plastic bag off my head and put it in my pocket. I ran slowly and carefully down the hill, picking my way between the large clumps of grass that made the ground very uneven. It began to get very steep and I could see below me a tumbling stream that led down to the reservoir on the eastern side of the hills. Against the skyline that was tinted orange by the lights of the roads and the towns, I could see that three of them were following me, coats billowing as they raced down at full speed. I couldn't see their faces, but I could sense their anger and I could hear their cries as they urged one another on. I headed down the steep gully, which was ridged with sheep tracks and speckled with large rocks, and half slid down to the last rock, which I judged I could probably use as a launching pad to cross the stream and reach the other side. I turned to see them, but by now could only hear them.

Just as I landed on the other side of the stream, I saw them begin the descent. I didn't wait to see what they made of it, but started the scramble up the other side, pulling with all my strength on every little outcrop of rock, every large clump of grass and pushing with all my might to gain some ground, before they reached the bottom. I knew that if I didn't put some distance between them on this ascent then I was in serious danger of being caught. Halfway up, I felt something land just below my feet. One of them was throwing rocks and was good at it. Then, the sound of someone shouting as he lost his footing and tumbled down the slope and the splash as he hit the water at speed. I didn't turn to look. I just kept on going, as the dark crept in and the sounds of other people faded into the distance.

I stayed out all night, nestled under a overhanging rock, full of sheep droppings and tufts of fleece, curled up and warmed by the soft earth below me. And woken by the sun and the bleating of the sheep passing through.

When I got home, I expected a welcoming committee, but no, nothing. No messages from Kate, no people waiting for me, nothing. I decided to pack a few things and keep out of the way for a few days.

'Where have you been, darling? I've missed you.'

'Kate...'

'Is that all you can say to your favourite ever person?'

'Kate...'

'Yes, sweetie, what would you like to say? I can feel something coming my way...'

'Kate...Don't ring me. Don't speak to me. Please.'

'I thought that's what was happening, but I wasn't sure why. What's happened?'

'Nothing. I just need to not do this for you.'

'Shall we meet, would that help?'

'...'

'Well, I need to see *you*, ok? There are things we should have talked about before, and maybe now would be a good time. Really would like to see you.'

'Kate...'

'What about tonight straight after work? Pick me up at my office, say 5.30?'

'...'

'I know you'll be there. By the way, where have you been?'

'Cleethorpes.'

'Lovely. See you, sweetie.'

I hated myself for wanting to see her so much, for wanting to see only her, out of the eight billion people on the planet, hated her so much for what she could do to me. But I get out a white shirt, the sort she liked, and went running for two hours to get her out of my system.

'You don't have to speak, if you don't want to...ok? It's just nice to see you and not have any distractions or...How are you?'

We're in a little, old-fashioned, milk bar down a side street, not far from her office. It's so old-fashioned it's actually trendy, and the red leather diner benches squeak every time we move. She has a cream satin blouse on that makes me wish I had the hearing of a bat and could hear the gamut of swishes it makes every time she moves. Her eyes are grey that ebb into blue, depending on the light and the mood. Some people think words are too vague to communicate what we mean, but I think words are too fixed and too solid for me to want to go anywhere near them for a while yet. I like it when she talks. I like it when I am at the centre of her world and she tries to tease me out of the mood I am in or tease out of me what I am thinking. I simply like this being of the *being with her.*

She wipes her hand on the table where her elbow has been.

It's sticky. She tries not to pull a face. Coming here or to my house must be an amusing diversion for her. *Slumming it*, as my mother used to say. I don't know why, but I tell her I'll wash it for her.

She laughs. 'The table or the blouse?'

'The blouse.'

'You have your own dry cleaner?'

'I'll do it by hand.'

'That's very kind of you to offer.' It felt like the most honest thing I'd heard in ten years.

'I can feel a 'but' coming...' I wish I hadn't said that.

She paused. She pursed her lips and her eyes sparkled and she looked past me at the landscape of her life, then looked straight into me, to a place that held the switches in the darkness. 'You are a very strange man, you know, most men run a mile at the thought of a handwash in a bowl and getting stains out of other people's clothes...' she laughed.

'I have a hoover, soap, a spare pack of foam pads and more than enough cleaning agents to wipe out the opposition.'

Then she laughed again, out loud, and picked up her milk shake with a stripey straw in it. Between draughts, she said, 'Is that a very strange proposition?' and laughed again out loud, so that chocolate bubbles floated across to my side of the table.

'Sorry,' she said, as one landed on my white shirt. 'So sorry...' and dabbed at it with a paper napkin.

'This one I'll never wash.'

'Oh, come on,' she said, laughing. 'Do you want me to buy you another one? I can put it on expenses.'

'No. It's this one I shall keep. Unwashed, till the collar has bonded with the hairs on my neck.'

'You can't wear a hairshirt in our business. No one has ever asked for a hairshirt. I keep thinking I've heard it all and then someone comes along and well, there you are...'

'You're on the phone to me...'

'I'm on the phone to you...'

This time it was my turn to stare past her at the staff lolling behind the counter, one with a phone in her hand and a cloth in the other and the other one wiping down bottles.

'Kate...' She lets me dawdle. 'If I get another phone, for example, would you ring me on it so that we could meet up like this...' She was looking intently at me. ''Cos I'm about to throw the other one away.'

'Mmmmm...I thought you might. Which is why I wanted to see you –'

'Don't mention work or another job, please, Kate...don't.'

'Of course not, no, I wouldn' –'

'We should never have met, not by all normal ways of measuring paths and circles and orbits and nodes or whatever –' she's smiling at me as she sucks the straw, 'but maybe the best people in our lives are the ones we should never have met.'

She slurps loudly as she drains the bottom of the glass. 'Sorry, didn't meant to...'

I smile. 'I love the way you do that. You do it so unaffectedly.'

'Milk shakes always make me feel so young. Take me back, you know, to the good times...'

'It's difficult to imagine despair with a chocolate milkshake in your hand.' She waits again for more from me.

'I once had a friend who was old when I met him, in his seventies. Never married. Eventually, after a few years he trusted me enough to tell me about why. It was way back before the war, he met a woman on a ship. Quite what happened he never told me. But what he did say struck me as odd at the time: 'I wish I could live without the sex impulse,' he said. I didn't know the full compass of what he was saying. I know a bit more now. I wish there was a way, when you were ready, to have the place that needs it, the sex impulse in its widest form, that's what he meant, everything from wanting to look nice and have someone laugh at your jokes, to rubbing yourself against a chair seat and shagging ten times a day and all the way to the need for someone to be with who you can trust...'

'That'd be the end of my business, wouldn't it?' she said. And then, 'Not sure I'm completely getting what you mean.'

'Kate –'

'You know how often you've said my name?'

'Kate...you never answered my question. The one about throwing the works phone away and starting with a new one, a definitely-not-for-work-one.'

'Well, I'd rather you didn't throw your first one away, of course, and I can't stop you or make you do anything you don't want to do –'

'You can make me do anything you want me to do, and you know it...'

'Look, I do feel guilty that I forced you into this. I realise that now, but when I met you, I thought you would, I don't know, deal with it. I thought you'd just think, *Fuck it*, literally and metaphysically, if that's the right word. I thought you'd laugh in the face of the insanity and just take the money and have fun...'

I realised that she wasn't going to answer the question. Not in a way that wasn't a Kate way of answering anything.

'But I understand you're getting more and more difficult to pay.' And started laughing. 'See, you are a strange boy, you don't do it for fun and you don't do it for money. So...'

'So, why am I doing it? Why do you think?'

'You can't think of anything else to do? You're a bit lost? You're disillusioned and want to be ever more disillusioned, as if sinking downwards might lead you to the light. I don't know, I'm just guessing. And maybe a little bit of you wants to keep teasing littl' ol' me...' and smiled, like the words were getting in the way, 'which you do very nicely.'

‘That’s just the carrot for the next time. I don’t believe you.’

‘I can’t be the answer. I’m flattered. Immensely flattered. I’m old enough to be your aunt,’ and laughed, ‘or something worse.’

‘We better go,’ I said, ‘auntie.’

When she stood up, she turned her back to me. ‘I’ll pay,’ she said. ‘Go, go...go, ok? Please.’

She walked towards the counter with her coat over her arm and I did as she asked.

No calls for a week. No messages. No pleas to fill in, or take a job, or any sort of message from her. I thought of every word of our conversation in the milk bar. I went over and over it. I ran all the way into town in the worst of weathers dressed in a hoodie and a scarf, and second-hand running clothes past her office every other day. I found a little newspaper seller, Kev, and made friends with him so I could stand outside for fifteen or twenty minutes and stare up. Her light was on every day.

Once, she left her office when I was there, talking to Kev at his stand. I bent down at his kiosk so she wouldn’t recognise anything about me. My heart raced to bursting, watching her stride down the street and cross the road. After another couple of weeks, I forced myself to stop going on that route and chose another one, over the hills and down the steepest tracks onto the moorland, running without a map, till darkness slowed me down and I found myself fifteen or twenty miles from home, in places I didn’t know.

And replaying and replaying the sight of her leaving her office, walking down the street and crossing the road. The tap of her shoes and the swish of her skirt and her grey eyes coolly summoning armies at will.

One afternoon, a text arrived. It read like the ones I used to get from Kate with job details. It finished, *Please confirm.*

I texted back. *Who's this?*

The reply came, *It's Jo, from Ssshh! how are you doing?*

I wrote back straight away. *Where's Kate?*

Jo: *Kate's busy, we've reorganised, expanded, lots of work.* Smiley face.

Me: *Oh. I'll take the work. I'll take as much of it as you can throw at me.*

Jo: thumbs up and a smiley face.

I'll show her who can deal with this shit. And I'll take her money, all of it. I wrote to Jo, *I need a pay rise. I'm charging 10% more. Make sure that is ok before I do tonight's job.*

Twenty minutes later. Jo: a thumbs up.

I worked four or five nights a week. When I wasn't working, I ran and slept. I piled up the money. Everything done by text, everything from Jo. I gave no cause for complaint. Never met any more Marianas. Was given the nicer jobs. Some of them were very nice. I saw the hand of Kate everywhere and every night I kissed it. I was more lost than ever before and every night I relived the conversation in the milk bar and the last time I had seen her, till the sun came up or the sun went down, whichever was the sooner.

About to leave the house one morning, I sat down to put my running shoes on. The right one had worn so thin that there was no sole at the point where I landed on every step. When I checked my right foot, it was calloused and thick-skinned and when I put a match to it, I could hardly feel the heat of the flame. I put my head on my knees and when I raised it ten minutes later, I had a plan.

Firstly, I went to the travel agents in town and bought a flight to Chad. Great music, lovely people and possibly a war going on. Ideal. It took a while for them to find out where Chad was, but I eventually got one. 'Single please', I said. Monday would be ideal. And paid cash and gave her a hundred quid tip.

Then, I went to the estate agent and gave them the spare set of keys with instructions to sell the house at a figure I had in mind.

Then, I went to the little office in the back lane where the nearest solicitor lived. He was a ruddy-faced fellow, all-hale-and-well-met. I told him not to speak and gave him his instructions, 'Like a will', I said, 'but I'm not dead, but might be soon'.

I told him about selling the house, and to contact the estate agents and I gave him Kate's name and address and contact details. I told him why, and that I wanted her to be the sole beneficiary of everything I had, to be held by her in trust and after one year she was to have everything, unless I contacted him, the solicitor, within the year. He thought it was highly irregular, but I told him I was paying. Then, he thought about it quickly and said that it was actually quite simple, all in all, and he would let me know the outcome. I said I would be in touch, within an hour.

'Don't piss about, like you lot normally do – sit down and write it, now.' It was Friday, pay day. The last pay day. Then, I bought one of those padded envelopes and wrote Kate's address on it, ready to put my phone in it when I set off to the airport for Chad, on Monday.

Jo texted me when I was out running. *We've had a cancellation, I desperately need someone this evening. Very well paid.*

As long as it isn't Mariana, I'm available, I texted back.

Big smiley face back. Number. Plus all the details.

I put on the white shirt that still had the chocolate spot on it, the one I was never going to wash. Key, phone, cash, no wallet, keep it simple. This time next week, all I'd have would be the clear blue skies of Africa and the heat of sub-Saharan sun and the relief of listening to the sounds of voices speaking mellifluously and unintelligibly. I floated into town, dreaming of the sounds and smells at the very opposite of these of Leeds.

The bar was in a hotel, a good sign. Her name was Anna, 35 and blonde. The sign was a black pair of gloves on the coffee-table. The woman who was there had a black bob and was probably fifteen years younger, but quietly friendly. She didn't want to sit downstairs but said we could order room service in a room she had booked. In the lift, she was very cool and sort of shy, didn't want to talk about anything personal, which was fine. She let us into a room on the fifth floor, at the back of the hotel, I noticed. I could hear the trains passing somewhere in the dark. She offered me a seat and asked me what she should order to drink. A bottle of water, I said, but she insisted on a bottle of wine. While she was on the phone, her friend walked out of the bedroom, fiddling with her hair. She looked like her twin sister, was even wearing similar clothes. 'Are you twins?' I said. All I could really hear was the desert wind and the sound of the Arabic of Chad. I have no idea what she said back.

'We're gonna have a bit of a party, do you mind?' said Anna. I nodded and smiled, thinking to myself that I am out of here, on the dot, at ten. The girls talked about this and that, and I went to the toilet and through the door I heard them talking Polish. When I came back into the room, one of them, I couldn't actually say which one it was, said she had to go and bring up a friend from the foyer.

Then, room service arrived. There was no water, so I asked for a bottle, 'A cheap one, please,' I said. Then, another knock at the door and another woman was let in, and the other twin went out, without much of a goodbye.

'They're off to get some friends,' she said. This must be Anna, much more like it. Smelled of fags, pale face done up a bit, hair coloured, but it looked tired. 'Hi, I'm Anna. Wanna drink?'

For no clear reason, I didn't believe for a minute her name was Anna. 'I don' know about you but I'm knackered, mind if we just sit for a minute an' 'ave a fag break?'

I nodded. Of course, it was her night. Or their night. She took a few swigs of the wine, then switched the telly on and threw her shoes off and sat with her legs tucked under, on the settee, staring at the TV. 'Been a right week,' she said, not looking at me at all, in between flicking channels and game shows and reality shows.

'Wonder where the girls have got to,' I said, after twenty minutes.

'Probably having a drink.'

'Are they mates of yours?'

'Yeah. Work, you know...'

'Oh.'

Then, she looks at her watch. One hour and I'm off. Forever. She starts to take her skirt and top off, and comes over to me to take my shirt off and unbuttons my trousers. I grab her hand, 'Sorry, luv, not tonight...' but she pulls her knickers off, and before I know where I am, she's wrapped her legs around me, and I'm on the bed on top of her. She is pulling my hair wildly and sinking her fingers into my shoulders, my back, my head. 'Hey, I say, hang on a minute,' but she won't hang on, and I'm running a hundred storylines through my head at this point, wondering what I'm going to have to do to get out of her grubby grasp. I needn't have worried, because the door is thrown open and a guy comes straight in.

'What the fuck you doing, pal? That's my girl you're shagging, you fickin' freak.'

As I look up, I feel his fist graze the side of my head and I roll off the lovely lady with a false name. At the door, I can see he has brought back-up. He jumps onto the bed and kicks me in the side of my head, which stuns me. Before I know it, I'm lying face down on the floor of the hotel room with a tie holding my hands behind my back.

'No, no, no...' but he has no way of knowing why I'm saying 'no.' I already know the dream is going, the packing, the leaving, the flight, the arrival, the whole bloody escape is going, and something just tells me it's already nearly gone. I want to scream.

'Call Security, this guy's a fuckin' criminal and I want him out the hotel.'

'Who are you?' I ask, 'I thought you were her boyfriend.'

'You fuck my bitch, man, you get what you deserve,' he snarls at me, from three inches away. I can hear her on the phone. I feel his knee in my back. I hear him telling her to wet her eyes, to look dishevelled, and he smacks her across the face.

'Just so you look better, darling...'

Within minutes, two Security in black leather jackets are picking me up and escorting me to the lift. 'Shall we call the Police, Madam?'

'I'll ring them later, pal, but thanks,' she said, 'just get him away from me, the fuckin' weirdo.'

'Have we got everything?' asks the boyfriend.

'Yeah, he didn't take anything out, it's all in his jacket,' she says. I watch him close the door and smile, oddly, unevenly. 'See you soon, darling.'

In the lift with the boyfriend and his mate and the two Security guards, I have the opportunity to feel the serious headache. I can't talk easily, but I try, 'Listen, Mr. Security Guard, why am I tied up like this?' and turn to show him my hands tied behind my back. He ignores me.

'Take him out the back way,' says one of the Guards when we get out of the lift in the basement of the hotel, and I see a fat envelope change hands and a bump of the fists. Mates. Great.

We walk down a low corridor, where I keep having to lower my head to avoid banging it on the pipes. They're dragging me sidewards, one behind me and one walking ahead. I can think of nothing to say.

Outside, they throw me into the back of a car, face down in the footwells. 'If you move, I'll slice the back of your knees,' says the one who has not yet spoken from the front seat, but has a Very Squeaky Voice, and I'm startled by the urge to laugh out loud. I remain very quiet, pondering just how I got here. Kate? Mariana? Fate? Stupidity? Wrong-person-wrong-job-wrong-life type scenario? 'Cancellation,' said Jo. My arse.

We drive for about ten minutes, and I can hear them talking shit about people who they're having aggro with and who they're going to hurt next. They pull up under a streetlight. The back door opens, and they pull me upright by my arms, which really hurts.

'Cut the tie,' says the Boyfriend to his mate. When my hands are free, he puts a knife to the bottom of my nose. 'One word, one move, one anything I don't like, I'll cut your nose, then I'll cut your mouth.' He's up close and personal, and I can smell garlic on his breath, mixed with something odd that I can't quite place. Something about his mouth is wrong, as if he's got gum issues and holding a pad in place for the pain.

'Get your jacket off. I want your keys, wallet, money, phone.'

I give him everything I have.

'Where's your wallet, fuckhead?' he says.

'Don't bring one out with me.' I wanted to add, 'In case this happens' but luckily, I didn't. 'Only got one house key, no car key, one card and some cash. Everything you see is there.'

He makes me get out the car and empty my pockets. Then he slams me against the car, which winds me and I have trouble catching my breath to reply.

'Where do you live, shitfucker?'

I consider my options, with him pressed up close and a knife nicking what I remember being called the columella, the bit of tissue that separates my nostrils. I'm not seeing too many ones this side of positive, at the moment.

‘Where do you live, ’fore I slice your face off?’ He waves the card at me, ‘and the number for this fuckin’ thing?’ pressing the blade of the knife millimetres from my eyes.

‘Card number is easy, 9 1 2 8. Please, don’t go to my house, I share a flat with two offal butchers, they’re lunatics. Please, don’t go there.’

They put new ties around my wrists and sit me on the back seat of the car, and we drive to a dark spot near a supermarket where Very Squeaky Voice gets out, leaps over a wall and goes to the cashpoint. He comes back a minute or two later, ‘Cards been fuckin’ declined, innit. He’s gone over his £500 overdraft limit. He’s a fuckin’ wanker, I tell ya.’

‘Is that right?’ said the Boyfriend.

I don’t want to sound too pleased with my overdraft, but I have to say, ‘Yes.’ Just one word.

‘We can’t let this arseshite get away with it,’ says the Boyfriend. ‘Put the blinds on him and put him in fuckin’ face down. And fuckin’ give him a fuckin’ kick for not having any fuckin’ money. Fuckin’ fannyfuckpedo.’

He throws my card out the window, at that point.

I wonder what they’ll do with my overdraft if I ever get out of this. The back door opens and Very Squeaky Voice tries to launch a kick at me but struggles in the confines of the back of the car and instead launches a punch at the back of my head which takes me by surprise, and I topple over making it easier for him to put a cloth around my head and push me back into the footwells. He folds up my legs to allow him to shut the door, but not without deliberately catching my foot in the door first.

We drive what must be back through town, because I can hear crowds and laughing and we’re having to go slowly, then stop start, and then, slowly again in the traffic, even at this time on a Friday night. I consider my options, which are still zero, as a way of dealing with the thumping headache where he punched me, without worrying if the damage is lasting. We seem to be hitting some sort of motorway, and the lights flash by as if we're going at speed and then we slow down and hit a series of traffic lights. I can hear their voices in the front, but I can't hear what they're saying. After a moment, the sound of the engine as he goes up the gears, then indicating to turn for a long time, and cursing the traffic, then he takes a right turn and we seem to almost go back on ourselves and upwards, upwards, upwards.

All I want to do is to take some paracetamol and sleep, but I know at some point I'm going to have to feel the knife across my face and listen to his ridiculous range of swearing, putting any two random words together, like a child experimenting. I try to memorise his features – I would say light brown skin, flat, wide nose, high eyebrows, weak facial hair growth. I would never go to the Police, but I would never forget him, either. I'm thinking of revenge, even before escape. After a series of shuffles, twists, turns, pauses and hesitations, we pull up in what seems like an unlit corner, silent, soundless. Even the rain has stopped.

They pull me out of the car, drag me across some tarmac and a gate is opened, I can hear the squeak, and after a few steps, a key is placed in a door and I'm pushed, stumbling up two or three steps, into a house, where we go into a room on the left. They throw me onto the floor.

'Right, wankstain, where do you live? I want the address.'

'20, Maine Road, but it's outside Leeds, it's miles away. When you get there, you'll see a big drive. Sometimes, they let the dogs out, so be careful.'

'Check that, will ya, innit,' he says to Very Squeaky Voice and then to me, 'what's your name?

'Kevin Baxter.'

'You're a fuckin' wanker, Kev, innit, but you're a good lad.'

He bends over and wipes my house key inches across my face and the gingivitis radiates from his mouth. Then a jab and a whoosh in my right arm. I shout out in surprise.

I hear the door shut behind me and locked. I could not be sure, but I hear no sound a human might make in the room with me. Then, the front door opens and shuts, and the car starts and drives away. I must be alone. But it's all drifting away, losing control, going somewhere. My head is spinning out of control.

It's the sharp shots of pain that wake me, the same ones that I've felt jar me to consciousness over the last...day? days? night? I have no idea now how long I've been here. I can't open my eye but it's watering. I come to consciousness, like fighting through undergrowth. I want to get out, away from the prickly leaves and the sense of being crushed but I'm not getting anywhere. Everywhere I turn just takes me deeper into the darkness. I wake again, sometime later. My mouth is so dry I panic. Gasp, try to shout, I can't swallow, I can't swallow and start to gip, start to raise myself up onto all fours. Jesus, I can't move, I've got no strength. My tongue is like a cardboard tube in my mouth, much too big for the space, I can't breathe, I can't swallow, I can't make my mouth produce saliva. I collapse down again and feel the gip gip gip of streaks of vomit tearing out of my stomach and roll onto my side and a little string of some foul-tasting stuff drips out of my mouth. It rolls slowly from the corner of my mouth and I don't have the strength to wipe it away. All I want to do is to sleep, to sleep, to wake up and feel better.

Next time I wake up, I'm watching someone shaking my head by the hair. I'm above everyone, looking down. Someone is screaming at me, but I don't know what he's saying at all or what he wants. I smile, I really want to help him, to stop him pulling, but I watch myself just grin. Grin. Even though I'm no longer in my own body and looking down and watching, I can feel the pain in my eye, I can't open my eye. I need a drink. Drink. Please. Water. Someone is saying it. Someone is trying to say it. Someone is helping me. Maybe I'm saying it, watching from above, trying to help this person lying on the floor. I don't really know who it is, I don't think. Even though I'm floating and free, I just want to sleep. Let me sleep. Let him sleep. Stop kicking him and stop shouting. Please, let's just all sleep.

Later, later still, who knows how much later? They've propped me up against a radiator. I know, because as I try to move, I slide down it and there is a strange pain, like an axe might make, going down the back of my head and going deep inside, making my eyes throb but spreading and making my pulse throb. When I look up, I'm staring at the underside of a radiator. It must be underneath a window because there's something flapping gently above it, like a curtain, maybe. I lie like that for a moment and then try to move my arm, but it won't move, so I try to sit up again, using the other one, which somehow works. I can open both eyes, but I don't know why that surprises me. The pain of moving anything is an electric shock every time. From somewhere, I can hear sounds, like wood banging and something being dragged. When I finally manage to sit up, my head is banging and the memory of the searing agony at the back of my head flares up again. But I see where I am.

It's the front room of a squat or a derelict, abandoned house. I'm in the bay window, lying on bare floorboards. Some of the floor is missing and I can see the joists below. There's a big slab of light coming through the front window where it hasn't been boarded up at the very top, and a slither of light coming in from underneath the door at the opposite side of the room. But there must be a broken pane or something, because the curtains twitch in the slight breeze. It takes long moments to be able to focus my eyes on the details of the scene around me, and it doesn't make any sense: the syringes, the plastic packaging, the rubber strapping, the lighters, beer cans, just piles and piles of shitty stuff, just inches from me. And I've not got a shirt on. But I'm still in my own trousers, but piss-stained and fouled. And my right arm is painful and tender to the touch and in the soft part, just below the inside of the elbow, are several ugly, big scabs. What the fuck has happened? The sobbing comes out first, then the screams that scrape my throat and burn my eyes. And I can't move more than a few inches from the radiator.

When the anger subsides and my throat and eyes are racked dry, I can hear clumping around, as if something is falling very slowly downstairs. I wait and the door opens, and a figure appears, 'Hey man, this room is empty.' He's hanging on the doorknob, very unsteady, with a voice that's dry, raspy and unused.

'Come here, man,' I say to him. 'Come help me, get me some water, please.' I sob quietly. 'Please, please, please...'

He comes over, and I think he's going to find me something in the piles of filth around me. 'You got any gear in here. Gear, yeah?' He stumbles around the room and then loses his footing and slips into a hole where the floorboards are missing. He gets up and kneels down near me, scraping around for some 'gear.' 'I can't find nothing here. You got something.' He's shifting through the stuff around me, like some zombie-hamster and I start to laugh but finish coughing.

'Nothing, mate. But have a look for yourself.'

'Where's the gear, mate?' he says, so gone that he's copying my speech. 'I go. This room's always empty. AK says.'

'Who's AK?' I ask him, 'Who the fuck is AK?'

'AK, yeah' he says, 'yeah, AK,' and struggles to his feet and then struggles even more with the gap in the floorboards, and just as he looks as if he's about to make it across the room, he misjudges it and slides down into the gap with one leg and then, just as soundlessly, slides out, and very quietly shuts the door behind him. The shuffling up the stairs, like someone dragging furniture, tells me where he's gone.

The house goes back to soundless. Having some contact with another human, even one like that, has slipped a few cogs into place and I can feel my senses flowing back, slowly. I need water and I need to get out of this house. And I need to make sure that I do both things before AK gets back. AK's got to be the guy with dental issues. He probably did this to me, as well.

It's me against the raw plugs. If this is a squat or a drug den, then clearly maintenance hasn't been a priority and with some effort I should be able to remove this radiator from this wall. But every movement requires monumental effort and despite pushing and pulling with my arms and shoulders, nothing moves. Just out of reach of my unattached arm is something metal, half-hidden under the rubbish. I use my feet to get it and drag it to my free arm. It's a spoon. I start to dig at the plaster around the radiator with it. The plaster is damp and old, but even so, my arm aches with a fire. After some time scraping away, I'm exhausted and there's a small pile of plaster on the floor underneath my efforts.

When I look up for a breather, I lean forward to rest on the windowsill and my head nudges the board cutting out the light in the window, and it moves slightly. I try to get my fingers under the bottom edge, but I can't. When I scrape my nails in the gap all the way along the bottom I get to the corner and I can see why it's bowing. The window frame in the bottom corner is damp. When I force my left hand around the side of the board, the wood is wet and flakes into nothing. I'm at full stretch, but I claw violently at it and within a few minutes the board is loose at the bottom. In this situation, anything is a win. I can only use one hand, but I pull with all my strength, the strength of panic and fear and flight compounded into desperation, and pull the whole left-hand side of the board away from the window. I can just about half-stand up if I stretch my right arm that is still tied to the radiator. I take a deep breath and a step or two backwards and then, when I am ready, I pull at the top of the board with a huge cry to force it away from the frame. Nearly. The nails squeak but it twangs back in my hand into place and the ricochets go up my arm. I'll give it one more go. One more painful effort and the board snaps off the upper frame and is thrown all the way back towards the right-hand wall. I can see outside. Memories that I can't pin down come back. Was I trapped inside a car and face down in the footwell? And why was I in a hotel room with two girls? Did I have my hands tied behind my back with those nasty little plastic ties? Did I meet AK before? Why am I here? How long have I been here? I can't really remember how I ended up here. And where the hell am I?

Outside, there is absolute quiet. No sound, no cars, no people, just houses, staring as if they're waiting for something to happen. There's a circle of trees with the houses looking onto it, looking like a huge roundabout without the traffic. I had an idea that I could call for help to a passer-by, but there are no passers-by. Some birds twitter in a hedge, but no people, no sign of life, no everydayness. Then, I see why – most of the houses are boarded up like this one was, waiting for something – love or death, comes to mind – and I start to laugh. Even the houses are waiting for love or death, like humans. It strikes me as really funny and I have to kneel back down to stop from getting too light-headed. When I stop coughing, I feel very weak and take some deep breaths. I stand up as best I can. I have an idea, which is probably not a good idea, but you can't always have good ideas in a drug den.

I pull with my free arm on the board that is now hanging on by one side only. After some pulling and twisting and heaving it comes away. I try to pick it up but it's very awkward with one hand. Eventually, I manoeuvre it, so that my left hand is behind it and my right hand is below it, and then aim it, with maximum force, at the front window. It bounces off and jars my wrist. I pick it up again carefully. In the impact, something has happened, and my right hand is looser, and the radiator has come off the wall. Not completely, but almost. I pull furiously at the radiator and the right-hand mount comes out. This time, I use the board as a lever and force the other radiator mount off the wall. Great, all I have to do now is to get the radiator off my wrist, but at least I've got more freedom to do it. I look for the weak spot – the copper piping – and set about twisting, turning, bashing, hammering and bending the pipe so that it splits, and with a few more movements backwards and forwards, the joint gives and I'm left a free man. Except there's a four-foot, white, single-panelled thin radiator attached to my wrist by a handcuff, that's worn a deep channel in my wrist, making it bleed.

Before I do anything else, I look amongst the rubbish on the floor for anything that belongs to me. No keys, no shirt, no money, no card. But I do pick up about 6 used syringes and a couple of filthy rags and an empty can of Bulmers, and wrap the syringes in the rags and bend the can so it splits. The jagged edge looks wicked. Then, the door opens, and I freeze. It's the loser who came in last time.

'You found some gear, mate? Give us some, will ya?' He comes right up close, but this time he's less spaced out and more aggressive.

'There's nothing here. Have a look yourself.'

'If I find you got somefin' and you don't ain't sharing, I ain't goin to let that go, mate. Just so you know. Yeah?'

'What, you want me to agree with you?'

'Just saying, any gear in this house ain't yours, it's fuckin' got my name on it. AK says. Yeah?'

'Yeah, of course. Anything you say.'

He looks at me like I'm speaking a foreign language. His lined, pock-marked face with the collapsed jaw and the eyes that are wary and alert, but twitching and drifting in and out of focus, just, draw my pity.

'How long have you been here?' I asked him.

'None of your fuckin' business.'

'Who's AK?'

'None of your fuckin' business.' He's focusing right on me now.

'If I tell you where there's some gear, will you tell me?'

He looks at me for a minute, then mutters something. He's having a bad moment. He nods.

'OK, see that pile of rags near the lighter there, just there, yeah, well, there's some under there.' He sets off walking with that dead-furniture-shuffle of his. I follow him. I'm stood behind him. 'Yeah, there. Just there. Under that pile.'

He stumbles onto his knees and starts to rifle through the filth. That's when I hit him really hard on his back with the edge of the radiator. He collapses to the floor and is winded. He coughs and splutters and brings up a big wave of bile. I turn him over so he can see me.

'My friend, I hate doing this, but you see, I don't have a choice. You need help. But I need help more.' To reinforce the point, I put the edge of the radiator against his throat.

'Who's AK? Is he the guy who gets you gear and stuff? Nod if he is.' He nods. 'Does he come here ever day?' He shakes his head. 'Is he coming today?' He nods. 'Why am I here?' When I pull the edge of the radiator off his windpipe he coughs and splutters.

'Man, what you doin'?' he says, in between gasps and coughs. 'What you hittin' on me for?'

'My friend, I'll slice your throat, or you tell me who he is.' I run the rusty edge along his Adam's apple. I was shaking badly.

'Ok, ok, ok,' he shouts, 'please...I don't know what he does, I just live here, trust me, he brings us gear, gives me a few jobs, I look after you and the others...people he brings here. Don't tell him I told you, ok? Please.'

'Why does he bring people here for you to look after?'

'I don't fuckin' know man, honest, believe me, but I...he, I dunno really. God man, I need some stuff, I'm feelin' like shit.' I apply the radiator with a jerk that almost chokes him.

'I'm getting sick of this, my friend. Tell me, tell me...'

'He brings a load of wankers here, takes their stuff – keys, cards, money, everything – whatever shit they've got – fuckin' whacks 'em with any old fuckin' gear he can get in them. Gets 'em high, like you was. I dunno after that. I dunno, fuckin' steals everything they got. Who knows, they're just wankers, I dunno who they are. You just one of 'em. Believe me. I've seen him give some right beatings, he has some fuckin' animal friends. If he thinks you got away, he'll fuckin' never leave you alone.'

'How many are there with him? When he comes here.'

'Him and one more – sometimes two of them and him, no more. He keeps this fuckin' set up sealed, man. No one here gives him trouble.'

'And anyone live here, in these houses?'

'Just a set of fuckin' ghosts, man. You never seen anything like em, weirdos and that. Spooky twats.'

'Are they AK's twats or just sharing the same toilet?'

'Dunno, whatever, just fuckin' wander around like space cadets. He never speaks to them, they don't fuckin' speak to him. There ain't many of 'em. Council want to shut it all down, turn it all into a warehouse or sumfin, innit?'

'Right, I ain't gonna hurt you, ok? Do as I say, and you'll be fine. AK is gonna blame me for all of this and you won't get a beating, ok? If you do anything stupid or make a noise, you won't be alive by the end of today. You get it?'

He nodded. I looked into his eyes for something to like.

'Roll over,' I said. I tied his hands behind his back with a piece of wire. I led him upstairs to the bathroom. I pushed a rag in his mouth. 'Sorry,' I said. Then gagged him with another rag. 'Tell AK I did this to you. Tell him you were just giving me some water, as you were told to do, and that I kicked you and tried to cut you. That I tied you up here. OK?' He nodded. I put a cloth around his head as tight as I could and laid him face down on the floor, and put one leg either side of the toilet basin and tied them together at the back with a bit of barbed wire I found being used as a chain for the blocked toilet. I had a few more questions for him, but they'd have to wait for another time.

I looked out of the back window of the bathroom and saw a black BMW pulling up, slowly. This didn't belong here. The two guys who got out were laughing and joking, and one lit a cigarette as the other one checked his phone. This is them I thought, this is them. I rushed downstairs, and back into the front room where I'd been chained. I closed the door carefully and silently. I made a big pile of rags and shit look like a figure was sleeping over where I'd been chained. It would take him a few seconds to register something was wrong. Then, I picked up the board that had been used to cover up the window and propped it against the wall and got inside it. This was the best I could do in the few seconds I had spare.

I held my breath and listened to them come in the back door. I heard one of them open a door downstairs. 'I'm dying for a piss,' he said. I recognised his squeaky voice. I took my chance and made a moan like a man in pain. The door opened. When he was inside the room, I let him take two and a half steps and then ran at him as hard as I could using the board like a huge shield pushing him backwards to the opposite wall. When he hit the wall, I kicked his ankles as hard as I could with a sweeping kick. He went down easier than I thought. While he was down, I shut the door behind me and jammed the board underneath it to stall Squeaky Voice trying to get in. Just as AK was wiping his head where the bang against the wall had split it, I grabbed all six used syringes out of my pocket with my left hand and rammed them into his left eye as hard as I could. I even managed to make sure that I pumped a few millilitres of oxygen into his head with a few of them. He looked at me, stunned, as if to say, *Who the hell are you?*

'I'm the man with a radiator,' I said, and hit him as hard as I could with it across his head. He went down properly this time. Behind me, Squeaky Voice was trying to force the door, and I saw his right hand appear as he tried to force the top half against the hinge. I chose my moment as I felt the wood squirm and bend and just start to crack, when I rammed the edge of the radiator as accurately and forcefully as I could against his fingers and the wall and I heard him yell in agony. He held his hand there just a little too long, and I sliced at his wrist with the edge of the rusty can of Bulmers. The spurt of blood took me by surprise, just like the shock did him, because I saw his hand slide back into the hallway, still spurting, and heard him sink to the floor.

'Fuckin' hell, what do I do now? Help me. I'm bleedin'. Someone, help me.' It sounded so prosaic.

I really didn't want to see his face, I didn't want him to see mine and remind him of who I was. I just wanted this to be over, to get out of here. I couldn't walk through that door and face him, slumped there, staring pathetically at his slit wrist, possibly with a gun or a knife. But, when I turned around and saw a person in the front garden looking into this front room, my first thought was, how is he going to hurt me? How can I hurt him first? I walked to the cracked glass.

'Yeah?' I said.

He looked at me. I wondered how much of this he had seen. He moved his hands in front of his chest, slowly, as if to signal, *calm down, calm down*. He was wearing a hat. No one wears a hat like a top hat, do they? He motioned for me to come forward. His eyes were hidden. I heard the moaning from the other side of the door and the sight of AK lying out cold was beginning to worry me. He motioned again, *but do it calmly*, he said with his hands. I pushed the radiator through the window, and the glass parted, and I kicked away a piece of glass left sticking up from the frame and stepped on it, and in a push, I was out of the house, free. He strode off around the corner and I followed. Is this the wisest thing to do? Or is it the only thing to do?

As we walked, I felt my legs begin to wobble, the adrenaline to fade, the insane efforts of the last hour take their toll and the experience of the time chained up in the room, all begin to hit me. As we turned another corner my legs gave way and I sank to the ground, slowly, slowly, and there was nothing left, no energy, no strength, no way I could raise myself up. He turned to look at me and waited. When he saw I was stuck in some unseen quicksand, he turned again and lifted me up with both hands and held me upright. I have no memory of how I got to the house, hidden in trees. I have no memory of walking through the door or laying down in this bed. I have no memory of the removal of the chain attaching me to a radiator. Just moments of waking and sleeping and dreaming, not sure of the difference, but lying, conscious of remote pains moving around between my arms, my neck, down my back, in my stomach, throat and down my legs. The strangest panics of gasping for air and drowning in shadowy waters, whilst floating and watching the body abandoned below me, flailing around in no-man's-land.

When I finally landed back into my body, I snuggled into it like an old glove, wearing the familiar again after a long time, knowing it was mine, with all its comfortable frailties. The room was plain and dark, lit only by a table lamp on the floor and I was on a small metal bed, straight out of an institution. The air was cool but fresh. I sat up, rubbed my wrist, saw the last of the scab and bruising on the skin and felt the tenderness of the bone underneath. It took me several attempts to stand up, as my legs just wouldn't do what they were supposed to do. When I did make them work, I teetered around the room but felt exhausted and sat back down on the bed. My footsteps must have made a sound because I heard the stairs creak and someone walking towards the door. I couldn't have done anything even if I'd wanted to, so I simply sat and waited to see what came through the door.

The door opened very gently, the handle turned so quietly. My heart started beating wildly. A face appears as the door opens. I don't recognise it. He nods. I nod back. The door shuts just as quietly, and I climb back into the warmth of the bed. A minute later and he appears again, with a cup of tea, and hands it to me without speaking and then, he leans back on the wall. I struggle drinking the tea because of the dryness of my mouth and throat, and it catches me unexpectedly, making me cough. I look at him wondering what sort of lunatic or saint he could be. We are like this for a while. Then, he leaves the room and comes back, moments later, with a bottle of water and passes it to me without speaking. He goes back to leaning on the wall, looking at me. I like him, but I don't know why. I sit and don't speak. Without asking, he brings me another cup of tea. Half an hour later, he brings me some food. It's steamed vegetables, chopped finely, and noodles. It's very easy to eat, but as he watches me, he makes that sign again, the *slow-down* two-handed sign that he made when I came through the window of the drug-den. He's not wearing his hat. When I try to say thank you, he cuts across me with his hands, making the sign, *That's enough*. When he left the room, I barely heard more than three or four steps, and then silence again. I liked this silence. And in between the silence, the disconnected sleeping and disturbing dreaming and then I realise that being awake is the time of peace and silence.

I was woken by the most appalling stomachache I had ever felt and at first, I thought I had been poisoned, then I thought appendicitis and then, I tried to remember the last time I'd had a crap. I read somewhere that addicts get terrible constipation. Now, I had the most violent need to empty my swollen stomach. I stumbled to the door, but before I got to it, it was opened, and he read the signs and led me to the toilet door. The relief was like Luther's when he finally nailed his 'Issues' against the Roman Catholic Church. It was a life-changing experience. Was this a turning-point? A rebirth? The release of more than just weeks of deprivation finally passing through the human system? I felt emptied, as if I'd had an enema or a scrape. I was so relieved that I broke down on this strange toilet in this strange, unspeaking man's house, without any real idea of how I'd got there or what I was going to do next. I muffled the sobs with a towel I found on the bath side. When I stopped, there was the same soundlessness as before, and I felt guilty for disturbing this peace and an uncomfortableness at revealing my weakness. I made my way back to the bedroom and slept again. I slept fitfully for hours at a time and then would wake in sweats with his face staring down at me. For how long I have no idea.

A hand pressed hard on my lips startled me awake. He was making a sign not to speak or make a noise. I nodded. He threw a shirt and trousers at me and told me to follow him when I was ready. All the time in absolute silence. On the landing, he led me through a door into a bedroom. In that bedroom, was a wall of pine panelling, and he knelt down and pulled out what looked like a knot of wood that dangled on a string, and into it put a three-way Allen key and part of the wall, only a third of the size a door, opened. He gestured, *We're going next door*. He opened it and we stepped through. He closed the door very carefully behind us, and pulled the knot on the string back into its place. I felt a draught of cold air. *Be careful*, he signed. Absolute silence. He stepped very carefully to the door opposite and opened it, and without doing so himself, he told me *Look, just look.* I could see the landing of a normal semi with doors leading off, but no stairs, the stairs had been removed. I pulled my head back inside. He smiled and closed the door soundlessly.

In the room was a rope ladder and he stepped up effortlessly into the roof space. I followed. Then, he pulled the ladder up and let down the hatch. Up here was another world, a small, cramped, but safe, other world. Tins of food, bottles of water, sleeping bags. And best of all, two or three little windows on each side of the roof. *One-way glass*, he signed. *We can see out, no one sees in*. He produced a pair of binoculars and pointed where to look. A black BMW, a black Ford and a black SUV. Eight blokes hanging around. He touched my arm and made two letters with his fingers. A and K. *Plus*, he signs, *Not good.*

They spread out in pairs. They've got baseball bats. They go very carefully, slowly, as if they're expecting something. Soon, they've all disappeared from view behind houses and into alleys that I can't see. I tell him what I see, but he knows. *They probably got guns, knives. I've seen them with a taser*, and for the first time he laughs, as he mimics being tasered. I ask him his name. *No name*, he signs, *no names.*

OK. Why are they here, do you think? I ask.

Looking for someone, probably you, he smiles. He points me to the books on the little bookcase between the beds.

No sleeping, not yet, he signs, *got to stay awake.*

I settle down onto the bed and pick up a book that looks a

hundred years old. Red cover, from a school library. *The Selected Poems of Oliver Goldsmith.* I let its easy canter of rhythm and old-fashioned, poetic language slide along for a page or two, and flicked back and forth, wondering if it mattered at any point if I moved verse 2 on page 56 to follow verse 4 on page 89. Then, out of nowhere, me reading from the middle of a page up, and then the proper way round:

'Ill fares the land, to hastening ills a prey,
Where wealth accumulates, and men decay:
Princes and lords may flourish, or may fade;
A breath can make them, as a breath has made;'

That stopped me in my tracks and I read the lines again. There was a small introduction outlining his life and his career. 'Ill fares the land, where wealth accumulates...1770. *The Deserted Village*. An Irishman, son of a clergyman, addicted to gambling and living by playing the flute. Author of *The Vicar of Wakefield.*

'Ill fares the land, where wealth accumulates...Ill fares the land where wealth accumulates...Ill fares the land, where wealth accumulates...'

I was startled out of my thoughts by the movement from across the other side of our attic space. *Two people*, he signed and pointed downwards, directly below us. *Silence. Absolute.*

I strained to listen and caught some voices, and a door opening and then the sound of feet stepping on bare floorboards. Then whispering. Maybe fear. Can you hear fear? I thought. They start speaking out loud when they discover that there is no staircase. They stop, and the smell of cigarette smoke drifts up to us. Stay still. Breathe as lightly as possible.

I realise I didn't even know his name...

Click. Click. Click, Click. The tape end goes around the machine. I have used one whole tape up on one of those old reel-to-reels that I like. They remind me of nicer days. Was I going to say *better* days? The common phrase echoes and becomes strange and dark and full of shadows that move.

Click. Click. Click. They remind me of a different time.

I turn it off, pull the reel off the machine and label it. I put today's date. As long as there's nothing else bearing the same label, then the label has a meaning. I look around at all the hundreds and hundreds of tapes, all neatly labelled and the 'Book of Labels', which tells us what's in the room, stored on tape, what's on the tapes and who recorded them and when. In another book is a written summary of all of the accounts and stories on tape. And there's a computer programme that cross-references all of the labels of all of the tapes to make sure none are replicated. I check to make sure that 'About the Circle' isn't taken. It is taken. There's another tape called 'About the Circle' recorded five years ago. I check who recorded it. It doesn't say who recorded it. I must check. I must ask Smoothie to check. I don't have time now.

It'll have to wait.

12

About Wonder

Wonder look at his watch. He was supposed to meet his friend, Felix, at 6pm. It's after six already, and he's still at work. He shouldn't even be there, but his brother is sick. His brother younger than him, him just fifteen, he loves to work. He is sick now, real sick, he's been off and on, off and on for weeks now. Wonder the one suppose to go to school, suppose to study for the family, and his brother like the work, but he lying at home, real sick now. The Green Tobacco Sickness is the name of this. He been going out and working with the wet leaves. Mama told him but he just want to work. He throwing up, he shaking, got a fever and he can't even take water but don't know what to do about him now, because Mama sick already and just stay at home and if one of them don't work, then they don't able to pay for no doctor. Mama sleeping, he hopes. Wonder likes to see his Mama at peace and she only at peace when she sleeping. Sleeping on the floor when the rain comes makes her sick. He don't know who going to die first.

Father say years back that black man can't go Nairobi. *Nairobi for Whites Only*, he says, *we got to do the work for the railroad and the building* so his old family build a house in Kibera, before it got so big. But then the jobs come to Migori and they move there, plant tobacco, cultivate tobacco, tobacco save everything.

They put a sign up just away from the house, *Know Your*

HIV Status. It's only wooden thing and now it's leaning down. Wonder know Felix will be there, waiting by the sign.

Wonder say to his boss, 'I gotta go, boss. I don everything.' Boss say everyone do overtime, new contract. But Wonder ain't got a contract, Wonder's brother ain't got no contract.

'Tobacco leaves keep coming in,' he says, 'you gotta keep feeding the fire.' Sometimes he speaks Luo, when he gets angry, but Wonder don't speak Luo. He speaks it when he don't want an argument. Wonder don't argue. Wonder keeps feeding the fire for drying the leaves. He needs every shilling he can get for rent, food, doctors. Every day he can feel school slip slip away. He can't think of another way.

After another two hours, the boss has left, and Wonder get his things to leave. He walk in the dark along the farm road. Felix will have got sick of waiting and gon home. Felix won't hold it against him, but Wonder don't like letting his friend down, they're both strangers in this place.

A car pull up in the dark. There are two workers from the farm. They ask him to get in, it's better than walking. These are good men who have families, although he knows them most by what people say. They are talking incessantly and speak Kiswahili, so Wonder feels happy.

Enzi is from Tanzania, he has a big, big voice and come to Kenya for work. Chandu asks Wonder about himself, how old he is, his family and his school. Chandu wants Wonder to be a doctor for Kenya, Wonder says he doesn't know what he can be.

They drive on the dirt road and the big spatters of rain drum on the car. After a while Enzi pulls over and tells Wonder he has to get out if he wants to go home. Chundu says, 'No, no, it's too wet, there's a storm coming, maybe.' He wants Wonder to come to the meeting, just up this turn here, not far. Enzi says he's too young. Chundu says no one is too young to decide on their fate. Wonder likes these people who take him seriously.

They laugh and start the car again. He hears them say they need youngsters to keep the movement going.

In the meeting room in an old school, three mile down the track, there are sombre men sitting quietly on wooden chairs. There is one light bulb. It sways when they open the door and shadows move all around. There is greetings, handshakes, brothers embrace, laughing. Then they turn to show Wonder to the crowd, and everyone slap his back and shake his hand. A brother. He sits down on a bench at the front, between Chundu and Enzi. For the first time in a long time, he miss his father. His father would be king here, he thinks, everyone would love him.

There is a lot of talk. Nearly everyone stand up, talk, the men clap, shout, hiss. Some sit silent, as if every story they hear make them feel worse, not better. As if the words are their words, too. Wonder doesn't understand all of it: the Company, certain men from the Company and some women, the Government, the loans, the debts. One man worked all year and by the end of the year, after he sold his crop, he owed them more money than he did at the beginning of the year. They cheered this. He didn't want sympathy or a fight with anyone, he want to know who could allow this and who could bear this and what they going to take next.

One tell about cutting down wood, cut down all his wood and after all these years of cutting down wood, to fire the kiln, to dry the wood, there ain't no more trees he own for to cut down. He can't buy wood to burn and he don't have no more left, so who gonna cure his leaves?

One old man start singing a song in Kikuyu that the old men sing when the British rule things. Everyone go quiet, let him do it. When he finish they each shake his hand and tell him to teach the song to his childer, his grandchildren and all the childer in the village. He laugh and say that there is no childer left in his family.

Chundu thank them all and introduce Enzi. Enzi talk about Tanzania and what they do there to get a voice. Enzi very good at talking like this. He make you feel strong, thinks Wonder, he make you not feel like a slave earning less and less every year, but he tell us all about what they do in Tanzania and how they beat the company, how they work for one another, how they get help from other place. Enzi says that we have to ask for more from the company and to all ask for the same thing, and that if we don't stand together we will not win, but we can win because we are the power in the machine and without us there is no machine and the big bosses need us to keep them rich and the Governments of the world need us to keep them rich with taxes and the people need us to keep them happy.

'Everyone needs tobacco,' he says, 'everyone. Everyone needs tobacco farmers.'

When he finish we clap him. Wonder stands as well, wants to make his father proud and make things better for himself and those he living and working for. Chundu calls everyone for a cup of tea. The cups and the water is prepared on a table at the side.

A big light comes shining in through a window. Enzi tells us to shush, be quiet. The look on Enzi's face isn't good. It sounds like a car engine being switched off. Wonder looks at Chundu and Enzi. They are shouting in English at one another and Wonder doesn't speak English. The door is smashed down, and a policeman comes in wearing a uniform and a beret. He's carrying a big stick. Everything happens so quickly for Wonder to grasp. More men come through the door with batons. Wonder stares because these are not looking like policemen. Wonder hears cries and shrieks and screams and curses and sees two policemen smashing their batons on Chundu's head. The hot water pot for the tea is turned over and someone is burned by the boiling water. Enzi rushes at the door and is beaten back by three of them Police. Wonder is amazed at the size of the clubs. He stares at them. Four feet long at least, thick and untrimmed, not from a factory, he thinks. Home-made. Wonder stands and watch as Enzi is reduced to a pile of silence on the schoolroom floor. As they drag him out by his legs, his beating leaves a trail of blood on the dirt floor. As an afterthought, Wonder feel a hit from behind by a powerful blow to the side of the head and then crumple into unconsciousness with a blow on top of his head.

When all the bodies are dragged outside the Police Inspector orders the school to be burnt. The conscious and the unconscious are thrown in the back of the big truck. The driver and owner of the truck does removals when he isn't doing this. He drives for three hours to Bondo, then smaller and smaller roads. If he can get the bodies dumped over the border, he gets a bonus.

All the cries and moans are ignored. Wonder lies face down in the dirt, unconscious, the life flowing out through the brokenness of his skull and a man he has never met is dumped on top of him.

The driver is back in Migori by dawn. He washes his lorry down clean and takes a coffee and a cigarette. A guy comes by the coffee shop and passes him an envelope.

13

About Tim

It's hot tonight, even up here looking down on the city. Great views. Nice little spot, all in all. They've got these big blower things discreetly hidden, so, even out on the terrace, it's very pleasant. He calls for a cigar. Thinks about turning off all three phones. If just once in his life he could bloody get away from the things, he'd feel a bit better. The boy comes with a cigar. Here, he feels, he can treat himself to one. He takes bloody big drags of it to spite her. He holds his glass in the air to signal he wants another one, but nothing happens. He turns around awkwardly, but there's no one around. When he stands up it's uncomfortable. He aches after the long flight and has to stretch his back for a minute or two to take away the deep twinges. Where are the lazy bastards? If his father were here, he'd be flaying someone with his tongue by now.

He steps through the doors into the lounge area. Big old leather couches, card tables, slow, creaking old ceiling fans and walls drenched with the heads of dead animals. When he was a kid, he counted seventy-eight heads on wooden plaques, waiting for Papa to finish and take him home, before he lost count. Ranting about the perverted savages, even after Kenya was independence, was the next memory that came to mind when he thought of his father. And endless reminiscing of his service days for the Kenya Police, steadily deteriorating with the endless gins, as they turned the former HQ of the colonial police into 'The Club' that they call it today. And now, he thought, you can't get a drink for love nor money. He set off down a corridor of black and white photographs of men on horses, men hunting, cricket matches and parties and all the memorabilia of a colonial military force. Tim realised now that there are many ways to run a country. That was just one of them.

He caught sight of a boy in a white jacket disappearing around the corner and called after him. There was no response, so he set off to catch hold of the blighter. When he turned the corner, there was no one in sight. A silence that was odd. And an icy shudder went through him, that odd, unexpected shadow of fear that ran through him he couldn't place. It was like that in Africa, he thought, chasing shadows. Hearing voices at the edge of the thicket. Something that could be a light through the trees. He told himself to calm down and that the best thing for it was a drink. He took a deep breath and walked back to the terrace. 'Calmly does it,' he said out loud.

By the time he got back to the terrace, they were all there, all smiles, all jokes, all handshakes and fey comments and teasing remarks. The General, Hilary, Bob, Aki, and a new guy, Frank.

'To think your father hunted my father from here, Tim-*kitwana*...hahha.' The General said this every time he met Tim. Everyone laughs. He goes on to remind everyone that there was a house just behind the main house, out of sight, 'that was a kind of torture-house, but you British burnt it down before we could get to use it...hahhaaa...'

The General has a big warm laugh. Everyone laughs.

'I'll have a double Bombay and tonic. Ice. And bring a couple of bottles of water.' Tim orders. 'And bring some canapes or whatever you've got for us to nibble on,' he adds. The staff are visible again.

They sit around a large, glass coffee table, out on the verandah.

Hilary begins in her tense, Afrikaaner way that always half-irritates, half-fascinates Tim. 'It's getting boring, gentlemen, as you know. Sorry to jump straight in, but I'm on a deadline, I have to catch a plane to Jo'burg in two hours, the place is like the wild west at the moment. We have to stop it spreading here. We know that tobacco prices are low, people are getting restless, the farmers and workers are, well, getting more demanding, the Government down there (she sweeps her arm in the general direction of Nairobi, sprawled out below) is all over the place, we're fighting on several fronts – against the NGOs, the Cancer charities and now there's unionisers and – well, you don't need me to tell you – but protesting is everyone's latest hobby –'

'Tell me about it, Hilary, my men are exhausted, the press is on our backs, every day we go anywhere there is a shit of a reporter or someone asking questions – we are the Army for god's sake –'

'General,' said Hilary, 'we appreciate what you are doing for the company and the economy, we really do.' She touches his knee at the point and smiles, like his mother should have done more often for him. 'I'm thinking we need to shift our perspective a little.' She waits for him to be ready for what she's going to say. 'What do you think?' she says to him, but smiles at all of us, and waits for him to nod.

He smiles and nods, knowing she is a very busy lady.

'OK. We are suggesting – well, we have agreed these as possible strategies at board level, possible ways forward. All the Directors of TobacAfric are behind you, General, we trust you implicitly.' She smiles and he nods and thanks her. 'Tim, since you and your businesses own substantial players in the Tanzanian, and now Kenyan, tobacco markets and have a lot of experience in the mining industry down there as well, just give us a flavour of what we need to happen.'

Tim never quite knew what to expect from Hilary, but he

presumed she wanted something like this: 'General, gentlemen, it's true to say that we are having some difficulties – staffing difficulties, you might say (laughter) – and it's true to say that there are some signs of declining markets in tobacco sales here, but – we do need to change the way we do things. General, I don't know if you're aware, but to cut a long and very boring story short, your country is seriously undervalued in terms of the content of your geology. People have said that Kenya is poor, minerally, for a long time. But, and it's still a big *but* – we have very good reason to think that we may be sitting on some very interesting possibilities. Chief amongst these are what are called 'rare earth metals', amongst other things, so, we need your help. With your help, Kenya could become very rich indeed, if we could just get on with business.'

The General smiled. 'Kenya is a beautiful, bountiful and very mysterious lady. No one has ever found out all her secrets. But I'm very interested in what you are saying, Tim. We are here to serve Kenya and her people and to make her preeminent in Africa. How can we help?'

Hilary stepped in. 'Get out of Kibera, and all the other slums. Leave them be, don't waste any more police time on them. But we need you to recruit the boys from the slums who are desperate. Make up some sort of nonsense about new regiments, new opportunities. Short training period, keep it all nice and shiny and pay them enough to keep them loyal. A sort of National Guard. On the side of order and Common Sense. Good so far?' The General nodded. 'What Tim is saying, 'she carried on, 'is that we're going to need access to the land to start the mining, but we're going to do it before anyone can object. OK? We need you to encourage the tobacco farmers to cause some issues – local uprising, rioting, looting, burn a police station in Migori County or something – big, but not too big, but enough of a distraction to warrant your intervention, give them a few guns, if you think – get in the news, then, you and your new boys go in to restore order, sensible policing, protecting the nation. Police are the heroes. You're on your way to being a presidential candidate and we've set up our first half dozen mines under the radar. What do you think?'

Bob spoke with his strong Afrikaans accent. 'Real bit of bother, Hilary, eh?' He laughs. 'You never do anything by halves.'

'I'm going to take that as a compliment, coming from you,' she said.

'We are going to need some incentives,' said the General. 'And there are a few gentlemen of the Government who will need winning over. Persuading them that it is good for the country.'

Everyone laughed.

'General,' said Tim, 'have you thought about moving into the Presidential Palace? I really do think it would suit you.' Everyone laughed. 'Lots of bedrooms, I hear.'

"Tim, hahaa, *kitwana, kitwana,* you have more sense of humour than your father.'

'I'm not joking about the Palace. And I'm only guessing about the bedrooms.' Everyone laughed. Tim continued. 'General, we need a good story, we need nice photos, we don't need any martyrs or Malcolm Xs, we need a headless chicken for an opposition. It's so difficult with this social media and every little incident being videoed, so General, please be very, very careful to protect yourself. We need you to look like Jesus...'

'Now, you sound like my father, Tim,' said the General.

Hilary kept the show moving, 'I know you have all met Frank, but Tim, Frank is your man for this. He has vast experience of this sort of operation and I'm sure, General that you'll enjoy working together with Frank. He can bring a lot to a project like this.'

All eyes turned to Frank, who smiled and raised his glass.

'Nice to be here, nice to meet you.'

‘To our next little project,’ said Hilary and everyone raised their glass.

‘Bob’s word is good enough for me, Frank,’ said Tim, ‘but what exactly do you do?’

Frank laughed. ‘I work in liquidity,’ he said. Everyone laughed.

‘To liquidity,’ said Tim. They all raised their glasses.

Hilary made her excuses.

Five minutes later, Tim was left on his own on the terrace. His flight back was tomorrow, so he sat back in the big chair on the empty terrace. Tomorrow was Parents’ Evening in his daughter’s school back in England. He wished he could ask Frank to deal with some of those teachers. They’re so full of stupid ideas that have got nothing to do with the real world.

Economic Offender's Register	
Name of Person, Aliases & Alternatives incl. Sir, Lord, Lady etc.	
Name(s) of ALL Companies, Corporations & Bodies incl. Directorships and Responsibilities Ever Held by Offender	
Details of ALL Previous Convictions, incl. Bankruptcies, Other Parties involved, Amounts of Public Money Accessed	
Details of ALL Bank Accounts to which Offender has Access incl. Spouse's and Immediate Family	
Names of ALL Victims, incl. Direct and Indirect Parties Affected by Offender's Financial Crimes and Details of Offender's Plan to Repay Victims.	
Details of ALL Property Held by Offender and of Property to be Confiscated or Currently Held as Compensation for Offender's Crimes	
Details of ALL Passports held by Offender	
Details of Work to be Assigned to Offender as Rehabilitation and Details of Work that Offender must NEVER be allowed to undertake again	

14

Ceadd

> And she went away a moment and brings me back a metal cup of the sweetest water I have ever tasted. I drank so deeply that she was moved to go and fill it again and I saw the place that she went to, and it was lined with stones and water emerged from that flat ground unlike any other spring I ever saw, and above it a wooden stake with copper ladles hanging from it... And it was the time of King Edwin, when a woman could walk across the whole island from sea to sea without receiving harm from anyone.
>
> About King Edwin, d.633
> from Bede's *Historia Ecclesiastica* (adapted)

Like a stage set in an amateur production when someone rips the backcloth. It won't change the acting or the words said or the plot, but it will change the way the audience look at it. The nagging shift of focus until it's forgotten or parts slightly, with unseen forces. The Circle sits beneath comforting darkness. Leeds ticks away in the background. Just far enough away to still be heard, a train picks up speed with the endless to-and-fro-ing of carriages attached reluctantly. No voices from within or without, leaving the thousands of city lights to whirr just below human hearing. Even the bats are disturbed by the lack of insects bobbing up and down the usual channels, lost in a sea of unlit, gravitational letting-go.

I sit down on a wide bench under the open sky and flop onto my back. No constellations, no scudding clouds, too much pollution from man-made lights, just a nothingness of muddy greyblack. I doze, but when a voice breaks the silence I feel as if I've been fluttering against the lamp and am shuddering.

'You ok?'

'Yeah, just dozed off.' But I'm glad to be woken.

'You were shaking your head and twitching. Looked like you were having a fit. A little fit.'

It's Picnic. His dark voice pierces me. 'You were saying things. I was a bit scared. I once spent some time with a man who...no...'

'Who was he?'

'Just some bloke got himself arrested for being in the wrong place at the wrong time. Like me. I spent three days and four nights with him while he went in and out of being someone else other than himself. At first, I didn't know what was happening, then I got to really fear it. Felt like he was making me...'

Picnic was back there. I could hardly see his face, silhouetted by the single light coming out of the doorway of Soho. I breathed in like I was going underwater for as long as I could.

'Doesn't matter,' says Picnic in his Cape Town black voice. 'Doesn't matter. He ain't gonna hurt me. It's gonna pass. He's just letting out his pain. He's twitching now. He's foamin' at the mouth. He's shoutin'. He's really shoutin'. Take it easy, take it easy. Come on, breathe, breathe... I'm shoutin' to myself to breathe, really deep... Breathe, breathe... this ain't about you. I try to watch myself watching him. I'm screwed up tight in a ball, as small as possible. The cell is nine, ten foot square. It's daylight, but no one's around. I don't know which prison or police station I'm in. There are bars and a metal-bar door. No one in the corridor. No guards, nobody around. Just me, huddling, trying to get out of this lunatic's way. They brought him in a few hours ago. He hasn't spoken till a few minutes ago. He seemed really small when they brought him in. They threw him on the mattress like he was a kid. Now he's shouting in Xhosa, but not shouting like anger. This is like the devil shouting, like a king in battle giving orders. He's grown huge and can touch all the walls of the cell from wherever he stands. He ignores me, or he can't see me, or he doesn't want to see me. I ache everywhere from my own beatings. My right ear aches so badly that it feels like I'm in a permanent sea surf and my ribs are bruised from the kicking, but still I cover my ears and hold myself into the tightest ball. I just want to cry, die, give up. I have no strength left. I don't know his name, I don't know how to speak to him, I don't know what he's doing...I feel his touch on my arm and I dare to look up. He's grown so big that he's spread his legs, so his feet touch both walls about a foot off the ground. With his arms he grabs the bars. The incantations pour out of his mouth in fluid, super-human fluidity, as if the language is the fuel for the power and the words are the force of the spirit. His feet scrape backwards and dislodge me out of my hiding place in the corner, and I can feel the expression of strength ripple down his legs and bounce off the walls again, in one tidal wave of exertion, to go up his thighs and through his waist and fill his upper body with extraordinary focus. Seconds later, he bent the two bars he was holding slightly apart, and even more extraordinarily, within parts of a second, he had stopped speaking and was visibly, before my eyes, deflating back to his normal size. I stared in utter awe at this thing I have never seen before or since, but the next thing he did was even greater: he composed himself with one calm, enormous breath and reduced himself with the opposite effect of his earlier efforts, and in an instant slipped through the bars and stood facing the room that was no longer his cell and gently reached for his foul little mattress and pulled it through the bars, with all the struggle of a normal man pulling something too big through a space too small, before, with much exertion, he was curled up and asleep on the outside of the cell. He made no effort to move, nothing, no running or escaping. He just didn't want to sleep in a cell like that. I didn't sleep for hours till the guards came and woke us up. They asked him lots of questions in Afrikaans and slapped him around a bit, but he had lodged himself back inside and didn't answer. He never spoke to me for three days. I wasn't there as far as he was concerned. Just another intruder in his country. I don't know what became of him.'

I waited to see if any more would come.

'Do you think we are alone in ourselves? Do you ever wonder why we are so obsessed with ideas of character and personality? Are they just fixed, in order to keep us fixed?'

He wouldn't let the gaze fall, even as it was warm, intrigued and challenging.

He kept on talking. 'You have a lot you don't talk about,' he said.

'Everyone has,' I said.

He didn't reply but waited without moving. Nothing moved at all, and I tried to think his thoughts. Several more moments.

'How good is your Latin?' he asked.

'Poor,' I said.

'I'm surprised because I heard you speak it just now. Sounded very fluent to me.' He smiled.

I couldn't answer straight away.

'Do you always hear Latin when you hear someone mumbling in their sleep?' I asked.

'That was the Lord's Prayer in Latin. Didn't think I would hear it out here, in West Leeds, after all these years...you've got to remember that I had a good old-fashioned, classical education and the Lord's Prayer in Latin is one of those things you don't forget...and since I'm a trained actor, trained to remember things very quickly, I could repeat exactly what you said:

'*Pater noster, qui es in coelis; santificatur nomen tuum: Adveniat regnum tuum; fiat voluntas tua, sicut in coelo, et in terra. Panem nostrum cotidianum da nobis hodie: Et dimitte nobis debita nostra, sicut et nos dimittimus debitoribus nostris: et ne nos inducas in tentationem sed libera nos a malo*...and this is how it ends: '*Quia tuum est regnum, et potestas, et Gloria, in saecula. Amen*.'

'Amen', I said, but couldn't say anything more for a long moment.

He looked at me, passively.

'Do you believe in coincidences, Picnic?'

'I think I do, but they can often be easily explained away.'

I get up off the bench. 'Come with me if you have a minute. I want to show you something. Some things.'

He follows without speaking. We leave Soho and walk back to the Square. He has a very peculiar gait and rolls from side to side. There's an oddness to his steps that sounds so relaxed and distinctive I want to copy it, and feel my hips let go and roll along, letting the ball joints work so much more roundly in their sockets and feel the sinew and muscle holding it all together, so much more animal than urban human wretch, tied up in trainers and conventions. It was like being followed by a very lazy lion padding behind, with years of power, treading his kingdom, under each paw.

I stop at the top of the square.

'Years ago, there was a house fire here and some people died. We didn't want to rebuild the house, so we demolished it. With it being a semi, it also burnt next door down, so we had a big plot of land to do something with. We didn't know what to do with it, so we let it alone, the weeds grew, and it became like a big staring hole. This is way back when this place was a different place to live, before we began to change everything. Anyway, we had a little discussion, thought about what was missing and put this up. I know you probably know some of this from what the others say, but it's not quite what you think. Come on in.'

I walk up the drive, past the garden with the memorial to what we want to forget and stand in front of the semi's frontage.

'I sometimes feel everything is a lie hiding a lie, covering a bit of truth perfumed with a little mendacity and some smiling Janus-memory deep down. Picnic, you know what lying is all about as an actor. But there are good lies and bad lies and some lies that are somewhere between. This is a truth.'

I make him step forward to see that these two beautiful, bay-windowed 1930s semis are exactly one brick thick. The wall is supported from inside by two small side walls of similar brick, but there is no house or front-room or front door you can go through. Instead, there is a much smaller, entirely prefabricated attachment to this house.

'We like symmetry. We like to present a good face to the world when we have to, and well, I'll let you judge.'

I walked up to the door of this attached building and got out the keys. It's long and low and a bit crude 'cos we were still learning how to do it. There are no windows, and the roof is now covered with grass.

'I hate keys and locks. This is one of the few buildings that we lock and that we don't unlock to everyone or share the key. Maybe I'm wrong. I imagine you haven't been here before? We have lots of names for it. I like the idea of a place having more than one name. It's closer to the truth of a place to be known by more than one.'

'No, didn't imagine it wasn't the same as everywhere else.'

'There is a reason, bear with me. At its core is a massive static caravan that we found and didn't know what to do with.'

I open the door and flick on the light.

'Have a seat,' I say.

'Wow,' he says, 'still not sure what this has got to do with anything, but I'm all ears.'

'Perfect metaphor,' I say.

'It wasn't meant, but I can see what you mean.'

'Every story that I've ever had a chance to record is here. On tape. On real old-fashioned magnetic recording tape. We call it 'Fritz's Shed', in honour of Mr. Pfleumer, who added ferric oxide powder coating to a paper strip and well...the rest is history, or not, of course, depending on who tells the story of history and who records it and who steals it and who passes it off as their own and who believes the stories, until they stop being lies and are the stories we live by. There's also discs and files and flashdrives and, well, you can see all the stuff in here. But that isn't why I brought you here.'

'Hang on a minute. What is all this?' asks Picnic, pointing at the walls of this caravan depository.

'If I ask you to keep what I say to yourself, then immediately I'm asking you to create another story and partly to live with another lie, but I would like you to keep all of this to yourself. Do you agree?'

'Yes, if that's what you want,' he says.

'Haven't you ever thought about all the words that come at you – particularly in your profession – and are lost because no matter how much you want to remember that brilliant bon mots or bit of repartee or moving incident that someone tells you about a life or a death or a love or a joke – you don't have the time or opportunity to record it. Life gets in the way. The bus stops at your stop and you have to say goodbye. The director shouts it's time for the next take or the line runs away with you in your head and you can't quite tell it again, as you did when you first told the funny story to your friends, of going to kiss your first love on the neck, but in the dark get a mouthful of puss where you've broken the head of a blackhead. You tell some stories so often, that you can't remember any more if they're true, or which bits really did happen. If only you could go back to the original story and listen to yourself telling it again and learn the truth about yourself, once again.

'You know when you walk down the street you grew up in, played with your mates in, fell off your bike in, had a fight in and then go back to as an adult – for the very first time you see it as it is as it was – how the hell do you ever go back to the stories that you've lived by all your life that mean so much to you, that are you, that define your experiences, your way of responding and dealing with other humans? The thing that makes you the hero and the anti-hero of your own *Odyssey*. This is my feeble attempt.'

He turns away and walks along the walls, scanning the titles and dates and colours of insert cards. 'How many are there?' he asks, without turning.

'Ask Smoothie. He knows. He thinks I'm wasting my time with these tapes. He has them all stored digitally somewhere. 'In a cloud, but not as you know it', he says, 'but very safe'. He gets fed up having to source the tape for new stuff...do you think it's interesting that *story*, noun and *store*, verb and noun are connected?'

'And what's that at the end,' he says, 'that room?'

'That's where I do the recordings or listen to them or work with them.'

'And am I in here?'

'Of course, you are.'

He looked like he was trying to frame the next question.

'Out there,' I say, 'as you know, it's, well, when they come here with their troubles and their questions and their doubts and they need help, I'm not like Solomon, not some wise bastard who's got all the answers, I'm just struggling with it all myself and I've come to something like a conclusion, it's not totally clear but it's beginning to feel right...'

'And what is that?' he asks, carefully. 'But wait a minute, isn't this unethical? Do you tell them they're being taped? Isn't it like spying on people, in a way?'

'In answer to your first question – not just at this moment, but bear with me, we'll get there. Unethical in terms of whose ethics? Could it be just as true that since no one owns words, any words, thank God, they belong in the communal sphere? If so, then it follows that you can't own your own words, all you can do is choose which ones you choose to say or which ones you choose not to say. And be hanged or be damned by them. If you choose to come to me and talk to me, then, am I not also simply choosing to do you the honour, not the right word, but you know what I mean, of allowing myself the opportunity to listen to them again?'

'Well, yeah, but all you have to do is tell them it will happen.'

'I do something better. I tell them to choose very carefully – exactly – what they're telling me and to mean exactly what they're saying.'

'And what if they were to say no, or to find out that you had recorded them?'

'They never say no. No one ever says no if they're the only one speaking. And could you ask for the conversation back when you first made your mother cry? Hardly. The primacy of the spoken word. Plato wasn't alone when he stated to worry about what writing was going to do to the way we think and work.'

'I never made my mother cry. She made me cry enough, but it didn't seem to bother her.'

'You see.'

'And why have you brought me here?' he asks.

'Coincidences.'

'You asked me about them. Whether I believe in them.'

'And you said, 'I think I do, but they can often be easily explained away.''

Nothing for a minute or two, as he fiddled with our conversation in his mind, then he turned to me, 'Are you taping this?' he asked.

'You're not telling me anything,' I smiled.

'Turn it on,' he said. 'You talk for a change. See what it's like.' Another pause. 'I bet there isn't one single minute here where you aren't asking a question or listening to the answer, is there? Turn it on.'

He stands up to find the switch. 'The whole place must be live. Come on, how do I turn it on? Come into the spotlight, Mr. Burgerman, whoever you are. Tell me what made you bring me here. Speak.'

The actor turned director. The visitor turned Inquisitor. The silence within all this whirring potential to record meaningful human sounds. I can go blank. I have to admit, I can freeze. I imagined the tape desks turning in the control room, the VU meters shivering, measuring the disturbance of space as the human lungs propelled out air between narrow gaps and wider gaps, between vocal chords, tongue muscles, hard palates, soft palates, alveolar and dental ridges, teeth, lips and nasal passages.

Nothing had come because no one needed to know. This was not my personal space to add vulnerable words to their libraries of suffering and anxiety. This was all about them, the ghosts of the speakers fixed in little boxes and trapped on magnetic strips of brown evidence. I picked up the tape that I had labelled just an hour ago, 'About the Circle'. There it was, recorded and labelled, but not in a catalogue. That story felt like the easy one to admit to, the crime that I wouldn't mind people knowing about, but what Picnic was asking was something else, deeper, the real secret at the heart of the place. I didn't know where to begin. Except the compulsion to tell it before it was lost.

'It's not here, is it?' asked Picnic. 'Yours is the one story that no one knows, no one has heard, has never been recorded. You're just The Man, aren't you? The Big Daddy who asks the questions, who doesn't have to stand and be in front of everyone else. The best place to hide, right in front of everyone. That's why you brought me here, because only an actor would know what you've been doing for all these years. Only an actor would know the lies of performance and the truth of acting.'

I didn't speak again. I was mesmerised by my own little setting in this lean-to caravan, disguised as a house, behind a false front, on a piece of land we didn't own, with more lies and deception in this promised land honesty than maybe even in any Lardland. That's why I couldn't tell my real story anymore, because I had become everyone else's story of me, of Burgerman. Of the man who listens to everything and is eaten by honesty and is eaten by lies. The only truth I know is the instinct to lead by example, of wearing the humblest coat that is no more than an actor would put on in *Henry the Fourth Part Two*, to create the effect, but to hide the unsubstantial personage, shouting across the stage.

'There is no rush,' he said. 'No rush at all...' He turns off all the lights except one. He has found the remote that turns on the mics and the spools. For several minutes the tape goes through the heads pointlessly.

'How do you normally start?' he says. 'Tell me your story? No, that's not great. What about, 'When you're ready,...' a bit better, but not quite. You are the master of this, I'm just learning. Bear with me.' He watches me, as I fight with my composure.

I pass him the tape labelled, 'About the Circle'. 'You're right,' I say, 'but only partly right. Before you found me on the bench, I had recorded this, 'About the Circle'.' I shuffled it in my hands and put it down.

He picked it up and looked at it and read the title. 'You haven't argued with one word I have said to you in here,' and laughed lightly, 'and remember we deal with all of the things that are unsaid as much as what is...so, what is it you really want to say? You didn't know what I was going to say when I finished off your Paternoster, did you? This,' and he waved 'About the Circle' at me, 'this is not the thing that is the coincidence, is it?'

Silence.

He broke it. 'When you were talking about that stuff about telling a story till it is true...what was it you said? 'If only you could go back to the original story and listen to yourself telling it again and learn the truth about yourself, once again', that was it, wasn't it? There's another story, isn't there and you daren't tell it, because you don't know if it's true...is that it? Tell me, please.'

I couldn't look at him. I could only look at the rows and shelves and lines of other people's stories.

He waited, having spent his life waiting for the cue from his fellow actors. He waited until he knew it was right.

'Tell me the 'Pater Noster' again. When you're ready.'

'*Pater noster, qui es in cœlis; sanctificatur nomen tuum; adveniat regnum tuum...* But that's not the point, that's not the point,' I say.

'What is the point?'

'Wherever I go, whatever I do, I can't get away from this place, that's the point. Part of me hates it so much, but I have to be here.'

It all goes quiet except for the sounds of the machines made by humans.

'What you say will not betray you,' he said, quietly.

'You are right, there is a story of the Burgerman here in the catalogues, of how someone ends up somewhere, but there is no record of this place and why we're here or what could be said about claiming the place as our own own. The place we are rooted, that defines and outlines and explains the attachments.'

I pause.

'Picnic, this is the story of why this place matters so much and the coincidence is that I'm telling the story of why it matters so much on the eve of losing it.'

'One day, years ago, I set out from home. No maps, no route, no guides. I didn't know where I was going. I had rung in sick in the morning and that was that. I put on my walking boots and took a small bag and set off. I got a bus out to the East Coast and got off at Hull. I walked through the evening to Aldbrough. It doesn't matter, it's not this that matters. I slept better than for months, wrapped in all my clothes and a thin sleeping bag, on the dunes behind the sea. I woke up and bathed at first light in the sea and then walked up the coast to Hornsea. I slept with the sound of the sea thundering, whipped up by the waves, and I hadn't felt so alive in days.

At dawn, I got drenched in a downpour and took refuge in a bus shelter. Later, the sun shone again, I bathed and shivered in the sea and for no reason I know, I turned due west to follow the sun. It was early April and warming and blustery. Walking without a map is the best way to read the landscape. I got wet and disorientated by the dykes and watercourses and canals due east of the Mere and picked up the straight road near Etton and felt captivated by the purposefulness of this narrow road going straight across a flat landscape, particularly after what I had just had to fight my way across. I had no idea where I was going. I had never been to this part of the world before. Everything was visible and went on for miles and miles, or so it seemed to me. It felt like it was going straight up to heaven and for me, who had nowhere else to go, heaven felt like just as good a place as any. For as far as I could see, forwards and backwards, the road went straight as a die, sitting on landscape as flat as any prairie. It was utterly bewitching to take steps that barely made any impact on distance or perspective.

Imagine it. Almost completely lacking human housing. No cars, no walkers, no travellers, no livestock. Nothing. Nothing, it seemed to me, was alive that day. And it seemed that the more I travelled, the more the road egged me on, the more I looked behind, the more there was to see in front. The more I stepped out, the more the road was laid at my feet. This was like a wonderful dream of moving and standing still, just as Eliot dreamed of, in *The Four Quartets*. That was where my end and my beginning was. And the more I walked, the less I saw there was to see. The fields seemed to get bigger and the trees at the edge receded and the slightest of hills on the horizon shivered and diminished in the bluster of this midmorning, as the wind and the showers danced around my back.

Eventually, I hit the first rising of the land and trees that break the landscape and swallow more of the sky. This is different country, and the paths take the first of many turns till I come to a road where I have no choice but to go into a village either side of a sloping lane past a church raised up on an oval mound supported by a wall to a man's height. After a slight dip and then a rise, the road takes a right-hand bend before it drags me down into somewhere much deeper and older. I stop at a spring and remember the coloured ribbons tied to the branches of the elder trees.

I drink the water and I'm so elated, whether from exhaustion, hunger or what, I barely know what I'm doing or if I'm going east or west, up or down and sit to rest...

I must have fallen asleep in the sunshine and a woman's voice wakes me.

'Ceadd, Ceadd, wake, wake up,' hissing at me in the old tongue, 'you have fallen asleep again. You cannot be here asleep when they come, they will mock you.' She's busy with the effort of cutting flowers on the steep bank.

'Were you drinking again? Everyone says that your drinking is the cause of your sleeping.' She talks whilst she cuts the stems of the wild garlic. 'How many days and nights of drinking, Ceadd? How long have you been here? And they say the King was asking after you. What do you say to that, Ceadd?'

I cannot speak for thirst. I make myself sit up and feel the nausea again.

She comes down the bank to where I sit. She feels my forehead. 'What is it you carry in you? You act more like a woman with your ills.' She strokes my face with her hand, and my head is filled with the smell of the leaves.

'You have the fever. Where have you been?' she asks. 'You look like a wildman of the islands. Like one of those Frankish heremits. This will not please the king. Come,' she says.

I follow her downwards along the stream to the well. All my limbs ache and drowsiness befuddles my thoughts.

'Drink,' she says, and passes me a copper ladle full of sweet water. And I drink, so that the water falls out of my mouth, and filled with such need for cooling water, I rise and half fall into the little pool that catches the water from the spring. And I drink, and I drink, and I breathe in the water, like an ox after a day in the high summer's harvesting, till I am full. I wipe my face on my tunic, but the old woman tuts and passes me a cleaner cloth to dry my hands and face and neck.

'Ceadd, you are filthy. The king and all his men and priests came yesterday and will expect more than this from you. Clean yourself.'

And I let the cool waters of Saint Helena's Well fill my guts with sweetness and look down to behold my bearded face in the mirror of the water and splash it and try to remove the dirt.

'The garlic's making me feel sick,' I say, in the old tongue.

She doesn't reply. I hover over the stone and water of the spring between the spells of blurring and the weakness of my knees. There are lizards and bees and ladies with fine hair carrying water in pots, lining the pool in clever adornment, but now they are moving around, released from their stone prisons. Each movement is repeated so that they don't leave their position and don't stay still. I cry out, and the old woman comes to me. She feels the heat of my neck and my arms. I shake from head to foot, bent almost double over this stone pool below the spring, and I cry out for her to help me.

'Auntie, are the lizards moving? Why are the stones moving?' I cry out.

She shushes me and calms me and touches my hot face and then eases me down to the floor. I feel the wet of the water splashing over the stone bowl. She presses her hands to my chest, as it to make the devils in me come out.

'Let them out if they want to come out,' and pulls her hands away.

She calms me again. 'Listen to me, Ceadd. Stop. It is me, Vinda. You know me. Your heart is running faster than a horse runs. The devils are not in you. The devils are in other places but not in you...'

She presses both hands onto my chest above my heart to stop the pain of the galloping horse dragging me to exhaustion and a death by bursting apart. 'You are in fever. You are not well. I don't know if what I know will save you, but there is one thing I know, if you don't do as I say, you'll almost certainly die. If you do as I say, there's a chance you won't die.'

She motions for me to get up and puts her heavy arms around my shoulders and tries to lift me.

'I'm glad it's so early. It may be that no one sees us.'

We hobble off together to her hut. I can hear the other beck of Godmunthingaham whistling past us, as we cross it to her cottage. She lays me down on her bed. It smells as always of pine around her doorway and inside of lavender.

She brings me water in an ancient beaker of metal.

'I think you've been poisoned,' and stands above me. 'Take this with your water. If you're sick, I'll leave you this pail. Eat all of it.'

She turned to go away. Crumbly black powder on a platter of wood.

'What is this?' I ask her.

But she's gone out of the door. My head's swimming and my heart is trying to catch the hare while the waves of thick, blanket sickness cover me and make me sweat and drip saliva. I scoop up large clumps of the black powder and force them down. Charcoal. I force down three more fingerfuls with gulps of water from the beaker and then lay back, waiting for the sign of death to show itself clearly and allow me end to this suffering. Off I drift into a sort of sleep, and don't know how long I am there before I wake with a spewing that spurts all over the cottage floor. It's black and vile and smells so foul that I do it again and again. I hang like that for ten minutes, on all fours, retching and crying out for air, then sobbing with the force of the spewing. The minutes pass, and carefully I wilt down into the bed, wiping away the saliva one last time, before I drift off into a sleep.

When I wake, the room is clean and the pail cleaned out. No sound except sheep and pigs, but not nearby. I lie, wet and wrapped and shaking but not deathly, not in fever, not racing with the horses anymore but exhausted, with only a rough pain in my stomach and throat and a wide ache in my chest, like after a blow from a blunt instrument. I rest like this till she comes in again, half-awake.

'You have a strong heart, Ceadd,' she said. 'Very strong. You also have strong enemies. Do you know that?'

'I have good friends, Vinda. Maybe stronger than my enemies.'

She stands in the doorway, holding swathes of cut wild garlic.

'Are you hungry?'

'For those, no,' I said, pointing at the garlic leaves.

'Good,' she said, 'then you will live. But fate is chasing you these days, Ceadd, since I have heard that King Edwin, his men and his priests and the Latins came to the temples here yesterday. There was much shouting as they are wont. He asked after you and he was curious to know where you had got to. I could not say, Ceadd, I did not know that you were lying in the woods, blackened like a beaten dog, and I could not say to the King himself if you were amongst the living or had left this world for reasons, light or dark, fair or...' and she trails off.

After a long pause, while she cuts the garlic and puts some in her mouth. 'Who would do this to you, Ceadd? I cannot think that the King knows.'

'I need all my strength to speak with Edwin,' I said, 'he will have to wait till I can go before his company.'

'Go before the All-meet is over, Ceadd, to Edwin. People have come from every corner of his kingdom and all are now here, enemies and friends alike, to hear what he has to say. You must be there to make sure your words are among the last he hears, before he makes the wrong decision. Hear his words, Ceadd and make them hear yours. You speak with the care of your father.' She paused and looked me up and down, 'Catch him before he starts drinking.'

I don't speak. I feel raw-mouthed and weak. Once, when I was a child with my father in Gwynedd, we helped a fisherman, tossed in the waves for half an hour, fight for his life on the beach. We couldn't get the water out of his lungs quickly enough for him to catch his breath. My father had the strength of a bear and still couldn't wrench the water out, nor force the breath back in him and he died in his arms. I have felt that same exhaustion of battling for life and all I want to do is to sleep.

'Eat. This bread is dry and will not cause you to spew again. And drink this. Edwin must not think you have been drinking.'

She passes me the beaker full of cool water and passes her hand over the offering, to remind us both of where it came from. She sits and watches me, all the while I eat.

We do not speak as the manner of the old ways dictates. The harmed man lives by other rules. After I finish, she doesn't rise to take it away, but starts to speak as if she has much thought to share, and has long been thinking of such things.

'Is there any hearth anywhere in this world for us to warm ourselves when we are old?' she asks. I have to ask her what she means, since she is using the strange forms of the language of the Men of the North. 'I can't say if even the trees are listening and telling tales in these times, Ceadd.'

'I am always so far from home that every hearth is home.' I try to use her words and they seem strange on my tongue.

'My father remembers these Angles coming here, up our little valley, from the south. Then, they started coming here from the north as well. He used to tell me tales of the last Latins who were in their army. He claimed to have met them and been able to talk to them. He said that they were the men who were not men, but more than men, giants who left stone walls higher than oaks, roads as wide as rivers and had more gold under their dragon flags than is now left in the whole of the Island of Britain.'

'I've heard this, many times, from many people, Vinda. But what is this to me, now? They're here, they fight with everyone. They fight each other. The Latins – the *real* Latins – are gone.'

'But the new ones are worse.' Her voice flies at me. 'As my father said, they came with their swords and emperors and their taxes and their men with paper and their measuring of every kind, but these new ones are worse. They are worse than all the armies put together, sent from Rome.'

I let her speak and lay back to ease my discomforts.

'You have travelled with Edwin for several seasons now, you have seen how he has grown and changed. He sought refuge with your father in Gwynedd. He learnt some civilities with your family and with your people. He came out of that time a better man.'

'You're kind and speak well of my family. I shall tell them of your special kindness, Vinda, when I return. They shall honour you, in the old ways,' I said, calmly.

'May you live for them, Ceadd, may you live for them long. But you are a poet, you master the language of these Angles and Northumbrians. You can set words together that make them laugh, you know their wordcraft.'

'It is much simpler than ours,' I said.

'Yes, but not everyone can. You make them listen. I remember you with the King and I knew he held you dear, although old friends become something else when a man gains authority. But I've seen something else since you arrived here.'

I wait for her time.

'You have heard everyone has made enemies amongst them. I have heard say that they envy, that you, a foreigner in our own kingdom, could make the King dance with your thoughts and how he let his power become your power.' She sways on her haunches.

'Think on it. The Latins, with their words like slippery rocks and how they leap from one to the next without pause for breath. How they have such fire in their hearts for burning and destruction, and when they speak out about devils and evil and set such fear into the hearts of our people, of everyone. They are full of madness that they have learnt in their book. They shout it from every hillock and large stone. If you reply with a simple thought, they foam and they rage and they pull out their hair and they shout that you are to be seized and to be drowned or burnt. That is not enough for them, Ceadd – they say that once you're dead from their stones and blows there's another sort of death that is much worse – like an everlasting death, where you suffer death every day, but are somehow kept alive to suffer your new death. Think on it properly, Ceadd. I ask you – is this the ways of our people?'

She recedes back to give me air to consider her words. Time passes between us, sufficient for the fullness of her words to become in me good words.

'For twenty, maybe more generations, the Latins came and built their houses and sent their soldiers to take our possessions when they willed it. At times, there was peace between us and them. At times of wars, there was slaughter and blood on both sides. But never did they try to take our minds. Never did they try to make our hearths like their hearths. Never did they strip us of the things no one can own. These new Latins with their devouring god do this, heedlessly.'

'Speak with Edwin, Ceadd. Speak for your people, not just for now, but forever. Think of all the ways we love the earth – not with books and foaming mouths and rules and shouting and tearing at clothes and the force that wrecks men's minds but think of our ways of loving the earth and honouring the spirits of all living things and all dead things.'

She pauses and takes a stem of wild garlic. 'Think of all the bards before you and the stories that they will poison and think on our old ways. Look at us now, speaking in the ways of our dead fathers being pushed back to the other side of our land, because we trust no one.

'Think of the hearth that you knew, Ceadd, the hearth that is your birthright. Of your place before the people, to fill them with the majesty of being part of this world, not in fear of everything for fear of madmen with their books,' and she began to iang from the old songs, the low keening barely moving amongst the notes:

Mountain snow,
Frost on graves,
Stones cover our fires
Our kinsmen on a covered path

And so, I joined her in the song of watching the world pass before us into something changed, and we sang out our birthright, songs that would bind everyone in our people as tight as rods of forged steel, the singing that takes the way when speaking has no usefulness:

The mountain snow
The waters rising through ice
The men of our hearth
Longing for the feuds
To cease, the warm hearth

The mountain snow
Strong our arms and shoulder
Shield laid for the first crops
The sun shines on the lake

The mountain snow
Has gone in rags over the hill...

...and we sang on, hovering in that space that is lighter than our bodies, where communion of thoughts can help us understand everything that is to be shared. As we sang more, I drift onto my back and close my eyes and feel the touch of lightness like angels' wings carrying lavender and balm to my forehead and nostrils around my temples and the tilting of my head to drink honey-flavoured water. The taste was not the sweet water I had tasted before but something else, unfamiliar to my tongue and charging my mouth with an urge to repel it, but I can hear Vinda's voice soothing, like a lullaby for a child,

'Drink, drink and chase the memories, follow the shadows where they take you, like dogs with the scent, follow the source of your thoughts to all the places you could have been to the centre of the dark wood where the doers of this evil are, to where the place this evil lies and who did this, Ceadd, sleep and dream to see who did this and you will know what to do, to those who would have you dead, let the memories lead you into the darkest places and the light into the pathless woods and remember all, remember all, let the memories receive you...'

So, I drifted off to sleep, as she eased the balm of herbs around my fading mind and the casing of my thoughts, around my temples, skull and my eyes and ears.

Seven days earlier

"It is told such peace there is in Britain, where King Edwin's word extended, that a woman with her new-born babe might walk throughout the island, from sea to sea, without receiving any harm.' My father's words to remind me I would be safe. I shielded my eyes when he spoke, so fierce was the spring sun.

'Go to Edwin and give him warm greetings and tell him we wish him well from our people here and are keen to hear what he has to say. Entreat him to be as wise as to consider the words of each man equal. I know you will find the words, Ceadd, but do not let him do anything in haste and moderate his recklessness, for the sake of all of us.'

'I will remind him of the many times you spoke to him and me when we grew up together here, in Gwynedd, father. How the fate of so much lies in his hands.'

We both knew, however, that steering Edwin to the wiser

course was like riding two horses at once. It would depend on the hour, or the shape, of the moon which part of the man would take what, as counsel.

'You'll have company, Ceadd, but we'll follow you in spirit, as well. Return as soon as you can.'

Then he paused. 'You wear the red cloak because you are the blood of this royal house. I want to see you in it, coming over the estuary like the Dragon of the Islands, your great, great, grandfather, Maelgwn, King of Gwynedd and –'

'Great, great, great-grandfather, father, you forgot the third great – there are five generations between me and King Maelgwn of Gwynedd...'

'Your mother says that the sooner you go, the sooner you will be back. Make haste. Go. Come back safe. Go, go...' and he nodded to my two companions, Cadog and Idnerth.

The wind carried his words past me and whipped the cloak around my legs, and I scanned the walls of my father's house and thought I could see a pair of eyes staring out of the darkness, but in this light, in this wind, I could hardly be sure. One last time, I turned to take in the view from high up here, of the sea to the north and the river to the west, glittering into the mountains to the south. Below, I could hear the wind striking the rocks of the shore like the smith. The woods were coming into leaf and the birds were busy finding mates, and I felt the beat of the day as we took the steep path down from the hill of my father's house, now the King's house, to the road above the beach.

For two days we travelled. The spring wind brought in good weather until we crossed the Dyfrdwy where we took ferry with a boy whose father was sick. We are used to it, but once the rain starts the roads become muddy. Every year the roads gets worse, the old stones looser, the gaps bigger, the bridges weaker. We tire more easily with the effort of staying on the road, the nights are fiercely cold in the rain, and we sleep where we can.

One morning Idnerth doesn't wake up. When we go to him, he is fevered and clammy and his teeth chatter and he will not rouse. The rain is falling like from an upturned bucket.

'Cadog, we cannot stay here in this weather. We must get him to shelter. I reckon we're just three or four miles from the old fort at Rigodun. If we can get him there, we can leave him with someone.'

'There are few people who'll help since the wars,' he replied.

'Well, we cannot leave him here. Come, lift his legs, we will carry him between us. An hour's march away, at most.'

In the distance, I could see the line of the big moors against the grey, swirling sky and the road rising slowly to a gap in the mountains. Somewhere on our left, in a broad hollow before the road swings upwards steeply to the right, should be the place I had in mind. I hoped it was only an hour away in this rain. Carrying Idnerth was exhausting and we began to rest every few hundred paces.

Rigodun. Where we had been welcomed before, before my father became king when I was maybe twelve or thirteen, and it was my first expedition outside Gwynedd.

Twenty years ago. The memories come flooding back. Twenty years have passed since I was here. All those years ago, but time leads us down such narrow roads:

We were only a small band and we had horses to make the best speed. I remember asking, 'Father, why do we have extra horses?' and I remember the question getting lost in the wind, as his eyes took in the whole scene of our home and lands, on that rock above the river and the sea. No-one there to say goodbye, as he insisted. Just the eyes, perhaps, of my retreating mother, as she melted into the darkness she favoured.

In my mind. we flew along the coast, crossed the Dyfrdwy and within less than two days we arrived at Rigodun, the sun setting on our backs and warming us as we made our way up the same road as this. Smoke and red roofs we saw, and children running in the fields and horses grazing. Then, I saw the walls: huge, grey and black and the towering pillars of a formidable gateway. But, where there once in the time of the Latins would have been stone, was now a simple wooden crosspiece linking the stone, that looked temporary and quickly thrown together.

As we came into view, I remember the children shouting and rushing for the gateway, the horses agitated and shinnying and men appearing from the huts and on top of the walls, some with spears and others running to hastily gather shields and swords. My father stood up on his horse, 'In peace, in peace, do not be afraid...' then in one moment he astounds me when he switched to a language I had never heard him or anyone else speak, and he bellows out strange, harsh words and waves and shouts what must be greetings, and even though they are two or three hundred yards away they reply. I am astounded that they drop their weapons and walk open-armed towards us. When we are much closer, he shouts what must be names and I hear them shout his name, Cadwallon, back. But so strange was their pronunciation that if I did not know him myself I would not know their saying of his name...and this was how we arrived in Rigodun, more than twenty years ago.

By the time we reached the gateway we were surrounded by a crowd of women, children and dogs, whilst the men waited to form a guard to greet us as we passed into the courtyard and inside those huge, black walls. I can see my father as if it were yesterday, more strange than I had ever seen him before, everything that I had ever known about him had gone. All his actions, his smile, his face, even, was shifted into other forms, as he spoke this strange tongue to these people who we did not know, who clearly revered him with all honours fit for a leader and a king. I wanted to know who he was and why I had never seen this version of him before. Since my last question to him had been the one he had ignored at the start of our journey, I had not dared ask him another, but now I had even more. Why had we started this dangerous journey? Who were these people? Why had we come to this lost, unlovely spot under these dark mountains, away from the sea and the light of our home?

Before we could enter the courtyard, they took our gear and set the horses out to a separate pasture. They had clearly been expecting us, because food was being prepared and tables set for a feast, and they bade us sit. The roughness of their cups to my lips and the freshness of the wood was something I have carried with me for all these days, as was the first taste ever in my life of their ale, sharp and bitter and not sweet like our mead, which they drank and made them louder still, almost instantaneously. Very soon we were being backslapped, cheered and toasted and still no food had been served. Whilst I was thinking of home and how we would never have done this to honoured guests, all I could do was sit in wonder and watch my father at the head of the table match their leaders, mix with them like an old friend and make them laugh with every utterance as they made him laugh with the loudest guffaws I had ever heard come from his mouth. All the time the women served this ale, and I felt myself slide into a place of smiling stupidity and inarticulacy, and watched the sun set far away in the sloping west.

As the light faded, I remember thinking, why are there no smoking fires, no roofs, no sounds, no sign of anything close or far that resembles the things that are everywhere in our Gwynedd, that makes us love what we have and share? In the darkness, the flames roared up and the laughter died down and the food was cleared, and the men and women gathered together to talk and tell stories, when I felt an arm under my shoulder, and I was pulled to my feet. I wanted to resist but I had drunk too much, and I was pulled gently behind the benches and placed at my father's side. Someone had already begun his song as the others around him shouted for quiet. My father pulled me close, as I sat down. 'Know them' he said, in our tongue, 'watch them, drink with them, this is what they are.'

In the morning, the ravens in my head were pecking at my eyes and what was behind them. I must have fallen asleep, unnoticed, because I woke between two huge creatures who turned simultaneously, so I always had a great brush of a beard in my face, no matter which way I turned. When I tried to get up, everything whirled me round and I fell over and threw up all over the feet of one of the huge creatures, but he didn't notice. My mouth ached for water and tasted like I had eaten refuse. I slunk away out of the hall as quickly as I could, hearing barely a snore or a sound. Outside, the air hit me like a cold slap, last night's warmth had been replaced by a drizzly, fresh chill that pierced my tunic. I was glad, this was good. Just what I needed. From the well, I drank and drank and then sank my head several times in the bucket. When I came up for air, there was a face in the mirror of the water, one that was not mine.

'We must move, Ceadd, very quickly. Do not speak, just listen.' It was my father with his ear pressed to mine, hissing the words at me. The smell of the Northumbrian ale was still on his breath. 'News has come that means we have to move very quickly. I want you to get your horse with our men over there, prepare to leave and leave nothing behind. Leave nothing behind. Tell the men. Within half an hour we have to be meeting the horizon,' and pointed back the way we came. With that, he pushed me roughly towards our men, who had gathered around a bench. I did not have the mental power to speak or ask, I just did what I was told.

'We must get the horses. Do not leave anything behind. Come.' I sent two of them off to check our gear and baggage.

There were two men at the gateway, but they did nothing, as we stepped through the already opened gate. As I turned to look at where my father had gone, I saw now how much the first image of the place of the huge, grey-black walls was only partly true. There were also gaps and cracks in the masonry, places where the walls were leaning perilously close to falling except for some makeshift supports holding them up; stunted trees grew into the base of the walls and inside, the roofs were leaning and losing tiles, some of the buildings were open to the rain, and water sat in stale pools, slowly receiving the soft drip of this September shower. The feeling of abandonment made me glad we were leaving so suddenly.

Outside, on the shaded side of the fortress, were small huts and houses, nothing like we have, but roughly constructed. People stood in gardens making ready for the day or in their doorways, staring as we walked past, the good mood of yesterday had evaporated but throwing stares or nods or nothing at us, as we walked out to the paddocks, where they had put our horses.

'What has happened? Why is everything changed?' I asked Cynon, one of my father's old companions.

'You will see. We all will see. But I have challenged your father at the wisdom of his plan.'

'Is there a plan?' I asked.

'There is always a plan, young man, but whether it is a plan that has sense is another thing.' Then, he was off, bridling the horses with the other men.

I did as I was told. I was ready to set off and take the path we had come by and reach the horizon with the hour and was waiting on my horse outside the gateway, ignoring the stares of the local people. Cynon padded up to me, holding his huge horse, with a hand curled around his ear, like it was a child.

'Ready?'

'Surely,' I said.

'Are you sure? I think you might regret leaving in this condition?' and smiled as he said it.

He leaned towards me. '*Hasta, tua hasta...*' I was so surprised that I didn't at first recognise the Roman words. 'Your spear...'

'*O, duwia mawr!*' I leapt off my pony and ran back to the courtyard, cursing myself and my carelessness, cursing all the while and hoping that my father never found out. I rushed into the hall where we had eaten and drunk and listened to the old stories and songs. It was still completely quiet, and I searched all the places where I could remember I had been last night but found nothing. I stopped for a moment and tried to remember what exactly had happened when we arrived last night and what order we had done things – the horses, the gear, the greetings, the food... They had taken our gear and our weapons before we had started the feast.

I stalked back outside as silently as I could, not wanting to disturb the sleepers. Around the courtyard were lots of smaller rooms, and I thought that somewhere there must be our stock of things. There was a strangeness in the air, as if some black fire or fantastic beasts were about to come over the horizon, or out of the air, any moment now. The ale these people drank did not settle the mind.

So, I stepped carefully around the fallen tiles and masonry of the inner wall of the fortress, feeling like a thief and I knew not exactly why. Where there was a door, I pushed it gently, looking for the spears stacked up and the few pieces of baggage we brought for the journey. Nothing in the first one, just broken, dusty pots and cobwebs. Nothing in the next two. I stepped lightly over the fallen earth and pushed the door of the next room aside. I heard a voice, but in the instant it took to get used to the dark, I saw no one to produce a voice. Where? I cursed my befuddlement, this was not like me. What is happening? Am I hearing these things? I heard the voice again, hissing this time in that yawning, hissing way of geese that I have come to know so well. I stepped into the dark, as lightly as a hunting cat and settled into the space, making myself part of the space.

The voices were in the next room, and now I could hear everything that was being said, except I could not understand one word. Then, my heart leapt again as I heard words I could not make out come from a voice as familiar as my own. It was my father's. At first, I thought I should leave this room and announce my presence to him by going to the room next door, but something told me to stay still, do nothing, wait.

Listen, find a sign.

Soundlessly, I stepped across the beaten earth floor. To the right, and high up, was a fallen roof beam that was now leaning against the opposite wall. It left a gap between this room and the next when it had fallen all those years ago. I just needed something to stand on and I would be able to see what was going on. In the darkest corner of the room was a small table, which I could move into position if I was very careful. I stood for what seemed like an age, trying to picture the scene next door and then chose my moment to pick the thing up and move it to below the gap between the two walls. For one terrible minute I thought I was going to let it slip and trip just before I could manage to set it down, but I did it. Slowly and breathlessly, I eased myself up onto the table, hoping it would bear my weight and hardly dare extend my full height, in case what I saw was something too awful.

Through the gap left by the rotten beam, I can look down at a steep angle into the room next door. It's dark and cramped, apart from a slit of light coming from a half-broken window in the back wall that just about illuminates the scene. There is a man with his back to the outer wall, and he is holding a knife to the throat of someone who is taller than him by several inches, but the person being held has their face covered by some sacking. The knife-holder is sweating and is having to bend the body of the person he is holding, and it looks faintly ridiculous, since he also appears to be supporting this person without letting the knife slip too near the throat, as he holds him in place. All the time there is low, threatening hissing and shouting in the language of the Northumbrians. My father has his back to me. I curse my lack of knowledge about what they are saying. Out of sight, but also facing my father, there must be another man, because I can see the dangerous end of a spear pointed very close to my father's chest, and in return he has his hands raised so that they can see he has no weapon.

Out of the darkness comes a bag of money, jingled provocatively by the spear holder, and my father speaks in calm terms and with gestures for everyone to put their weapons down, and he makes a gesture with his hand near his head, as if it's time everyone started to think before they do anything very unnecessary and stupid. The unseen man has a deep voice, perhaps even with a foreign accent, even though my understanding is almost non-existent, it sounds like he is struggling to express himself and I can tell my father is listening intently to him, as if he too, is struggling to understand everything he says. This seems to frustrate the spear-holder who starts jabbing the spear closer and closer to my father's chest, and after a few of these threatening moves, the end of the spear catches my father's tunic and it rips. With that, they force him to his knees with shouting and the spear pressed into his chest, slowly turning on its point to produce blood. The whole thing is happening so quickly, and with so much being said, that I don't understand. I'm just helpless and angry, still cursing the slowness of my thoughts.

I sidle down from my perch and step soundlessly out of this room, hoping that if they haven't noticed my so far, then I may have a chance. The courtyard is deserted, and for the first time I notice the gate is closed. But I cannot see the guards. It's as if the whole world has left this place to rot. I need to get out of here without being seen and I need to do it very quickly.

I'm desperately trying to remember anything I can of the layout of the camp: the walls, the doors, the access points. The hall. If I can get in the hall, there is bound to be a window or a door out on the outer-side. But when I get there, the hall is locked from the outside and there is only the gentle sound of people sleeping inside. At least from here I cannot be seen by anyone. I walk along the side of the building and then, all of a sudden, I stub my toe against something really hard. It takes all my strength to not cry out. I look and there in the grass is a short ladder, unused for months, judging by the length of the grass that concealed it, and I pick it up and lean it against the sloping inner roof of the courtyard and within an instant I'm up on the roof tiles as light as the wind and walk up to the outer-wall, where there are some remains of ramparts. Just before I jump, I make a note of which of the rooms my father must be in. When I step off the wall, although it must be more than twice my height, the landing on the soft, springy moorland turf is easy.

Everything sounds the same. I run along the outer wall and in my haste, I miss the shallow run off and pit that must be used as the outlet for the latrines, and splash my way knee deep into and out of the foul sludge in an instant, but the smell makes me retch. Another hundred yards, and I approach the corner very carefully. Straightaway, I catch Cynon, looking anxiously in my direction and our eyes meet. I put my finger to my mouth, and he looks away. I thought he hadn't noticed and was about to hiss his name when he spoke something to one of our boys, who were now all assembled around our horses, and he walks over to me as if excusing himself for a piss. Like every good soldier, he never puts his spear down. He walks over to me, already moving his tunic and his cloak, to relieve himself, unimpeded.

By the time he gets to the corner, I can hardly make the

words come out in any order, my breath will not stay with me long enough. He puts his spear down. I force the words out.

'Do not speak, do not do anything except the piss and then go back. Listen for a shout very soon, in our language and be ready with your weapons and watch the guards,' I said.

I don't wait for him to speak or ask, but as I run up the side of the fort, I check he has understood and as if nothing at all was wrong in the world, he finishes his business, and slowly and casually, rearranges his outerwear. The only difference is he no longer has his spear. The rain is still drizzling and there's a very fine mist, as if everything is closing in around us. I can move silently in these conditions, but around the final corner my heart is banging like a smith's mallet.

Looking down the line of that wall, I calculate roughly where would be the room that my father is in. I knew I didn't have much time and begin to run, bent very low down, pressed against the wall and counting every pace I took. When I felt I was twenty paces away I try to remember exactly what it is I'm looking for. Slowly now, on my belly, I crawl along the wall to the first little slit of a window and strain to hear any voices. Nothing, no sound, so I crawl on, barely allowing myself to breathe. Then, ahead I can hear what sounded like scraping or scratching and stopped.

The mist is now coming down in big, soft waves and there is almost total silence. I wait.

Inch by inch, I move forward to the little window, that at this point, is just half a man's height above ground because of the slope where the outer rampart had collapsed. I strain to hear the sound of conversation. Slowly, I move myself to within a hair's breadth of being able to just look around the corner of the window. There is the sound of one voice, saying what, I do not know, but repeating something in the face of my father, whilst the knife-holder is now breathing with even more strain and I can see the back of his little red head rocking slowly, backwards and forwards, with the strain of his sagging burden. My father has his eyes forced upwards, as the spear point was pressed deeply into the soft flesh under his throat, whilst the eyes of the spearman are concentrated completely on taming the resistance of my father. For one moment, his eyes flash as he sees me place the spear at the best angle and seems to understand that if he is to survive, he must act like lightning striking.

With all my nerve, I line up the spear in perfect sight of the man holding the knife to the Hooded Man's throat, and with all my might, I stick it perfectly and venomously to enter the skull above the ear and to move through the brain instantaneously, and emerge somewhere near the left eye or below. As soon as it did so, I would remove it for fear of catching the poor victim wearing the hood. Even before the spear has moved one thumb's length, my father gestures with his head and eyes to the window where I have appeared, and in the instant that the spearman looks away, he is up on his feet and smashes his elbow into his tormentor's ear and then wrestles his spear from him. As the knife-holder's knees buckle, the victim in the sacking hood also falls, with shock and in instinctive self-protection, and all three end up in a pile in the floor.

My father hisses at me to grab the hand of the hooded one and pushed him through the window and turns to pierce the former owner of the spear in the space between his eyes with his own weapon, then pulls himself through the window, with my help.

'Move,' he said, to us both, bent double and breathless. 'Move, as if the hounds of death are coming for you...' and he pushes me and pulls the Hooded One along the wall of the fort to the place at the gate where our men are waiting.

He hoists me onto my horse and hoists the hooded one onto the back of his own and tells Cynon to take watch at the rear of our small party and with a silent command we are off, raising wet soil in wild lumps as we ride off down the way we had come.

Not one word from anyone for five hours. Hours riding the upper road to avoid Mamucium, the place we call Manceinion, leaving it well to the south, stopping only to rest the horses and water ourselves. Cadwallon had asked for peace, and we honoured his command. And as the day wore on, the day grew brighter and the rain and drizzle lifted, unconsciously.

It was as if the spirits themselves were watching us and we could not commit to our existence with words that anyone could hear and pass on. Overnight, this had turned into enemy territory, and I could feel the urgency of leaving these lands, in my father's face. We could not admit we had ever been here, and we could not name ourselves or anything about us, for fear of the spirits.

At last, as the sun was setting, and the insects hovered, and the swallows wheeled in the silent air, we turned off the highway off to the right, to higher ground. Below us was a river, and the bats were already up and down, ploughing the hidden fields of midges and moths under the canopy of trees along the waterway. Wretched with exhaustion, we dismounted and pulled ourselves off the road. My father dismounted more slowly, and picked up his charge and sat him down on a milestone, before he took three of the men on foot and set off up the bank towards a holt of trees tucked into a little hollow, nearly out of sight.

I could not help but stare that the Hooded One made no move to remove the covering on his head. He was not bound and did not have any signs of bloodshed or violence on his clothes. For the first time, I was able to see he was tall and gangly, judging from his thin, stooped chest and shoulders, he was not a man used to guiding a plough or holding his own with weapons. He sat silently and folded his long hands into the folds of his cloak and seemed almost more at peace in his hooded state, like a hawk perhaps, who trusting his master can relax, undisturbed by the horror and beauty of the visual world.

'Cynon, go and check the outlook from the top of the hill behind the trees. Make sure we are not going to be surprised from there,' said Cadwallon. 'Here will be as good as any for tonight.' He spoke to us as he stood on the bank above us, on the paved road. 'Ceadd, take some of the horses to the river for water. Gwion, help him. Then, bind them and let them eat.'

We laid down without a fire or song. I heard my father set the order for guards: change every two hours, two men with the horses, two men on watch above the trees on the brow of the hill. Last watch to rouse the men just before dawn to make the Dyfrdwy well before the sun sets tomorrow.

And home and safety.

In the very last light of dawn, I heard my father, not far away from me, mutter to the Hooded One, but couldn't catch his words, and I swear that the long, slender fingers moved upwards to push the covering off his face and off his head, but I could not swear to it truly, nor did I see his face, for the dark had swallowed the light, and here in this little valley, the dark had swallowed us.

When I awoke the next morning, I was the last to rise and my father almost pulled me up. Not one word had he spoken to me still, except to command me like one of his men. They were all mounted and waiting to move off. I stumbled up and grabbed my horse and rolled on to his broad back, grateful for his forgiving nature.

All was unchanged from yesterday. We rode in silence. I rode in the middle of the group just behind my father and thus, just behind the Hooded One. We rode more deliberately this time, less anxious of what was behind us, less anxious of what was in front of us. But still the signs of devastation were there: the farms burnt out, the corpses of some dead cow or dog, half-devoured by wolves and crows, fields of crops going to waste or seeing one lonely figure far off, trying to harvest a whole field and looking lost, almost drowned. We saw no crowds of families, or groups of neighbours singing as they worked, or standing in groups to make a heavy task light, no, this was a borderland again, patchy, damaged, uneven, unclear. It felt dangerous on this side of our river and yet we had ridden with such purpose and focus, albeit on a different route, but only twenty miles to the south, on our way here, but this felt like a different country.

It was well we did not speak, for by mid-morning the hand of our leading rider rose, and we slid off our horses like snakes off their rocks. The air was taut like a drum, and we were in a broad valley that was still well-forested, only pierced by this old Rhufeinig road. Gwion's father, Gwythyr, the oldest of my father's friends, turned at the head of our column and signed with his hands, *A small group, thieves, probably, marching at speed, five or six hundred yards away, out of sight but moving towards us...*

Cadwallon signed back. *Turn, no fight, mount up and find a place in the woods to hide, quickly. Go*, he waved, *turn and go.*

And was on his horse again, wading through us to take the lead. Within moments, we were moving at that distinctive pace our horses had that was one pace below a gallop. They would see our tracks, but in the confusion of the going and the coming, and in their haste not to be caught by mounted men, they would move through this narrow strait as quickly as we wanted to move the other way.

After two or three minutes of this urgency, no more, my father turned and signed again, *Keep going, keep going...every twenty paces file off, one right, one left, find dark place to hide, wait for signal ten minutes after they've gone...*

We nodded and began to file off, one discreetly at a time to the right, one to the left, one to the right, then me to the left, across the small ditch, through the bracken and the high wayside grass and into the deep anonymity of the woods. Once I had gone fifty paces into the woods, the sounds dimmed and the light closed in and it was easier to slide off the horse and lead him through the trees, ducking as I went and winding around the back of the low hill that on the other side let the road slide along it. I stopped when I could hear nothing and see no sign of the road. I tied the horse to a tree and slowly picked my way, making no sound, back to where I had sight of the road.

I waited for a minute or two, thinking I had missed them since there was no sound at all, just a few goldfinches flitting colourfully around, and somewhere on the other side of the road, a woodpecker emphasising the silence with a ghostly, rapid *drddrdrdrrddddd* of his beak. Then, silence again.

The birds darted and danced closer and closer to me, forgetting that once I had moved. I suddenly felt very exposed here in my little viewpoint above the road. I should have stayed further away, gone deeper into the woods, lost myself, so as not to endanger my companions. I knew that moving would be the worst thing to do and I sat hoping that these men would simply pass through and we could get to the river and return home.

Above me I heard a crack, the unmistakable sound, of a twig being broken. Not the sound of a deer or a badger scratching in the leaves or scuttling quickly as they do on their foraging runs, no, this was the weight of a human cracking a twig in this early autumn forest. I froze because the sound came from above me. How had he got there? Why was he there? Was I visible from where he stood? I had expected everything to appear before me, not come at me from above or behind.

I shrank down into the earth as slowly as a leaf drying. I focused on him and all the sounds he could make: his breathing, his walking, the movement of his arms and neck to avoid the branches and the fallen trees, the fear he would carry. His fear would carry before him. I closed my eyes the better to picture him. He walked very slowly, like someone who was expecting danger, he moved awkwardly, as if he was carrying something that made him shift his weight often, he breathed heavily like a man who has not done this sort of thing for a while, and once or twice, he slipped and cursed, but not in our language.

Ahead of me, two hundred paces, I began to hear the sounds of men whispering to one another. Gwythyr had said a small group coming our way, but what I heard coming was not a small group. I tried to imagine how many of them there were, just by sound. Fifteen, maybe more. At least one above me and surely the same on the other side of the road, in the trees. That's nearly double our number. We would be lucky to escape with our lives.

I shrank into my space between two trees and in a hollow of leaves and exposed roots, but I opened one eye to watch what I had only heard so far: outdoor men, not walking, more like wrestlers bracing for the rush, knees bent, weapons at the ready – staves, knives, a bow, an old javelin – these were the weapons they carried, one even had a sling and was ready to fire a stone. Behind them, guarded by a little rear-guard of their own, were some women and children, unkempt, cowed into silence, dragging their feet as if they were tired of walking like this. On the slope above them, on the other side of the road, were two men with bows looking this way and that and gesturing at the group below to keep together, to keep going. I urged them on as well, silently, fiercely, *keep going...just keep going.*

Above me, the sounds grew closer and closer, even as I sank into the hollow and embraced the earth and the roots of the ancient tree. He stopped no more than three paces above the tree. I could hear his breathing and the ruffles of his clothes as he moved slowly, looking for clues and danger. Then a shout, as he lost his footing and slipped. I could feel the echoes of his weight slamming against the tree come down the roots to my little hiding place and feel the *Ufffgggh* of his breath as he stopped himself with his chest and arm around the trunk. If he hadn't grabbed the trunk as he did and released the weapon in his hand, he would have landed right on top of me. The men below shouted, and I could feel their gazes and fears, even though I could not see one face, the focus of their energies was like a deadly spear and he shouted back with words I did not understand. For as long as I could, I did not breathe, and for as long as I did not breathe, he stood above me and steadied himself on this treacherous forest floor. He shook his hand a few times, which he had obviously bruised, before bending down only an arm's length away to reach for his bow. I was as still as the winter corpse, but I felt him stare for longer than I thought I could bear, before shaking his hand and blowing away the dirt and the leaves, he set off down the hill towards his companions, obviously thinking that the flat, paved road was a safer bet.

When they left, I put my face in the earth and blew out a storm's worth of air, gasping like a diver who has been down for far too long. I blew so hard that I felt faint and light-headed and raised myself up, and then gasped and rattled for air, like someone in my grandmother's stories dying of the plague. I knew I must wait for the signal and I knew not what I would do if the signal did not come. But it did not come.

Then, I saw Cynon passed on the road in silence, like any normal traveller and I wanted to cry out, but I didn't. I watched him pass. Then, silence again. And the goldfinches twittering and the sound of the woodpecker, all oblivious to what had just passed. *Such it is, this life*, I heard the old monkish Irishman my father employed to write things in books, say in my head, *Such it is, this life.* Whatever happens to each one of us would take more pages than there are leaves on the forest floor to tell.

And then Cynon came riding back, and out of the darkening

woods came each of our men silently, one after another, and we took our place, as if nothing had happened.

Two days later, we rode into Deganwy just after the sun had set. My father had spoken to me on our last day of riding.

'Ceadd, whatever has happened is not to be spoken of amongst men, or at home, do you understand? We will arrive home just after dark, as if we have simply been out fishing on the river. In fact, we will stop a few miles from home and fish so that we can account for ourselves well. You will say your words to your mother, and we will eat, then rest. Whatever you have seen or done is...' he hesitated, 'to be spoken of later.'

And so we did. We fished only an hour from home, caught some fresh salmon and perch and gained admittance from the watchman at our home, said our greetings to our mother and our household and we ate, in discussion of the harvests at home and the prospects for the winter and its preparations.

The Hooded One was out of my mind almost as soon as we arrived, and I thought nothing of who he was or what we had done. This was why my father, Cadwallon, was King of Gwynedd and respected throughout all the territories we neighboured and honoured with the kings of Powys and Deheubarth and even amongst the Mercians under Penda and Cearl and even further, to the places that I still did not understand. He had reasons for journeying so far out of our lands and bringing back this boy to live amongst us.

One morning, a month later, before *Calan Gaeaf*, I came to my father's table, after feeding and cleaning out the horses and there was a stranger at our table. In my place. My mother bid me sit next to him, and to do it in silence. I saw his hands first, the same long fingers I had seen before, reaching for the bread, as if it were something precious. My eyes followed his hands bring the bread to his board and then to his mouth. I caught my mother telling me with her eyes not to stare, as she often would.

‘Ceadd, serve Edwin whatever he will take to drink.’

I rose, as I always did when she spoke like that, in an instant.

‘What will you have?’ I asked him. He did not respond.

‘Ceadd,’ she said, as if I were looking to make trouble, ‘how can he understand our language? You must help him, as we always help a stranger.’

I stood like a fool, with a jug in my hand in front of them all. I was angry that we had gone through such troubles and dangers to bring him here amongst us. And disturbed by my mother, who would never invite a stranger to partake directly at our table without the greatest efforts of my father. And annoyed that this Edwin looked so tall and gangly and awkward and could not even answer a simple question about what to drink. But I was the one being made to look stupid in front of them all. More than all of this, I was angry with my father for not saying one word to explain his actions or his thinking, but instead foist this jutty-chinned, smooth-skinned, big-eyed, overly-long-limbed girlish giant on our family and expect me to serve him.

I stood and showed them nothing of my thoughts. And for a long series of moments nothing happened.

Then, my father said to the foreigner, in Northumbrian, ‘What do you want to drink, young man?’

For a moment, nothing came back.

Out of nowhere came a sound which no-one caught.

‘What?’ I said.

‘*Dwr*,’ he said, in our tongue. Then, a moment when we looked for the meaning. ‘*Dwr*’, he said again, as if we were the stupid ones.

My father laughed the first, then everyone followed. He was so pleased that he stood up and slapped him on the back and shook his hand. Even my mother told him what a clever boy he was. Thus, Edwin came to become one of us, here on our little hill jutting out into the ocean, far away from wherever his father and family were. If, indeed, he had father and family.

Despite his face lacking in proportion, and his limbs that were always too long, and his laugh that was too shrill and too infectious, I found Edwin of Northumbria to be the finest of brothers, a foster-brother, but bound in the same unspoken ways as brother with brother until the time he chose to leave after seven summers. He was part of our family and when we said goodbye my mother wept and my father and Cadfan, my grandfather, were sorely afflicted and urged him to stay.

'But I shall be king,' he said, 'I have no choice.'

And thus he left, in the company of our men till he reached the borders of Gwynedd, where he was met by his own men. That was a decade or more ago. Now, I shall return to Northumbria with a heart that is heavy and a heart that is glad, in equal measure. I carry my time with Edwin like a gift. And remember the times I came before when he was a king and I his fosterbrother.

We came again up the same road. Rigodun, where we captured the Hooded One, the future King Edwin, from kidnappers, who would have sold him to the highest bidder. Or slit his throat for the same amount. Except my father saved his life, and I saved my father's.

It's twenty years or more since I was last here, but truth be told, I have been here before many times in the stories I have shared, and in other times, when my father and our allies bid me and the soldiers do what soldiers always do – unpleasant, dirty, secret tasks that never see the light of day or even the darkness around the makeshift campfire.

Yes, I had been here before.

We toiled with Idnerth up the last sections of the old road to the fort with those wondrous walls and that gateway with the rough wooden pieces stretched across, which had so impressed me as a youngster on my first expedition. We were flagging under the weight of carrying an armed man. Several times we put him down, sweating and vapoured like draft horses in the spring rain. The exertion of carrying him was taking its toll, so we barely noticed we had arrived, so dense was the fog, coming down off the invisible hills in waves. It was only when we heard voices that we could tell where the place had disappeared to.

After wandering around in the direction of the voices I found a hut, and all of a sudden, another five or six small huts appeared out of the fog. From one, hobbled a man, thin and old.

'What you want? Who are you on a day like this? We have nothing, so take it if you find it and leave us,' then retreated into the dark of his dwelling.

'Wait,' I said, 'we will give you something,' and produced a few coins from an outer pocket. 'I have a sick friend, he just needs warmth, food and rest and no more. Please, friend, I ask your help in this man's name. He does not carry the plague, he is just fevered with travel and damp and the chill. There is more money on my return. More.'

Silence. But I knew them better this time, and waited.

'You know our tongue?' said an old woman, who had moved into the doorway of the house, with two youngsters around her skirts. 'Let me see your coins.'

And thus, I passed a night once more in Rigodun. This time without seeing anything of the place, since when I left at dawn, the mist was worse, and it was a task just to find the old road. I left my friend, Cadog, with Idnerth, his need for protection greater than mine.

'Don't worry about this mist,' the old lady had said in the morning, after a night of sleeping with dogs, children and strangers on earthen floors, 'twenty minutes up the road and you'll see these clouds like a bird sees them,' and laughed.

'I will return soon. Care for my friends as I expect.'

‘You have to arrive and do your business ’fore you come back,’ she laughed again, and sent three of the children to see me on my way.

And she was right, twenty minutes toil up the stony, muddy track, through the thick mantle of fog and all of a sudden, like walking through a door, I emerged into sunlight and spring. Turning to look back, and below me was a sea of white covering everything as far as the eye could see. Out of it nothing emerged, no feature, no sound, no light, just an undisturbed blanket of air, thick with damp.

Another hour, and I had crossed the highest ridge, past the boundary stone that now marked no-man’s-land, belonging now to a different time. Another two hours and I was in a steep, wooded valley with a twisting path that rose and fell as it accompanied a river, fed by countless bounding streams. Sometimes, I would catch sight of small hamlets and the scent of woodsmoke and voices and then, I would freeze for a moment, not wishing to meet any man, or account for who I was or where I was going. Several times, I hid from travellers coming the other way, often just in time.

By evening, I was camping in the forest that is called Loidis, that they say was once huge, and no one could pass through, and was full of rivers that flowed backwards and where they joined into one river, they would flow out of another. Here, I felt sure would be no prying eyes or too many travellers, but if I met anyone, they would probably be people of no good.

In the shadow of a dark rock, way off the slender paths, I sat and made a fire. I sent my thoughts to Idnerth and Cadog and saw the spirits emerge from the old trees and their hiding places and could sleep burrowed into the good earth, wrapped in my cloak and leaves, knowing I was safe.

What woke me was the sound of a dog. Then the smell. For a moment, I thought I was at home, and the smell was my favourite hound, Broch, sleeping close by. But I did not normally sleep in a hollow of raw earth and remembered where I was, in an instant. I desperately set my ears to fix where he was, this dog, or whether there were other sounds, revealing other creatures. The dog was moving a hundred paces away, maybe less, moving towards me but not directly, nose down, trailing leaves. As I lay there, I heard the master calling the dog back, and then the tell-tale scampering of a dog running back to his master.

I lay a while longer to listen in case the man was not alone. For the first time in a long time I felt, only fleetingly, what a lonely death might be like, away from anyone loved who could witness it and tell the tale. Even the unheroic death, of an old man in a comfortable bed surround by loved ones, would be better than a lonely death.

I rose quickly, when I was sure it was safe and made sure the space I had slept in looked undistinguishable from what was around it. Checking the sun and the moss, I set off eastwards again, regaining the path I had left at sunset last night. I did not want another night out in the open and knew that my father was expecting me to greet King Edwin by the end of this day and be in time for the Spring celebrations and the conference with the Latins and the Christians, that would begin very soon after the new moon. The business with Idnerth had slowed us down. I would have to make up time, so I began at the pace we march when we are accompanying the messengers. They have to change horses and if they cannot, they have to slow their pace. That is our pace on foot.

It was easy to lose one's way in this density of coverage. The trees were so closely knitted that sometimes, literally, I had to climb through them where the path had simply come to an end, as if the way had died decades ago. At one point, I climbed an easy tree and standing in the higher branches, all I could see were more trees extending in every direction. A few miles on,

I came to some marshy, willowy ground and a river that was slow and brown, swollen from rains days earlier, that took my breath away as I waded up to my shoulders and stumbled on the unseen rocks below.

On the other side was a little structure, like a hanging-place, with a wild boar's head dangling from a pole. Draped over and covering the wooden structure were the long, intricate branches of two or three closely planted birch trees, adorned with little pieces of coloured material. Behind it was a stone well, and beyond that, unseen from the river, was a little clearing with a house in a very distinctive style that looked like our people's cottages.

From the house, came a keening, as low as bees around a hive. Time was pressing and the day would be a long one. In the next moment, through the trees on the path I was going, the voices of men shouting and laughing disturbed my indecision. Instinctively, I dived into the cover of the trees just beyond the low fence that separated the garden from the forest. I was just in time. They were on horseback and behind them they had a prisoner on the end of a rope. He was stumbling to stay on his feet, even at this slow pace. The two men stopped at the gate, one pulling the rope so that the prisoner was at his side, before he pulled out a knife and sliced through the rope and roughly kicked the young man into the gate.

'Come out, you dirty, idol-riding pervert, mend your ways. This is the last warning to you,' in the harshness of the South Saxon tongue.

The young man picked himself up from the ground but was wildly disorientated. His right eye was now just a socket and his face was brown, not with sunburn, but with blood and dirt matted across his face. He was holding his left ear and when he moved his hand there was no ear, just the stump of it, cut right back and still trickling fresh blood. He couldn't stand up, the agony of shock written across his face, as he sank back to his knees in silence. For long moments, just silence hung there.

A woman appeared at the door to the cottage so slowly it was hard to tell how she moved. Her voice carried on keening without any shift, and she walked to where the young man was, and her face did not break its fearless melancholy. Now that she'd moved outside, it was clear that there were other voices singing the death song, as the sound of the keening continued from inside the house. She picked up the broken young man, without acknowledging the existence of the riders, and gently led him inside the house. As she went inside a small child appeared in the doorway. Its face was painted with ashes and it carried a wreath of yew.

The man who had held the rope turned his horse and went to the little shrine with the boar's head and aimed another kick at it but missed, and his friend burst out laughing.

'Careful it doesn't bite ya,' he said, 'come, come...we can't be late for the arsehole-faced King.'

He aimed another kick at the dangling head and missed again.

'I've a good mind to piss in the well,' he shouted to make his companion laugh, but off they turned and rode away, having delivered their cargo.

I waited awhile again. Unwilling to meet those two on an open road in this mood and unwilling to break into what must be a place of mourning and now of suffering.

This was not my business. My business was with King Edwin on behalf of my father.

I waited for a further while. Then, I set off down the road but after only half a mile or less, I turned around. When I got back to the house, the keening had stopped. I told the little child to fetch the lady of the house.

'I am sorry for your troubles. I am Ceadd, son of Cadwallon

of Gwynedd. I am on my way to speak with King Edwin.'

'I am gladdened that you have come, Ceadd. You are always welcome here.' She spoke in the old tongue, the one that was once the same as ours, but more like what our ancestors spoke, when the Romans were here.

'Thank you, lady, but what I witnessed was unjust and cruel. It's none of my business, but I can help you, if it is right to do so.'

'There is water from the well, we have prepared some food, you would be welcome. We are simple, but please stay and tell me of your people and of your father, Cadwallon,' and turned and walked inside.

At one end of the hut was a body laid out, ready for burial. The young man I had seen was sleeping in a cot with cloths over his eyes and ears and hands. There were two older women and a child around a table, eating, eyes lowered. One admonished the child for staring, very quietly. And the young man moaned in his sleep and shifted his position and winced. 'Give him more medicine, he needs to be numbed and sleep,' she said to the old lady, who dutifully got up, lifted his head in her hands and put a clay jug to his lips.

'I am very honoured to share your table, thank you.' And they gasped a little in surprise that we could speak to one another and understand one another. And they offered me bread and a pot of vegetable stew.

'After sharing a table and your generosity, it is only fair that I ask you how I can repay you, you have been most kind.'

'You owe nothing. We are honoured with your company.'

There was a slow silence in the room. Even the child was fixed and didn't fidget or ask for things, like other children would. Only a sound of disturbed breathing from the chest of the bandaged man broke into this space. I looked over at him.

'Why did they do this to him? Is he your kin? Your family?'

'Ceadd, it is better that you don't know.'

I felt I had asked too many questions already, maybe stayed too long and I felt the nagging of my greater task and thought how to leave, graciously.

'A man may have been unjustly treated – maimed – I saw them bring him here and this is no way to deal with – well, I do not know him or why he was punished like that.'

She held my gaze, then looked over at her patient, and I let myself look at her profile framed by the dark hair and thought how she did not look much like a woman of Northumbria.

'We will care for him and hope that he can return to his family and be of use to them.'

She paused again and looked right into my living eyes.

'I think you are going to the east. In a little more than an hour you will pass through his home. Tell them we have him here and we will care for him as we can. Tell them in love and respect that we honour his people.'

Then, she walked to the door and made the slightest movement with her hand that I was to leave now. 'You have far to go, so go. Tell them as I said.'

Then she turned to go, and once again I caught the shape of her face and my heart just skipped and struck me like a thudded punch. With her back to me she said, 'The slender one, they call him the slender one, Tanau, by this name he is known.

So, without wanting to, I was on my way, conscious again of the sun lowering behind me, pushing me as quickly as possible to find Edwin, but careful of the brutish pair who were maiming people for sport, somewhere on the road ahead. It was with a heavy heart I set out, without looking back at that cottage in the forest by the wayside shrine, and it was with a smiling heart that I thought of the strange, dark lady. If I'd watched her float across the trees, I wouldn't have doubted what I was watching was real.

Sooner than I thought, I was in that pace we used in warbands when speed was the essence, when we were running and could make nine, maybe ten, old roman miles in an hour. On a good road and with a good captain, more. Now, I was going even faster, spurred on for more than one reason. After half an hour, I reached the brow of a low rise with a view eastward to the hills that I was heading for. I crouched down, conscious of being seen or heard in this treacherous place. I waited in the edge of trees with a view back where I had come and forward where I was to go. Nothing to cause me concern, but still I waited.

After a little longer, I started off down the slope to the bend in the road and the few stepping-stones across the little beck that was just a muddier, higher version of its normal spring self. Then, down the road, hemmed in by tall ash and alder and the dampness of moistened soil and the first whiff of burning that made me melt into the cover again. The smell of burning was not what I expected in this place. I strained for sounds or any sign of things out of place, but nothing. Slowly, more slowly than before, I stepped onto the road and skulked along the side, keeping low. This would be a very easy place for an ambush of any kind. I wish I had chosen the higher ground, but there is no higher ground in this lower part of Elmet, protected by thick bulwarks of forest and a myriad of rivers, marshes, streams and inlets descending slowly to the Humber, that is the southern boundary of Northumbria, still a way to the east. This is a land that is best gone around and here am I going through it, a stranger in this dangerous place, where laws and customs have been abandoned.

After another half a mile of hiding as best I could in the hedges and cover of the edge of the forest, I rounded one last rising bend and crept to the best place to see the terrain in front.

Below me was a cluster of buildings in a clearing in the forest, like so many others. At one end was a stone farm building that looked like a very old common barn and below it, the smouldering remains of houses, enclosures, sheds and animal pens in different states of destruction. Some had clearly been razed to the ground, others left half-standing, one smaller one with an untouched wall and most of the roof left sagging and half-burnt.

By the well, near the top of the enclosure, at the foot of a small escarpment, was a figure. I didn't notice the figure at first, because only the feet and legs were visible. Was it a corpse? I was so wary of getting myself caught up in these troubles that I crouched for a long while in my vantage point and tried to make sure that there were no hidden dangers.

There were some cattle wandering around grazing, and some dead animals that had been caught in the fire, but other than that, I couldn't see any other living things. Then, I saw the corpse at the well move, wiggle and grunt. It was a woman, with her upper body draped into the space of darkness above the water.

I ran along the edge of the clearing towards the top of the home-fields to the well, but slowed and spoke from a distance, knowing I might frighten her if I appeared without making a sound.

'Good-day to you.'

She slid away from the well and instinctively reared up and swung herself round to the other side of the well to give herself some protection.

'What are you, stranger?' she said. She spoke our language in the same way as the dark woman in the last place.

'I am Ceadd, son of Cadwallon, King of Gwynedd. You have nothing to fear from me.'

'Why are you alone, if you are son of a king?'

'That is a long story.'

She leaned her head to one side. 'Why do you speak our language?'

'Because we are kin, but that is also another story. Why are you looking down the well? What happened here?'

It was then that she seemed to remember where she was in this scene of fire and destruction, and slumped into a softened shape and lost her fear.

'They threw the men down the well...but, I don't know what to do...I don't think they are alive...' and all of the life ebbed from her face, and she slumped before my eyes into a staring shell that shocked me.

I walked to the well and looked into it, but it was deep and dark. I could make nothing out in the depths.

'Hello, hello...let me know if you are there...hello, hello...can you hear me?'

And waited to let the echoes drop and come back from the water. No human voice.

'Are you sure that there are people down there?'

She looked up from her despair and nodded.

I looked around for a rope There must be a rope for bringing up the water. It was lying some measure away, having been thrown out of the way. I tied it to a hook in the side of the well and let it over. It had been a long time since I'd climbed a rope, but I eased over the side. Going down into darkness was easier.

The walls were dry, and I stepped down, pushing out as I had learnt when we were hunting puffins and their eggs on the cliffs of Gwynedd. There we had good ropes and little hooks that would steady our descent and we could see exactly what we were doing. All my life I had done it. But I braced myself for what I would find, as much as bracing myself to bounce easily off the soft chalky stone of the well.

What I could see below me was only black and what I could see above me was only brightness. It can't be that much further, I thought and stopped to listen. Just a drip of water somewhere and a little stone scudding off my boot into the water below. Very near. It came into my mind to doubt the woman at the top of the well. What if this was just a trick to lure me to my death?

What if she was simply mad and had imagined everything? What if the burnt buildings and smouldering animal corpses were just imaginary? I stepped slowly now, anticipating the first touch of water. What could I do but believe her?

Slowly, slowly, I inched down to where I was anticipating the level would be. Nearly there, surely. I could almost feel the shock of the cool water wrap around my boot and ankle, reassuring me that there was an end to this act. As I slid down slowly down the rope, I felt a hand curl like a tentacle around my ankle and I slipped and lost my grip on the wall and jerked my arms nearly out of my sockets with the shock of the drop. I let out a scream and tried to kick it away. But dangling there on the end of a swaying rope left me weak and unable to lash out and free myself. The hand, or whatever it was, had simply clamped around my ankle and was not letting go. I shouted out, instinctively, 'Let go, let go...who are you? Wait, wait...wait and I will help you.'

But no response, no words back. I took a deep breath and looked downwards into the darkness and let my eyes adjust to the place and the gloom. If I moved to the side and let the light from above fall undisturbed, I could catch the reflection of the water, just. And if I held onto the rope with just my right hand, I could lower my left side, and arm and hand and try to feel what was gripping my foot. I steadied myself with one leg wedged against the wall of the well and one arm holding on to the rope and inched slowly down my own leg till I met the thing gripping me. It felt for all the world like a human hand, but clammy and cooler.

The terror that ran through me of the thought of that human hand reaching out from a deep well was the worst fate I could imagine for a dying soul. The memory that would echo through my night dreams for the rest of my life. But the grip remained strong. So, I descended, and only then did the grip lessen, and as I felt the waters of the well embrace me, I also saw the face of the gripping hand, pale, bruised and with one swollen eye appealing and a mouth opening, making no sound. Floating in layers were several bodies in the water, and these bodies were stopping me sink fully into the water. All dead, unspeaking, already swelling and departed. And in their midst a living soul.

I knew I did not have much time here, so I tied the rope under the arms of the man with the gripping hand and secured a very strong knot under him and told him to wait. He did not speak. 'My friend, whoever you are, I will get you out. Wait.'

The climb to the surface was easier than the descent. The old youthfulness of surging up the cliffs with the bag of eggs and birds came rushing back. The firmness of the rope made the climbing easier, now that it was fastened to the man floating on the surface of the well water below. When I reached the surface, she was there and looked astonished, like she had seen ancestors from the spirit world come back to visit her.

'Help, quickly, help me pull up the rope,' I shouted, drenched with water that was reddened.

Together we pulled, trying all the while to keep the man steady and not cause him further injury by banging his head against the wall. He did not respond to my shouts or those of my companion but eventually, with exhausting effort, we pulled him to the top of the well and laid him on the dry earth. She bent over him and immediately started to tend him and bathe him and speak sweetly to him, but he had faded into unconsciousness.

For a long moment I lay on my back and let the strength return. I felt the thirst of a mariner and stumbled around looking for water. When I found some in a little pail meant for the horses, I drank it almost dry. When I turned around, she was stood right in front of me.

'I need Alwena, I can't tend him back to life without her.'

‘Who is Alwena?’

‘You must’ve passed her house, near the shrine by the well.’

‘I have to be in the court of King Edwin tonight, I cannot go, I have been too delayed already.’

‘Look what they’ve done. That man is my husband and he’s all I’ve got left. If you go now, Alwena will save him, if you don’t then I will throw myself in the well.’

I calculated that I was a day at most away from Londisbeorg, Edwin’s meeting place. Even if I rose before dawn, I would not be there in time to speak to him tomorrow. My hopes of achieving my father’s wishes would be nearly crushed.

By then, she had moved to the edge of the well. ‘I beseech you as if I were your mother. Go to Alwena. He will die and I will die down there.’

‘Your son lives, if it is your son I saw. He was dragged by two men to the cottage of the woman you speak of.’

‘What?’

‘Yes, she called him Tanau, the Slender One. Is that what you call him?’

‘How do you know?’

‘Because I saw him when they gave him to Alwena and she took him inside and tended his wounds.’

‘Now you must go. Every moment he walks nearer to death,’ and she walked over to him lying there. ‘Tell her to hurry. She will know what to do.’

There was no choice, and knowing the road and the distance, I put my pack to one side and carrying only my spear, I set off back down the road I had just come, cursing my luck on this journey that was slowly sinking into failure.

When I arrived at Alwena’s house I did not wait for an invitation. Inside, all was calm and as I had left it. ‘My lady, you must come, there is a great need of your skills to save the life of his father,’ pointing at the young man in his bandages, ‘and his mother. She sent me. Please, we cannot waste a moment. He was thrown in the well and is very near death's door.'

She gathered her things, and we ran to the road and I was surprised at her speed and grace. She could easily match me. By the time we arrived at the place of the well, I knew that she was slowing for my sake and sank to the side of the man with the gripping hand, barely out of breath. She commanded us to bring her water, blankets, some herbs and strips of cloth and make a fire and to make him a bed and take him to the old barn to be properly tended.

Hours later, we finally sank into sleep, the earth had closed in and we left the door a little ajar to keep the air clear and the smoke out and the light of the next day in.

Before the dawn, I felt an icy grip sprawling up from my right ankle, like a hand with monstrous fingers, and pulling back so violently, I woke myself up. Gasping for air, I was wide awake and gulped in air with the relief that it was not real, rubbing my leg anyway, just to make sure.

I felt the need for a piss and slipped out of the barn as soundlessly as I could. A shadow of movement caught my eye and I started, in the dullest of drizzly dawns. Across the clearing was a figure moving. I instinctively crouched down to watch what it was doing. It moved very slowly, on haunches, bent down in the grasses. I watched it for a while, wondering if I was dreaming. Then, it stood up and walked slowly towards me, all the time intently staring at the ground, heedless of anything else. I watched her transfixed once again, even at this distance, in this state.

'Why are you about so early?' I asked her.

'The best time for finding what I want,' she said.

She put her basket down and started to sort the little herbs and plants she had found.

Through me flashed a little river of thoughts that would not rest. The ones I wanted to pick out were slippery and I knew I would look like a man letting go a fish, so thought it best to not start.

'What happened here?'

She laughed a very low laugh that was lacking in warmth. She looked at me as if to weigh me up with the burden she was going to pass. 'Ask your Edwin.'

'He is not my Edwin. Please, do not doubt me.'

She bent down again to prepare her ointments for the man with the gripping hand. She talked, but not to me.

'They come with sweet words, the Latins, the Romans, the one with the hooked nose. He has a powerful voice, and no one speaks against him, but he has sweet words, and messages of kindness and love and he speaks like a merciful general but pretends to be a blessed one.' She looked up at me with fierceness in her eyes, but her voice was plain and dry, like when you talk to someone in authority. 'Then they leave this...' and swept the burnt out place with her gesture, 'this you will find wherever there are those who will not agree with them, or say a word in defence of their own beliefs, or talk about the world we know here which is our world – the spirits, the gods, the seasons, the earth that we respect and worship in simple ways,' and bowed her head and whispered something that was not for me.

'So, ask your Edwin why he allows these men to do this in the name of love, with messages of hope and heaven and living a better life in the next life – ask him why he lets these men burn, maim, kill and destroy in his kingdom, when we have lived here for more generations than we can count – ask him why he lets these priests kill and maim men who have done no harm but plough fields and women who have tended families and children who have played in fields and woods. Ask him, Ceadd. What is the true message of God's messenger who blinds, maims, kills and burns in a madman's rage when he hears one word of challenge? Ask your Edwin, ask him, and see if he has anything to say,' and she lets her eyes burn me, coldly, fiercely.

The drizzle of the forenoon had turned into a late afternoon of unexpected, mild spring as I marched up the low hill to the entrance to Edwin's estate at Londisbeorg. Ahead were the impressive staples at the edge of the royal lands, adorned with carvings and faces of animals and men, set strongly into the earth and guarded by three men. Marking off this land were stones set into the ground, trailing off to the woods to the left and to the river below to the right, as a sign to all that this was a space set apart. It was only fitting to pass through these wooden pillars, only fitting, that is, for honourable travellers.

'You travel well,' said the little fellow, 'we've watched you now for nigh on ten furloughs and you move as if you've a band of slavering Ulstermen at your back.'

The other two laughed as if they were well-trained.

'I give my greetings to King Edwin and bring him greetings from Gwynedd and from Cadwallon, his foster-father, and I am Ceadd, his son.'

'Ooooooh,' he said, and turned to his friends and said something in a form of their tongue I did not understand, which made them guffaw with laughter.

'You better come through, Welshie, before you catch your death of cold, particularly if you the son of a Codswalloper, we don't get many of them in these parts,' rolling his eyes in mock servitude, the other two snorting.

'Go with him, escort prince johnny-foreigner' he spoke to the youngest one with a flick of his head, 'make sure he gets to Ed, an' no harm comes his way.'

More guffawing.

'He's always making jokes, is Beorhtric,' said the young lad, sent to accompany me, with an accent of a man of the far north.

I still had a way to go, so resumed the marching pace. 'Hey, hey,' he shouted after me, 'come back, wait for me, I'm supposed to show you the way, so you don't get into 'arm's way.'

By the time I had climbed the low hill and had taken the left-hand fork through the thickets, I had left my 'guide' behind and could see the curls of smoke above the trees and could hear the voices of men laughing and vying with one another through the soft spring evening.

I had not expected this: horses stabled under the trees, tied in rows in hastily made-up paddocks, tents like the travellers use, who move goods around the country, pitched as if in a fair, food being cooked and wandering between the tents, hawkers selling ales and tidbits of delicacies – flavoured eels, pies of every meat, squirrel legs, dark, black fruits like grapes that I'd never seen and little pieces of flour baked with honey that reminded me of home. There were groups of men talking who clearly rarely meet like this, and others walking purposefully in ones and twos. Lost in amongst the temporary buildings were the buildings of Edwin's court that I had known in earlier days, but now there were makeshift stalls and decorations to mark the arrival of spring, draped across every tree and down every wall and around every doorway. The cuttings of the silver birch and the branches of the freshest greenest leaves and the carved faces of the spirits of the woods, peeping out here and there to smile and catch out the unwary. And everywhere, too, soldiers wearing Edwin's livery and carrying Edwin's sign – the standard that was said to have been handed down from the times of the Romans that held a weaving of a picture of a circle, as bright as a sun, and around it a thousand feathers floating.

There was no one here to greet me, as my father had promised, no sign that they knew I was here, no acknowledgement from anyone, just the throaty scrape of the Northumbrian tongue clacking loudly all around, and others speaking languages that

I couldn't name or say from where they came, and some even speaking Latin, slithering and rapid, as if they were telling very secret secrets and two women whispering in a type of Irish, curling dark hair from a piled-up crown idly, as they chose some fine-wrought Belgian gold from a bear of a man who could only speak in numbers. And others of a striking type, with part-shaved head in undyed shifts and overshirts of woven animal hair, and plain men, darkened, even on these isles, by years of living outside and taut in their standing, leaning on large staffs, gathered in groups and marked out by not laughing. They eyed everything and spoke in a form of uncommon Latin, rough and accented, with all the sounds coming out through the nose.

I was so engrossed by these strange and foreign sights that I did not notice the clunk of the guards' spears across my chest, barring my way.

'No further today,' said one of them.

Then, from behind him, another guard appeared, the same short type I was beginning to recognise. 'Tomorrow, come back tomorrow, the King will speak then with everyone.' And turned to walk away.

'Tell him I send greetings from King Cadwallon ap Cadfan ap Iago, King of Gwynedd, foster-father of King Edwin, King of Northumbria and friend of our people.'

The guard turned around. 'The King is in an important meeting. He'll see you and everyone else tomorrow.'

'Friend, I am here representing my father, the King, as a brother of your King.'

'You don't look like anything but a travelling beggar –'

I flipped the legs from under him with the blunt end of my spear and within a second, I was on one knee had the blade of my knife to his throat.

'Up,' I said and pulled him to his feet. 'This is not how you welcome kinsmen...' and dragged him with me to the hall of Edwin, followed by a small commotion of guards. It had been a long while since I'd been here, but it wasn't very far to his hall, and I was certain he would be there.

The doors were open and the guard at the door commanded silence in the presence of the king. Edwin looked up when he heard the commotion and saw it was me and commanded the guards to go back to their posts. He smiled at me and bade me wait a moment, but the anxious look returned, and his gaze fell back on the proceedings in hand.

Before me was a most particular scene: on the left-hand side of the room a group of men, all clad in plain cloth and hair fashioned in that distinct style of a circle, shaved in the back of the head producing a curtain of wild, sprouting hair. When I walked in, they were lying face down or kneeling and rocking and muttering with shaking bodies, chanting their songs in a foreign Latin. And on the right, a crowd of Northumbrians, some Saxons and Irish all clad in different colours according to their fashions, but all looking in fascination at the muttering, or watching the contest in the middle of the room.

Edwin was slumped on his high seat on a dais between them, twirling his hair in his right hand, as he did when he was unsure. Often Edwin was unsure. In front of Edwin was the leader of the Latins, also in plain cloth, but a small hat of golden material sat on his long head and he held a great staff, fashioned at the end with some golden adornment. Opposite him, was the strange creature that I had heard Edwin speak of when he came to live with us. A huge figure in a large, black hat covered in feathers, teeth, claws and tails of a variety of animals. His face was soft, and he had no sign of facial hair and wore a long flowing gown of soft pale fabric, delicately covered in sparkling, valuable stones that looked like war-treasure captured from a Frankish princess.

At just the moment I walked in, the imposing figure in the gown and hat was passing to the Latin a large, wooden figure that he kissed before releasing. The Latin placed it on the floor near the hearth of the hall. It had huge, bulging eyes in a grotesque head and was a most astonishing creation. What became clear, after long moments of staring, was that it wasn't a figure of a head at all, but was a woman giving birth to a tree. The mood shifted at the passing of the carving from one side to the other. The mood of the locals now became dark and they began muttering amongst themselves anxiously over what was going to happen next. Some seemed to want to step forward and take it back from these unnecessary foreigners.

The Latin held it, and then let it slip to the floor, either deliberately or not, who can say? A huge uproar arose amongst the Northumbrians, affronted with the disrespect of these clumsy, sly foreigners. Edwin lifted his hand, and seemed for a moment to rouse from his slumber.

I could not wait any longer and chose this moment to walk forward and address Edwin, 'My brother, my King, my friend, it is me, Ceadd, son of King Cadwallon ap Cadfan ap Iago, King of Gwynedd –'

All he did was to hold up his hand. 'Ceadd.' And nodded, but I was to come no further. As if on cue, from behind the tall Latin with the staff, there was a movement and a woman stepped forward, the only woman in the hall, from what I could gather, and peered through the dying light and muttered something in the tall Latin's ear, then stepped back, like some vanishing spirit raised up by a travelling conjurer.

He was clearly acting on instructions, and from out of a box, the Latin produced a tinder, and looking around to make sure all eyes were fixed on him, he struck the stone and put it to the wood of the carving of the woman giving birth to a tree. The light flickered as he held the carving in the tongue of the flame.

The Latins began a chorus of chanting, the words runnning into one another, as words do that have been said together too often. Listening to their unfamiliar Latin, I struggled to tell more than that they were praising the god they believed would help them.

The Northumbrians on their side held their ground with deep breaths and folded arms, expecting the worse. Still the flame flickered and danced underneath the living carving, as the woman with her legs wide open and the cries of birth pangs coming from her stretched mouth remained forever caught in the moment of giving birth to a fully grown tree. All the candles in the room flickered and the chanting sounded out, fixed and unbroken, and Edwin watched as if he were peering into a packed cell of madmen, unable to believe his weary eyes.

Then the flame died, and the carving remained as it was before, unmarked and extraordinary.

To still the chanting, the tall Latin stamped his staff and demanded silence. The praying ones immediately fell quiet. For a moment, I caught his face. I saw the iron at the core of the man. Although he was tall, he stooped and his shoulders were rounded as if by worry and intensity of feeling and his face looked worn, thin with a hooked nose, that set him definitely as a man of Latin origin. He turned to look at the whole assembly, and I could see he was used to making an impression, his black hair framing his face, and his black eyes burning as he spoke with a most unusual voice, high and rasping and very loud that was pitched at street-market level, not the intimacy of this home of a Northumbrian king, 'The God see your tricks in your pagan wooden piece this here, like this.' He spoke in the local tongue, struggling for fluency and accuracy but powerful, nevertheless.

Edwin looked at him as if he didn't quite understand, but Edwin's man, huge, effeminate and otherworldly, stepped in, 'This is a piece of wood that can burn, but it will not burn because it is more than a piece of wood, it is the spirit of the earth bringing forth as it should, and for this reason it is to us sacred and will not burn for you. There is no trickery. It is you who mock and trick and will show the power you have by burning our sacred things. King Edwin, I beg you to make this stop, for the sake of your people that love you and our customs that they hold, that make our lives have meaning and form.'

And from the shadow stepped forward the woman and whispered in Edwin's ear, who nodded, and the Latin with the staff stooped even more, to bend his ear to her words. He called out, and there was a hurried movement that led to the bringing forward of a small earthenware jar, whose contents were poured on the undeserving carving of the birthing woman, at the same time as cries and shouts and protest erupted from the Northumbrian side, which Edwin stilled again with his hand.

Bending down to try again, the man with the light in his hands lit a flame below the now drenched, sacred carving of the spirit earth. The chanting arose again, this time louder and with more venom, more heartfelt singing and shaking and pleas for help aimed at this strange god, which was at the moment sitting on a golden throne high, high above us all, in a place called *Heaven* and would come to smite its enemies – and their enemies – if only they prayed hard enough. Having been smitten, these poor souls, who dared to practice ancient beliefs that belonged to this land since time unnumbered to generations unnamed, these poor souls would, according to the vivid Latins' imagination of this place, conjured up as *Hell*, which is a place of the worst torments that could be ever imagined are visited upon people day after day – even though in our mind they are dead...

I didn't really understand it, staring in despair, wondering how King Edwin had been led to allow this scene to play out in his court, and how much it was to do with the interventions of the shadowy woman who had the Latins' ear and the King's bed.

While the flame licked the outspread legs of the woman, then played with the roots as they emerged from her opening, I watched the Latin's lips moving furiously and his stooping shoulders forced upwards in a plea to the roof, and upwards and beyond, wherever his mind could wander, to the place where this god lived. Then, a huge cry arose from their ranks, as for one delicious moment the flame did its work, and the lower half caught fire across the places where the oil spilled over it and the whole thing burst into flames and he had to let go. Indeed, there was joyful exultation, and the Latins stopped their chanting and instead all stood up, and all in the same manner, lifted their arms upwards and shouted, 'Allelulia, Allelulia, Allelulia, Allelulia...' until the tall one stamped his staff and they fell silent.

Even before they fell silent, the flame had died as quickly as it had risen and several bodies moved around to peer at it and to examine it. A shorter, rounder Latin moved to pick it up, kissed his hands and offered them upwards, prepared to be burnt by the still hot wood. But he wasn't burnt, it wasn't hot. He passed it to the tall one, who examined it, then threw it down in disgust.

'Not wood, not wood, there is not wood if it no burning,' he snarled, in his piercing way.

The moment he threw it down, the Northumbrians surged forward angrily and moved across the divide to stand face to face with the Latins. Someone bent down to pick up and pass the extraordinary carving to the safe hands of the King's priest. The clamour served to rouse Edwin, and he stood up and threw his hands in the air.

'Stop, stop, this must stop,' moving towards the angry faces, pushing them back with gestures. 'Everyone go. Go, go!' Edwin shouted. 'Paulinus, stay and Coifi, stay, and Osfrid and Eadred and Cuichelm, please stay and my good friend from Ulster, Flaithbheartach – and the rest of you, go in peace. Any man breaches the peace tonight will be severely punished.'

And so, they all filed out, the Latins in plain clothing and the men of the North, the Saxons and the Irish together, muttering each in his own tongue and planning retribution to the affronts that had been made in public to their gods and spirits.

After a moment, he lifted his hand to me. 'And Ceadd, stay. Give me news, tell me anything that does not make me have to decide between these and these,' pointing with a weary flourish, like a man whose guests have stayed months longer than the expected time. 'A man needs a rest.'

When all but the closest of the court had left his presence, Edwin, King of Northumbria, the most powerful man in the North, came to me and hugged me, warmly.

'You are much missed.'

'King Edwin, I thank you for your warm greeting. I have been delayed on my travels but I give good greetings from my father and mother and they hope one day you will honour us with a visit to Gwynedd to see the family who are so fond of you.'

'Thank you. You can see that I have been plagued –'

'Hsssssss,' shot out the woman, half hiding behind Paulinus, the Latin. I had not seen her stay.

'Ceadd, I have been wedded since we last met. Please the Lady, Queen Ethelberga.' He smiled at her, but I didn't recognise the smile on my foster-brother's face. 'My lady, this is Ceadd, the Prince of Gwynedd, whom I have spoken of much.'

She nodded and retreated behind Paulinus.

'You are most blessed, Edwin,' and bowed to the lady. 'My father wishes you to know his thoughts, which he is sorry he is unable to discuss with you himself, but they are urgent, and I wish to fulfil my father's wishes and I know you would value his counsel.'

'Go on.'

I was very hesitant to speak these things, even in this select company. 'Could we speak in private, the better for me to say all the things that he, as your foster-father, has most closely on his heart and for to consider, in private.'

'On what matter?'

'The future of your kingdom and...'

He spoke too smoothly. 'Ceadd, speak freely here.'

'My father is concerned that you receive his counsel on many things, but chief amongst them is maintaining good relations with all our neighbours and keeping good relations with your people and...'

'Go on.'

'King Edwin, these are matters best discussed in private...'

'Ceadd, we are amongst friends here.'

I hesitated. Edwin was putting me in an uncomfortable position. It occurred to me that he was also putting himself at a disadvantage in front of members of the opposing parties.

'He wants to speak freely with you on the influence of the Latins and how best to proceed with the questions of Christianity and the respect for the people and their ways and gods.'

Edwin eyed me like I was a lowly shipwrecked trader who he'd never met before. He smiled, curled his lip and measured his next words. The warmth flowed out of him and I did indeed feel as if I was speaking to some foreign prince in Arabia, so remote had he become.

Before he could speak, Queen Ethelberga shouted 'Wait!' and hurriedly whispered in the ear of Paulinus. Everyone waited for the translation.

'The Lady Queen is much please for this your message from your father and thank you most-heartedly, but King Edwin has fine counsel and is making the many wise choice.' Even at this distance, he shouted and for anyone at the back of the hall, it may have felt a comfortable volume.

'My Queen, I thank you for your words. But, King Edwin, my father knows that you will wish to discuss privately his thoughts and asks that we can now speak freely together, as a matter of urgency, and as a matter of importance to all the people who serve the King and are proud to do so.'

'Ceadd, I thank you and I know you have travelled far. I am beginning to tire and tomorrow we will meet for three days to discuss this and other matters in one final debate. At the end of three days, I have said I will deliver my decision. My people and my company are most anxious that we do the best thing. Tomorrow, Ceadd, please let's meet at daybreak to eat together.'

He put his hand up to stop all further discussion. We all bowed as they left the hall, King Edwin, his Queen and her priest.

I sank to the nearest bench and felt already the failure of my mission. This was not how I'd imagined being reunited with my brother, the man whose life I had saved so long ago. I was exhausted with the effort of the last few days and the disappointment of this meeting. I rested my head in my hands. I don't know how long I stayed there.

'I've travelled times-without-counting through your pretty country, but I have sailed past it more,' said the figure who had silently moved to sit opposite me.

He just stared and smiled at me, as if waiting for a sign. I got up to leave instead, but he grabbed my arm.

'Edwin was an old mate of yours?' and paused. 'Just seems to have slipped his mind, for a bit of a long moment,' and laughed. 'He might come to,' then he hissed through his teeth, 'but I'm not much thinking it's very likely,' and picked at something in his teeth. 'He's more of a mind to run away to sea with a whore with the plague than listen to yous blowing in his ear about this nonsense,' and pierced me again with his staring blue eyes that weren't jesting.

He pulled me back down. '*Mo chara*, my friend,' he says smiling, 'I aren't knowing your father's message. Come to that,

I aren't knowing you or what you're a-cumin' here after. A word of warning,' and he looked around the now deserted hall in all directions before he continued, 'nothin' here's what it seems. Edwin's in a bit of a pickle, you might find yourself saying.'

Then, he stood up and held out his hand, 'Flaithbheartach's my name, Ulsterman as long as you're a Gwynedd man. Come, come, come, *mo chara,*' and pulled me upright, 'Ceadd they tell me ye are, let's find a better spot where there's a house full of blatherers and no one'll lift a windy cheek at what you might catch me saying,' and was as full of laughter as a yard of children.

He was as slender and as wiry as a queen's housemaid, with the grip of iron and the insane strength of the heath-dwelling madman, but I let him lead me.

'I know a little place to take your mind off things, we'll be there in as much time as it takes to park your arse on an empty bench an' get you settled with the cheapest ale to take your mind off yer troubles for a wee while. Might find you a bit of something to warm your hands as well, so we might.'

He was determined to get me out of the King's Hall, and so we went out of the hall, down a passage, out into the kitchens and the cookhouse and the storage yards and through a little gate that was locked on the inside with a block of wood, which when we were through, he flicked expertly back into place, as if no one had ever passed here at all. In the dark, and after all the changes and buildings added on here and there, I had lost any real sense of where we were and was surprised when we emerged into the fringes of tents and stalls through which I'd come just an hour or two before.

We walked till we came right to the edge of this temporary, strange gathering place and he lifted up the canvas door of a tent and half-pushed me into the gloomy, smoky inside. It took me a moment to adjust to the dark, before I was pulled down onto a rough, uneven bench that swayed whenever anyone shifted their weight, and he pushed the previous occupant away with a swipe of his hand and a curse.

An ale appeared in front of me, from a hand that didn't have a face. Three or four other arms reached out with similar drinking vessels and we all smashed them together as one and all cried together in thundering Northumbrian, 'Vigour to your sword,' and from somewhere across the room, another sweat of ale-oiled voices chorusing, 'and long may it rise,' amid cascades of laughter uniting them, and I felt their cold ale hit my throat comfortingly, despite my impending sense of failure and my travel-weary body saying no.

At some point, Flaithbheartach appeared again by my side, smiling, his little hands seizing my shoulder with his lunatic's grip, shouting in my ear, 'You don't know these people, or what they can do, if you know them you would be on that long road west as soon as your little legs could take you. You don't know these people, if you knew that they have no sense of what they can do or what they can't do...' but by then it was all just words that I thought were coming from a mouth that was too stupid to do anything but repeat the same things. I indulged his ramblings. This was just drunken words repeated in a different order, like a child playing with little blocks, without any sense or consequence to any of them...

I must have fallen asleep in the sunshine and a woman's voice wakes me.

'Speak with Edwin, Ceadd. Speak for your people, not just for now, but forever. Think of all the ways we love the earth – not with books and foaming mouths and rules and shouting and tearing at clothes and the force that wrecks men's minds but think of our ways of loving the earth and honouring the spirits of all living things and all dead things.

She pauses and takes a stem of wild garlic. 'Think of all the bards before you and the stories that they will poison and think on our old ways. Look at us now, speaking in the ways of our dead fathers being pushed back to the other side of our land, because we trust no one.

'Think of the hearth that you knew, Ceadd, the hearth that is your birthright. Of your place before the people, to fill them with the majesty of being part of this world, not in fear of everything for fear of madmen with their books, and she sang from the old songs:

> Mountain snow,
> Frost on graves,
> Stones cover our fires
> Our kinsmen on a covered path

And so, I joined her in the keening of watching the world pass before us into something changed, and we sang out our birthright, songs that would bind every one in our people as tight as rods of forged steel, the singing that takes the way when speaking has no use:

> The mountain snow
> The waters rising through ice
> The men of our hearth
> Longing for the feuds
> To cease, the warm hearth
> The mountain snow
> Strong our arms and shoulder
> Shield laid for the first crops
> The sun shines on the lake
> The mountain snow
> Has gone in rags over the hill

And we sang on, hovering in that space that is lighter than our bodies, where communion of thoughts can help us understand everything that is to be shared. As we sang more, I drift onto my back and close my eyes and feel the touch of lightness like angels wings carrying lavender and balm to my forehead and nostrils around my temples and the tilting of my head to drink honey-flavoured water. The taste was not the sweet water I had tasted before but something else, unfamiliar to my tongue and charging my mouth with an urge to repel it, but I can hear Vinda's voice soothing, like a lullaby for a child,

> 'Drink, drink and chase the memories, follow the shadows where they take you, like dogs with the scent, follow the source of your thoughts to all the places you could have been to the centre of the dark wood where the doers of this evil are, to where the place this evil lies and who did this, Ceadd, sleep and dream to see who did this and you will know what to do, to those who would have you dead, let the memories lead you into the darkest places and the light into the pathless woods and remember all, remember all, let the memories receive you...'

And so, I drifted off to sleep, as she eased the balm of herbs around my fading mind and the casing of my thoughts, around my temples, skull and my eyes and ears.

And when I awoke, I felt purged, as if someone had changed my blood, swept my lungs, drenched me in light and caused the very air to course through my body as if for the very first time and set me alive, for the very first day. I sat up in the little cot Vinda has laid me in. I cannot say for how long I had slept. She was dozing on a bench, but I woke her with my steps.

'I am going to the Sacred Groves, Auntie. The spirits have been with me, through you.'

She nodded.

The afternoon with a beating heart, its clarity in my every step, its singing breath in the birds on the budding trees, in the feel of the earth's blood pulsing through the rising sap from the roots finding space in the waning rock to the infinite drops of moisture blending into the greening leaves and grass, this was an afternoon that celebrated life in a beating cycle of returning and a beating centre of changing and a beating power of living and dying and shifting between the two that no man or woman like us could understand.

I came to the place called the Sacred Groves.

Before me is the entrance of huge upright poles, blackened by fire, arranged like sentries guarding the Empress, making an impenetrable screen so carefully fashioned were they, placed apart in a way everyone would have to brush against them, a reminder how insignificant we are. On the other side of the Sacred Groves was the women's entrance, screened with living evergreens, the branches adorned with the valuables of the previous visitors, hanging reminders of the faiths and hopes of those passing through. Of course, one can only go through one entrance in one life.

I stood to pause and find the internal peace to enter. As was the custom, I took a mouthful of water and rinsed and spat it out, washing away all the impurities of our speech. On the floor just inside the grove, was the water in the stone pool where I knelt to bow down and feel the place that all things flow from, splashing it on my face and palms, and placing my heart where the earth could hear it.

No dead things that once had hearts can be in this place.

Each offerer must make a choice from the sacred vessels: choose the smouldering leaves burning in the unwithering hollow for knowledge of the future; choose the seeds that are to be eaten for knowledge of the past; choose bitter waters mixed from oils and ground herbs for knowledge of love and families; choose the mix of pastes and dust to be smeared on all bare flesh for knowledge of war and business; and choose the darkest vessel of all, that was rotten wood and fruit where the insects fed, where the hand would grab for knowledge of memories and the weevils, the woodlice, the ants and the other creatures would feed on the drying decayed wood and the fruit and other small offerings that the priests placed for them to feed and do their work. I was reminded of the words of Vinda, f*ollow the shadows, like dogs with the scent follow the source of your thoughts to the centre of the dark wood, to where the place this evil lies and who would have you dead. Let the memories lead you into the darkest places and the light into the pathless woods and remember all, remember all, let the memories receive you...*

And so I put my hand into the hollowed-out trunk incorporating the three faces of memory melting into one exaggerated face: there was a hole above the eye where the woodborers and the woodlice and the pillbugs and deathwatch and woodworm beetles and all their offspring and fat adolescents and eggs had chewed through the wood and left nothing more but space for air. For a moment, I thought of the artist who had carved this, knowing that one day it would be not even dust, but would become instead the pulped and digested matter on which insects were meant to feed. Would knowing this make the artist do their finest work or produce instead something that was dashed off, made to look like it was what it was, but without the care or the pride? Out of his handiwork and the countless digestions of countless hours of insects devouring, I found my hand full of dry powder, flaky and crumbly and not easy to grasp. I could feel some of these earnest, busy weevils and beetles that didn't want to let go their feastings crawling over my hands. But as was the custom, I crushed the powder further in my hand, and then crushed another handful with my left hand and mixed them together with the lavender on the wooden pillar placed outside the willow tree, with its living branches woven into a wicker bower of stakes fixed in the ground, so that one could enter and from inside not see out. No one could say where the living tree met the dead wood, or where the human and the natural finished and ended. Inside, it was dark and smoky because of the embers preserved in a special way to burn constantly. I bent over the low stone bowl and lowered the mix of dying wood and herbs and lavender onto the embers, uttering my request for knowledge of those hours lost to me and why I had ended up here, left as if for dead. Then, I was to put on the hood of blackened cowhide that hung on a nail above the burning embers and to sit without moving, until I had the answers to my questions.

The thoughts swirl around me because the memory does not know what you no longer remember, instead it shows you many things that you might want to know, from childhood, youth, from battle, from the day to day and the hurts and the kindnesses that are the stitches holding you together and many things that you might want to forget or that you were meant to forget...

In the beer booth with the Irishman, sad men are drinking ale in silence, one drink and then I will find lodgings, first thing tomorrow I will get to Eadwin and he will hear the counsel of my father,   I am alone and am hunched up like everyone else over their cups, I take a few sips and need a piss,   I don't remember going for the piss, outside there are people in the shadows, but I am responding to the call of nature,   one of them greets me, it's the Irishman, Come, he says, finish your ale, slaps me on the back, I will be with you now, someone comes with a torch and lights up their group   the lady I saw earlier – surely not? and two others, two of the Latins, then she's gone, they're all gone as if they were never there,   I walk off to the privies, when I come back, he's waiting on my path,   Thought you had gone, he says   He's a friend I can trust, he says, We're almost cousins and tells me his lineage: I am of Síl Aedha Eaniagh, descendant of Niall Noígíallach, you must have heard of him, Niall of the Nine Hostages who took a daughter of every king he wished, and was King of All Ireland,   I have to go, I say, No No NOOO,

I can help you, I know Eadwin values your family's friendship, you saved his life, he has told me, smiles and we drink to Eadwin and we drink to all of our kin,   then I am floating above it all and have left my body seated and I can see the Irishman talking to the booth-keeper,   what is he doing? they are talking and laughing, and I can see a bag of something going between them, from the Irishman, they laugh,   he comes back with more drinks, Drink this, he says, I want that one I say, Nay, this is for you, my friend and I reach for the other one and then he loses his patience and grabs my cup and forces it to my mouth with his dagger at my throat, Don't doubt me, friend, drink this or you'll be dead by the time I walk out of here   and as I drink I float above myself and watch as I am carried out onto a dirty carrier's cart, loaded like a corpse dead from plague and I hover above my journey to the dark woods above the King's estate, up the track that no one would go   but he cuts a corner or two and counts me dead and does not go as far as he ought but stops on the edge of a steep-sided bank and down into the hollow and tosses me down the bank to the place where the wild garlic grows   and the sun shines first thing and where an old woman knows grows the most succulent cress   and the taste of garlic trickles into my mouth trickles like a rapid infusion and the stench fills my nose and the air around me,   the sensation of gagging begins to rise up and I pull off the hood as quick as I can to gasp for air and free myself from the memory of lying face down in the wild damp beds beside the stream where Vinda finds me,   I am losing track of where and what and who I am and what has happened to me.   Vinda, she said something about the King's men coming and asking after me and he came to visit the Sacred Groves,   I need to see Vinda, I need her to tell me what she can see...

No one can leave the Sacred Groves, having taken so much, without giving back. I give a thanks with a coin, at the place where the two largest branches part, and leave the mystery of this enclosure where memory is restored and make my thoughts turn to the power of the wisdom that can give troubled people parts of themselves back and the spirits that walk with us and guide us to make such things beautiful and possible. In due honour, I walk the paths with the gilded trees, the bare trees which are hung in winter with every sort of thing to bless them and keep them safe, because we have to keep our spirits safe as they keep us safe, our sacred trees: apple, elder, ash, rowan, oak, hazel and above all, the yew where people pay respects, give more than we take, leave something of ourselves behind, make our peace with the world around us as we make our peace with the people around us and finally, just before I smear the red dye across my wrists and neck and around my mouth and eyes, I must leave something valuable at the last altar at the exit pillars, something I value, and in return, I must pick up something left by a previous traveller, to remind us that we own is owned by all of us. I have money left that I have not used for this trip. I leave one of the small bags, unopened on the rough, blackened stone. I have no need of anything, but custom dictates.

Out of nowhere, some big drops of rain land on the table. I want nothing, but the rain comes down suddenly in lumps and I move under the shelter of the big spreading yew which guards the exit. On the other side of the table, my foot treads something hard like the knot of a root. I look down and in the bare earth, half-buried, is a shiny stone. After a few moments, it's in my hands and it strikes me like a bolt to the head, Alwena. Out of nowhere, her name becomes attached to the double band of amber beads that grow in size towards the middle. When I wipe off the dirt, I can see what I am holding – the figure of a hooded woman in bronze, hanging from an amber necklace

Now, I'm running to the King's estate at Londisbeorg. Vinda

tells me that today they will decide. She will come with me, but I say that there is no time. I am terrified of what they are going to do, of what they have already done. Three days, he said, three days and anything could have happened since they poisoned me and left me to die above the banks of the stream.

I am running to speak to the King. Vinda has told me that the King's mind is not made up, but it is not his to make up. That he will be forced to finally do what his wife wants, and the men with her. That the only outcome will bring death and destruction to all of the things we know.

When I arrive, the show is reaching its climax. A great number of men and women are gathered around Edwin and Ethelburga, raised up on a small mound for all to see. She is hidden behind the Latins, and Paulinus is prowling in front of them all. The open space in front of them is for the speakers. It is Paulinus who is ordering events. From his side of the space, a man is in full flow,

'O, king, it seems to me, in comparison of that time which is unknown to us, like the swift flight of a sparrow through the room wherein you sit at supper in winter with your commanders and ministers, and a good fire in the midst, whilst the storm of rain and snow prevails outside; the sparrow flying in at one door, and immediately out at another, and whilst he is within is safe and he immediately vanishes out of your sight, into the dark winter from which he had emerged. So, this is the life of man – it appears for a short space but of what went before or after we know nothing.'

And he stopped. Paulinus urges him to continue. He smiles as if to say he has made his point.

Paulinus stepped forward, again. 'This new doctrina contain something more than this man say. There is a heaven an' there is a hell on both side of this sparrow life. There is many sign and many miracle that God has wrought to you to see this truths, that without this God you are sparrows. Believe me,' and how he was thundering as the rain fell again in big spattering drops, 'your fata, your destiny, will become a choice between this sparrow live between dark and dark and the one true God who will give you all the light of heaven after you die and can tell you everything before you came to this world.' He is crying.

Coifi steps forward, adorned beautifully in his gown of blue and voice as sharp as steel. Edwin looks on like a man who has passed through the gate of death and had come back unwillingly. He twirls his hair like he did when he was an adolescent, in the way that used to make my mother so annoyed.

'Good people, how much have we heard from our friends about this new god. They have tried to discredit our spirits, our gods, our old ways, our friends, our communities, our relations with other people on this island with their words. Their endless words, angry words, threatening words, their uncountable words that we have endured with forbearance and respect. We have done as they bid every time. You have seen how we have allowed them to burn our statues, slander our laws and mock our oaths and we even hear the truth of stories of them butchering the outliers in our land. I have long been poet to King Edwin, servant of our people when they needed to make decisions, helped to make peace with the people we share this land with and with the spirits that guide us. What right have we to ask for these things that are being held up as temptations – their gifts of life, salvation in this world and the next and most laughable of all, eternal happiness? We do not need these things, friends, these are not our ways – ours is a long and deep understanding of the earth, the ways of men and the ways of our ancestors. We stand here in peace, we want them to go in peace, we have our own peace enshrined in our Sacred Groves. We know the nature of our place on earth, we know our place in this world, we know that there is more than we can see, but that the power of what we can see is greater than the power of empty promises for a world that is always going to be better, but, never is. We love the world we are in and we respect all those with whom we share it. We know our gods and they know us. That is all.' He smiled as if he knew nothing but love.

Sensing that Coifi was gaining the upper hand, on this the final hour of debate, incensed Paulinus so much that he seized a spear from a nearby guard of the King.

'Edwin, I say to you,' he screamed, and turned to Coifi, pointing the spear at his throat, 'this man is Conjuror of the Devil and he consor with spirits 'n' we seen him dancing with devils in his foolish and 'eretical sacred grofess that leads your people into sin.' Then he paused, and commanded triumphantly to one of his followers, 'Bring out the gerl.'

And a young girl that was not of the place, or known by anyone there, was brought forward and Paulinus spoke roughly to her, 'Is this the men you seen dancing with devils who seize you and make you perform such acts with him in the sacred grofess? This one...?' as he pointed the spear even closer to Coifi's bare throat.

Coifi wanted to shout out to defend himself but Edwin stepped forward. 'Is this true?' he said. 'Speak, girl.'

Paulinus spoke for her. 'Yes, tell him, yes.' He is fury itself.

'Yes,' she said, bewildered and uncomfortable.

'This is nonsense,' said Edwin. And was looking around as if he were in a place he did not recognise.

'King Edwin, you know how much we hold dear our bonds of honour and each of us holds his position based on that trust we owe one another. Upon my life, Edwin, never ever would I even think of such a thing,' said Coifi, pushing the spear away from his throat.

'It is true, she does not lie,' said a voice, and Queen Ethelberga stepped forward, with her rich, Frankish accent, 'she told the very same thing to me.' She lowers her eyes to the ground and a single tear drops to the floor in front of everyone. Silence.

King Edwin stood in the middle of the group and looked around him, unable to comprehend.

'She is my servant girl,' and she stepped back once again amongst the men in plain cloth.

At this, Paulinus seized his chance and struck Coifi with the spear squarely in the breast. As if by divine intervention, the Latins burst into pious chanting and moved near their leader and surrounded him with singing.

King Edwin rushed to Coifi's aid and called for help.

In the rush of people and the commotion, Paulinus left the group of singing men and taking two of them, he seized some of the King's horses, one of them a stallion for himself, and rode away from the scene as fast as they could.

Coifi was carried inside and two experienced soldiers attempted to treat his wound and medicines were given to him to stop the bleeding and ease his pain and his breathing. I followed them in and watched him begin his journey from the space of this life to the Otherworld.

I watched Edwin retreat from this scene of death and went outside, to see the rise of smoke across the fields on the hill to the east. At first, I could not believe what I was seeing as I computed the possibilities. The other Latins were still chanting like men deranged, but the crowd had dispersed. And all this time I was watching the smoke curl and thicken. I started to run, as fast as I could, madly in the direction of the burning hill. I still wonder what would have happened if I had taken a horse, but I think very little would have been different. I ran and ran, imagining what I would find when I got there. It is not far from Londisbeorg between the fields and the common land, up the brow of one low hill and down to a brook with a sacred well, and then skirting the woods, up to the site of the Sacred Grove.

When I got there, Paulinus was directing the men, the spear in his hand, setting fires under each of the sacred trees, all burning in the overcast day. They had already overturned the altars, the vessels and the wooden objects and everything loose piled up in a bonfire that was now past saving. They were even pulling the trinkets off the trees and the offerings from the altars and passing them to Paulinus, who was piling the valuables to one side. As I got closer to him, I rushed at him and seized the spear from his grasp. With it I swiped the feet from under one of the men, and when the other one turned towards me to defend his friend, I swiped him as hard as I could with the blunt end of the spear and he fell to the ground with just a tiny gash to his temple, that barely trickled blood. I did not mean to kill him. He did not move when Paulinus rushed to tend him.

'Murderer,' he said. 'You have murder a man of God, a man peaceful who was innocent and could not defend.' He spat out the next words, 'Murderer. Edwin shall your action be know.'

He bent down to begin his chanting and making his signs over the dead man's body.

I left them, bent over the dead man, walking away from a burning place, like a dead man myself. Nothing dead is allowed in the Sacred Groves. But in there lay the body of a man that I had killed.

When I arrived at Vinda's house, she was watching the smoke rise below. She bade me sit beside her. We sat while she repaired the bindings on a pair of shoes and patched the hole in the toe.

'I like doing this,' she said, after a long while. 'Look at them, I remember the father of the lad who owns them now getting them new. I remember his wife being taken ill. Now I help him do things like this.' And she finished the deft patching and felt if it would hold. 'Maybe, by the end of the summer, he'll be bringing them back. Nothing lasts long, does it, Ceadd?'

I looked at her to see what she could see.

‘If you go home, it may be wiser. If you go to Edwin, he will not be able to save you from the Latins.’

She creaked as she stood.

‘Nothing can save us now from the Latins.’ She paused. ‘Will you take food with you?’ but didn’t wait for an answer.

When she came out of her house, she gave me a small bag wrapped in cloth and held both my hands in hers. ‘I will not see you again, Ceadd, or your handsome father, but tell him we will share the old songs again in some place...’ and started laughing, motioning to the horizon, ‘maybe somewhere warmer, I always wanted to go somewhere warmer.’

‘Will you be safe? They might come for you. Come with me, then you will see my father again.’

‘If they come, they will find an old woman in a hut at the edge of the woods. Let them come. And you must go. The road will treat you kindly, as it always does, but it is a long way home. Farewell, Ceadd.’

Then, she showed me her back. And I stood like a fool, thinking of the kindnesses I had known from her, when I was here when Edwin returned all those years ago.

Due south, avoid the Latins, avoid the King’s land and his men. Avoid everyone. Through the woods on the narrow paths till it was dark. That was the plan.

The smell of the burning of the sacred trees drifting across my last view, as I turned to set off.

At the river next morning, I persuaded a fisherman on a rickety quay to take me as quickly as he could upstream, with the tide. The weather was windy and coming off the sea with showers of rain drifting in and then falling away, as quickly as they had come. I refused to tell him how far we were going, and he looked suspicious, but I gave him coins that would keep him for a month and told him that was half the fare, the other half when I told him to land. No questions, I told him, and you have never seen me if anyone asks.

We sailed for an hour or so, then the river stopped looking like the ocean and narrowed at the point where a large river met ours from the south. The river turned right and left, and we sailed along in silence, the wind and the rain sweeping us upstream in sudden and fitful ways, with no sign of people, apart from small clearings and smoke rising from hidden houses. When we turned away from the full brunt of the sea wind, we sailed into a more tranquil river, browner, sluggish.

'Here?' he asked. I struggled at first to understand him.

'No, not here.' He clearly was struggling to understand me.

Another mile and we came to the confluence with another river. 'Is this the Yr?' I asked.

It took ten minutes of talking around one another to reach agreement. Yes, it was. 'Go up this river,' I said.

'I don't know this river, I have never been this far before.'

But I dangled the next bag of money. I wondered if he might kill me and dump my body, so I kept my dagger just to hand and kept my eyes on him.

We passed a small, sad little place. 'Yrmun,' he said.

We sailed another half an hour. When it felt certain we were away from any prying eyes, I pointed to him to pull in where the river had doubled-back on itself and left an almost-island, well-wooded and undisturbed. I dangled the bag in front of him. 'There,' I pointed, and he steered his boat neatly into the little sandy bank, so I could step ashore without getting wet.

'I thank you. I give you an extra coin for your silence,' and pushed him away, with something like a smile on his face.

If my calculations were right, I could rest here tonight and be at my next stop in half a day's march west. The night was sharp and fresh, and the birds woke me early from my fitful sleeping.

There was no path, which made me feel more at ease, as I stepped as silently as possible through the spindly alders and birch that were just coming into leaf. I calculated that by now Edwin's men would have searched the estate and ridden out to Godmunthingaham and searched Vinda's house and ridden past the smouldering remnants of the place we once counted sacred. If I knew anything of Paulinus, he would be looking for a scapegoat, so that the focus of attention was the fugitive murderer of an innocent priest, not the death of Coifi, and he would be directing Edwin to send men out on all roads west. The roads I had travelled by just a few days earlier.

By the end of the day, I forded the sparkling stream and crouched to spy the lie of the land. I could hear the tinkling of the branches above the shrine and the drone of bees and insects in the late afternoon arching sunlight. Nothing moved at all in the clearing, and from here I could not see the front of the house. Crouching in the cool of the clayey bank, I tried to imagine what I would say and was astonished at the words that were coming to my mind, unannounced, like guests you had not dared hoped would come. Not wanting to arrive like a robber in the night, I waited for the sun to shrink a little more below the trees before I finally scrambled out of my hiding place.

Across the little meadow and around the back of the house, I hoped I would be unseen. I could hear better from here the low voice coming from inside, but only the one. Otherwise, all around in the air, on the ground and in the trees, no sound. I waited a little while longer and finally crept to the door at the front and knocked. No response. I knocked again. Finally, the door was opened by the little figure of the old woman who had served me food last time I was there. Once again, she did not speak but just let the door stand half-open.

At first, my eyes just saw vague shapes in the unaccustomed gloom. I closed the door behind me and stood against the wall, trying to take it all in. This was not what I had imagined.

In the same place as before, was the young man who had

been mutilated, lying motionless now. His eyes were closed. The body they had been mourning that had been laid out in the centre of the room had gone, and now in its stead was the little child, who had only a few days earlier been playing outside. The keening for the dead that I had heard last time was now only in the mouth of one of them. The other was comforting the bent-forward figure of Alwena, her hair falling forward to the floor, from whom no sound at all came.

I crouched on the floor, wanting to melt into the walls, uncomfortable with these strangers in these terrible times of death and suffering. I waited. The light outside faded into twilight and then into night. How long I stayed I do not know. But I became aware that, perhaps, my presence was stopping them do what they needed to do to vent their grief, so I stood silently and moved to the door and opened it. The cooler fresh air of the evening rushed in and one of the women looked up from a place that is the other side of our minds.

'Wait,' she said, 'not yet. Sit. Not yet.'

The door was closed, and I slid down against the wall and fell asleep with a thirst that tormented me all night and made me dream of water, bathing in water that was not to be drunk, and the more I sank into the lovely clear water, the more a hand stopped my mouth from bending to drink. When a hand held out a rough beaker to drink from, I drank it down in one.

Squatting down and eyeing me straight into the marrow of my eyes was a face that was flesh and blood and not from the land of the spirits. 'You were thirsty, you cried out in the night. But we were awake.' Then she took back the cup. 'It is good to see that we are not alone.'

She stood up and bade me sit at the table and offered me some breakfast. The dead child was still on the table, but the other two women were sleeping in their bed.

'When she wakes,' she said, chewing her food with some

effort and fewer teeth, 'you must take her away from here.'

She looked at me again, with eyes tired of seeing this world.

I must have reacted in a way that gainsaid her.

'You came back for her. She cannot stay here. Not now. We will look after one another till it is our time. But she is young. Take her from here, it isn't safe for her.'

She spoke sharply in the old way that sounds like the words our poets use. I have to gather the scatter of the sounds of her words and put them back together again.

She pushes me gently towards the door. 'She will resist leaving here but you are to take her away. We have known that Edwin would accept the Latins and their angry god for a while now.' She opens the door and nudges me outside. 'Who knows how long it will last, but they are ready to destroy everything that does not take the oaths or shows the least resistance. Even King Eadwine knows Alwena, which means that his Queen does, too. No, Ceadd, you must take her and keep her safe.'

Outside, the night had fallen with such an intensity. The blackness was almost tangible, and the stars so cold and remote. 'Go back to the river. Follow it, but stay on the north bank. There are few people, few paths, no roads. Treat the forest in the usual way, show respect, make offerings.' And as she stared out at the unmoving darkness, she said, 'I could almost imagine it was me, but it isn't, I am too old.'

Pause.

'You will come to one of the old roads that the Romans built, you will know it immediately, it is the only one you will meet for five days travel west. You will find there a ford. In my day there was a bridge. Beware the folk there, they are well-known for every conceivable crime. Keep going along the river.' Then, she looked at me, without sentiment. 'Roads and people are danger. Who knows now how far the power of the Latins will go? It will not come to a good end with Eadwine, I have seen it written.

But that was his choice.' She grabs my hands and clasps them to her lips and kisses them and whispers words of wishing over them, words so old that they conjure spirits.

'Listen,' she said, 'and trust them.'

The air moves and we hear the life in every living thing beat as if there is so much heart that the world cannot contain it. The space folds back and she looks up from the depth.

'I will give you this. I did not think I would be doing this to a stranger.' She put her hands inside her mantle and passed me something the size of a human palm, wrapped in a cloth of soft material. 'Love her, Ceadd. Take care of her. She has lost everything here and you may never find her. But be free with her. And this,' she nodded to my hand, 'was her mother's, and her mother's mother's.'

Pause.

'I have never been beyond where the river meets the road. But send word, Ceadd, when you find safety and can make a place to live.' Then, she went inside and left me outside to contemplate what she had just said.

And so it came to happen: Alwena resisted leaving the corpse of the child, and the kin she shared a home with and the stillness of the dead was rocked by her loud entreaties to be allowed to stay, until halfway through the morning a man and a woman came through, carrying large packs, who told the story in the fifty paces it took to walk past the house and its fields, of the burning of their shrines and their barns and their houses by men they did not know. and how hiding in the woods was the only thing that saved them.

Who were these men? we asked. The King's men?

'The King of Kings men, they had heard say. Brutes with no mercy.' And the haunted ones walked off into the woods, barely able to keep up with themselves.

And so, we left. We did not speak for days. She was weak

with mourning and carrying a very heavy heart that left her for long hours in a state of heedlessness and slowed us down, to the point where I would stop to let her catch up with me and then she would not be roused for an hour or two but seemed to sleep in a trance, but would wake and not recognise me or where she was. Instead, she would sit in dumb acceptance until roused to walk another mile, or as long as her heart allowed.

I began to despair that we would ever survive. I began to doubt the wisdom of accepting her on my journey. Worse still, I began to ask myself what my journey was.

We would both sit in silence, unspeaking for some unmeasured period of time until roused by some animal or the weather or a strange sound.

And so it continued, the longer we were together the less we talked. We slept at night in much the same manner as we travelled during the day: in a withering, cold, indifferent silence of separateness.

It took us days and days to reach the place where the river met the road. To be honest, if we had been taken by robbers and cut to pieces it would have been a blessing for us both.

The weather had taken a cold, foggy turn and the showers of April had become wretched and long-lasting until everything was always wet, and we had even given up making a fire, huddling together for warmth in the hollow of the roots of a tree or under some overhanging of branches that lent a little bit of shelter from the rain for a while.

I stumbled across the road without even realising it until I had almost crossed it. She was a hundred paces behind me when I stood in a moment of energy on the cambered paving, thinking that was all not lost and we had at least reached this point, alive and together. For a brief while, I felt the rain lift and something like sunshine fall through the trees, when from just around the corner, where I presumed the road met the crossing, voices and laughter drifted towards us. They seemed to be moving in our direction. I stood frozen for a brief moment, weighing up all the options. If they saw us, they would be upon us in an instant and there would be no escape and I could not trust what sort of people they might be.

As if the last few days had never happened, I leapt off the road and into the trees in the direction that I could hear Alwena coming, I just needed to reach her and still her before they saw us. When I spied her through the trees, she was motionless with her arms in the air, mouthing words, but to something that only she could see, her clothes ripped and sodden and unnoticed. It was her soundless crying and something like the despair of her spirit crying out to leave her body. For the first time in my life, I found how love must face terror and how beauty is only in a face for a while and love does not rest there. I picked her up and carried her in her soundless agonies to a place where she could rest, and she did not resist.

She fell asleep, wrapped around me. The voices faded and we lifted ourselves up, weary and hungry.

Later that afternoon, I found a place of clearings, where two or three meadows joined one another, gathered around a collection of rocks, and on top, a tiny hut, where once grass and hay had been stored. It must also have been a watch-tower commanding views over the forest for many miles.

Here we stayed for the days of the flowering, away from everything. Never in my life had I spent so much time surrounded by trees, birds, insects and all the living things apart from men. Never in my life did I appreciate how much the intrusion of men causes disturbance, unrest of the spirit, vexation, distress, unhappiness and all the things we associate with loneliness we associate with the negative, all of which are just as made in the minds of men by men. The world has other rhythms that do not change just because men might say them or gainsay them. This was the world that I had stepped into, unwittingly through a screen, into a world where we sank, both of us willing, into a place like a dream we could touch.

By day, I would find food, she would rest and recover and when I returned, I would find a new addition to our hut. A candle and a candleholder, or some sweet soup of things she found at the edges of the fields, some wild apples she had found from last winter. And I could count the words we used on the fingers of two hands.

The view from the topmost rock was like a view from the crag above our home in Gwynedd: a sea of green in every direction, on a clear day the outline of high ground to the west, flat unending green to the east. There was almost no break at all in the undulating flood of the trees going out in every direction. The river itself was not visible, nor were the sides of this valley clear. There was sometimes smoke visible, curling up into the air, but it never seemed to be in the same place two days together and the things I thought I could discern one day, I could never discern the next. All regal things and common things, all gods and all religions and all riches and all poverty seemed to just be meaningless words from a forgotten language that had lost their power.

One morning, I woke to a dog bark, coming from the south side of the woods. I woke Alwena and put my finger to her mouth. Within the time it takes to light a fire we had all our things packed and were at the door of the hut. The light was still just breaking over our hut, and our door was in shadow. If we were very quick, we could run down the slope through the meadow to the north and hit the edge of the woods before they'd reached the grounds from where they could survey the whole expanse of the clearing.

'Run,' I pointed, and she was the Alwena I had forgotten, running fleeter than me through the long grass, throwing off sparkles of dew as she whipped through the meadow. We threw ourselves into the thickest part of the wood and watched, hoping that the dog didn't catch our scent or was forbidden to seek us out.

We must find a place of peace, I said to her, but soundlessly, as we had grown accustomed.

Keeping the sun behind us we moved swiftly and rested often. Always the river to our left, always mindful of the paths and the people. Stay away from the paths and the people. Rarely did we see any sign of the intrusion of humans and we became adept at living off of the uncultivated, the unasked for, the untamed.

Through all this time, she led the way. I felt her flow back into herself. The peace we talked of flowed from her. It became her journey. We walked till sunset.

She woke in the sunrise and made the sign not to speak. I had grown used to her silent ways and her strangeness and put it down to our unfamiliarity with one another and her dealing with all of the things she had lost so recently and was still mourning. I had grown used to her absences and never asked why, but this time when she returned in the midday, she looked pale and said without words, *Today we stay. At this point here. And find me these*, and presented me with a very particular flower on a stem.

When I returned with a small bunch of the flowers, she was asleep, curled up into a tight ball. I placed them near her head and left her underneath my cloak.

I walked alone, an hour or two to the west, when I met a wall of stones hidden beneath the densest, most impenetrable, thorny thickets we had yet met. Try as I might there was no way around it to the north or to the south. There was no gap, no gate, no hole, not even a badger's hole visible for half an hour's walk in any direction.

So, I walked south, down the sloping woods through the

undergrowth that had long tentacles of thorny twines of wild rose or raspberry or some such, and after a good deal of effort I reached the banks of the river. Without realising it, we had hit some higher ground and the river below me was very fast-flowing. It suddenly occurred to me that we might not be able to go any further west without making some serious deviations.

When I returned to Alwena, she was awake but looked ill and the look on her face made me wary. She was sat up and looked feverish, rocking slightly. 'Leave me,' she said.

I left her. I spent the rest of the day imagining what I might find when I got back to her. What I would do if she passed from this life. I watched the place that she lay for the rest of the day for a sign of life. When I went to her, it was dark, and I lay down next to her and she asked me why I had left her for so long. She was clammy and sweaty and weak and asked me to warm her.

She was awake before me. Her fever had passed.

'Come with me,' I said, and took her to the place I had found yesterday that barred our route west, and we walked to the north and then we turned to the south. When we reached the river-bank, she took one look and smiled.

Perfect, she mouthed, and the next thing I knew she was in the water, clinging to a branch and pulling herself against the current up the stream. The icy water took my breath away as I followed her up the river, flailing for my footing on the bed of the river which was full of uneven stones I lost my balance on and deep holes, where I slid gasping under the water. She was laughing and moving slowly away from me, calling to me to catch her up and keep up. For long moments, I forgot all of the fear and wariness and sense of being caught by surprise ,and just laughed and shouted and waded behind her up the bed of the river, between the high banks of the densest woods, with the calls of the birds flitting high overhead and the crashing of water swirling all around us.

Ten minutes in the water and I was growing cold, out of the warmth of the sun. The river maintained its speed and depth, and then I realised in the shadowy light that I had lost sight of Alwena as the river disappeared around a bend and I could no longer hear her laughter. I panicked and ran and fell and splashed and shouted, desperate to find her, not to lose her to some terrible fate.

'Alwena, Alwena...' I was running wildly, and shouting wildly, heedless of the cuts to my feet on the sharp rocks in the river or the bruises as I fell from losing my footing. I rounded the bend, but she was not there, the sun slanted directly in my eyes now in a natural clearing of light and grass and I stopped.

'Alwena,' I screamed, in panic, 'Alwena, Alwena...'

Silence. Just the water's sound rolling over the stones. And birds, more distant, now.

Then, laughter, behind me.

'Alwena,' I shouted her name.

Laughter again and above me, now.

I turned and looked up. She was perched on a branch, hanging out over the river. She had watched all of the flailing, panicking moments. Then, she laughed, rolling in her laughter on the branch, stretched out over the river.

I fell to my knees in the middle of the river and laughed, too. I didn't know whether to go to her and punish her like a naughty child or go to her and push her off the branch. Instead, I walked to the bank and lay in the grass and stared up at the sky above this place. She threw herself down by my side and joined in this floating sense of sky and blue air all around, undisturbed in this little bowl of space, topped off by an uninterrupted line of high trees slowly spinning around us, trying to take it all in: the peace, the warmth, the enclosed shape like a huge palm of a protecting hand, the river, shallow and floating over a pebbly bed and full of fishes lazing in the sunshine, and the flowers and the insects and bees loud in the glade, loud enough to almost drown out shouts. Over on the far ridge, I saw a movement and pulled Alwena to me, and we watched as the little group of roe-deer followed well-worn paths down the slope to drink at the river and graze on the soft, sweet grass.

I whispered to her, 'The Lord and Lady of this place.'

We let them take their ease, until they climbed the other side of the valley and disappeared into the thick undergrowth.

That night we made camp. When I woke, it was dawn, and she wasn't there. I ran down to the river where we had stood earlier and once again, marvelled at the beauty of this secret place on this river, and stared out across the compass of the clearing and could not see her, could not discern one step of movement. Her not being with me was something that stuck me like a knife blade through my chest, the pain was violent, like a jolt that brought sickness and dryness.

I would listen. Just let me imagine the sounds she might make through the world. Nothing except sparrows chattering in the bushes across the river and the arc of crows up above my head. Like a whisper, less than the sound of deer's hooves, I caught the lightness of a step behind a large clump of trees on the other side of the river. I crouched into silence behind some trees overhanging the water. She was bending down and walking and picking at the same time, her feet hidden under a few inches of marshy water, gathering some plants as she went. She was utterly oblivious. Her dark hair was untied and hung down hiding her face entirely, her long legs like a wading bird as she placed her finds into the folds of her gathered skirts.

When I was almost in striking distance of her, I whispered to her from the branch of a tree, as the moon sank behind the ridge of trees above and the sun rose behind us, like an owl might, not with words, but in the call of the birds, *I will love you,* said the cry, *I will love you...*

And she looked up at the owl and kissed the flowers she had picked and called back without words.

There's a sound like a woodpecker just above my head. I freeze because I don't want to disturb it. It drums again, lightly. There's someone with me. *Where's Alwena? Don't go again, Alwena.* The someone isn't Alwena. I can't bear it if she goes one more time. The separation is like a stab wound. Picnic looks at me wondering if he should answer the door.

I rock forward, gasping for air. I am choking and can't breathe. I have been so deep and so long without air, I choke. Picnic stands up and pats my back, tries to get me to drink. To calm down.

'Take deep breaths, if you can,' he's saying, 'breathe slowly.'

The door opens. It's Full English.

'You OK, brotherr?' he barks, when he sees me coughing and spluttering.

'He's ok, yeah,' says Picnic.

'We've mebbe spotted yer man Milton. When yer rreddee,' he says, and disappears.

It takes me five minutes to get my breath back.

'Nearly had you in the recovery position, joker,' says Picnic. 'You were that close,' and puts his thumb and forefinger together with a millimetre to spare.

I take two or three glasses of water to calm down.

'Sorry,' I say.

Picnic shakes his head. 'No sorry. I'm sorry for doubting you. Need a coffee?'

I nod.

15

About Heather

It's well after dawn and the jackdaws are deafening. They seemed to have settled on some of our trees to roost. I walk through their chiding in the coolness of this May morning. I can always find a coffee and some breakfast in the Clubhouse and when I get there, I sit on a large settee in one of the dark corners we made and feel the urge to just sleep and let it all go. I wake up with the coffee cup cold in my hand, still three-quarters full. It's still quiet in here, and I resist the temptation to nod off again.

There's two or three people who come over, pass the time of day. MP, who's not been well recently, who landscapes our public areas with the most surprising stuff – glass leaves dangling in the most unexpected places that really look like leaves, or a jam-jar observatory for looking at invisible things like poverty and love and longing, or the wrecks of a few burnt out cars that he joined together to make a mini version of Blackpool Winter Gardens. He sits down and tells me his plans to make a maze of human pains in his own garden, which he says is based on his own body.

I met him years ago when he was being arrested for guerrilla gardening in a garden centre car park which belonged to a Lord Someone one or other.

'They should've offered me a job, rather than trying to put

me inside for doing what they're trying to encourage everyone else to do,' he said, as we drove him away in a borrowed car. He lived in a sort of half-way house, so coming to us was a step up, even back then, when we didn't know what we were doing. I said I'd come to find out more about what he was planning when I had a bit of free time. We shook hands as he left, an old habit from OTC.

I asked Chow Mein to join me and Smoothie after a piece of toast and another coffee.

'You ok?' said Chow Mein when he arrived. 'You look like you been up all night.'

'Can't hide nothing from you. I'm still thinking about all the loose ends from yesterday. Look, Milton's got a gun, so he says. He's lied to us, as you found out. And does he have some connection with the guys with the shotguns?'

I looked at Chow Mein to pull some miracle from the skies.

Chow Mein taps his phone. 'Wait', he says and spins a finger around his temple and goes up to get a coffee.

First Picnic, then Smoothie sits down with us.

'I wonder whether what happened yesterday was just a series of coincidences or they're coming for us? I know that sounds over-dramatic, but we should work our way through all the possibilities.'

They nodded for me to carry on.

'Ok, that makes me feel better. I say we act quickly. Find Shotgun Joe and his shot-up Beamer, try to find out what they really want, then get to Sid's, the clowns who gave Milton the gun, and try to find out what they want and then pickup Milton and, well, what do you suggest we do with Milton?'

'I've traced the Beamer. It drove down the M1 without stopping and then spent four hours at an address in the east of the city, towards Rotherham, probably being repaired. Parked up above Hillsborough and it hasn't moved since last night.'

‘Smoothie, you’re banging the drum, brother,’ said Picnic, ‘very impressive.’

‘Yeah, first stop, then. Thank you, Smoothie. I think we all go, in two cars. We don’t know what these guys can do. Agreed?’

They nodded.

‘What about Milton? Milton is a liar, we know that and potentially the gun thing is a big deal.’

‘Why do you think that?’ said Picnic. ‘If he’s just a loser, which he seems to be, he seems to have got himself into a lot of bother with a load of psychos and they’ve given him a gun. So what? We’ve got guns. Lots of people these days got guns.’

‘I know,’ I said, ‘but what if Milton isn’t what he says he is? We know he’s lying about some things and people who lie about some things can lie about anything. What if he’s not at all what he says he is?’

‘I’d buy that,’ said Chow Mein. ‘Every bit of his story that we’ve checked so far is a lie. I think we just keep checking and then ask him what he’s really saying.’

‘Gentlemen, think about what we’ve got here – we do what we do without bringing attention to ourselves. However many years we’ve been going, we’ve always done everything silently.’ I paused for the right words. ‘The worse it gets out there, in Lardland, the more I worry about what will happen to us. I’m worried that anyone could come up here one day, the Feds, the Council, the druggie gangs – even people like us looking for a place to escape – anyone, coming up that road who we don’t want coming up that road.’ I paused again. ‘I don’t want to lose it. And I don’t want to go mad with paranoia. I don’t have a Lady Macbeth taking me to the dark side, brothers, but I think we need to sink lower and lower into the ground. Pull down the blinds. Shut up shop. Disappear.’

Chow Main spoke, ‘You mean like close it down? Walk away?’

I looked at him, saying the unthinkable. ‘Kill off Burgerman.

Kill the myths about us. We have no idea any more about who knows about us or how they find us or –'

'Or how to kill the myths. Do we really know how to kill a myth?' said Picnic, his voice always so big.

'And we just turn people away who come here? Most of them with nothing or nowhere to go?' Smoothie said. 'Not sure we can do that easily.'

'I take what you're saying, yeah, but what if Milton happens to leave the gun lying around next time he comes to see us, and then, next day we get a visit from the Feds who've been tipped off there's guns floating around a community of non-existent people who haven't surfaced for years but are wanted for stuff? We know it's stupid stuff, but some of us can't go back out there. Not only that, but we live here without paying rent or bills or anything.'

'Hey,' said Chow Mein, 'just think before we do anything.'

'Let's meet in half an hour and try to get down to Sheffield before they set off again. Smoothie, if the Beamer does go somewhere, make sure we can track him while we're moving. Chow Mein, can you try to get in touch with Milton and ask him to come and see us? Picnic, can you make sure that we have all the equipment with us that we might need with these psychos? Also, we're out all day, so come prepared for a day trip.'

'Have you spoken to Full English about what he said to you this morning?' said Picnic.

'I haven't seen Full English this morning. Where is he?'

Picnic looked at me quizzically. 'OK, think we should go and see him before we set off, 'cos he thinks they've spotted Milton.'

'Why didn't you tell me before?' I ask him.

'You've got a lot on your plate, and you're gettin' old.'

Full English is bent over a computer and looks at me strangely as I walk in. 'You ok now?'

Not quite sure what he means, I say, 'Yeah, good morning to you as well. They tell me you spotted Milton.'

'Mebbe. Where would ye go if you think you're house is bein' watched? You canna go to Ibiza 'cos you're in the middle of a job. Hotel in town. You wanna be amongst people so yous feel safer. I checked the Queens Hotel, in Leeds, big, roomy, no one gonna notice ye. Nothing. So then, I checked the CCTV around the streets down there, in an' out of the hotel an' there's a guy I swear looks like him.'

'Show me,' I said.

So, he calls up the footage. 'It's a wee bit grey but he's wearin' the same clothes he had on when he was here, remember? Look, there he is stood outside, lightin' up, an' then he's on his phone. Ten minutes later, this guy turns up. Canna be a hundrred perrcent surre, but there's a lot of similarity.'

'Bloody hell, there is.' I'm peering at the screen trying to remember what he was wearing. 'Get Smoothie to check the pictures of him when he was here. And who's the guy he's meeting? See if we know him from before.'

I look at Full English, 'Magnificent work, brother. If we can find out who the other guy is, then we're getting somewhere.'

'Well,' he says, 'I followed him backwards, thinkin', the other guy must be in tuin if he can get there in ten minutes and I reckon he's come duin uit of this buildin' here.'

I follow the mass of shapes moving endlessly across one another on the footage and see exactly what Full English is getting at, and know exactly which building he's pointing at.

'That's the fucking Council buildings. Jesus. Can you get the best version of these two fuckwits and get us a picture of them both and send it asap? You done good there, FE. Very good.'

In the car with Chow Mein we've gone very silent. We're following Smoothie and Picnic. He stares at the road. We've gone over and over what Milton could be and what he's up to with his mate from the Council. We've gone very silent. We're going on the back roads, over the hills, slightly out of our way, no cameras, no traffic. I imagine holding a glass of beetroot juice out in front and focus on not spilling any of the staining liquid. Focus on what I want to happen next. Unpick all the possible plays before they happen. Have a simple goal that serves a purpose. I focus and focus and I focus again, but it's not emerging, the thing that I want most to happen is not appearing, the vision is not manifesting itself. Instead, the fields and the trees keep flying by and I feel the bumps in the road and the liquid running down my hand and drip onto the floormat in the footwell below.

Part of me wants to disappear inside another existence that doesn't exist. Part of me wants to put a gun at Milton's throat and ask him what he's doing and part of me wants to shake all the Miltons in the world and ask them, what combination of blindness, stupidity and despair makes you accept the world for what it is and not want to do anything about any of it but just carry on walking blindly into servitude, debt, powerlessness and the whole ugliness of compliance with the shit of the world? I can't hold the glass straight and I open the window and pour the imaginary liquid out of the real window and then throw the unreal glass as well.

A message comes through from Picnic. *Just here on the right.* We drive slowly past a 1930s semi with a black BMW parked in the drive. It's on a steep hill, looking down the valley. *Are you sure?* I text back. He's pulled over, just out of sight of the house and we pull over in front of them.

'According to the map, there's a back garden and an access road as well,' says Smoothie.

'We'll go and have a look there first, then knock on the door.'

Chow Mein leads the way. The house is in the middle of a

small row of neat, suburban, red-brick houses and at the back are long gardens accessed via a pot-holed lane, wide enough for a car to get down, and beyond the stone wall, there are woods rising up to the moors behind. We peer over the fence at the back. The garden of this house is twice as wide as the other gardens and there's a long row of outbuildings running the full length of one side. Some of the sheds have got wire fronts and what could be animal cages inside. We go back around the front.

'I've looked at the Beamer and it looks like it has a new sunroof!' said Picnic, rather pleased. 'Did it have a sunroof before? I can't remember.'

'I think they've annexed next door as well,' I said to Picnic and Smoothie. 'I think we just knock on the door, nice and calm and say hello. What do you think?'

'We'll wait at the gate. We don't want to get too close and personal just yet,' said Picnic.

The two of us walked up to the front door and knocked.

A young woman answered. She hung on the door, almost squashing her head in the gap. 'Yeah?' she said, 'do I know you?'

'Maybe,' I said. 'Your friends paid us a visit yesterday. We've come to say sorry.'

'Huh,' she said, and shut the door.

Chow Mein signed, *Move away from the door and come back with me to the middle of the drive*. We did. He always expects the worse. Usually, he's right.

'What's happening?' shouted Picnic.

Chow Mein signed him to be ready. I looked around: gardens, cars, a mother with a pram across the road walking down the hill to do shopping, a guy on a bike in blue lycra cycling up the hill, not giving up, not getting off. I once went for tea and cake to a colleague's house after school, years ago. She lived on a boring road, trees, birds, people shopping, women with prams, guys on bikes. 'Next door was cordoned off at the weekend 'cos they found a headless corpse in the boot of next door's car,' she said, as she presented me with a home-made lemon drizzle. 'Lovely,' I said, 'very moist, the way I like it.' I wasn't really listening to what she said.

The door opened again. Same head, 'Come in.' She opened the door just a little bit wider than a human's head and we squeezed in. 'They have to wait outside,' nodding at Picnic and Smoothie. Then she closed the door. 'Go through,' and nodded in the other direction.

Down the hall and into a room that's a lot bigger than I expected. There's a photocopier whirring away and spitting out paper at one end. In front of it, a desk with two people looking at us as we walk in.

'Welcome,' she said, 'an unexpected moment.' She stood up but just to wave us to a seat each. Her friend said nothing. 'How can we help?' From upstairs there were sounds of footsteps and voices, but nothing more.

'Well, I don't know if you know who we are –' I began.

'We do, yeah.'

'This isn't quite what I – erm, we – were expecting. Yesterday two of your guys turned up – one fired off a shotgun – and well, it could have gone either way. And now we're here.'

'No need for any apologies, but we accept them.'

'Listen, you sent two guys up asking questions and they were armed. Why? What is it you want?'

'Good question. Two good questions.' Then she nodded to her colleague who passed her a folder. 'Is this you? I mean, you plural,' and pushed the folder over to me.

I picked it up and opened it. Photos, notes, lists. Me, Smoothie, Picnic, Chow Mein, Malcolm. All of us. And photos of the Circle. I looked at her. 'What is this? You Police or some department of the Government? You spying on us? Why?'

Chow Mein was busy devouring it, memorising it, checking

the validity of all of it. He picked up every photo and piece of paper in the file.

'If I said that one of you was working for a department of the Police, would you believe me?'

'No,' I said, 'absolutely not. I would say you were lying.'

She laughed, without malice. 'I have to admit, you're right. I couldn't have those sorts of people here. We think you're safe, as much as anyone of us is safe. But we had to check.'

She nodded again to her colleague to pass another set of files, this time four or five thick bundles of brown. She didn't pass them to me this time, but flicked through them. For my benefit.

'As you can see, you aren't the only set of folks stepping outside the system. But more on that later. Would you like a cup of tea or anything? To be honest, we're a bit surprised to see you so soon after our visit yesterday. But we're glad, aren't we, Jenny?' Her colleague nodded. 'How did you find us?' she smiled. 'Bojo is going to have to explain how you found us so quickly. Bojo is the aggressive one you dealt with yesterday.'

'And the Spanish one, who's he?'

'Actually, he's not Spanish, he's Basque. His name is Ferdi to us. But as you know, everyone we know goes by more than one name. What are you going to do about this, Burgerman?'

She smiled again, leaning forward to encourage my answer. I felt like I was being interviewed by someone who knew I wasn't going to get the job. It was my turn to laugh.

'Good question. We threw a tracker in, just a cheap one and it led us here. When Bojo was losing his cool. But why the aggro and the guns? I don't see any guns, unless your friend here has got something hidden under her files.'

I smiled at her, but she didn't respond.

'Your place has got a reputation for drugs, violence – your Burgerman and some of the others have got reputations – '

I burst out laughing. 'You sure you got the right Burgerman?

We don't do drugs, Miss. And the violence was a long time ago.'

'OK, we wanted your interest. We wanted to talk.'

Chow Mein nudged me, and signed he wanted something. He got his phone out. 'My friend wants you to do something for us before we go any further. We need you to find out who this guy is, can you do that?'

I showed her the photo. Her friend took the phone and sent the photo to her computer. Chow Mein beamed at her but nothing doing.

'We'll let you know what we find,' she said. 'By the way, I'm Heather. Not my real name, of course. What's your not real name?' and she looked at us both, with that smile.

'Kevin Baxter,' I said, and Chow Mein looked at me. 'And this is Chow Mein.'

'Nice to meet you, Kevin and Chow.'

'You have to call him Chow Mein or don't use a name. Can't call him Chow, ok?'

'Sure,' she said. 'Cup of tea?'

'Yeah, just me, he'll have water.' And she got up to pour the tea herself and passed a cup to me and a bottle to Chow Mein.

'The tea's lovely,' I said.

'You still serving that stuff that says it's Fairtrade but isn't really?'

'We were doing till yesterday morning, yeah. But your friend Dotty changed all that.'

'Oh, Dotty, is a sweetie, don't you think? She can actually taste about 25 different brands of tea, blindfolded. It actually matters to her. Don't you think it's strange what matters to us? I mean, it, whatever the *it* is, seems to choose us, not the other way round, don't you think? Dotty thinks that tea chose her, not the other way round. If you ask her after twenty minutes of listening to her reasons, you'll be completely convinced.'

At exactly that moment, and only as she was finishing that

last sentence, that I sensed her youth and her innocence in the admiration a young person has for an older person.

'You would like her,' she added. 'She liked you,' and smiled.

'What do you do with what you've created up there, Mr. Kevin Baxter?' She wasn't smiling now.

'I don't understand, we don't *do* anything with what we have created, we just live it.'

'So, you and your merry little band live like Robin Hood and fuck everyone else? Because it's become a nice little club just for you and your merry men. And some merry women, I imagine?'

I laughed. 'There is no plan, there is no endgame, we just survive with the people we trust.'

'Survive? What about your hospitality, your advice, your help, your services to the poor and the downtrodden...are you forgetting those?'

'You make it sound like an accusation.'

Chow Mein nudges my arm, *Let's go, this is bollux.*

Heather laughs. 'Don't go just yet, I'm sorry, it wasn't meant as an accusation. Let me start again. You and your friends work together. You and your people up there all work together. It'd be impossible without doing that, wouldn't it, without working together?'

I nod. I sign to Chow Mein to sit tight for a bit longer.

'What if we worked together?'

'What do you mean?'

'Well, the more people you work with who share your goals means the more likely you are to achieve those goals. From the Mafia to the bankers, from the cartels to the headbangers at the football matches, cooperation is the way forward.'

'Is that a conspiracy theory?' I laughed.

'Well, isn't every meeting eventually a conspiracy? Conspiracy theorists are mocked because of that simple question – when does a meeting become a conspiracy?'

'What are your goals?' I asked her. 'In fact, what are our goals? I think I'd be more interested to know what you think we're doing up there in the Circle? You seem to have worked everything else out.' My turn to smile.

'Democracy is dead. For several reasons. But it's dead. It was only ever half alive,' she said. 'These times we live in are devoid of ideas. Nothing really changes because there are no ideas left, there is just *Stop this* or *Stop that*, which isn't really an idea, it's a reaction. Stop pollution or stop corruption – these are just responses to things, typical of a society devoid of ideas. People who have ideas aren't listened to because ideas are conceptions, thoughts based on mental awareness, processes or understanding and most people don't want abstract, in fact, they're taught that abstract is bad, or laughable, because it's idealistic or just irrelevant in a world of possessions and object-fetish status worship. And then there's money, of course. Democracy is dependent on the masses and the masses have to be manipulated and bullied and imprisoned. Good democracy is dependent on good ideas. We have been duped out of our birthright of responsibility and rights and good democracy and been given easy living in place of those things, like penguins in a shabby zoo. Our goals are the presentation of good ideas in a practical form put into practice. In other words, ambitious direct and non-direct action for good ideas.' She smiled.

'I don't disagree with you, Heather. I like you, and Dotty and your friend. You seem nice people –'

'Not nice,' she said, shaking her head, 'nice is an undemocratic word. It actually sits right at the heart of the problem.'

'OK, not nice, but what has that got to do with us? You think we're too nice? Wrong sort of tea and bumbling about pointlessly?'

'Do you think petitions work? Demonstrations work? Serving tea and buns works? Doing good works *works*? Teaching people about racism works? Letters to the paper? Charity? Voluntary work? Voting? Going to meetings? Do you really think any of it works? When they're in Davos or New York or Harvard Business School or at the MoD or Whitehall or some posh arsehole golf club in Sussex or Gentlemen's club in London that they're desperately working out how to counteract the good works of a night shelter in Paddington or a letter from someone in Fife about inequality? They can ignore demonstrations of over a million people against a War. All words and most demonstrations are contemptuously ignored.'

'You're far too young to remember that,' I said.

She eyed me without a smile.

'I remember this,' and pulled out another folder and passed it to me. I opened it, not really wanting to. It contained colour photos of injuries. And details of them written down, when they were inflicted and the circumstances.

'Everyone of those people is working with us. Every one of those injuries was inflicted by a member of the organisations policing us, here, in Britain, in the last month. There are over two hundred and thirty specific injuries inflicted on nearly fifty people. We have a folder like that for every month for the last four years. As you know, they control the media, the legal system, the police, the armed forces, the special forces, the secret services, the financial system, the ownership of property, the education system, the parliamentary system. I don't need to go on. The only thing we can really decide is whether we have red sauce or brown sauce on our chips. Don't think that they haven't even manipulated that choice. And you tell me you don't know what your goals are, still?' She smiled again. She had almost said what she wanted to say.

'We live in a one party state, Kevin. The political parties are just the circus, the distraction. Wouldn't you agree?'

I looked at her. The swept back hair, kept in place with a

headband, made her look like something on the back of Che's motorbike. Her smile that was just a chess move, the flashing eyes, the pretty little chin that was as fixed as the north star. She reminded me of someone from a long time ago. It wasn't the face, so much as the self-possession. That was her beauty.

'If you owned a bit of everything like you've just listed, would you give it up? I wouldn't. Not without a fight.'

'Not without one hell of a fight, no.'

I had nothing left to say. Maybe I didn't have the energy left to say it. Maybe I knew that all arguments of principle led to what she was saying. Maybe I didn't have the energy for this fight. Everything was such a fight anyway, why pick one you cannot win? My mind was racing, and my mouth was numb, my thoughts crashing into one another and nothing at all could come out.

'I don't know,' I said finally. I raised my head to look at her. 'I don't know what to say.'

She looked past me and she nodded at a photo on the wall. It was a black and white, half-poster size of a wedding. Judging by the hair and outfits, it looked late 50s, early 60s. Strangely the groom was looking at the camera, but the photograph showed his profile only. The bride was smiling, weakly. There were three or four other couples and they all seemed to be keeping their distance, except for one man who was smiling, excessively, like he was making up for something.

'My grandma married a man who came back from one of the wars with a leg blown off, half an arm blown off and half a face blown off. He sat me on his knee and because I didn't shriek with horror like the other kids, he loved me. He let me touch the skin that was stretched over where his face should have been. He suffered so much, and in some ways, being at home was worse than being at war. I can only imagine his life, but when I think about not doing what we're doing, I imagine living with only half a face. That's what it would feel like. Take away a life where I'm not doing something decent, then you can take away my face.'

'I admire you for that.'

'I remember when my Dad took me to the Legion club where they all knew my Grandad, and what I remember most was not the things they said about him, but listening to them when they began to forget I was there, and listening to all of them lined along the bar and listening to their rage. The anger and the violence of what they felt, the half-articulated ferocity of disgust at the inequality and the injustice and the baked-in grime of the class system. And all the other shit that kept them down.'

Pause.

'The club is just over the hill, I could take you there. They're decent people, a lot of them. But the rage is still there, and the rage is the by-product of powerlessness.'

She looked at me again. 'I worry that you might end up in the bar of the British Legion raging to your mates.'

Then she laughed. 'Maybe not.'

16

About Mr. Nosey

In the car on the way out of the city, I asked Chow Mein what he thought. He shrugged.

'What about what she said about me ending up ranting on at the bar to anyone who'll listen?'

There's worse options, he signed, then out loud, he said, 'at least it's warm in there,' and laughed.

'Don't you have to done something military to get in there?'

He laughed. 'Kevin Baxter's got a great CV. Wasn't he in the SAS?"

I like it when Chow Mein talks. It means he's poking his head out of his shell and seeing what's passing. That's good.

'Have you got anything back from Milton?' I said, after a moment. He shook his head. 'One thing for sure, Heather didn't send him. How many of the others have just come to see what's going on?' I didn't let him answer. 'I did feel spooked when she said that she doesn't think any of us is undercover. That would be the end, brother.'

He nodded. I wish I hadn't said that because I could feel him disappear into his shell again.

When we pulled up behind Picnic and Smoothie, it was early afternoon, back in Leeds. It's red-brick country, ignored and dirty below a flyover. Plenty of space to park. We went to sit in with the other two.

'The pub that Milton calls Sid's is just round the corner, about fifty metres down the road and on the corner of another little side road,' said Smoothie. 'It fits in with everything that Milton told us.'

'Is he leading us into a trap? Is he leading us to something he wants us to know? Is he working for someone else? Is what he says, after all our doubting, true?' I asked. He had really got under my skin.

'No one comes here,' says Picnic, carefully, 'you wouldn't know about it unless you knew about it, it's in a deserted part of town. I mean, look, it's busy all over town but there's no one here. No traffic. Difficult to spy on it. You could come here if you didn't want to be seen.'

'Let's say that some of what he's saying is not true, and he may have his own reasons for that, and let's say that this bit about Sid's and getting involved with these psychos is a massive mistake and he's worried where it's going to lead him, and let's say he has come to us genuinely. What then? What we aiming to do here?'

Ten minutes later, I find myself hobbling through the doors of Sid's on my own, leaning on my stick, dressed in my worst old mac, with the newspaper sticking out the pocket. Chow Mein's gone for a stroll around the block to see what he can find, and Smoothie and Picnic are off to pick Milton up at his home. If he isn't at home, they're going to wait for him.

The place is smoky and cheap, and there's a central bar with three or four separate little rooms, each with its own access to the bar. I have a little cough and keep my hat low. I order a half from the barmaid who can pull a beer without looking up from her phone. I take a seat where I can see along the whole of the bar and who comes to get served at the other hatches. The lounge here is almost deserted, apart from a big guy with a big beer belly reading the paper. Something tells me that he's Sid.

His daughter behind the bar has got his weak chin and body shape. She looks like she can't smile at all.

I open the paper and stare at the story about a member of the problem family in Buck Pal who has supposedly been banned from seeing some of the others who live in another big house somewhere. All I can think about is what Heather said and my weak words echo in my head. She's right, and Chow Mein would agree, I have lost sight of what we're doing because I'm so frightened of it all coming tumbling down. It's not how he sees it, I know. I don't answer my phone, which is on silent, but I know it's ringing. I want to keep it simple. Old man with mobile phone is what attracts irritated stares.

I cough, stand up and shuffle off to the bogs. When I get there, I check behind every door and every cubicle. I'm alone and can see who's ringing. Heather can wait till I'm ready to consider my words, carefully. Smoothie texts that he's checked remotely on the cameras and seen someone driving round the Circle in an unknown car and given the order to stay indoors and watch what happens. And that Milton is still not replying. Chow Mein has texted, *Four dudes outside in suits, two cars, Range Rover and Audi A6, coming in now.*

Take photos of everything, I reply. I wash my hands. The place is foul. Why don't people flush toilets? Call me old-fashioned, but that is way below the human minimum.

I shuffle back to my seat and hear the door to the bar next to me open. Sid raises his eyes and stands up. His belly sways and plops over his waistband and below his untuckable black t-shirt. He goes round to greet his visitors. I can make out the shapes through the frosted glass of the partitions. I can hear a lot of what they're saying, but not all of it. I can hear Sid and another voice.

I can feel another text come through. *Forgot to mention one of them has chauffeur.* From Chow Mein.

I go for another half. At the bar I can hear the voices better, but I can't see them. I wait patiently. The barmaid comes over but just as she's about to pour my half, Sid shouts at her to get some more drinks for his party, so she turns on her heels, pours their drinks first and one of them comes to collect them from the bar, then he's joined by another one who orders some cigars.

'On the house,' shouts Sid.

I look up from my paper and get a good look at both of them. One is jowly, slow, his nose looks like it's peeling, and he's got a three-piece suit on that must have shrunk in the wash. I know his face. The other one I don't know, he's darker, sleeker, sharper. We need photos. These guys aren't here for the fine dining and the sophisticated interiors. Just as I'm about to sit down, two guys walk past me straight to the bar. I can't risk a text here now, so I go back to the toilets and tell Chow Mein that he has to get photos.

When I get back to my seat, the lads are sat right next to me. They obviously want the banter and take the paper from my hand. I don't argue, but stand up and am out the door before they can begin more of the same. When I get outside, I don't look for Chow Mein but turn left to walk past the other bar where the five of them are sitting. Sid is busy puffing and blarting out something, but the third one, whose face I haven't seen yet, looks straight at me. He's the one, I think. I will remember that face. He may well have been trying to picture mine.

I take a left down the side street and see the chauffeur in the Audi. He's on his phone. He doesn't have a peaked cap. There's only one other car on the road, the Range Rover. I know that Chow Mein will have the registrations already, but I make a note of both of them. Just in case. At the end of the road, I take a right towards the main road. Then left, as if I'm going back into town. A minute later a car turns into the next left. I follow it. It's Chow Mein being careful.

‘I got some photos, not great,’ he says, ‘and I got both registrations and I got a description of each of them, before you ask.’

‘I knew one of them, but I can’t think where. Tell me, why would you go there at lunchtime to have a drink and a bit of banter?’ I paused and looked at my friend. ‘Do you like crossword puzzles? Why do I ask, I know you don’t, they’re just annoying, I’d rather creosote the fence or take a cat for a walk than do a fucking crossword puzzle. This is like a crossword puzzle. I don’t want to do it. I just want the answers. I don’t even want to know the answers. I just want to be left alone. Chow Mein, I keep saying to myself that I just want to be left alone, I want us to be left alone, I want nothing to change or be challenged or ruined. Is that wrong?’

‘You’re becoming a Friedbread, brother, I knew it was in yer,’ and he laughs and pokes me in the arm.

‘Let’s go and pick Smoothie up and get him to do the background on these knobs we’ve just been lucky to cross paths with.’

When we get to where Milton said he lived, Smoothie and Picnic are still waiting for him to come home. They have obviously been talking and Picnic asks if we’re all going to get a chance to talk later.

‘Of course, it’s everyone’s decision.’ I thought about how to say this, but it just came out, and it wasn’t the best thing to say, ‘I don’t know what to do next. Honestly.’

Picnic nodded. ‘We talk later, then.’

‘It doesnt look like Milton is coming home soon, so would you two go back to Sid’s and see what’s happening there.’ I spoke to Picnic and Chow Mein. ‘Me and Smoothie will go back to the office. Call if you need us.’

In the car on the way back to the Circle with Smoothie, I ask him what he thought, knowing he wouldn't be happy.

'Do you really have no idea what to do next? Not sure I buy that,' he replied.

'If you could decide what we should do, what do you think we should do?'

He looks at me and then, out the window, when he answers. 'I've been here with you so long I don't have anything else. If the Army find out where I am, I could get two for leaving them and ten for mugging off the twats who beat me up. They were superiors.' He looks at me, the tension's in his face. 'B-man, you see what I mean? This ain't no joke.'

Pause.

'I can't go back to nothing, can I?'

'I thought so.'

'I mean, from what you say she saying, she talkin' a lot of sense, I know it, you know it, we all know it, but it's stacked like a mountain against us. I know what these fuckers can do and if you do start against them, you will come up against them, and I can't afford that, no way. That is a street I do not want to go down. You gettin' me?'

'Totally. One hundred. Yeah.'

When we get back to his rooms with his piles of computers, I talk him through the little episode at Sid's. He shakes his head but carries on without saying a word.

'What's wrong?' I asked.

'Nothin', jus' –' He stops.

'Do you remember two days ago?' I could feel his anger. 'Can you tell me what it was like here two days ago, three days ago? Three days ago, it was like a sleepy town from a movie in Alabama. Nothin' happenin', no one comin', no one goin'. Now look, everyone wants a piece of somefin' we don't have. Fuck the lady's revolution, fuck this Milton dude. B-man, I tellin' you, I don't like this way and – guess wha'? – I don't like that way.'

'I am with you completely. I can't remember half of the reasons or thoughts I used to have about why we doing and what we doing and all the rest of it.'

My turn to pause.

'Part of me thinks that doing nothing is the best thing to do when you don't know what to do. Then, when you have to, do what you think's best.'

There was a ding on one of the many screens that Smoothie operated. Screens, servers, towers, files, backups everywhere, but nothing in the cloud. The cloud was their space, he said. Smoothie ran every bit of his space like a prison governor. And he had everything we needed in this little room overlooking the main square of the Circle.

He sweeps over on his wheeled chair to the screen that's been racing through the data the most. 'Bingo lingo, B-man. Here is something useful. Reg of the blue A6 is – wait – is this right? It belongs to Mrs. A Morrison, address is some village up North Yorkshire. Is that right, boss? Have we cocked up?'

He goes to search through his database and starts clacking on his keyboard. I'm calmer when he is absorbed in something he likes, not fretting about the shit that's happening all around us.

'He's using his wife's car?' I asked. 'What about the other car? That was a Range Rover, wasn't it? An old style one.'

'Still working on that.'

And he's away checking out the sporty A6 again.

I think out loud. 'The other thing that's bothering me is this: we turn up, out of the blue, at a crappy pub that no one goes to and then four other guys do the same at more or less the same time. Who are they? We don't know who they are or what they doing? It could just be coincidence. Four ordinary blokes having a beer and a bit of pork pie with an old friend.'

Smoothie pulls a face. He has printed the photos that Chow Mein sent him and is waving them at me. 'That car was gotta be worth more than the pub, the suits were worth more than what the pub take in a year and these jokers don't do pasties or pork pies except if they're payin' more than a ton for one in a five star gaff.'

He passes me the photos. I stare at the full portrait outside the pub of the one I thought I knew.

'Any details of the other car, the Range Rover yet?' He looks over, then he types furiously into another machine.

I must check on Chow Mein and Picnic.

'Smoothie, can you check who was snooping around when we've done this? I don't want to forget about that.'

He nods but he's staring at the screen.

'This is all not right, B-man. Some Mrs. Morrison, who appear to be eighty year old grandma, from what I can see about her. Maybe there's more than one of these Mrs. Morrisons. Then, this Range Rover, which is registered to a company, South High Holdings, registered in Edinburgh. It's a limited company but – wait –'

I text Chow Mein to see how he's doing.

Ok, bro. Chillin. No sign of anything is the reply.

'What do South High Holdings do?' I ask Smoothie.

He doesn't respond because he's delving deep into the carcass of Russian dolls that is the back country of our commercial brethren.

I imagine myself standing next to the guy with the bad nose I've just seen in Sid's. I try to recollect the scene. We were in a building with lots of stairs. I wasn't sat next to him, I was watching him, that was it, I was sat down in a place like a museum, a gallery, a courthouse, something like that. I shut my eyes and replayed the scene where he had walked past me, deep in conversation with another person. I remember something odd about the interaction. Was it a funny handshake, something passed between them? I remember that I was waiting to speak to the other guy, that was it. The jowly one with the peeling red nose was talking and talking and talking and I didn't have much time. I tried to think about why I wouldn't have had much time – these guys are officials, that's it. Was it when we were first organising ourselves at The Circle and we needed some permission or some paperwork or some discussion? Something official. The Council.

'Smoothie, the fat, jowly one with the peely nose works at the Council or something. He either works there or has some connections there. Can you check that out? Can you also check as far back as when we first came here if we have any paperwork or letters or anything that has to do with the Council or Planning or anyone official? Anything from that first year when it was still a shit tip?'

I thought of those days and didn't want to go back to them. But, I thought of all the stories and all the people and all the records we had of everything and I'm the one who cannot remember. I went outside into the fresh air to find the peace I needed to go that far back. The sun was shining but it was windy, and I felt the sharpness and a taste of dampness in the air. The clouds were piling up over on the Pennines to the west and when I sat in the overgrown back garden on a little wooden bench that we inherited from the previous dwellers, I felt cold and sapped and wanted, for the first time in a very long time, to be somewhere warm, where I didn't speak the language. I don't know why or from where it came, but Chad came to mind. No idea why.

Then, comes a call from Smoothie, asking me to come back upstairs. And a text from Chow Mein to say that the three dudes leaving Sid's

'The dawdling-maudlin car that was seen sniffin' on our streets earlier today I have found. Call me Shylock, Mr. Holmes.' Smoothie is very pleased with himself.

'Sherlock, you mean?'

'Whatever. Them ballers must be doin' well because that car and those plates have not known one another for very long. The plates belong to a Mr T. Jones, who was born in 1933, for his pride and joy, a Ford Fiesta. Whatever it was they drivin' up here in, it wasn't a Ford Fiesta.'

'So, that means that whoever was driving around this morning wasn't paying us an official visit. We're becoming Britain's Number One destination, for lunatics, revolutionaries and criminals. Wonder why they like it here so much?

'Ok. And sit here,' he said to me, 'and scroll through these files, names and addresses of companies attached to them South High Holdings. See if anything ring a bell. I'm going to look for those ancient records you ask me about,' and he left me in his room, in the dark.

I started off looking at South High Holdings, but my mind was wandering. What if this was all a complete waste of time? Ok, so four dodgy blokes meet up in a losers' pub to plot some scheme, what has that got to do with us? I was playing the permutations in my mind that went something like a computer programme: Milton – good – go down this route, Milton – bad – go down this route. I went down the good route and eventually came out with another twenty-four permutations, at least, of what could happen. I did the same with the Milton-bad route and came to the same endless number of permutations. Then, I remembered Full English. I rang him.

'Brother, what happened to the photos you were going to send me of Milton meeting that guy last night? Remember?'

'Yeah, I've got them here. Better for ye to see them in rreal life. Where's ye naow?'

'I'm in Smoothie's office.'

Three minutes later, and we're poring over grainy images of guys on CCTV cameras. Eventually, we find a magnifying glass to get the detail. It is not easy. It isn't really black and white, more like white and grey with splodges of dark.

I hesitantly suggested, 'I think those are Milton's shoes. I remember them 'cos we made him take them off. No one wears slip-ons anymore, do they? And the other guy doesn't show his face so well, but that nose I would recognise anywhere.'

I put Chow Mein's pictures from outside Sid's next to these pictures from the CCTV and it looked like same height, same build and same nose.

'Looks like yer man,' said Full English.

'So, Milton's working with them,' I thought, out loud.

I wasn't really paying more than a ten-percent game with South High Holdings. Companies spawning companies in all parts of the UK, including the Channel Isles and the Isle of Man and reference to companies that I couldn't find anywhere else, as if the whole lot was part of a much bigger package of shell companies going ever deeper into other companies that were running out of registered addresses on earth. Open an office on the moon seemed to be the next inevitable step. Why have I never heard of South High Holdings? Then again, would I want to? I have never smelled fraud at this magnitude before, I didn't know it had a smell to it, but this is it, coming out of the computer at me, in waft upon waft of financial wizardry using human body parts and tax avoidance lawyers, who may not have any human body parts left. That is still being debated.

I realise I should have made notes earlier, so I started again. I tried to follow a sensible thread and find out who sat on the board and whether they sat on boards of other companies that they were connected to. There seemed to be a recurring set of three or four names and the shifting of tenure and position.

Just Google 'em. So, I began with the first man's name, James Hart Nevinson, and within seconds he appears just like that.

And he's just as fat, flabby and with a gorgeous peeling nose as he is in real life. This time in a tux and a dickie bow, with his arm around someone half his age. Bingo! Wings 'n' all! Weaving across a couple of other little sites I was able to piece together his distinguished career.

Smoothie comes back and shouts over, 'I can't find nothin' like what you lookin' for, but what you got?'

'Here he is, the lovely Mr. Nosey that we're looking for.'

I showed him the images and described his career: 'posh house, Scottish education, army, but not for long, police south of the border, then goes into business, building, security and then about twenty other businesses and then...what do you think comes next?' Pause. 'Yes, he's gone into politics to serve his community. First wife seems to have taken him to the cleaners, so does the second, so there he is, nose peeled, ready for action with whoever can line his bedsit kitchen diner with nice queen's head wallpaper...'

'Looks like the same jerk to me. What next?' says Smoothie.

'Cup of tea?'

Five minutes later, we're holding our teas.

'Do you think we gotta change our tea brand?' I asked Smoothie, taking a break from the computer screens.

'Is that top of our agenda, at the moment?' he said, wisely.

'No. I like this one.'

'It's gritty,' he says, 'but do the job.'

'What about this agenda – tell me how to make it better: find Mr. Nosey's Range Rover and get a tracker on it. Find the other car and get a tracker on it. Then, go and meet Chow Mein at Sid's. Then, see if Milton is in and if not, break in and see what he's up to and then...meet up and see what everyone thinks. Anything I've missed? Or to remove?'

'I could get a couple of the guys to look through these files you looked at and check all the names against the photos of

Mr. Nosey's friends from the meeting at Sid's today. What you think? While we're out?'

'Yeah, great idea. Don't forget the two trackers. Meet you back here in ten. I'll tell Chow Mein we're moving and see if he has any more news of our lovely, duplicitous Milton.'

'Let's start looking for Nosey's Rover at the Council,' I said, as we drive into the town centre, half an hour later.

We park five minutes away and walk separately to the Council Chambers. The building looks something like a Central American Republic's main cathedral, but only dates from the 1930s. There are several car parks dotted about to choose from. We eventually find the Range Rover with the right reg after about forty minutes of looking, on a deserted piece of enclosed waste land advertising parking for a fiver a day.

'It's definitely the right car, isn't it, Smoothie?' We were looking at it from outside the flimsy fence, in the shadow of a railway arch.

'It mighta been resprayed and had the plates changed to look just like the one we want it to be, but other than that, I'm not too sure.'

'Cameras?'

'There's one over there but he's parked in the shade and it's a long way away. Not sure. I'm thinkin' I'll say goodbye. See you back at the car.'

Off he walks, as if he's just an ordinary worker taking a short cut across the car park, when he bobs down in a flash to pick up a piece of paper he dropped, disappears behind the car and then gone again, not hurried at all, to disappear over the far fence and round the corner into the next street.

Back at the car he's already clocked on to his latest little attachment using a little Chromebook. 'Bangin' little things, these,' he said, 'already tickin' tickin' away, hahhaa.'

He looks up at me and I have to smile. He's not ready for a job at Tesco's yet. I worry about him though, like he's family.

'Time to pay Mrs. Morrison a call, I think. And if the car's not there, then we can at least see where they live. It's a little village called Thraykston. The Old Hall.'

'Boss, that's more than an hour away. Maybe more, it's like North Yorkshire. What about doin' a dawn raid, see what happens then? We can't let Chow Mein and the boys sit there for much longer.'

'You're right, let's go and see them. We could always follow Old Nosey when he sets off?'

I get a text. It's three emoticons: a brain, a finger pointing up and a body with the right arm raised. It's Heather. No idea what that means. Will ask a youngster, at some point.

When we get to Sid's, Chow Mein is dozing. Picnic is doing all the watching.

'An old couple, a guy with a dog and three bruisers in suits,' he says, 'before you ask. And this is the reg and the photos.'

Picnic likes using a real camera, a digital one. 'Not passing through anyone else's hands, you see,' he says.

I look at the pictures. Old couple look genuine. So does man with dog. One of the bruisers looks like a fitter Sid.

'Could that be Sid's brother?' I ask them.

Picnic asks what Sid looks like. Smoothie nods.

'Who is this Sid? He ain't just selling old pies and bad beer, is he? Smoothie, can you check him. Name should be on the licence outside the door.'

Smoothie puts his hoodie up and jogs around the block.

'Arthur Sidney Forrester is the name,' he says, getting back in.

'Thank you, Smoothie. I think you'll find that one of the bruisers is Arthur's thin brother. Smoothie, do you want to take Chow Mein home and see how much you can find on this list of arseholes, while me and Picnic will stay here a bit longer. Chow

Mein, any news of Milton?' I can hear the weariness.

Chow Mein stirs in theback of the car. 'No.'

'I thought not. See you later, gentlemen, and Smoothie, could you get everyone together for a chat later?'

'Will do,' he said.

'What do you think?' I asked Picnic, when they'd driven off.

'About all this that's happening now? I think it's inevitable. Just got to make the best decision, based on what's in front of you. Heather and her crew are what you might call, *people of principle*. I saw the men of principle in South Africa. I've seen them pick up a machete and act on principle. I think, if you keep going long enough with your principles, you gonna have to pick up a machete. The ones who survive don't think about it too much when it's done.'

He stared out the window being brushed with light rain. 'You know what, I ask myself this for years, though – where would we be without principles or ideals leading us out the dark cave? Without something like collective good, we might still be fighting the mammoths. Now, we just fight one another. Ain't nothing else left to fight. I just don' know about you, B-man, if you're a man of principle or how you gonna get out of that one.'

'Yeah. Good question. Collective good. Great words, great idea.' I start laughing. 'Putting yourself second. Not even sure that's an old-fashioned idea, you know. It was dead long before we probably had a word for it.'

We sat and watched the rain land in bigger blobs down the windscreen. We sat in silence for half an hour. Picnic slid down the seat and rested his eyes. I watched as the pub lights came on. Nothing was any clearer, nothing emerging, nothing except the feeling of slowly being encircled by things that as yet have not appeared. That's the scariest point.

Picnic's thoughts buzzed around my head. *You gonna pick up a machete if you have principles.* Sooner or later.

manifesto

I would believe in every poor man in jail if there were two rich men there in his cell or I would fight for my country if it was my country and I shared it equally with all who lived in it and I would eat at the table of the poor for the rest of my days if I could bring more than I ate and if I could count myself amongst the servers and the preparers along with all who would share it and we would worship any god and all gods that were blind to revenge and blind to riches and deaf to loud voices and blind to false acts and could justify nothing except planting seeds in the ground and love in the hearts of all gods and all people who would sit at the tables of their neighbours and bring more than they left with and I would worship their customs and tread shoeless on their sacred places built of stone or wood or the air of their belief and I would carry my friend for as many miles as he needs and I would listen to a man of principle maintained for a lifetime or forty lifetimes whose silence drowns out all shouters and ambitions and anyone who casts down arms against all orders and raises arms against all orders I would hear his wrath and I would write her words for all to consider and I would ask the quietest voices to rise like thunder and give judgment against the raisers of the causes of war and against injustice and I would share my house with the downcast and share my voice with the downcast and I would not be alone if I would be cast amongst the despair of the world forever having company for those who would speak out for those who would drop their arms in battle or speak against those who raise their arms falsely or would do as the multitude do or would speak truth until the multitude seize the principle of making thought beaten like the finest sword on the anvil of truth by the unflinching hammer of principle into something I would raise in judgment and I would hold in pride and I would share with the hands of love and all my neighbours and all my friends and all my enemies and all the spirits that linger in our world who would share the necessity of changing everything.

m a n i f e s t o

17

About Tim

Tim smiled at Lady Antur, Chair of today's meeting. He apologised for his thirty minutes of lateness and blamed the traffic from Heathrow. She nodded politely. Very like her mother, he thought, who had just died, who had been a good friend of his mother.

She was in the middle of a presentation about this year's flagship project for PLANT, the children's charity of which Tim was a director. She was outlining the successes this year in building and equipping a hostel for teenage children in Lafey, sheltering them, and providing some basic education. Lady Antur was terribly passionate about it, but Tim wasn't sure where Lafey was.

He'd had a terrible journey (and night) coming back from Kenya and still had dozens of messages stacked up on his phone that he hadn't dealt with since landing. After this thing here with the charity, he had another meeting in London, before trying to get to his daughter's school to give a couple of teachers a piece of his mind about upsetting Caroline, his daughter.

He excused himself with having to go to the bathroom and had ten minutes in a cubicle when he had to urgently sell some shares in Bondolit, the GM food developers, and buy more in KANdos Ltd, the bulldozer and demolition people currently supplying Israel and Brazil with every type of heavy plant.

When he got back into the presentation, she had moved on to other work closer to home about raising money and interest for the development of what she called, 'a rainbow of prospects in the fight against child poverty and homelessness in Britain.' Tim had turned his phone to silent, but no matter how many times he ignored it, the same caller kept ringing.

'Do you know that more than 110,000 youngsters were facing homelessness in Britain last year?'

Tim nodded and shook his head. *Terrible*, he mouthed to her. He looked at his watch. If he did another ten minutes then he could say he had family issues, which would be true, and leave.

Next meeting he was on time for. He was rather proud that he was a Non-Exec on a charity with a 'royal' in its name – the Royal Association for the Development of the Arts in Disadvantaged Groups. This was the one with the Royal in its name that he was hoping would get him noticed for at least an MBE, and possibly more. He had made a point of being at every major social gathering of this group in London and had met a range of types. He spoke in this meeting when they were discussing getting some celebs on board to raise the profile, and Tim offered his services in organising a glitzy fundraiser where tickets to sit next to famous arty types – musicians, artists, actors and actresses – that sort of thing, were going to be auctioned off. His ideas were warmly met, and Andy, the Chair, nodded and smiled. After the meeting, Andy made a beeline for him and asked him if there was any way he could give it his best go and give him a date, in say, six weeks. Tim nodded, knowing full well he would be making excuses in three.

He did the third meeting in the back of his car, on Zoom, and turned his mike off. Ray, his driver, was told to put his foot down. It was a very boring NHS Foundation Trust thing, and Tim had only got involved because he was told it was essential for any sort of public recognition. He always voted in the same way as Michael Mac, the only one with any sense. Michael usually kept him in the loop quietly, explaining to him what was going on. Anyway, reception wasn't always very good, and he had to continually log back in and refresh. Caroline's teachers and Head of House were going to get his ire.

When he rang his wife to say he was going to be slightly late, she was less than pleased.

'Don't know why you had to go to Kenya, when you knew how busy this week was going to be.'

He put her on reduced volume, whilst he dealt with incoming from Jim on his business phone.

'I know, I know,' he says to her, in between, 'I'll do my best. I'll be home soon.'

To Jim, who was an annoying twat most of the time, he tried to be patient and listen to him, 'Yeah, Jim, I get it. I agree. You want to move fast, good. I'm happy if you do it at 3 o'clock in the morning dressed as fuckin' Santa.'

To Lottie, his wife, 'Why didn't you tell me that about our daughter before today? What do you mean –? No, you listen –! For fuck's sake, Lottie, why didn't you tell me –?'

To Jim, 'Ring one of the brothers, get some muscle and do what you have to do. It's up to you, when, and how and everything else. Sorry, Jim, I've got my wife on the other phone, yeah, I know that you've pushed the paperwork through, yeah, I get that – but, yeah. I get that a lot is hanging on it for you – yeah, I'm not sure – if you let me finish – I'm not sure what you're getting so het up about – yeah, yeah, it is – yeah, it is a big deal to me – ok, sorry, we need you yeah – ok, good.'

To his wife, 'Lottie, Lottie, Lottie, darling – I'm listening, I truly am listening – well, you said that our daughter is having issues at school – ok, she is causing some issues at school, and that it's Parents' Evening tonight – no, not Parents' Evening, I didn't mean to say that but you fu – ok, sorry, sorry – look, I am sorry, ok, I have said I'm sorry – and I'm sorry to Caroline as well for not being there – as you often remind me – and to Jim, 'I will be there, I have promised you I will be there, darling, please listen – oh, fuck, sorry, Jim, yeah fucking old lady giving it some big, mouthy blow off down the phone – yeah, no, yeah, no, Jim, no, I won't be there – no, I can't be there, ok, you have to sort it without me – ok?'

And thus, Tim was not looking forward to going home as much as he had thought he was when he set off up the M1.

After another hour, Ray, the driver, lowered the screen that separated passenger and driver, and asked, 'Sir, just to let you know that we will be there in about twenty minutes. Shall I call ahead?'

Tim had fallen asleep and woke with a start and a crick in his neck.

'Oh, thanks, Ray, thanks for the shout.' Then, he knocked on the glass again, 'Take it steady here and when we get to the top before the gates, just pull up, eh?'

These last few miles were on narrow country roads with a few hairpin bends, but about five minutes from the gates was a spot that Tim loved. Ray knew where to stop. The big car floated into the viewing spot and came to a halt. Tim reached into the drinks cabinet and pulled out a half bottle of vodka and a packet of cigarettes. It was his little treat before facing Lottie. He went round to the driver's door and offered Ray a swig and a cigarette.

'Thank you, Sir, but...'

'Yes, of course...'

So, he walked off to stand in the evening light angling in from the south-west and drenching the scene below. Fields, cattle, some sheep, even a pair of hawks, calling high up in big circles as they rode the rising warm air, as if these moments were made to remind him that this was his country, that he was doing it all for the right reasons and whatever happened, he could retreat here to this place that was out of all harm's way, the place of peace that he had worked so hard for, that he deserved to enjoy, considering all the tolls on his time and energies. This was his little bit of heaven and he, of them all, had earned it.

He took a couple of deep swigs of the vodka and drew in big draughts of cigarette smoke, knowing how much she disapproved, and he flicked the still burning butt over the hedge. He got back in the car, Ray pressed the starter button and they crunched softly over the gravel and eased onto the tarmacked road again. Tim called these last couple of miles, 'The Mint Run'. He might even change into his other jacket to meet her. *If* she came to meet him, that is. Bloody woman. Bloody daughter. All he did was work for them, and if it wasn't one of them kicking off, it was both of them.

Ray came to a stop and pressed the buttons of the remote control to open the heavy wrought iron gates that led into the grounds to the house. They always juddered slightly when they were pressed into action, and Tim had an extra moment to savour the pink-hued sandstone columns with the tasteful, restrained geometric shapes carved into the outer face to extend the height. Looking down from the top of each column was a plaster sculpture that had the face of a man-lion with a mop of wavy hair, caught between yawning and roaring. Tim loved the way the eyes seemed to follow wherever one moved. He watched the gates close slowly behind him as they wound their way to the house, hidden behind trees and a low ridge of a hill.

He turned his phones on. The pings kept coming all the way till he stepped through the main door of the house. Sometimes there was a signal, mostly not.

There was no one to greet him.

Caroline's school is set into a secluded valley, so secluded in fact, that unless you knew which little unmarked, single-track road in the woods to turn off, you would never find it. Lottie was now striding to the front doors of the building which Tim was sure was a monastery and not a school, such were the buttresses, the windows, even the hushed quad that Lottie had already reached, while he was still checking he had turned off his phones. Lottie had said she would throw the bloody lot out of the window if she heard one beep out of any one of them. He decided it was wisest if he didn't beep either, considering her foul mood.

They were not allowed to meet Caroline immediately, but ushered into the Head's study. He was ex-military, so very courteous and did not waste time on unnecessaries.

'Thank you for coming, both of you, but think we needed to do this in person. Do you know how your daughter is, at the moment?'

Tim wanted to tell him what a stupid question because looking after his daughter on a day-to-day basis was the school's job, wasn't it? He kept his mouth shut, just in time. Lottie was much more realistic.

'Well, we hope she is well. She certainly hasn't said anything to us. Is there a problem? Something wrong? Has someone upset her?'

'Your daughter is a bully, to put it bluntly.'

Lottie looked aghast. Tim was less shocked. 'I'm sure it's nothing too serious, Mr., erm, Mr.?' said Tim.

'Mr. Buccleugh. B – U – DOUBLE C – L – E – U – G – H. If it weren't serious, you wouldn't be here.'

'Like my husband, Mr. Buccleugh, I'm shocked, to say the least. This is not at all like Caroline,' offered Lottie.

'I think we need to speak to these people making these comments, straightaway. Have you interrogated the culprits?'

'Your *daughter* is the culprit, Mr. Westhuizen. I think the real word for these other people should be victims.'

He stared at Tim. Tim stared back. He wished Lottie was more reasonable, and he didn't have to fight her before he fought everyone else.

'I am sure it's just silly teenage misunderstandings, something said in the way young people do,' offered Lottie again, looking very flushed, as she did when she was about to explode. She looked at Tim like she expected him to say something.

'Where is our daughter, anyway?' asked Tim, 'I think we should be talking to her and hearing her side first, don't you?'

'Of course, you can speak to your daughter in a moment, but I would like to make very clear the nature of the allegations first, if you don't mind?'

'You've just said 'a bit of bullying'. Ok, we get it. We will talk to her. End of. Don't understand what all the fuss is about. Kids will be kids, surely you and your chums here should know that.'

'Tim, please...' said Lottie.

'Well, I've told you about this school before. All these pompous fools running around a pretend monastery who have never had a real job in their lives.

'Tim, stop it,' shouted Lottie. 'This is not helping.'

'Mr. Westhuizen, do you want to hear what I have to say, then you may be in a position to help your daughter? Or shall I, as some members of the Senior Management Team would like me to do, shall I simply hand her over to the Police?'

At that point Lottie uttered a loud gasp and started quietly to cry. 'Oh, no, please God,' she said, 'what has happened?'

'It's not what has happened, Mrs. Westhuizen, it's what Caroline has been doing. She has been bullying members of the school and we know that because she has started bullying members of staff. She has been using other children in her class to extort money, solicit indecent photographs – some of them we think have been sold and published online – and has used information against members of staff to coerce them into altering her marks, writing favourable reports and has even engaged in some sort of relationship with one of them.'

Lottie is aghast and simply stares at Mr. Buccleugh. Tim is absolutely furious and is standing over Mr Buccleugh's desk, demanding to know the identity of the swine who has seduced her daughter and demanding that he be allowed to speak to this pervert of a man.

Mr. Buccleugh doesn't speak but simply asks Tim to stop shouting and to listen to what he is trying to say, and to sit down and listen civilly, while the issues are outlined.

'Mr. Westhuizen, please take your finger out of my face and stop shouting, otherwise I will have to either ask you to leave without seeing your daughter or call the Police immediately, and they can deal with all of you.'

Tim sits down, ferociously angry.

'For your information, Mr. Westhuizen, the member of staff is female, not male, and is once again a victim of your daughter's immoral and highly inappropriate acts.'

After another ten minutes of this humiliation, Tim is left alone in the office with the Head. Lottie has gone off to get Caroline. The Head sorts out his pile of papers relating to the case. Tim turns his phones back on. They are strangely silent. The Head looks up.

'You won't get a signal here, I'm afraid, unless you're with the network provider, BO3, you won't get a signal.'

The Head's phone rings, and he puts his hand over the speaker, 'Would you mind stepping outside for a moment, Mr. Westhuizen?'

Tim leaves, but the door to his office is left slight ajar and he is sure the conversation is about him and his family. Tim can hear some smug laughing and he's sure he hears him say, 'your officers,' and 'this school has a reputation,' and 'unpleasant, unsavoury...' somethings like that, and then a couple more of those smug little laughs. Tim waits for him to put the receiver down and walks back in and straight up to his desk.

'Don't fucking laugh at me and my family, OK, you jumped-up shit with your smug little bollux. If I hear one word against my daughter or my family you won't ever fuckin' work again, do you hear me? Do you hear me, Mr. Bolloxs Headmaster?' Tim is now whispering about half an arm's length from the Head's face. '*Work* again, sorry, I meant *walk* again, silly old me. Now, I hope that is an end to this bollux and we can all move on.'

Tim doesn't wait for an answer. He marches the long way down the corridor and out into the quad and then to the main gate and the visitor's car park.

Lottie's car, which they came in, is not there. There is no sign of it at all. He instinctively grabs his phones from his jacket pocket, stares at them, presses the usual icons on the screen. No response. He does it again. No signal on either of them. He throws them onto the floor in frustration and walks around the car park shouting 'Fuck' at the top of his voice.

It takes him several minutes to calm down.

Then, he walks back to his phones, which are still beating, but the screens are scratched and scuffed.

Two lads appear at the main door of the school, wondering what all the noise is about. He runs over to them.

'Either of you got a 'phone? Really need a 'phone, lads, that fuckin' works, yeah?'

They look at him, and then at one another. One of them pulls an old-fashioned phone out of his pocket. Tim grabs it off him. He bangs in the numbers.

'Jim, fuckin' get yourself up to this shithole here. Do it as quick as you can, ok?' He gave him the directions. 'Don't fuckin' hang about, ok.'

18

About *Enta Geweorc*

When we get back to The Circle, it's busy. People milling around, some setting up chairs and making food and laughing in little groups. The stage is still set up from Uncle Kevin's Extravaganza last night. The moon is out in full cheesy glory, shining through the trees and the leaves whisper and rustle and shimmer. I have in my hand a memory stick containing a single file, and I turn it around and around in my hand, listening to all the sounds of this lovely place and the people who fell in, blew in, were dragged in or sailed in or sank in gradually, as they go about the business of being together.

I walk under the Three Elder Trees, in the Sacred Grove, which means that I must become part of my silence. The leaves are dense and the space inside feels warm and dark. From here I can remove myself briefly from the world. Outside, I can still hear what's going on.

Soon, someone, Peanut, I think, judging by her voice, starts the chant. One of the few things we all have to do is learn the chant. Our rules are ideas based on bringing us together, not for punishment or isolation or threats. The chant is a communion. It begins very softly, with the first slivers of sounds from the rainmakers, mimicking the skittery pitter-patter of rain on a wooden roof, then the first note at the heart of the song, hummed softly, longingly, before the voices gather together around the second note, sliding between the two, till the volume rises, and then the homemade drums, lightly, as skittery, at first, as the rainmakers. Everyone has an instrument to bring to these times of inseparability. When the leader signals, so the tempo doubles and the melody rises and falls and the feet begin their stamping, followed by the sudden sound of the voices singing the melody of the drums and the point when we all will rise and sing till we rise with the moon and see all the things she sees in the slender light of her sight and our people. Then, it ends with the boom of voices like distant thunder and we thank the people who we share things with. And we thank the things around us for this place that is ours.

As always the chant ends on a wave of love and laughter. It really is lovely and sets my skin rising and tingling every time I hear it. The more I hear it, the more I sense the sound working best in a place of trees. The wood and the branches act like amplifiers.

But I have no choice, I have to come out from the protection of The Three Elder Trees. I walk in front of the gathering and open my hands and arms wide, 'Our words should always be songs. We carry our songs lightly. They are not a burden. Without them we are not people. This land is our song, and this land is the spirit of our song. Our song, our land.'

And they respond, 'Our song, our land.'

I put the memory stick into the computer at the side of the stage. *Memory*, Greek, having sense of remembering, care, anxiety; *stick*, Old English, a twig, spoon, rod, cognates all around Europe; the verb has early meaning of, fastening something in place. How apt. There is only one file on it.

The opening slides begin with images and stills from today, this evening, with a black and white shot of the trees and the moon with wolf's eyes staring through. The theme: this place. This very place, within metres of where we are sitting. In the background there's a simple guitar line, hypnotic, relaxing with a little melody in minor chords following the breeze round our little grove of trees and playing hide and seek.

Next, photos of the people who are sat in the gathering tonight appear on screen, going about their lives this evening, getting ready for this evening, without knowing they are being pictured. Then, as they see themselves, the whoops, the surprises, the little exclamations and the lost comments and the laughing and the whispers and nudges as the slides slowly turn into the conjuring of memories of things we've done three months ago: scenes of the past reminding us of the music, the lectures, the food, the cooking, the events that just make up any collection of lives lived next door and down the road and just round the corner. The people in their ordinary glory.

More slides appear, going further back in time, documenting the buildings we've changed, the overgrowth we hacked down, the laying out of plans and gardens, the planting, the growing, the things that died, the things we grew and ate, the competitions, the people and how they looked last year and then the year before; the guitar has faded into our singing now, the nights we sang in the summer evenings, the silly songs, the funny ones, the ones we loved when we were teenagers that we're still singing now, the ones we brought to this place.

The music stops and there is only hush, as all eyes stare for clues as to what is being put before them, what memories in these photos from a time we can hardly remember: the first photos, the first of us, the first time we dreamed we could do this, put the Circle up like the first settlers going into a dangerous place, full of unpredictability and threat and daring, just because that was the only thing left to do, daring to lay out the first idea of how we could live here, of the first house we changed and rebuilt and where the fence would go and looking at one another knowing that without you, my friend, and you, and you, and you and you and everyone else, we are not going to do this. A field full of folk, more than a dream.

And the last photos, back to the place where we're sitting now, as we see it every day: a lovely space surrounded by trees and grown so we can sit in comfort, and watch or do or listen and speak whatever we have planned together.

Thus, the screen fades slowly to black and everything stops: no sound, no pictures, no music and they, the People of the Circle are waiting. When the music starts again, with the same lingering, looping guitar piece that flits and turns through the branches of the trees that want to whisper another story, out of the blackness comes a photo of the road that once curved round here and a burned-out car and a man in a hoodie, his face nearly all covered.

The next photo shows the same burned-out car from a wider perspective, with the same house gables, visible in the background. To anyone who knows the Circle, it's clear we're sitting exactly where that burned-out car is. The lovely people with whom we share so much are looking at one another and at me and talking quietly. I'm certain they won't have seen these photos before.

In the foreground of the next photo is the burned out car, but in the background now is an enormous upright stone, the size of a man, and in the next photo the same stone is shown from a different angle but this time including what looks like another upright stone amongst the trees.

Some of the audience are pointing, looking, trying to work out where these stones are. What are they looking at? What are they being shown, really? Why?

In the next photo, the man in the hoodie with his long, loose hair hanging down, is digging furiously at the ground with a pickaxe. A different man appears next, on his knees, scraping between two exposed slices of stone laid on their side. The man is looking up, smiling in the rain. It's a younger Chow Mein. Somewhere in his wardrobe, he still has the long black leather coat he's wearing in the photo. And the top hat.

I start talking, as two words appear behind me on the screen. White background, black letters, gothic but simple:

Enta Geweorc

'I've often wondered if I'd ever stand here in front of you and say this, show you this, celebrate with you all the things we've just been reminded of: the laughing, the eating, the good times, the way we've moved this place along to what it is today. Since the day we planted the first tree and tidied up the first place and made it our home, I've wondered about today. Often had moments of asking myself, how did we get here? How is it going to feel for you and me to watch what we've done pass before us in a few photos? How do you measure what you've achieved? All these questions, and more, have swum around my mind. Hoping that this day might never come. I'm really proud and I'm really sad.'

Pause.

'When the poets looked on what was left of a disappeared civilisation, that's what they called it, the work of giants, *Enta Geweorc*. The newcomers, the migrants, the refugees from the old homelands who'd walked here, carrying with them whatever they could to this island. And when they got here, on the easiest routes up the river valleys and on the higher ground, avoiding the wetlands, they'll have built some huts, started farming, cutting down wood and in between, they'll have sat around, in their groups of families, relatives, kinsmen, friends, and clansmen and told stories of the homeland they'd left behind of gods and forests and the old ways of doing things and foremost amongst them were the poets, for even they had poets.'

Pause.

'*Enta Geweorc,* the works of giants, in the words of the grandmother of our language – *Enta Geweorc.* What one anonymous poet called the ruins he sees, built by a people who have now gone. The work of giants. The baths, the walls, the cities, the temples of the Romans in the eyes of the people who landed here in their wake. What better way of praising the things from the past that we can hardly build or imagine now? The ruins of a culture that has gone, the mystery of a world that has passed, the things left behind after the people have gone.

Pause.

'That one day, other people will come and look at what we've done here and stare and wonder what the people were like and admire us, is very unlikely. Not because it isn't beautiful and amazing, but because what we have built is so much more than bricks and stones placed pleasingly together. It's unlikely they'll come and wonder at this, our world, because our *Enta Geweorc* are the things that are invisible as well as visible: a way of living together outside of Lardland, the system that has failed so many of us and those who lived in it. But that day is closer than we think.'

Pause.

Sounds of whispering, little exclamations of surprise, then questions, asked, shouted, whispered.

'What do you mean? What are you saying? Who is saying that? Why? What's going on? I don't understand,' and the surface of the gathering churns up, like when the wind comes quickly to the waters of a lake.

At the back of the group, standing with Chow Mein in the ring of the glow of candles, I see for the first time Heather, and wonder how long she has been there.

I flick the remote and Milton's face appears on the screen.

'I will try to explain. You remember this guy who came here

yesterday? His name is Milton, and he wanted some help because he said he'd got involved with some local gangsters. We're still trying to locate him and speak to him, but we have since turned up these people.' I flicked to the next slide showing pictures of the four who were in Sid's when we first went there. 'One is a multi-millionaire businessman landlord, one is a gangster, one is a city councillor and one other. Nice little collection.'

Someone shouts up, 'Are you sure?'

Then, everyone is firing off questions. 'What has that got to do with us here? What are we going to do? Can't we just sit tight and do nothing? Who are these people?'

Some were just shouting, 'We're not going anywhere. We don't have to do owt. Fuck them, they can't move us, if we don't want to go.'

I waited for them to calm down.

'I get what you're saying and yes, we need to act carefully. We don't know the full story. We don't know what they're planning. We don't know for certain if this's got anything to do with us. But Milton came with a story about being given a gun. He won't answer our calls. He's not at home. He lied to us.'

From the back of the group, I heard a voice, and when I looked around, Heather had her hand up.

'Can I add something?' she said and walked forwards and moved to the front.

'Hello, everyone, my name is Heather, we met with your man here earlier today,' pointing at me. 'We're on the same side,' she said, smiling and producing a couple of photos of a man with a beard and our man Milton, and held them up, side by side. 'We've done some digging and we think – we can't be one hundred percent sure yet – that these two men are one and the same, bearing in mind a few years has passed since this first one was taken, but minus the beard and add a few years.

'This man,' she points at the Milton with the beard, 'we

have evidence to prove that this man is an undercover police officer who infiltrated a sister organisation in Sussex in order to gain intelligence on what the Government calls, an 'extreme climate change organisation'. We think that the Police and the Government are stepping up more proactive approaches to any counter-culture organisations by infiltrating and subverting and eventually arresting, disbanding and disrupting any form of what they call, 'subversive activity.'

Pause.

Silence, then whisperings, then questions. 'Are you sure? Why would they care about us? We don't do anything like climb buildings or block roads or attack animal labs...'

Silence again.

Heather looked at me. 'Can I?'

'Of course,' I said.

'You guys are in a major city, but you're off-grid. You don't exist on paper, but here you are, living lovely lives, but don't pay taxes and don't have jobs, you don't have any paperwork and some of you are hiding from things that have happened.' She realised that she was saying things that an outsider shouldn't.

'Perhaps I should explain. We have a very similar set up in Sheffield and you'd be welcome to join us. The only difference is, we don't live together, like this,' and opened her arms out to indicate all the things around her. 'We live in little clusters, but in a similar community to yours we've built on shared values. We live outside the system, we live freer lives, but we don't have your space, your lovely space,' and smiled her lovely smile. 'But – and I don't mean this negatively – we are more militant, we take actions of a different sort and we're aiming for certain political and social goals. I'm sure you'd agree with all of them. That is our way. It may have to become your way.'

She smiled again, like a doctor might.

It all went very quiet again, like all the air had been sucked out of the evening, the sky, each of us. It felt like it was slipping away, before my eyes. We needed to reach a point where we all understood what was happening to us.

'Heather,' I said, 'is it true what you are saying to us? Is it likely that he's undercover?'

'There's a crowd in Brighton who are very closely connected to us. Several people in the group said the same thing about your man, Milton. One, maybe two, of the women had a sexual affair with him. We're talking a few years ago. The Police say it isn't happening anymore, but it is. Anything could have happened in between.'

'What do you think happens next?'

'You want the honest answer or the difficult answer?' she said.

'Whatever you think would help us here,' I said.

'I would say, be ready to go with half an hour's notice. Pack only the most valuable things in one bag. Have an exit strategy that makes sense. Find somewhere safe to go where they won't find you. Decide if you're going in ones, twos or a group and who's going to look after who. Work out what you're going to do after this. Keep in touch afterwards.'

'Are you serious?' I was speaking for all of the silence around me.

She was ready for the resistance. 'Have you seen what they do when they move into a place like this? It's like a fucking invasion. They hire gangs of thugs to go in before the JCBs and the diggers and the loggers and the demolition crews. I'm surprised they aren't using tanks. Just be grateful they aren't firing on us. Yet.'

Uncle Kevin stood up. 'I'm not going anywhere. You can' jus' come here, young lady, and tell us to pack one bag and be ready to go in 'alf an 'our. Who the fuck do you think y'are?'

'Kevin,' I said, 'no one's telling you to pack a bag and go. What we're saying is that we may have to move quickly and to be ready, because *if* – and remember, it's a big if – if they do come, it's likely, from what Heather's saying, to be unpleasant and probably violent.

Kevin was still stood up. 'Tha' don't change nuthin'. I were here before all of yers. Simple, I'm not packin' a bag, I'm not off in 'alf an hour and I'm not movin'. My feelin' is, it'll blow ov'r. E'en if I wanted to, which I don', it'd tek me three week to pack.'

Claps and cheers went up around the audience. Part of me loved Kevin even more. 'Here, here,' and 'well said,' and 'Kevin, you're the man,' were shouted out. The frustration was palpable. This wasn't supposed to be on the agenda.

'I completely agree, Kevin. You haven't said a word I could argue with. This is your home, our home, you were here before all of us and you've got all the material concerning your Project. Kevin, it's heartbreaking. Taking this place and destroying it without asking, without discussing and without any thought or concern for us or for the place makes me scream and rage and want to fight for every inch of what we've got –'

'Do it, then,' shouted Kevin, 'do it. Put up a fight. Don't talk about it, do it. Natterin's not goin' to get you nowt.'

He was staring at me and beyond me, watching his life's work fluttering around a burning building.

He was right and I knew it. He knew he was right. I knew he would lose. The silence was the worst moment of all my time at the Circle. The silence when you know both truths are wrong.

Heather stepped forward. 'Kevin, forgive me for suggesting those things so abruptly, please. Everyone has the right to choose and to make the best decision for themselves, you are right. Let's take a break, grab a coffee and think about what's been said, talk to one another and we can meet up in an hour and discuss what our response will be to all this.'

They looked at her, Kevin sat down, and others stood up for a break and a coffee. The air was full of whispered conversations and some disappeared into the darkness. I could feel the eyes looking at me and I couldn't look back.

'Thank you, Heather, that was just what was needed,' I said a minute later, when we had moved away from everyone. I am not sure how much I hated her for saying what was possible and what was awful.

'You always get one,' she said, 'and who can blame them? They're just saying what most think and they're right, but, well, you know what I'm going to say.'

Picnic comes up to me, 'Don't take it like it sounded. Think about who it came from.' He was smiling. I nodded.

I called over Chow Mein, Smoothie and Malcolm.

'Would it be a good idea for you all to talk to Heather about what she's just said and give her your thoughts. Then, we can talk through how we can protect the place, what we can do as an exit strategy and what other options we have.'

They walked off with Heather to Smoothie's office.

I sit in the dark, on the far side of the Circle, trying to deal with what is happening. It's all too fast, too uncontrollable, too inevitable. This doesn't feel like the way we should be going. I put my thoughts into words, to myself, to the darkness.

I'm as shocked as all of you by what has been said tonight. It's difficult to imagine that only yesterday morning we were all doing what we normally do and didn't have too much to worry about and now, thirty-six hours later, we're looking at exit strategies and packing in half an hour to save ourselves from thugs, JCBs and the rest of the Lardland vultures.

It's difficult to imagine what has taken us more than ten years to get right is going to be lost in a couple of days. There is no logic that explains this other than greed, power, money and selfishness. And a system that stinks. From every angle it ain't looking good: up against all of them, in the end, the law, the police, the planners, the council, the thugs and the gangsters, difficult to tell where one set ended and the next began.

They just take what they want because they're all in it.

I want to list the options but what's the point, they all lead to the same place, walking out of here as silently as you walked in, at best, or walk out of here with no choices, no options and a few broken bones and bruises and a span at Her Majesty's pleasure. Heather is right, get out while you can, fight a new fight in a different place. Kevin is right, don't fight the first fight and you lose all the rest.

I am right, leave me alone, please, please, please.

Leave me alone isn't an option anymore. Not for a group of people you care about. If only Moses had put that at the top of the Ten Commandments: Leave Everyone Else Alone. Not that Thou shall not kill has any effect. Nor any of the others.

No options. Let's make up some options. You can do this, blah blah blah *and then you'll get crapped on, you could do a different* blah blah blah *and get crapped on and if you do options C and D the crap will be sprayed at you till you drown, suffocate or breathe it in and start to worship it. How can I think like this? How can I ever look them in the eye again? I shout out some expletives into the night air. I feel marginally better.*

I know I am going to begin with some bullshit and give them options when really there is no option. Same since Eve told Adam some bullshit. The choice is the illusion, I could already hear myself saying, 'Look, we don't want to act too quickly but we don't want to be caught out either. We've all had some time to consider the options we have...'

Above and around the darkness, the trees, the leaves, the stars and the city glowing to the east. I fuckin' hate the people.

Thank you, Kevin, you are always right.

When I got up to Smoothie's room, Heather was in the

middle of answering a question, and they were staring into the ground or looking at her as if it was her fault.

'The first of them will arrive at dawn. These are the guys with the bats, paid thugs who soften up the people left inside. There's usually cops on the sidelines to make sure that the residents don't fight back and since this is public property and it isn't enclosed, they'll just walk in and knock on doors. Then they'll bang the doors down. There will be uniform and non-uniform and possibly other sorts of snoops, depending on who they think they might find.'

'What do you mean, snoops?' said Malcolm.

'Dunno, but dodgy ones, army ones, special branch ones, undercover ones, filming ones, secret service, anti-terrorist, hired security, cheap guys in yellow hi-vis, could be any of them or none of them, but if you say that one of the contacts with Milton is Police, and we think Milton is undercover, then they may come looking for specific people.'

'How do we know they will come at all?' asked Picnic.

'We don't,' she said. 'But we know they might, and you have to be prepared.'

It went quiet.

'I feel like I've let all of you and this place down,' I said, 'standing there without a plan or an answer or an idea about what to do in a situation like this. I'm sorry. We've been so busy just making it work that we didn't get round to thinking about walking away from it.'

'We aren't walking away,' said Chow Mein. 'Not yet.'

'Exactly, we're just making plans. Necessary plans.'

She just looked at me to see if there was anything to say.

'Can we fight them?' asked Smoothie, 'you know, legally, squatters' rights, houses for the people, I don' fuckin know, affordable homes, somethin' like that?'

'Well, you're not exactly tenants are you, paying rent?

You're squatters of sorts, but to be honest, they're going to probably bulldoze the houses, so if they smash a few guys up with baseball bats and lose a few windows or doors and a few, scrounging doley-druggies like you – that's the angle the press and the authorities use so the courts and the public have got no sympathy, and if, just if, they have a scheme to replace what is here with homes of some sort, then, well, you can see where you stand.'

She smiled again, this time as if she lived in a world where news like this wasn't bad news, it was just news.

'What about buying some time?' asked Picnic.

'That is a good idea,' she said. 'Buy some time.'

That sounded like a plan.

An hour later, we're all gathered again under the single light, swaying in the wind. You could hear a chair creak. I started talking again, trying to sound like there was hope.

'This is our home. This has been our home for more than ten years. This is our community, and all around us are the things we've built, made and planted, the visible and the less visible things.'

I looked at the faces of my friends and wanted to not speak but to stop and hug them. These words are just perfume blowing through.

'I'm as shocked as you by what's been said tonight. It's difficult to imagine that only yesterday we were all doing what we normally do and not worrying about how and why, and now, thirty-six hours later, we're looking at exit strategies and packing in half an hour to save ourselves from thugs, JCBs and the rest of the Lardland vultures.

I signed to Chow Mein, *I am so shit at this*.

Carry on, just speak.

'I think there are four options. Option 1 is do nothing. Wait, carry on and see what happens. Option 2 is to find out as much as we can about Milton and the guys we saw at Sid's. And carry on as normal. Option 3 is to prepare to defend the place as best we can from this moment onwards. We can always go back to normal if the threat goes away. Option 4 is to leave safely, under our own terms, but as quickly and safely as possible.

Everyone started shouting at once. I had to ask for people to speak in turn.

Most spoke, most listened. Views were varied, some talked practical sense:

Dr. Forager: If it is anything like this young lady says it is going to be like, then we are too old to run away or anything like that. I am sorry, but we came here for safety and for the ideas. My husband and I are not for fighting anyone. We just want to garden in peace.

Claps. Cheers.

Jalapeña: We have fought the system in Argentina, in Chile and in Spain. We will fight for the rights we have here. You can count on us to do everything for the preservation of these essential rights of our existence.

Claps. Cheers.

Molly: We have heard a lot of opinions tonight about this place and what it means to us. We must remember that nothing lasts forever and we must always adapt and move and preserve the best of what we have. I am not too old to fight but I am getting too old to lose. We must look after one another and be ready to do that in the next place.

And so, it went on. Almost everyone got claps and cheers, even when they had just cheered for the opposite response.

Within an hour the silence had descended.

I summed it up: 'This will be our home until they force us. If you want to leave, if you have to leave, if you fear for what will happen, you must leave. We have friends and places who'll look after us. I'm sorry this isn't better prepared. The blame rests with me. From now on we have to prepare. From dawn, expect the beginning of the fight, the fight to make it as difficult as possible for our home to be taken from us.'

There was no reaction now, just that feeling of having moved on to a new normal, there was no going back for a while to the old.

'If you're staying, we're going to have to work together. We're going to work in teams to prepare. If you're leaving, then we will help.'

No one spoke. No one moved. One or two people started to hug and one or two started to cry. I couldn't be there any longer, I turned around, and my last slide was still on the screen.

Enta Geweorc

I left Picnic calling out names and organising the teams.

I told Malcolm and Smoothie and Chow Mein to meet me at Smoothie's.

I asked Heather if she could help us get people out of here and to somewhere safe.

'Of course,' she said.

There was nothing left.

No walls, no works, nothing. No giants.

19

About Mansions and Scrapyards

Sitting quietly in the back row of the gathering was Molly, and I introduced her to Heather.

'Molly, could you call on the ones likely to leave before it kicks off, or the ones who aren't going to cope. Take Heather round to their houses, she'll make sure they get out of here safely.'

Molly smiled. We tried and tried to give her a nickname, but she wouldn't be named. When she arrived, she was Qareema and would talk of nothing but the day ahead. After six years of keeping out all trespassers from the past, she quietly asked to be called Molly. 'Molly. My name is Molly,' she said, 'I'm just Molly.' Then, about a year ago, she came to me and said, 'I understand that you collect stories. I'm 78 years old and I want to tell you mine. It's not that much of a story, but I don't know how long I've got left so, if not now, then when?' she smiled.

Now is not the time to let you listen to Molly's story, but I will tell it later.

In Smoothie's IT suite, all three of them are staring at screens.

'Gentlemen, what I'm thinking, I can't tell if it's real or not. Is this a dream?'

'Bad dream, brother, bad,' said Smoothie, clacking away at two keyboards at once. He reminded me of Rick Wakeman, live in a stadium somewhere, operating stacked keyboards ganging up on him in an arc. But without the music, which I was glad of.

'What you want?' he said, without looking up.

He always made me laugh. 'Don't ask me what I want, but what can I have?'

'You can have the address of the Range Rover, you can have the movements of the Range Rover over the last three hours and you can have all the backed-up dirty pants information about anyone you want.' He made himself laugh.

'Spray that dirt, then,' I said.

'OK, Range Rover registered in Edinburgh, owned by South High Holdings does a lot o' slickin' around Leeds and up in Yorkshire. This time it left Leeds, gone north, park in a little specky place with no name I can see, then set off for a bit of chasin' sheep or whatever they do there and go to a place, even smaller and speckier and now come down Leeds way again and park it lil' self here.'

Smoothie showed me the spot. It's just outside Hunslet, the old industrial quarter that is being gentrified. He showed me on Google maps where the car was. It was a breaker's yard. We went onto Streetview and could see it looked quite large. *Forrester's Scrapyard*, it said, in a tatty sign. ***Scrap Paid For!*** is what it originally said, but now it said ***Crap Paedos!***.

'What's that big building there?' I said, pointing at a four-storey red-brick mill without windows.'

'That is, let me see,' said Smoothie, 'could be ***Forrester's Demos***. I can't read it.'

'Chow Mein, who can we send to do some reccying? Someone reliable.'

'Send Taco, he's a fox. He doesn't mess.'

When Taco came up to see us, I gave him his little task.

'This scrapyard and this building and anyone who's there. If it's safe, hop over and have a look, but only if it's safe. I'm looking for photos of cars, people, faces, registration plate numbers, anything and see if anything is happening in there, ok? If you find anything, ring me on this phone, the number is in there. Asap, Taco. *Hasta la vista!*'

Taco smiled and nodded and ran out of the room.

I asked Chow Mein, 'Who is he? Why don't I remember him?'

'He's safe, completely sound. He was a student who overstayed his visa and ran away from the detention centre where they put him when he was caught working a few hours in a restaurant in Nottingham. He's lost his passport and doesn't know how to get out the country without being caught. He's very bright.'

'Chow Mein, do you fancy a drive up to Thraykston? We need a tracker on the A6. When you've put the tracker on, can you set the house alarm off or something and see who emerges? We need to see who they are. It's a scenic drive.'

Beautiful at this time of night, he signed, and was gone.

'I'll be back,' I said to Smoothie and Malcolm.

Outside, it felt fresh, some westerly wind that was left with a little bit of moisture whipped around, fitfully. There were the sounds of voices and I could hear clanking and the sounds of hammering and banging. I found Picnic in the middle of it all.

'You look very sexy with a clipboard,' I said to him. 'You should wear one more often.'

'Might be all we got left this time tomorrow.'

'Don't tell me that. Tell me good news.'

'Heather and Molly got quite a few people who gotta leave, and we're taking everything that they want to save but can't take with them to the lockups, hidden at the back, near the fields, in case we want to come back for some stuff. Then, we're boarding up the houses when they gone.'

'Good. How many going?

'About twenty-five plus. They all got good reasons. No one jumping ship, just yet. Heather is getting some transport for them and they going out of town. Then, we going to get started on the road into this place, but not yet. Before that, we're blocking up all the entrances they might find, like the path out of Cromwell Court that goes through the woods and up to the road, they might find that one because it's obvious. All of them places we can find, we going to disguise and fill them in.'

I nodded.

'Then, we going to make sure they can't find the electricity supply and cut it off. Water is easier because years ago we cut into the supply to the new estate over the hill, do you remember, so that doesn't exist on any plans? We should've done more with the electricity.'

'It was on the plan,' I said weakly, 'but we've got a couple of generators. We should make people move into houses together then we won't need as much of everything. Maybe move everyone to this row here and the houses behind?'

'Makes sense. Then, we'll have to move more people and things and board up the other houses.'

'Great idea. Picnic, you should be running a country.'

'No, thanks,' he said, 'what would I do with all the stupid people?'

'Is Heather around?'

He nodded in the direction of the café.

She was on the phone when I found her. There was a small crowd around her, bags stacked up behind them.

'I've got a minibus and cars to take them down to Sheffield. We've got space for them all tonight around the city, but we'll have to move them on tomorrow or the day after. I've told them that they have no memory of this place, that there was no Circle.'

'Thank you,' I said. No memory of being here. Already.

I looked at them all, sitting around, in silence. How can there be so many refugees who cannot find a place to be in Lardland, their own country? Refugees from the laws, the systems, the violence, the injustice, the inhumanity, the unforgivingness of Lardland. Friedbreads take more on a two week holiday to Alicante than these people were taking with them for the rest of their lives. It wasn't the leaving, so much as the single suitcase, that touched the nerves.

I shook hands and hugged them all, promised we would meet soon and next time it would be even better and who knows, we may all be back here sooner than we think.

I make a note, to list all of the people going, on a monument to remind ourselves of them. But how can you list people who aren't on any other lists?

'The transport should be here within the hour,' she said.

We set off walking back to the IT office, Smoothie's room.

'You can be quite cold, can't you, Heather? Callous, almost.'

'What? We're helping out, providing a safe place for people we don't know. That's not callous. That's not cold.'

'Telling them that there was no Circle, that they have no memory. That is callous. This was their home. For some of them this was the only place they ever called home.'

She shook her head. 'Well, it's about to be taken away from them, they have to deal with it. What else do they do, sit and talk about how good it was as they're handcuffed in the Police vans and thrown in cells?'

'They can keep their memories, can't they? Or does the state own them as well? What's the point of any of this without attachments to give it some sort of meaning?'

'Well, maybe you can be too attached. Too sentimental about it all. We're all just passing through, aren't we? Even the bastards who think they own it all, they're just passing through, as well.'

'You have no attachments, then?'

She stopped and looked at me in the darkness and pulled the wind-blown hair out of her eyes.

'Look, what you have done here is amazing, I get that, but it's not the aim for me, or us. It's just a place for the ideas to live.

You've got to keep them living before you do anything else.'

'For me, the place is the idea. The walls that make the spaces are where the ideas live and grow or die. I love this place and these people because they and the idea became the same thing, here, in this place over all this time.'

'I have an idea,' and laughed, 'a different idea, something that we've been working on that you might want to contribute to.'

'OK.'

'But let's wait and see what this morning brings and the next few days.'

'Are you staying?' I asked.

'Try getting rid of me.'

When we got into Smoothie's room, they're still bent over computers. Smoothie spoke without looking up,

'Chow Mein's sending through some bad stuff about Mrs. Morrison's yard. It's lucky we got an address because the house is about five miles from the doorway, man. Hahaahaa. It's bigger than Harrogate.'

'You never been to Harrogate, how would you know?'

We look at the pictures on the screen that Chow Mein has sent through. Big stone walls going on for miles, a couple of impressive entrances with huge wrought iron gates at opposite ends of the grounds.

'He says the signal comes and goes, so he's gone over the wall and he's going to try to get near the house and the car. He don't like dogs, so he's hoping they ain't got wild hounds,' says Smoothie, 'and that if we don't hear from him in an hour then to come and find him.'

'I hope he's ok. Should we send someone up there now in case he needs help?'

'See how we goes, you know da man, B-man, he love this type of thing,' laughed Smoothie.

‘And our Taco has got to the scrapyard, and the Range Rover is still there, and the lights are one and,’ Malcolm’s reading the messages, ‘the scrapyard is huge, and the photos are vague but there seems to be a meeting going on, but he can’t see into the portacabin. He can’t spell portacabin, but that’s what I think he means.’

‘Tell him to stay there and see if he can get any car details or more photos. Ask him if he needs help.’

Heather is studying the photos and info that Chow Mein has sent through. ‘What’s this?’ she asks me.

‘This is the house of a certain Mrs. Morrison. She owns a blue A6, very sleek, if you know your all-road sports cars. Spotted outside a pub that Milton ended up in, which led him into all sorts of stuff that led him to us...except Mrs Morrison wasn’t there, but some sleek geezer was driving her car when he met his mates for a beer and a pie.’

‘Wow,’ she said, ‘perfect.’

Smoothie suddenly shouts, ‘Whooo!! Yes, yes, I knew it. Look at these wastemen, B-man. I knew I seen that name before.’

On the screen were two mugshots of two men. Jowly, square-necked and a little bit like seeds in a pod.

‘Forrester. It’s the same name. Forrester, yeah, the scrappy paedo and the fattieman in the pub, Sid’s. They’re brothers. Remember the name above the door of Sid’s? Seems like they both been caught for this and that but always seem to slime out of everythin’. Look at them. I want to punch both fat faces. Just for no reason.’ He feigns a double-smack in the two imaginary faces, then repeats the blows only harder.

‘There you are, Heather, on the right is Handsome Sid, who runs the pub and his younger brother, even more handsome Raymond, who runs the scrapyard.’

‘And why are they important?’ she asked.

‘Very good question.’

20

About Mrs. Morrison
(from *Wikipedia*)

Education and career

The daughter of Gerald and Gwendolyn Morrison, née DeAth, she was educated privately at St Dampener's Girls College in West Frickham and at the University of the Arts, Colchester, where she received a Bachelor of Arts (Third Class) in 1993, receiving the Bourne-Foulke-Witt Prize for Equestrian Services. Morrison started work at The EU Council of Arts from 1994 to 1996 in Brussels and was a consultant in Hand on Art art gallery in Peckham from 1997 to 1998. Between 1998 and 2004, she was a member of the Kent Utilities Board, between 2004 and 2007, vice-chairman of the Voluntary Organisations for African Wildlife Hunting & Tourism and between 2012 and 2014, chairman of the Royal Educational Consultative Council Pre-School. Between 2011 and 2014, she was a lay member of the Southern English League of Breeders' Wives Council.

Current Memberships and Directorships

Matti Morrison was also a member of the Advisory Council on Dance Curriculum from 1999, of the Shoyt Inquiry into Local Planning 2007 and the Home Office Advisory Panel on Licences for Experimental Practices 2000-2010, and of the Rail

Franchises Select Committe Wales and Eastern Board from 1999-2015. She was director of Seaboard Television from 2001, Director of the Shark Newspapers Holdings Ltd and of Dance TV Africa and since 2003 of London Holidays for Mental Health, becoming Director of GAGA Charity CEO Recruiting in 2004.

In 2005, she received an Honorary Doctor of Business Administration from the University of Edinmont and a further Honorary Doctor from The University of the East Coast, where her husband is Vice-Pro-Chancellor.

She is currently in receipt of a Lady-in-Waiting Bursement from the Privy Purse and holds 43 further Directorships.

Personal life

Since 1999, she has been married to Mr. Tristan Rupert Gothanger Clones-Dyke. They have two daughters and a son. She owns a noble title entirely in her own right, but she chooses to use her husband's title as Viscountess Clones-Dyke.

Lords Select Committees Membership 25

Overseas Communications Wildlife Tourism Charities 2013

Transnational Mental Health Organisations 2013

Pre-Legislative Scrutiny on Monopolies Listings 2013

Scrutiny of Comparable Ownership Schemes current

Styles

Miss Matilda Dorothy 'Matti' Rosemary Morrison 1975-1998

Mrs. Matilda Dorothy Rosemary Morrison 1998-2014

The Hon. Mrs. Tristan Rupert Gothanger-Clones-Dyke 2014-present

The Rt. Hon. The Baroness Clones-Dyke-Morrison 2009-present

The Rt. Hon. The Viscountess Clones-Dyke, Baroness Clones-Dyke of Morrison 2011-present

21

About Tim and Mr. Nosey

By the time that Jim found Tim walking around the lanes of North Yorkshire, and what with the narrow lanes, the intermittent phone signal, angry texts from Lottie, Tim's wife, and a number of phone calls which had all been terminated because of the poor signal, Tim was incandescent and Jim was steaming by the time they found one another.

'Where the fuck have you been?' shouted Tim, as he opened the door of the Range Rover.

'Well, where the hell have you been?" asked Jim, a little less aggressively. 'I thought you said you were near Ayrsborough Yarrick and that you were near your daughter's school? You're nowhere near either. Middlesbrough's just over that bloody hill.'

'Fuck off, *draadtrekker*' said Tim. 'How do I know the name of her school, it's not near anywhere. I told you to come to Ayrsborough.'

'There are three Ayrsboroughs – Ayrsborough Nethers, Ayrsborough Parvae and Ayrsborough Middlecock. There's no such place as Ayrsborough Yarrick. So, don't lose your temper with me, Tim, you're bloody lucky I found you.'

They sit in silence for a while. Tim is banging away on his mobile phone and swears either because it is working, and the messages are winding him up or because it isn't working, and he can't respond to anything immediately.

Why won't she back down? thinks Tim. *Don't ever drive off without me ever again and make me look a fool like that or*...On second thoughts he removes the *or* and finishes with a full stop. And a *Please*. And a smiley. He even removes the *ever*. The he presses send.

He can't help but send her another one, *Why aren't you answering my calls?* Immediately, a headline appears of a story about an unnamed royal sending pulses racing with bikini selfies and a blackmailing undercover journalist, who was working with a cop to get a scoop. And more news about the Queen's horses and three current members of the royal family voted Best Dressed Ambassadors of Britain.

Next text was from Tris, *What's going on? Sort it out, there's a good chap. Just heard from Lottie that you've had a row. I'll do what I can for you. Don't mess up.* His brother-in-law.

Just a little mix-up at Caroline's school. All sorted. Don't worry. See you tomorrow.

He hated when she got the family involved. No winning then. It made him so pissed off that he opened the Range Rover's rickety window and screamed in anger.

'What you do that for, Tim, the bloody thing won't go back up. Why didn't you ask before doing that?' shouted Jim.

Forty minutes later, they pull up at the scrapyard.

'You've come to the right place then,' said Tim.

'Eh?' said Jim.

'You might get a couple of hundred for it,' said Tim, 'I'll speak to the boss.'

Jim ignored him and spent the next five minutes coaxing the ailing electric passenger door window back up. When he got to the office, they were all there, Reg, Sid, Bri and now him and Tim.

'Change of plan, slightly,' said Reg. 'We've brought the date forward. I'm sure you gentlemen'll be pleased.'

'Not ideal, Reg, I'll need a bit of paperwork,' said Bri, 'something to get some lads there for yous as back up. Something to give us a reason to be there.'

'Jim,' said Tim, 'for fuck's sake, fill in something, anything, about what sort of undesirables, druggies, drug dens, yeah, go down that road. Just feeling like hammering the hell out of these lowlifes. I can write it for you and ask for police escort for our men. Bri, do you want me to send you some bullshit you can put on a form and get your wankers out there. It always looks better when some blue and white turns up. More legit.'

'OK,' Said Jim, 'but please, can we get in and out very quickly, please. Done deal. All over quickly. No dead bodies or anything. No publicity. Keep them all out. Got to get a positive news story out of this.'

'Send me something over,' said Bri, 'our DCI is happy to do this sort of stuff as long as there's paperwork that's kosher.'

'Can't say, kosher, Bri, you should know that. I could report you for racism,' said Reg.

'Fuck off, Reg,' he said, laughing, 'play the bloody white man.'

'Sure,' said Reg. 'Nice and easy.'

Then he stands up and goes to a cabinet at the back of the cabin. He pulls out a bottle of Talisker and pours everyone a drink, into plastic cups.

'Your health and your wealth, friends.'

They all drink.

Bri says, 'How long this going to take? I need to project something for my piece of paper.'

'Depends,' says Jim, 'what happens, depends how quickly we can get in there. I would have thought by the end of the week we could have begun clearing the place. Two days max, I would have thought.'

'If we get the twats out in a day, we could send in the demo boys, Reg, by the end of the week, and some of it could be gone over the weekend. I think it was a fucking good idea getting in earlier than we'd planned, make everything a lot easier. Reg, do the honours, you *draadtrekker*,' and laughs out loud.

Reg pours everyone another round. 'Your African language stinks, dickhead. To Tim, the Zulu warrior.'

Tim shakes his head. Bri stands up to leave. Reg stands up as well.

'Oh, Officer, I forgot to show you what I have recently acquired. Step back a moment.'

Bri sits back down. Reg pushes a small cabinet away from the wall and behind it is a small, locked door which Reg opens, but he makes sure he stands in the way of any prying eyes, and then turns around, looking very pleased.

'Look at this little beauty, gentlemen of discernment. Direct from Germany, at a very good price.'

He passes it to Bri, looking for the approval of a respected peer.

'For fuck's sake, Reg, I don't want to be holding this,' says Bri.

'Go on, it's fine, it's not loaded.'

'Wow,' says Tim, as Bri hands it to him.

On second thoughts, he takes it back and starts to try to wipe off his prints. '*Wat sou Jesus hiermee doen*?'

'Speak English, man.'

'What would Jesus do with that?' and whistled. 'Nice, very nice.'

'It's a Beretta 1301 semi-automatic, and what I love about it, more even than the sleekness and the grip,' at this point Reg has taken his rifle off Tim and is holding it up in a comfortable way, and pointing it out of the portacabin window, 'it's got a fuckin' magazine the size of a pair of 44 Double Hs. It just keeps firing itself,' and laughs again, as he does a mock-Rambo goon-slaughter.

'I really should be going,' said Bri, pushing the barrel of Reg's new toy downwards. 'Reg, mate, keep that locked away, please. I don't want to ever hear or see that again.'

'Quick one for the road,' said Reg, and poured another round in an instant.

Bri drank this whisky and crumpled the plastic cup and said his goodnights. When he stepped out into the night air, his mind was already working on tomorrow's plan: who he'd roster, what he'd write and dreaming secretly of who he would most like to have in the sights of the Beretta. He walked all the way to the gate of the scrapyard, setting the dogs barking furiously. He opened the gate and stopped for a moment. He was sure that he caught a movement over in the railway arches a hundred yards away to the left. He stared for several seconds. But nothing moved. Must have been a rat or something.

He turned round and got into his car. Before he drove out of the yard, he thought about ringing Reg to ask him to go and have a look, but he got distracted by a message from Claire. She was a dirty girl, sending him messages when she was topless.

22

About Heather

As Taco's pics appear on our screens, Smoothie's whooping with joy, 'The ugly bro live in a council house next to his mother in Gipton, and the *really* ugly bro live in Scarcroft in a palace with a swimming pool inside and a battypool outside.'

Smoothie is having fun on various maps and street view apps.

'Yeah, that looks like a nice place for relaxin' as a gangsta.'

Heather is leaning over his shoulder.

'Impressive. I mean you, Smoothie, not that house. You know your way around this stuff. Amazing.'

Taco's pictures from the scrapyard are coming up on Smoothie's screen. The last one is of a big, muscular guy with light hair cropped very close to his scalp, just as he's coming to the big, wire gates.

'That's Jarhead,' I say, 'that joker was in Sid's when I peered in through the window. Who is he? Why is he out so late looking for a second-hand battery? Is there a picture of his car? Smoothie, get Taco to send a picture of Jarhead's car, asap, please.'

'Will do.'

Picnic comes through the door. 'We got a plan going down there, if you want to see what we doing. I'm going to have a coffee and then I'll take you on a tour.'

'Thanks, good stuff. Heather, come down and give us the benefit of your thoughts.'

'Yes,' she said, 'of course. Just one thing before we go down. I want to show you something. Not here.'

We walked downstairs and out into the cool night air. There was the sense of people still busy and lights on, waving in the wind, and people talking in unseen groups. She stopped when we were out of earshot of everyone else.

'I wanted to show you this, it's a bit all over the place, and there's more than one camera so it's been edited together, but you'll get the point.'

She passed me her phone and the video clip had started. 'I've turned the volume down.'

It takes me a few seconds to tune into what is happening. The camerawork is dizzyingly difficult to watch as it shows people and faces and a tangle of different bodies, all accompanied by shouting and cries for help and swearing. That clip ends and it melds into the next one, which shows people running and gasping for breath. Someone is being pulled along as the camera tilts up for a few moments and there are men in balaclavas carrying big sticks and plastic riot shields running at and over and through a crush of bodies and lashing out in every direction. There's a whirr of student-types in duffel coats and woolly hats and girls with dreads and a dog on a lead, everything spinning around as the camera-holder flips over and over, then comes to a stop, amid shouts and muffled screams. The shot is held for seconds before someone else picks it up, and for a brief moment, there's a shot of a long trench in a muddy site with faces in balaclavas banging sticks against plastic shields.

I shake my head as I pass it back. She doesn't speak and I cannot ask.

'How do good Christian people get up and go to work and put their children in schools that preach Christian values and wave that flag and tolerate so much injustice, institutionalised greed and even more institutionalised violence on a daily basis?

How can any man pick up a club to beat defenceless men and women the same age as their sons and daughters? How can a human who has pushed unarmed, innocent people with broken skulls and bones into a muddy trench and watch them pass out with pain and unable to breathe ever find peace? How can any judge or politician sit in judgment on anyone anymore? How can anyone judge anyone else for any act done for the greater good that challenges the extraordinary greed, misuse of power and laziness of the few? And worst of all, how can the many sit idly by and live in their boxes and side with their oppressors?'

I had no answer.

She looked up at the trees and then back at me.

'You should protect what you can from this place, save what you can and let them have it.'

I looked at her outline in the inadequate light. The eyes shone like things that dwelt not in air. That was what I wanted to tell her. As if she had come up from the deepest part of the ocean and didn't know how to belong here.

'You are an exceptional person.'

She smiled.

'Those are not the words I want to use, but they sum up the feeling.'

She laughed. 'That's not fair. What are the real words?'

'Have you ever lived miles down in an ocean and found coming up to this world an incomprehensible, unlivable mess?'

'Does Aberdaron count?'

I laughed.

'I want to do something with you.'

'Are you sure?'

'No,' she laughed, 'but it could work. If they come and take and destroy your homes, as it looks like they're going to do, do you think we should show them what that means? Get under their skin. Old testament type of thing?'

'Not sure I get you. Old and a bit slow, sorry.'

'I mean that we disrupt their homes, their living space. In the same way they're destroying yours.'

'Wow, I like the way you constantly push me.'

'You will notice that I am using disrupt and destroy. Disrupt their lives. We are not ready to destroy their homes, but believe me, I would if I could.'

'Heather, Heather, Heather, hang on a minute – what you're saying is – if I'm getting you in any sense is –'

'I'm not sure quite what I mean, but in principle, would you think it would be just for the person who destroys communities and homes to have his or her home – affected, disturbed, bothered, disfigured – I don't know what the word is exactly? When I saw those pictures on your screens up there of those people living in palatial luxury in hundreds of acres of beautiful parkland and gardens and fields and woods, and I saw the horror and despair and the loss and the terrible disruption being done to you and your community here in the name of profit, I want those gangster-capitalists to feel the shock of seeing everything they have worked for damaged. Fucked.'

'Heather...'

'Stop saying my name and tell me what you think.'

'Not sure what I think. First thing that comes to mind from the Old Testament is, an eye for an eye, and all that, second thing that comes to mind is, that actions like that will bring the full force of the Armageddon squad down on you and the third thing is, tell me more.'

Now she laughed. 'Not sure yet. But if they come, and it's those people pulling the strings who we think it is, then, well, the last thing they'll expect is that while they're here destroying this community and these houses, someone is up there destroying theirs. Which is a sort of advantage. Then, it depends on what we want to do and how we do it.'

'Let's talk to them,' I said, 'but I'm not sure what they'll say.'

'One more thing that has been on my mind.'

I waited.

'You put together an amazing collection of photos telling the story of the place. I wish I had known you earlier. I mean *you* as in the place. At the end you showed some photos of your friend in what looked like a dig and a coffin. Perhaps it was nothing, but I heard one or two of the people talking about it afterwards. They've never seen those pictures before.'

She stopped and left it hanging.

'Do you have a very safe place for us to store some things with you? It has to be bomb-proof. Very secure, dry, very safe.'

'We do. And the coffin? What's the story?'

'You don't give up, do you?'

She looked straight back at me, then through me, like she had turned around on the shore, caught like a mermaid between this world and her world and looked away at the stars and the leaves and the orange arc of the city, while the siren of an ambulance pierced the frothing of the wind and held us there.

'I think you have planted so beautifully,' she said, 'that makes me want to cry.'

Imagine what I am feeling, was what I wanted to say.

I let her stare for a few moments more.

'I need you to help me.'

'Do what?'

'Talk to Uncle Kevin. I know he's going to stay and I think it will kill him to see what they'll do to this place.'

'I'm not sure I'm the person to convince him to do anything,' she smiled. And acted out exactly how he would react to her turning up on his doorstep. Accent, swearing and grammar were note perfect. She could really make me laugh.

'Take someone else. Molly would be perfect.'

'I'll take Molly.'

About Tanya

Education and career

The daughter of Jane Morris, née Morris. Acting father for frequent periods, Gus. Currently estranged. Biological father, unnamed. She was educated periodically at St Dunston's Primary, West Hill Lane Primary, Holy Mother Catholic Primary, St. Chad's Primary, Newgrange Road Primary and Stockton Primary in Newcastle, where she went after being thrown out by her mother aged 9. She was housed at more than 7 institutions in an effort to educate and support her between the ages of 10 and 15.

Morris was first offered cannabis at the age of 8 by one of her mother's customers and was involved with varying degrees of drug use until the birth of her baby last year. She started work as a prostitute to fund her absence from a Residential Unit in North Yorkshire at the age of 13 and has had several convictions for drug use and violence involved in crime and drugs. Morris has no known qualifications.

Current Memberships and Directorships

None

Personal life

One child with Lee Wilkington. Currently receiving Child Benefits and Universal Credit. Forced to use local foodbanks.

Styles

Tanya Morris current official style
Tan to her mates, *Lee's Missus* to Lee's mates

23

About the Circle

I watch Heather make a coffee. She grasps the jar and shakes the granules into the mug. No measuring. Picnic passes her a spoon, but she waves it away. She pours the milk and as she does so, she lifts the milk higher above the mug. I'm almost sure she twists the mouth of the milk carton as if she were pouring wine. She watches the undissolved granules float to the surface of the deep greeny-brown liquid. People think coffee is brown but it's more than just brown. It's funny watching Picnic's big frame fawn before a young woman. Funnier still how she brushes him away and sits on a seat he didn't indicate. He's become Othello to an unwitting Desdemona. I can feel his impressive flourishes finishing his sentences. I sit fascinated, wishing myself away to an outdoor theatre, in a warm evening, with a candlelit stage.

Heather reaches out and cuts across, 'Picnic, just tell me what you've done so far. We need to be ready if they come at dawn. These guys have a nasty habit of turning up before you've even woken up,' smiling, studying the paperwork on his clipboard.

She went straight to the map of the Circle at 1:2,500 showing the individual plots. She's taking in every detail as she speaks.

'Do you know that between 1919 and 1924, houses for ordinary people, like what you have here, sort of, were supposed to offer around 93 square metres of living area, but within five years the same people could be squeezed into 58 square metres? Funny, progress, isn't it? And that they were supposed to be able to fit in about 3,000 houses per square kilometre,' eyeing us both, 'but Sandringham, for example, second home of the twenty-four belonging to Elizabeth Saxe-Coburg-Gotha, is about 20,000 acres, which is about 8,000 hectares which is 80 square kilometres, so instead of a house for one family plus servants as at present, you could, theoretically at least, build 3,000 houses x 80 equals 240,000 houses on the Sandringham estate – wow, that's a small city in a nice place for nice people. Instead, they claim there's no land, so we'll put them in a tower. Not the Tower of London, of course, but a cheap, crappy tower block where the average size of 50% of them is 50 square metres.'

'Wow,' we said in unison.

'That's amazing,' I said. 'Soon we might be living in zero square metres, so if you have any thoughts about Picnic's work, that would be great.'

She laughed. 'Is there really only one road into the estate?' she asked, sweeping the map with her hand. 'And all of this is green land, woods or open space and all of this over here is housing?'

'Yes.'

'OK. And you have fenced off the only road in? And blocked the paths here and here and here? All of them in fact?'

'Yeah, blocked with barbed wire, fencing and whatever else we could find.'

'What are you going to do about an escape route?'

'We have two, 'I said, 'one is there, at the opposite end to the entrance road, the other one is there, the nearest point to a road. We built some garages and fences along that part there,' pointing to an empty space on the map, 'but three of the garages have false walls at the back and small doors that lead out to the road. The same over there, leading into the woods. Picnic can show you. Everyone knows where they are and how they work.'

'Do you want to see what we've done on the main road?' said Picnic, proudly.

'Great, but before we do that, a couple of things, which you need to think about. What do you do if anyone gets injured? What are you going to do about all that gear you have in Smoothie's office that puts you on a par with the Pentagon? And at what point will you think, *Yeah, time to get out?* I've got other things as well, but they're the most pressing.' She smiled.

I couldn't answer straightaway. I looked at Picnic, who shrugged. 'How old are you, Heather?' I asked, not knowing where it came from.

'Twenty-six, B-man. Why?'

'No reason. Very impressive, being so young and so –'

'Bossy?' she said.

'Definite, is the word I prefer. Let's go and see how they're getting on.' I looked at my watch. 'What time does it get light at this time of year?'

'Soon,' she said.

When we got to the main entrance it looks unrecognisable. People putting up fences, digging holes, stretching wire and pouring concrete.

'If they don't come, we're going to have some cleaning up to do,' I said, 'without demeaning your excellent work, Picnic. Wow. It looks like the entrance to –'

'Hell?' offered Picnic.

The only road in is now completely blocked. The burnt-out cars are now three in number and have been pulled across the road and the wheels taken off so that they would have to remove those before they get a vehicle onto the Circle. Then, there's a freshly dug ditch going the whole way across the road, and the verges at each side to the edges of the walls of the terrace houses either side. Into that, they've poured some oil to make it nice and slippy. Now there are two layers of interlocking fencing, topped off with barbed wire and interlaced with more barbed wire like vicious, metallic ivy. Just inside all of this, is a group digging around a small square. Picnic noticed me staring.

'That's a water main. Dirty water. If they are nice, they can have the clean dirty water from over there, but if not, they can have the sewage from over here. Just a thought,' he said.

Heather nodded. 'Everything helps. Let's face it, by this evening you might not be here.' She saw the reaction on our faces. 'Sorry,' she said, 'it was meant lightly.'

Smoothie was in full flow to Malcolm when we got back to his office, but swivelled on his chair and beamed at me.

'B-man, have I done, well? Yeah, I have done well. Chow Mein is on his way back. And look at what Taco has sent through.'

We all crowded around his screens. Lots of pictures of cars and people in the grimy streetlight at night.

'Recognise anyone? Or better still, don't recognise anyone?'

One by one, the figures we have come to know emerge from Raymond's portacabin. Taco is doing us proud, digitally. We count five people in there – Jarhead, The Handsome Brothers, Mr. Nosey and then one more we haven't seen before.

'You know what, the bison-wrestler there with the fake tan looks like the key to all of this. Who is he, Smoothie? Malcolm? The way he walks the walk and the company he keeps makes me think that he has the most to hide.'

Heather asks, 'Really? Why?'

Taco has sent us some video footage. 'Play it again, Smooth Sam,' I say, 'that clip of him saying goodbye and getting into the Range Rover. He swaggers. They're all nodding in deference to him. Look how Mr. Nosey is smiling, like this guy is the Mob. He is leaving saliva on the pavement. Disgusting. But who is he? I'm guessing he's out of town, big bucks, rugby player, ex-military looking at the way he walks. Spends a lot of time abroad. I mean, if you can see a fake tan in streetlight at night, it might not even be fake. Malcolm, can you get onto all the people who are on the Board of South High Holdings and find if he's in there? In fact, can we get a profile of everyone on South High Holdings and see how far their tentacles reach? And tell Taco that he's done brilliant and to come home.'

'Yeah, will do,' says Smoothie, 'and one more thing, you remember that car maudlin-dawdling here earlier this afternoon, with the plates that belong to a Mr. Jones who is now in his eighties, well, Taco took a picture of it outside the scrapyard. Well, here it is, and guess what, your Jarhead dude get in it. So, that's your proof, man, that this them, they, those, whatever you wanna call 'em, are connected with my home. They been here and they comin' back.'

Smoothie gives a whoop. He has made the connection.

'Smoothie, do you need a coffee?' He looks at me, quizzically, because he doesn't want to leave his machines at this critical moment. 'Just a quickie.'

Outside, I stop him from walking off to the café.

'Listen, I didn't want to say this in there, but you have to do something very important from now on.' He looks away. 'We might not have much time. Once we have found out as much as we can about these arseholes and what they're doing, we have to prepare to leave. Even if we don't leave, we have to prepare for it.'

'Yeah, of course. I know what you sayin'.'

'We need a plan, and you will need help. Whatever you need, we can do it.'

He didn't reply. He looked away again.

'What's wrong?' I asked, 'You ok?'

'Yeah, I'm good. I don't think I can do it. I can't leave all this. This my life, you know. So much stuff. We spent years putting this together. Never gone be the same if we just walk away.'

'I get what you're saying, Smoothie, I'm hearing it. But do you want to get pulled out of this house by the lunatics with guns and uniforms who are then just gonna put you in a room with a magic fist that you're gonna keep using on yourself till you appear one day in a psychiatric hospital and you don't remember whose legs you wearing, never mind what your name is. Or my name is.'

Smoothie sat down on the damp ground. I looked up, not knowing how to say this. Smoothie is family, like Chow Mein.

Way out over the North Sea there was the bit of pink streaking the grey, and the new day was coming.

'Look, brother, over there, dawn. We got one day, maybe two and we're going to be bulldozed out of town. If we lucky, we going to get away with our souls, our friends and some happy memories. If we spend a bit of time now, we can save a bit more, but you're going to have to think not about this life, but about the next.'

He was plucking some bits of grass and sprinkling them like grains of salt between his fingers.

'Please, Smoothie. For me. What you can save now will be the foundation of the next place. Remember me saying about the *enta geweorc* earlier this evening, the works of giants? You are bigger than the giants, 'cos you have it all stored, ready to be rebuilt.'

He looked up.

'Give me five. I'll press some buttons. Just give me five now.'

So, I let him be.

Of all of them, the old ones, the young ones, the illegal ones, the half-mad ones and the lost ones, it was Smoothie I worried most about.

The heart of a child.

24

About Alwena

For half an hour, I fell asleep on the sofa in Smoothie's living room. Chow Mein was coming through the door at the same time as Heather was coming down the stairs. I sat up on the edge of the couch and for a moment couldn't work out where I was, or who they were.

Chow Mein had a coffee in his hand and passed it to me.

'It was for me, but you look like you need it more.'

'Oh, thanks. How you doing? How was it up in Theakston?'

'Thraykston was good, don't know about Theakston. I talk to you about it when you've had a coffee.'

'Thank you, did we get what we needed?'

Chow Mein walked off with a *catch-you-soon* sign.

'Heather, sorry, I just fell asleep.'

'No worries,' she said, 'I found a couple of interesting things. Plus, I've made some phone calls and the ones who set off from here have landed safely and are tucked up in beds in Sheffield. I have also been through all of the directors of South High Holdings and their directorships and their mates, and as you might expect, it's a spider's web of mateyness – the same faces keep cropping up, the same names, the same reimbursements, the same endless set of fraudsters, swindlers, con-men and liars running all of the businesses and charities and god knows what else, where they can sniff an opportunity.

'Anyway, I think I have found our kingpin, you remember the rugby-playing, fake-tan swaggerman, who was sitting in that portacabin in the scrapyard? We're all agreed that it could well be this man – Tim Westhuizen, director of South High Holdings and at least fifteen other companies, probably more, and on the board of other institutions. I lost count how many. There isn't anything he doesn't put his filthy hands into, and I won't bore you with the details, but real estate and guess what, property development, are right up there. Unless we're sitting on some valuable dyspropium or tungsten they're probably going to redevelop your – this – place. He has several little palaces where he likes to hang out, but strangely enough, partly because he loves hanging around posh people and being seen to be seen, I found a picture of him in a local North Yorkshire paper and there he is, sponsoring a rugby competition for the youth of the area, and handing out the prizes. That made me wonder what Mr. Nosey was doing in his Range Rover wandering around North Yorkshire this evening, until he eventually turns up with Tim at the scrapyard. If I'm right, and I'm really not sure about this yet, but I think he's married to Mrs. Morrison's husband's sister. And guess what, they are seriously ficking posh. Vi-fowcking-count level posh, you getting me?'

I shook my head. 'Not sure, give me five minutes.' I stood up. 'I need some fresh air, do you mind?'

We walked outside and sat down on the edge of the circle of trees at the very centre of the Circle. The light was grey and streaky, split by a strange wash of dazzling light like foil pinned down in the furthest east, ripping and piercing the meek branches of the trees.

'You know that here are all of the trees that were sacred to our ancestors, laid out very carefully, so that we are reminded every day of the power of the earth around us.'

She looked at me for the flicker of an edge that she didn't

want to miss. 'Yeah? This is your world, I suppose, so you have to try to explain what you're on about.'

'What do you see? Tell me. Just a load of trees, haphazard, in the middle of a big circle of tarmac on a slope?'

She turned to the trees and stared at them.

'There are lots of them, I don't know the names of them all, but I think, the more I stare, the more I'm maybe missing something. Like one of those images where only some people can see the intended picture, and everyone else can only see it when they're told what it is.'

'Yeah, sort of.' I laughed, 'I wish we'd met earlier when you could have seen this place in better circumstances.'

'Tell me what I should be seeing,' she said, 'please, I know we have so much to do, but I'm sensing something important.'

'Stand up,' I said, and I set off walking around the edge. 'Count the width between the outer ring of trees. And what sort of trees are they?'

She measured with her stride the space between each tree, and I could hear her counting to herself. After a couple of minutes she said, 'They're all the same distance apart and all the same tree but, inside them there's another circle. Are they different trees? Or are they the same? I failed Biology GCSE.'

'No, you're doing well. The outer ring is blackthorn, to keep people out, but there are three ways in. Inside, is a ring of rowan. Rowan trees are a protection against enchantment, and some people say it is a portal tree, the way that leads between this world and the other world.'

'Really?' she said, again.

I laughed, 'Really.'

'Do you believe all that stuff?'

'Not sure that's the point. It's to do with the context of the thing you call *stuff* – where it is, how it works with everything else, how you treat it, how you let it become part of you again. If you see a tree in a featureless desert it becomes the Tree of Life, if you see a tree in a forest, it's just a piece of wood spoiling the view. If you aren't looking for them, you don't notice the yews.'

'What?"

'The yews? What are you talking about?'

'Look how clever they were, the developers of this estate when it was first built. It took me a while to work out why the roads didn't run in straight lines but made funny kinks and went in loops. It was as if they were avoiding something.'

She looked at me again. 'Am less with you now than I was a minute or two ago.'

'Come with me.'

We walked back to Smoothie's house.

'Look over there, past where everyone is working, stacking the chairs, dismantling the little stage, where you told us what to expect when they came for us. Do you remember? Seems like a long time ago. You see that tree poking up between the houses? It's got flat, dark green leaves that look much greyer close up.'

'Yes,' she said, 'it's sort of enclosed by all of the gardens around it.'

'Exactly. It's a yew tree. And it's as if the yew trees are the centre of the place and the houses are built around *them*, not the other way around. That makes them special and our place special. We've found twenty-one of them, scattered around. It may be that this was once a big grove of yew trees. Years ago, there used to be a pub on the top of the hill called, The Yew Tree. Gone now, no sign of it.'

'I've been thinking about what you said about this place – that this place is the idea and that now, as you're talking, it's making more sense. There's something else now, but I don't know if we have time? Or if you want to tell me.'

'Not much time but not much point in hiding either.'

'Those photos you showed at the very end. You and Chow Mein digging – it looks like something archaeological. That yew tree is in it, isn't it? Why did you choose that as the last picture? What were you digging for?'

My turn to look away. 'It sounds insane, ok, it sounds more insane than anything you've heard before from me or anyone here.'

'Tell me, anyway,' she said, 'because nothing you could tell me would begin to compete with the madness of the things we're dealing with all around us. Most of us just letting it happen. Tell me.'

'I was looking for the reason I was here.'

'That doesn't make sense. Looking for the reason you were here. What do you mean?'

'The reason that this place is the place I have chosen. I was looking for the reason when I was digging in those pictures.'

'Not with you yet.'

'I've been here before. When I ended up here, at the very beginning, I realised that I'd been here before.'

'That is strange, but it's not that strange. Maybe you came here as a kid and have forgotten about it? Or read about it and, I don't know, let your imagination run riot?'

'Yes, maybe.'

'That's not what you're telling me is it, that you came here as a kid, or read about it?'

'No. But I don't want to feel like I have to convince you. It's the truth. You have yours, mine is this.'

'What makes you think that?' She's being tactful.

'Come with me,' I said, 'you might as well, because it might not be here by tonight.'

She follows me up the road, away from the Sacred Grove and to the top of the square. We go into the sloping garden, past the *Memorial to All that We Forget*, which uses solar light and mushroom mycelium to constantly create new shapes and forms, depending on what we want to do. She looks at it, fascinated.

'These two houses here burnt down ages ago and only this one's front survived.' She follows me around the side. 'So, this whole thing is just a front with no substance. The real thing is hidden in a building that is an old caravan shell that we recycled into this.'

I unlock the door, and we step inside.

'Our House of Stories, or The Caravan Depository. It's got more than one name. Lots of names actually. Every story on tape and then transferred to its digital equivalent. Stacked, titled, catalogued, listed. If we had more time, I'd give you a taster. But listen to this. 'Ceadd'. Might answer your questions. It's the latest addition to our collection. Here's some headphones, a couch. Listen, relax, doze, let it wash over you. Here's the controls. When you've finished turn it off and pull the door to. No obligation. No need to say a word. You won't be disturbed.'

She sat down with a quizzical look and curled up on the couch and put the headphones on. I liked the lack of questions.

Back in Smoothie's office, it's very quiet. No one looked up, no one spoke. As if they'd just been discussing something they didn't want to discuss in my presence. Chow Mein didn't speak either, even though I'd forgotten about him. I looked at them, but they all kept their backs to me. Not a word from any of them. Even though we'd had disagreements and there had been misunderstandings or people had got annoyed, I'd never ever felt uncomfortable with them. Now, here I am when I need them most, facing the backs of all three of them, feeling their uncomfortableness but not knowing why. For the first time ever.

Malcolm spoke first. Not looking at me.

'Everyone kicking off about what we do next.'

'What do you mean?' Thinking, *Is that aimed at me?*

'Rumours, people talking – they're saying we might get attacked in our houses, that there might be some real psychos coming to soften us up, that we might not be safe, that this ain't just the Council with the slow, fat ones who don't care what happens. Is this true?'

'Where did you hear that?' I said.

No one spoke. Everyone kept their backs to me, everyone staring at their screens. I let it stay silent for a couple of long minutes.

'Come on, Malcolm, you know we can't keep things to ourselves,' I said.

'Your friend, that new lass who turned up after sending over those guys a day or two ago – what's her name?'

'Heather told you that?' I asked, not quite sure if she would. 'Are you sure?'

'She said something like that,' said Smoothie, 'so people started doing their own research and this company that we digging around now, they don't have a good reputation. Man, we found some scenes and it's shit scary. They seriously bashing heads of anythin' tha' move.'

'Which company?' I asked.

'This one,' said Malcolm pointing at his screen, 'SoHiHo Reconstruction. *Specialise in turning brownfield sites into living spaces for all.* That's their slogan. And we found it because, when we put all these names into the database, this was one of the businesses that came up. They have an office down in town. Officially, they're high-quality redevelopers, unofficially, if you look at stuff that's going around dark corners of the web, they use really dirty fuckin' tricks to get stuff through. They got some very rich friends. Look at this,' and he pressed play on a grimy clip on a big old mill site that looked like a pitched battle between a para-military and some hopelessly outmatched hippies. The hippies had a few bits of piping and sticks, and the thugs were carrying what looked like shillelaghs and cudgels. Some of them were using tasers.

'Malcolm, please, turn that shit off. We don't know that they will do this or even if they'll come at all.'

He turned it off.

'We have to be ready for this,' he said, 'though I'm not sure I want to get a busted skull jus' yet.'

'Let's do the other things we need to do before we get to dealing with this shit.'

'What are we doing, B-man? You didn't see the other stuff they were doing. Imagine, today, in a couple of hours this place is swarming with those headcases – you really don' wanna see what they're doing in half of the other videos – Jesus, they're doing it for the fun of it. We have nowhere to hide. I don't want to say this, it doesn't sound like me speaking, but my vote is we get out of this place and escape into the morning sunshine. Let's jus' go, save ourselves and meet up later when we got it all together. Sorry, man, B-man, you worked hard for us, but that ain' gonna help when they smash our heads and the coppers mop up the ones still standing who're gonna get a rap as well. Ain't no other way this going to end, my man. You know it, Smoothie know it, Chow Mein know it. Even your friend know it, what's her name?'

'Heather,' I said, 'I don't know her second name.'

'It's over. It's finished, you know. I'm outta here, gotta go.'

And he pushed past me and disappeared through the door. I didn't speak and sat down in his chair.

Smoothie turned round. 'Leave him, you know how he is. He get like that.'

'Yeah, but I get the feeling you been discussing things.'

'We just about to lose everything overnight, B-man. People gonna get worked up,' said Smoothie.

'Not me, then?' I said.

Smoothie turned round to face his computer and started clacking away, and to no one in particular, 'Don't matter what people saying unless they say it to your face.'

'You're not saying it to my face.'

'Then don' matter what I'm saying,' and he started to chuckle. 'Just tryin' to do my job.'

I smiled. 'Smoothie, you are a serious piece of dude. For that I will praise and honour you all the days. And what is your job?'

My turn to laugh.

Chow Mein signed behind Smoothie's back. *His job is to lose weight and do what the hell he wants.* Made me laugh out loud.

'100%, Mr. Chow Mein. That is his job,' I said.

No one listen to The Chow, he typed on his computer screen, and a little dog appears with a high-pitched bark.

'What about Malcolm?' I asked. 'Anyone want to find him and speak to him?'

Their silence said, *Leave him*.

Chow Mein broke it with a sign to come and look at what he had found up at Mrs. Morrison's. He talked me through the slide show of pictures he took.

'Thraykston is small but they live outside it, in an enormous house called Thrayke Hall. So, I type in Thrayke Hall and I get Mr. Morrison, and here he is.'

On the screen is a picture of a man in his forties in good physical condition in a shirt and trousers which look far too thin for most types of English weather. He's got that tanned look that his brother-in-law, Tim, has.

'Yeah,' I said, 'very good work, my friend, I think our Viscount likes hanging around crap Leeds pubs because we saw him in there with Ray the Scrapper and Mr. Nosey. He was the one with the chauffeur. And you're telling me he's a Viscount or something like that?'

'Yeah, says here his family have owned Thrayke Hall since

1200 an' something,' said Chow Mein.

'What the hell are these guys doing working together? They're from opposite ends of the system. Borstal boys playing with royalty, that ain't what normally happens, is it?'

'It says here that Mr. Tristan Clones-Dyke is, or was – mmm, not clear whether he still is or not, or what he's doing now – a professional soldier who reached the rank of Colonel then, suddenly, all the information about him stops about five years ago,' said Chow Mein.

Smoothie swivels on his chair, and asks, 'You got all this, B-man in your head? All I thinkin' is that there ain't no one left out there who ain't lined up against us, jus' look at 'em all, like something from a Jason Statham movie – Viscount Star Trek or wherever he comes from, Mr. Nosey and his Council power ranger job, Tim African Lion King who kill bison and anything that moves with one hand and two gangster brothers like them Kay twins who saw through you eyeballs and then ask you stupid questions when you don't know nothin' anyway – and we sittin' here and waiting for the Police and the gangsters and the thugs with sheilas and – B-man and Chow man, you winding me up to Malcolm-levels and I aint sayin' it lightly, you seein' me? I beginnin' to sweat my own blood.'

'Smoothie, apart from a few minor details I think you have summed it up just about perfectly,' I said.

'Police. You said Police. We haven't got the Police on our list, have we?' said Chow Mein. He starts raising his voice, 'Tell me, why you mention Police? No one else mentions Police. Smoothie, you mention Police. Why?'

Smoothie looks at me and I look back.

'I don't know, I suppose I took it for granted that they'd be comin', joinin' in the fun, someway.'

'I don't think we've thought how that would work before, have we? Who's left? Is there more of them? Smoothie, why did you say Police? Police is brilliant. There's got to be Police here.'

'Well, your friend, she say that after the thugs come, then the Police come and that, din't she?'

Chow Mein is flashing through all the photos that we have gathered, all the people and lists that we have compiled. All the recent info that has come in.

'Hang on, Chow Mein, you weren't here when Taco sent back the photos? Well, then he brought back some more. Smoothie, find him the photos that Taco took.'

Both of them scrambling through all the photos until we find that one that Taco took of Jarhead leaving the scrapyard and getting in the car with false plates. And comparing that to the ones that we took of the meeting at Sid's, when I was sat just the other side of the partition to them. And the face that looked out at me as I walked past the window. The face that I thought I had known. The face that seemed to know me. Set in stone. He's a copper.

'How do we find this guy? Come on, come on...Think out loud.' I am shouting at myself. 'He's in with these gangsters, he likes hob-nobbing with the gentry, he's probably got in bother before, he probably pretends to do good works, like the worst of them. He's probably been up on disciplinaries.'

Chow Mein is listening, and before I've finished talking out loud, he's trawling through all the pictures in the news involving Tim and the Viscount on websites that do charity events, Yorkshire Post and Yorkshire Life sort of smug stuff. I'm looking at stories about coppers reprimanded before the IPCC, corruption charges that were dropped, anything that gets you to where the dirty ones are. He's got to be there. Ten minutes. Nothing. Chow Mein is burning a hole in the server. Nothing. I'm running out of cases on the usual sites we use. Even though there's a case a day, I can't find this Jarhead nowhere. There's piles of coppers implicated in everything from fitting people up to petty corruption to losing evidence to fabricating evidence but not a single one of them looks like our man. Nothing.

Chow Mein pushes his seat back and shakes his head.

'Guys like him like a profile. He's got a big ego. A big cock of a bully and a dodgy fucker,' he said.

'Yeah, exactly. Tim's into rugby and probably shooting animals. What other hobbies do these wanker's egos like?'

'Golf. Shooting. Rugby. Gambling. Boxing.' He barked at me.

'Brilliant,' I said. 'You do golf and shooting and I'll do gambling and boxing.'

Ten minutes later and I'm beginning to despair. Nothing that looked like a lead. Chow Mein's keeping his head down.

'Do you think there's a bent copper,' he said, five minutes later, like a swimmer who's just won gold at the 400m, bursting to speak, 'in every golf club in Britain? Mr. Brian Scailles. There he is.'

I jumped over to his computer. There's a picture of him receiving a big fancy cup, dressed in the golfer's uniform at the poshest golf club in Yorkshire. 'Last year Mr Brian Scailles won, for the third year in a row, the Yorkshire Allcomers Open Championship by the finest of margins...' Chow Mein is reading.

Ten minutes later we had him nailed: DCI Brian Scailles. Big bad boy of the Drugs Squad. Commendations coming out of his hatband. Nothing at all that would suggest he's ever done anything bad at all. Never. He's even the force's Champion of Fullbore Target Rifle Shooting and something called Popinjay Shooting.

Chow Mein stood up. 'Need a break from this.' *Need to sleep,* he signed as he walked out. *Wake me in an hour.*

Smoothie pushes his chair back and stands up. 'I'm going for coffee. You want one?'

'Yeah, please. Anything.'

I think about asking him to go see Malcolm. I don't. I'm alone in this room and can't remember when I've ever been alone in this room. Flashes of scenes from a different life. All those years ago and we're putting the system in place that was designed to listen in to conversations all over the Circle, not to spy on one another but, just in case. Just in case, yeah, just in case we were attacked or taken over or what, exactly? But the fun we had testing all the mikes we'd planted in the trees and in some of the walls and at road junctions and on street furniture. Laughing till we cried as we sat and listened to Malcolm or Smoothie having stupid conversations, talking in strange voices and mimicking one another.

Out of nowhere a few days later, came that sudden extraordinary moment, listening in awe, when we realised that there was another consequence of all of these mics, an unseen one, literally. Sharing the Circle with us were millions of other beings living lives more secret than ours. Just how much secret life there was going on that we'd never been able to take any notice of before: the insects whirring and buzzing constantly, night and day; the birds chattering in endless fluid song in conversations and competitions; the blackcaps, nightingales, woodlarks and mistle thrushes and dozens others; the more we listened to the things we couldn't see, the more the place cast its spell and we began to listen out for their symphonies and poems, read the shape and progress of their lives, plant flowers, bushes, trees that would encourage them to grow and most subtly of all, to leave spaces for them to complement our human soundscape. In his wondrous ways, Smoothie started to lay sound traps for the scuttling spiders over the gravel or places that different types of bees would land or encourage different types of crickets and grasshoppers and sawflies and moths and dragon flies...we have so many of their stories of the time they were with us recorded. *The Works of the Tiny Ones*, I suppose.

The longing to catch that world again gripped me, to go back to the loveliness of those days. I was sure Smoothie would have something easily accessible on his computer and I wanted to connect, in any way I still could.

The first one I found was called 'Midsommer's Morning #20'. It begins with the faint dripping of water off the trees after a shower, and then the scream of a wild animal which repeats as the animal gets closer. It's a rasping and sharp sound, like a scream, but it's not a scream. It's a fox looking for its mate. This one we got to know, and we gave him a name and filmed him.

Binman, the fox who came to us a year or two after we set up the mics. It was as if he was waiting for the chance to get in the recording studio because he would have periods when he would signal his presence with his range of calls and then he would go silent, as if he was on tour, somewhere around the world. Binman produced several litters, but one year he misjudged the traffic on the top road outside of the Circle and we looked after his cubs. I'm listening to him now. Smoothie taught me how to distinguish his calls. He had the most peculiar mating call, like a Spanish woman shouting for *Raoul* at the top of her voice. Then, the birds take over and I drift off to doze and wake up to a shake of the shoulder.

I take off the earphones.

'What are you listening to?' says Heather.

'Wrens and robins mainly'.

'No?' she laughed.

I passed her the earphones. 'They were recorded around here a few years ago. Before that it was Binman, who used to make us laugh. He had a hundred ways of getting food out of us.'

She listened and smiled, then handed the earphones back.

'We have so much to do, but it's lovely.'

'Did you rest?'

'I was listening to your story about travelling back in time.'

'Oh, yeah, I forgot. Listen, I want to say something to you.

Malcolm walked out just a while ago. He showed me some clips that you'd shown him from some protests you've been on which made him do some digging, and he found some more which are pretty gruesome.'

'Yeah. And?'

'Well, he doesn't want to stay and fight armed men beating the hell out of people with sticks who have nothing to fight back with. Plus, Police and the law and all the rest of it. So, he walked.'

She looked at me if she was allowing me to say more. I didn't say more. She shrugged and sat down and span slowly round on Smoothie's swivel chair.

'That's how it is. But I have something to say to you.'

Neither of us spoke. I waited and she waited.

'Well, Malcolm has a point, doesn't he? If we wait to see if they turn up, as we think they're going to, and if they want to remove us and flatten the place, and if all those things are going to happen, what benefit would there be in fighting them? We aren't going to win, are we? Shouldn't we just evaporate into thin air while we have time?'

'You could, yes. You could let them walk in, take what they want, even when they have no right to do anything at all. From what we seemed to be finding out when we look into their so-called 'businesses', most of them should be in prison, if there was any justice. What they shouldn't be able to do is turn up here with the full force of the law and about to make endless millions from another corrupt deal involving our land. Using illegal methods. But hey, yeah, let them in, evaporate as you say.'

'These are gangster capitalists, Heather, as you yourself called them, with the full weight of the establishment and the law behind them. We are nothing. Zero. Never been heroes and still just zeros. We have no status, no rights, half of us have no legal existence, we simply ceased existing through no fault of our own years ago. We are better free and alive than whatever the opposite of that is – heroic and imprisoned. Or whatever people who stand up and fight are called these days. Dead and forgotten, or just simply forgotten.'

'Yes, I get it. You are right, in a way. But I was thinking about these people who are behind this whole shitshow,' she said. 'Wouldn't you agree that there could be ways of getting something back, disrupting their lives even in a little way, reminding them that they're not beyond a moral law, even if they live above the actual law? Let's move the battlefield but keep fighting the war.'

She looked at me with that look I'd seen before, as if she'd just surfaced from a place that was much more logical and kind, only a thousand metres below sea level.

'Please, don't just walk away because if you do, you'll have to live with it, and I'm not sure you will, easily. If they walk into nothing, just dead empty space, it will be as if you have never been here. Make a point. Make a stand. Don't make it easy for them. Make it unpleasant for them. In whatever way. *Then*, we can make another Circle somewhere else, and just because this one has been destroyed, doesn't mean the idea is wrong. Please.'

Pause.

'And I'll help you with everything else,' she said, 'when you tell me why you had me listen to Ceadd as an answer to why you're here.'

Then the phone rang. It was Jalapeña watching from a house facing out of the Circle near the only road entrance.

'Just seen a cop car drive past slowly. They've pulled up about 500 yards away, near the brow of the hill going to town.'

'Thanks, J,' I said, 'keep me up to speed.'

And to Heather, 'You heard that, I presume? Are we to expect visitors soon?'

'Give me the quick version,' she said.

'I ended up here against my will, without knowing where I

was or what I was doing here. Believe me on that. Chow Mein was living here at the time and he saved my life. On more than one occasion. The place was not what you see now, it was the place to come for action of every sort. We were in hiding in an attic and I spent a lot of time looking out of the Velux. One day, must have been around middle of June, midsummer's day, and the sun was at its furthest point from the earth and was casting long, strange shadows, just hanging in the sky, and as the day wore on into the long evening, I started to plot the features I saw out of the window. The air hung, quivering and there was no sound so, I left the house, even though I knew I shouldn't have. But there was something I'd spotted, and I needed to check it. Chow Mein was out. I'd never have gone out if he'd been there. It felt so good to be able to leave that space I'd been cooped up in for weeks and weeks. I looked at the map I'd made, now knowing the house faced due south. I ducked and darted and went over fences and down alleys, desperately trying to keep out of the sight of the gang members who I thought were still looking for me. We'd seen them using some of the empty houses and coming and going with people and cars and stuff, so we knew they were still around.

'Anyway, when I returned home, I realised I'd made a map. A map of trees. From my little hideout, I'd noticed the tops of a few trees that all looked similar, but when I went out on my survey, I found lots more, twenty-one of them. All yews. Do you know how old yews can live?'

'No,' she shook her head.

'Ankerwycke, Fortingall, Ashbrittle, Llangynog – these are yew trees that were one, two, three thousand years old when Christ was born. Here, I've found twenty-one of them, all discreetly surrounded by houses, so you have to be very bored or very keen to find that they form a distinct shape. But, they do. A circle within a circle, planted at regular intervals and interlocking. And right at the centre is a sacred space. This is a living temple. All around us.'

'This is very interesting, but not sure if it would stand up in a court of law, but what has that got to do with anything?' she said, with that pained look.

'In my mind I removed all the houses and then drew the plan with only the trees. There's a sacred door that lets in the sun at midsummer morning, facing east, of course, onto the centre of the Sacred Grove. In the middle of the trees we'd planted, we found a huge stone under a couple of feet of earth, but that was later. That is why we planted all those trees to protect that inner sanctum. We found other things as well, but I don't have time to tell you it all now.'

'This has to do with Alwena, doesn't it? It goes all the way back to her...and you?'

'Yeah. When we stopped running, built a place to live, survived a winter down by that bend in the river, we grew to feel we'd found the place where we would always stay, far away from any hostile eyes. We made a garden, we planted things to eat, we made a house of stone, we found peace. Such a peace. How many people really can say that they have known peace in their lives that lasts beyond a moment or an hour or an afternoon? Ours lasted years.'

Pause. Chow Mein walked in and shut the door, like a man who has just woken up. He put on his earphones and opened his computer.

'What happened?' she asked. 'The peace came to an abrupt end?'

'She died. And I carried her body beyond the ridge where we used to sit and watch the sunset. We had made different arrangements in the event of who would outlive the other. I carried her body up the steep slope above the river, into a little hollow of a place between two ridges in the endless forest that was even then all overgrown, where years before there had been a sacred place. We found sculpted stones and small figures and water bowls and all sorts of things that had belonged once to a people who had now gone. I placed her in a stone coffin that had been unearthed in a storm and dislodged from its place. She loved it and made me promise to lay her in it when she died, and then to promise to join her if I could.'

'She knew she was going to die?'

'Alwena was the most sensitive creature, who wasn't really a creature of this world but of another one that we sometimes glimpse. She knew about medicines, sicknesses, cures, the weather and the doors to the otherworlds and the voices that call to us in our dreams. She told me she'd only followed me this far because she could read my mind. Sometimes, she would leave me and travel further westwards and northwards to visit the sick and the old and the women in their labours and I never knew where she went, or who she saw. One day, she came back and said there was a sort of plague and told me how to treat her. But, by then she was too old herself and was weary and she died. So, I laid her in the old Roman coffin, as I had promised her, and buried her near an ancient yew.'

'Are you sure you aren't just wishing all of this. We all wish we were born in another time.'

'Do we? How do you know?'

Chow Mein pulled off his earphones. 'Because he made me follow him outside, whilst we were dodging psychos in drug gangs, to show me a big patch of earth, about, what he called, six paces, maybe twenty feet, due east of the big yew, hidden in that corner where we all meet. He spent half an hour digging with his bare hands and I told him we got to stop. So, we cover our tracks, and we go back several times and sometimes at night and he finds a big slab of grey stone. What you see in those photos is from a year or two later when we free ourselves from the gangs. He described to me exactly what he was going to find. He even wrote out those signs he said we going to find written on the edges. I shook my head and thought this was the maddest man I ever met in my life. When I first met him, he had a huge, great radiator cuffed to his hand. He made me laugh so much, running around like a bigger psycho than the ones that tried to kill him.'

'Wow,' she said. 'And where is Alwena now?'

'Same place she's been for nearly fourteen hundred years, sister,' said Chow Mein. From his pocket he pulled a phone and flicked through some files and then started laughing, 'We look so much younger then. Look, Heather, look how long ago we look so different.'

And she swipes through the pictures from ten years or more ago, of me and Chow Mein staring up from the grave while we are digging or looking down at it. Just us two. And some close ups of the whole exposed coffin, showing the shells and the leaves and the interlocking, geometrical shapes combining zig-zags and circles, swelling out of the flat surface of the stone to tell the story of the complication of time and the endless circles, the deviations and the unending progression that turns into an ever-decreasing circle. It was a prayer for another life, and a prayer for the person in it to reach a better life, on a different path.

'That's not a stone top to the coffin though, is it? The top itself is something else,' said Heather.

'Yes, it's lead. The top Ceadd put on.'

'And what's this?' she said, looking more lost than the competent, logical, unemotional Heather had ever done before.

'It's Ogham. It's the script we used for writing on stone in Gwynedd and Ireland. In those times. It's my spirit dedicating my name to hers. It's what we did. Both names are there.'

Heather looked at the long, thin line and the angular marks

coming off it. Slowly, she said, 'So, that means...' she seemed to be hesitating, 'that you wrote this?'

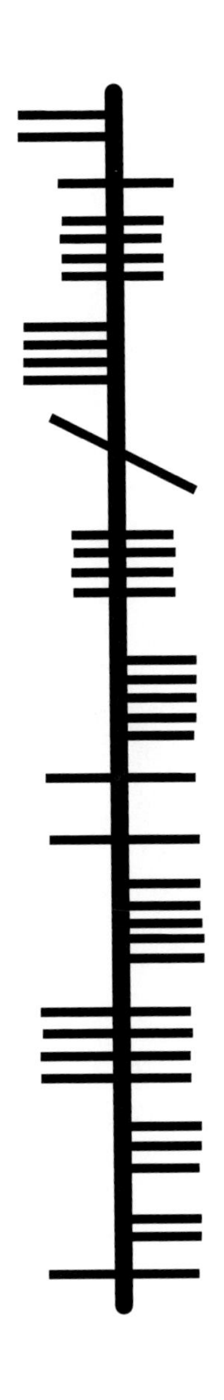

25

About Yrechwydd

O, Muse, tell of the Rother of the red-brown-water
Then watery Don, silent *Dana* of the river
Ouse, like whiskey, usso, *uísce* water
And from *Isāra*, the strong one to Aire, obscura
And Welsh at Walsden in the dale of Calder
Lived in the Valley of the River of Violent Water
And Derwent's echoes of the oak forest waters,
Or Dove, swarthy dark, sworn to pretty *Deva*,
While Snake-wearing *Verbeia* hides twisting Wharfe;
Elmet's hides and hundreds wrap'd in watery chains
Where mighty *Campodonum* home to kings
Ceredig, Gwallawg and *Madog*, heroes of tales
Of Doncaster, Catraeth and Heavenfield...
(from *Rivers of Elmetia*, (1721) unpublished)

Jalapeña rings me to say that two cops have stopped a pensioner on the way to the shops. She's taking her dog shopping with her, judging by the shopping trolley. Chow Mein says that they're tracking the Audi A6 as it leaves Thrayke Hall and heading south, and that Mr. Nosey's Range Rover has been parked outside the Novotel, near Leeds, and hasn't moved since arriving there after the scrapyard meeting.

Slowly, all the doors and windows of the last few houses

that will be occupied are being boarded up. I'm in the room with Chow Mein. Heather is organising with Molly the leaving. Smoothie comes in the room full of dark energy and thoughts.

'I say that we put all the equipment in boxes and label them and put them for now in the garages at the back, near the woods. Tomorrow we can find some transport to take it down to Heather's place. She says she has space.'

'That's a waste of time and I need mos' of it. Take one bit and the system fall apart,' says Smoothie, bristling.

'No, it doesn't. Just keep what you need that you can carry, if you need to.'

'But we need keep track of everythin' and keep findin' out what's happenin'. I can't do it if I don' have this stuff aroun' me.'

He's plugging things in as I unplug them. He's getting very twitchy.

'Choose the one thing you would take if they appeared right now at the gates.'

'You don' understan', I need all of it, I can' just take one thing... *one thing, one thing, one thing*, you keep saying *one thing*, but one thing on its own is best thing to useless. YOU un'erstan'? You ain' getting' what I sayin' to you. Either the whole lot or none of it.'

Smoothie looks insurmountable. A rock against which I am going to be dashed.

I try one last time. I turn off some switches on the wall supplying all the electricity. All the machines just die, the screens fade, the whirring stops.

'What the fuck you doin'? I haven' saved anything. All that work we done just gone, you fuckin' idiot.' He stares at me.

'Smoothie, we can't leave this stuff here. They might be –'

The thing about Smoothie was there was no midway point, no bit of leash that you could pull and tug and rein him in. No lead he could just pull on and test and see how far it was till breaking. There simply was no rope. He was the most placid guy and then he wasn't.

He picked up a monitor and it flew through the window. He picked up several more items which followed suit: a chair, a laptop, a lamp and then he picked up a metal computing box which was unfortunately attached by cables to others, so although he threw the first out of the window, the ones that were still attached were holding the first one back, so it was all left dangling a few feet below the window. It was at that point that I stopped him. He was ferociously angry, but I had his arms behind him and steadied him for a long moment.

When I let him go, he pushed me out of the way and walked out of the room and out of the house. Chow Mein came running up the stairs and into the room.

'Can you help me get this stuff together?' I said. He nodded.

When we had unplugged, unattached and stacked every bit of his system and got the window boarded up, we sat on the chairs at empty desks, with just a laptop each.

'Not quite how I'd envisaged this,' I said.

'Did you envisage it at all?' he said. 'How could you know?'

Exactly.

Outside, the sounds had diminished, just the knock knock knock of the hammers and the nails and no voices. The rain was fitful and squally, and the wind would pick up and swirl around for a minute and then die down, without a pattern, without any aim. I looked out of the window when we had finished putting all of Smoothie's kit into boxes. After all of the excitement of last night, this morning felt like the party had ended badly last night, and there were some bad memories that we needed to forget, like a hangover that wasn't preceded by anything like fun. I realised I hadn't eaten or drunk anything. I sat on a box when Chow Mein went off to find a coffee and some food.

Several years ago, we had decided to do without clocks in

the Circle. That just meant everyone used mobile phones or watches. But, we were spared the ticking of the clock or the vision of a wall clock or a digital clock and the drumbeat of the measurements as a backdrop to our days. Today, everything was different, stretched and twisted on expectation and waiting. By midday, a dull grey mop of cloud was grudgingly dragging overhead and dribbling cold rain that felt dirty, smudging windows and even leaving a wash on the woodwork. I couldn't imagine what was going to happen. It felt like we had already moved on. Like Lardland had come washing over us with the rain, washing away all spirit.

Worst of all, I remembered, worst of all, I found myself muttering to myself out loud, worst of all, was that I knew this feeling from many years ago. It was engulfing me, but how, from where, how did I know this? I was talking out loud again, asking myself out loud, *What is the memory that is holding me up against a wall with a grip around my throat and a punch to my stomach that winds me?* I am hurting in my stomach, but there is no one around, only me. And I step out across the logic of thoughts, like stepping stones across the stream – the doorway, the house with only emptiness, the rain that soaks with an atmosphere that chokes all energy and hope – the emptiness, yes – and Kate, oh, *Kate*, now I remember, how the breaking of hope feels, the discardedness of feelings, the little, brittle shards of feelings that don't work, that don't fit together and then the next stone, in the middle of the river – the longing, yes, the longing that will never go away, that wakes you in your sleep, slashes that moment of joy, leaves a cut in your index finger that you cannot ignore, the longing for something so strong that sickness overcomes you, despair sickens you – Chad, what is that word that haunts me – *Chad* –'

A hand touches my arm.

'Are you all right?' says Heather, 'you were talking, like you were in your sleep, but you're awake and standing up.'

'No, I'm fine, thank you. Thanks for bringing me back.'

'What's Chad?'

'A country in Africa,' I said.

She didn't laugh.

'You were talking out loud for about two minutes, as if you were in a trance,' she said, insistently.

'I need your help, please. Again. Come with me.'

And we went to the *House of Recordings*. Inside, I surveyed the shelves and piles and cases and cabinets lined with cassette tapes, CDs and DVDs of stories.

'Look at them, I can't just leave these. Help me. Tell me what to do with them. It's the last thing that matters.'

She stands and stares for a minute or two, whilst she slowly moves along the shelves, reading the names of all those memories.

'What about this for a thought? Imagine what the world would be like if we could have passed out a few tape recorders in ancient Athens or all those other old places, and the ordinary folk could have put down for evermore their thoughts and stories. Just imagine what the women would say.' And laughed.

'That is a spectacular thought, but it doesn't help me, here and now, does it?'

'No, but think about it – where do we keep the thoughts of those famous Greeks from millions of years ago?'

'In books?'

'In libraries and museums. Can't we take all these to a museum or a library and they can look after them?'

For some reason, that made me really laugh. The idea that we could share our stories with unknown people out there was very funny and strange. I wasn't sure what I thought about it.

'Would they take them? Why would they take them? It's just ordinary people telling the things that are about them, nothing more. I can't see how anyone would care for them or ever understand or attach any importance to them. It sounds odd. Mad. Mental.'

'Just imagine if we had the ordinary people of Athens speaking their truths in their words. It would be the most important thing ever collected.'

A message from Jalapeña arrives. *Another Police car driving past, pulling up next to the other one on the brow of the hill.*

Thanks, I wrote back, *keep me informed.*

'You sure you've not got all these stories backed up somewhere else? Digitally? In the cloud? You sure Smoothie hasn't got them on file, hidden away?' said Heather, hopefully.

'Too late if he has. He threw half of the equipment out of the window and then walked off. I don't know where he is. If I were him, I'd have got as far away as I could by now.'

She sat down and started writing in a book she had. It took her five minutes before she spoke. When she did it was like she was announcing the winner of a competition.

'I'll deal with them for you. You've won. It was close. They nearly all got burnt. But, in the end, every now and again, you have to be sentimental.'

'What happens to them?'

'Don't ask,' she says, 'you've got other things to worry about.'

We walked across to check on everyone that was left. Most of the houses were boarded up. We'd left a few to looked lived in, with washing hung out to dry, plates on the garden tables, clothes on the back of chairs, but empty of people. We'd boarded up most of the houses and painted some graffiti, amateurish, done quickly, across the boards and doors and walls, but emptied of people. What was left of us was squashed into a few houses. These were protected as best we could, as quickly as we could – locked gates, hidden little traps to trick the unwary. Some of the houses that we'd converted and joined together had exits in unexpected places and these were now full of people.

We went to check on everyone. Did they have enough food, water, warm clothes, protection, and bags packed for a quick getaway with instructions of where to go next?

We said goodbye to the next wave of those leaving. We hugged them all. I counted thirty-five people gathered together. They walked off in small groups into the afternoon. Heather had done her best, but space was tight now in Sheffield. People were going with nowhere to go but had decided that here was worse than nowhere: Sami, Linda, Dog and Hot Dog, Tomos, Eggbox, Pistol, Dishdash, even Peanut was going. And the rest. I had no idea where they were going. They were better at consoling me than I was them. Sami said being homeless ran in her genes, said they'd be fine. Linda promised to keep an eye on Tomos and keep him from rummaging too much in public bins. I walked them all to the edge of the Circle. Some went over the fields, some went straight for the road at the back. The afternoon was dark, the clouds coming over in big, grey piles.

The ones who were staying were getting fewer and fewer: Molly, CJD, Taco, Jalapeña, Picnic and others, berthed in houses that weren't theirs once more, facing another descent into other layers of worlds below. And god knows what in between.

In each house, no one was left alone. Everyone had someone looking out for them. Except for Uncle Kevin. No one had checked on him.

Back at Smoothie's house, the rooms are empty. Just Chow Mein on a laptop.

'I can't get anything to work,' he said, 'without your man we're lost at sea. The end of the information age.'

We sit in silence. The rain starts to make more noise against the windows. Heather is making lists. Chow Mein is writing on his laptop. By his desk is a bursting backpack. I'm fluttering from thing to thing, from face to person, to voice and laugh and then, to the words I've heard in the last few days and I'm panicking, I'm breathing in a strange way and I don't know if I'm imagining pains in my chest or am hearing voices. I daren't stand up, daren't look through the boards at the window, can hear the screams and the shouts already, again. There are great convulsing sounds like galloping horses and the endless crash of things banging together, mixed like when you're caught in a huge wave that smashes down and sweeps your feet from under you and nothing is clear but huge, indistinct roars in a watery cathedral. I turn away from them, so glad they are there. This time, I can't let them go and can't let them see me.

Elmet was one of the smaller kingdoms of the North of Britain. For references to this elusive place that defies definite geographical limits, expanding and contracting probably beyond the Norman Conquest, we owe a debt to Gildas, author of *De Excidio Brittaniae*, or *About the Fall of Britain*. He's writing a narrative, not history as we have come to know it, and even living around 540 AD, the memories and sources for what had happened in the previous hundred and odd years were dwindling down to names, legends and whispers of an unwritten people. Mainly, he's angry at the world he finds himself in and is looking at the rulers and churchmen of his day with an eye and a pen eager to blame.

Elmet was the elusive country between the Don in the south, the rivers of the Humber to the east, the Pennines to the west and gradually receding from Craven in the dales southwards, until the last stronghold would be the huge, dense elm woods and forests of *Loidis*, Leeds. A frontier state that Gildas would have known, destined to prevent the expansion of the German tribes into the middle of Britain. As such, it is recorded in a whole host of elegaic warrior poems describing the slow collapse of the old British kingdoms. In the old tongue of Elmet, Welsh.

The poets who witnessed and made legends and heroes of these warriors have themselves become mythic and legendary. With the loss of Catraeth, (Catterick) described by Aneirin Awenyd, Aneirin, the Inspired One, in the *Goddodin,* the longest epic poem of defeat becomes a national call to arms, a record of a world of glorious heroes living in another age as eternal symbols of resistance. In the *Gweith Gwen Ystrat*, the Battle of Gwen Ystrat, Taliesin records the victory in the White Valley, probably Wensleydale, against the men on horseback, who therefore cannot be Saxons, who fought on foot, but are probably Picts, from the far north. This time, the men of Catraeth are victors.

Taliesin speaks of battles with a vision that had seen battles in the flesh. That there were several battles in, and for, and around, Elmet cannot be doubted. That Taliesin wrote of Urien, king of Rheged, sometime king of Catraeth, who fought so often in Elmet is clear, and that in one poem, *Gweith Argoet Llwyfain*, The Battle of the Elm-Wood, where the great wood of elms is witness to the slaughter:

A rac gweith Argoed Llwyfein
bu llawer celein
rudei vrein rac ryfel gwyr...

Urien becomes Urien *Yrechwydd*, Urien of the Place of Cataracts, perhaps Catraeth, defeating the men of Lloegr, middle England, promising hardship, burnt houses and death to the invaders. Elm trees dominate the huge, dense forests that gave their name, over time, to the place. Elmet. Trees of Loidis.

Of all the places in the oldest Welsh poems, it is Elmet that is the scene of more heroism, more battles, more slaughter, more warriors clashing, more feasting and more sorrow and with the longest lingering sense of defeat and loss than any other place. Like the last place of a people who have no choice but to melt into the woods, the mountains and the spaces the newcomers or the authorities still can't reach. *Yrechwydd*, the place of fresh water, the place of the cataracts, made famous by its most famous defender, Urien,

Lleuuyd echassaf, mi nyw dirmygaf,

Most valiant chief, I will not deride him,

I can see them now, half-drunk with exhaustion, chanting the words that held their history together, the greatest bond of kinship, the people who are together, the *Cymry*, red-eyed in the smoky hall, telling tales of smouldering buildings, lost brothers and comrades and wondering how many enemies they would have to kill and how many retreats they could make before they were lost forever. There is no consolation at all in history, just a different place to relive the same.

The last place of a people.

Two hours later, Heather and Chow Mein came back carrying two plastic bags each and a big old rucksack, an old-fashioned brown canvas one. The label boasted bomb-proof.

'We'll put them in the car as soon as one arrives,' said Heather. 'I'm afraid that's not all of them. We ran out of bags. We'll bring the rest later.'

I thanked them. Kind of her to try. I picked up one of the CDs and read the neat writing, dated April, nearly eight years ago. The name rang no bells. 'Johnny Depp'. Everyone had a name given by us. I don't remember Johnny Depp, but I presume he was handsome or looked like a pirate or something.

Heather leant over to see what I was looking at.

'Johnny Depp was in Leeds, eh? Wow, wish I'd been there. Was he struggling paying his council tax as well?' and laughed.

I put it back in the bag. I shook my head. The dread again. The wrong decision, the wrong path, the wasted time.

'I've no idea,' I said.

She looked at me and then at Chow Mein.

‘That was the wrong thing to say. Sorry.’

‘*Da nada*,’ I said, ‘it was a good thing to say.’

‘We could listen to it,’ she suggested, ‘I would love to hear what people brought to you.’

‘Please, no, not now. Let Johnny Depp be. Nothing to be gained stirring through old shit now.’

The wind had dropped, but the afternoon was getting darker, the clouds heavier and the rain falling, the birds retreated. Apart from the sound of water gurgling, splashing, beating, running, being blown or murmuring in the trees, all other sounds were smothered.

We sat in the room in silence. Chow Mein on his laptop looking at football. Heather sketching and making notes and going out of the room to make quiet phone calls and coming back in, and looking for signs of a response. Then, choosing her moment, she passed us both a piece of paper.

‘I need your help. This evening. I’ve written down the details. Please don’t lose them.’

We both read what she had given us.

‘OK, we’ll do what you’re asking, but, Heather,’ I said, ‘why are you writing this down?’

‘Because I’m going now. I have to go. Trust me. We can do more even than this place, the Circle. Just do as I say, keep in touch. Follow your instincts.’

Then, she stood up and slipped her bag on her back. ‘Be true,’ and kissed me and shook Chow Mein’s hand and kissed his cheek and slipped through the door and out onto the stairs.

‘Heather, no, wait, please.’

I ran after her down the stairs, but she kept on walking.

‘Do something for me. Give me your phone.’

She turned and stopped. She didn’t question why I asked for her phone.

I walked away, out of earshot. On her Voice Recorder, I left a message. Five minutes of speaking. At the end of the message, I left her instructions of what to do with this message. When I had finished recording, I passed her the phone. I shuddered to think of what I had just done signified, but I couldn't tell her.

'Play it back. Check it's worked.'

She pressed play.

I heard my voice. 'Heather, if you don't hear from me within three days then I want you to relay this message in its entirety to –'

'Stop,' I said. 'It's fine, it works. Promise me you'll listen to it all the way through and do exactly as I ask?'

'If I haven't heard from you in the next three days, I will do exactly as you ask. I promise.'

Then, she put two fingers to her lips and then put them on mine, and nodded. And walked away into the rain.

26

About Ray

Ray has a new dog, Attila. Ray's wife told him not to get another one, but he got a name from a mate and rang the number, met him at the motorway service station between Leeds and Bradford and paid him a grand. Guy was a dodgy fuck. Should've known the dog would be mental. He took it down the yard and fed it, and the dog was obviously starving, so he gave it some more. Ghenghiz and Adolph were staring through the fencing at this new dog, so he shut the gates of the yard and let them out. They went fuckin' bonkers, running and running round in circles, chasing after Attila. After ten minutes Ray called them in. The two old dogs knew the score and went back in the cage. Not a whimper. Bastard Attila went running off around the yard like the other two were still after him. When he did catch the bloody stupid thing, he gave it a good kick and dragged it by its brand-new collar into the portacabin.

Phone went and it was his wife asking about the dog.

'Don't ring up and ask about me, da yer?' he laughed.

'Don't fuckin' care about you, bigboy, do I?' she laughed. 'Put the dog on, put the little doggie on the phone.'

'You having a laugh?' he said.

'Put little doggie on the phone, Ray, I want to talk to him.'

Ray grabbed Attila by the collar and put his muzzle to the telephone. Attila was wondering if he was going to get another kicking, so he dug his heels into the lino floor and tried to wriggle out of the collar and Ray's grip. Ray could hear his wife getting impatient, so he put the phone down and picked the dog up off the floor. Attila was now really vexed. He couldn't imagine what was happening to him, or what he was supposed to do. Ray felt his work mobile vibrate in his pocket. As he reached for this phone, he squeezed Attila a bit too hard and Attila responded by vomiting his dinner over Ray and Ray's desk and Ray's portacabin floor. Ray threw Attila instinctively across the room. Attila hit the filing cabinet and fell to the floor, but when he tried to stand, the pain in his back made him whine and his back right leg failed to support him. Attila heard Ray shouting and swearing, and as Ray went to open the door and grab him, he instinctively snarled and snapped at Ray's right hand and felt himself kicked out the door and down the steps, before the door was slammed behind him. Behind the fence, Ghenghiz and Adolph stared in silence.

Inside, Ray was shouting down the phone at his wife. Then, he slammed the phone down on his wife. He went to the sink and washed his hands and tore at his clothes till he was stripped to his underpants, and threw the rolled-up, dog-vomit clothes out the back window.

'When I get hold of that fuckin' animal, I swear I'm gonna shoot it. And if I get hold of that dodgy fuck who sold me it, I might shoot him, as well.'

No one was there to listen.

Still his mobile phone was ringing insistently, so he had to run outside in his underpants and scrape through the pile of clothes he'd thrown out the back window and pull the phone out of his sticky pant pocket. It was slimy, and when he lifted it to his nose, it smelled dog breathy. It was John. They were on site. Could he come down? Bit of an issue. Ray shook his head.

'For fuck's sake,' he said, I'll be there in half an hour.'

When he got there, the boys were gathered around the two transit vans, smoking, and talking shit. He found John.

'What's happening?'

"Well, we can't get past these fuckin' fences and whatnot easy. Bri said there wasn't nowt here yesterday when he came round. What the fuck's happened since?'

'Fuck it, gerrover there and crack some skulls and lets gerron with it,' says Ray, who's still rubbing the bite mark on his hand.

They were stood in the rain only a few yards from the only entrance to the Circle. The Police had let them in when they said that they were contractors for the Council.

Through the binoculars, Jalapeña is describing the scene to me. She tells me about the dozen blokes dressed in black who'd arrived in the two transits. *Half of them are climbing our fences and got their sticks thrown over the fences by their mates.*

Then, I saw for myself how they walked up the entrance road and fanned out in ones and twos, calling to one another, one guy holding back, on the walkie-talkie, directing them. How they'd walked around expectantly, tapping their clubs against the trees and the lampposts and the garden walls, how they'd bristled and shouted and called out, like beaters on a pheasant shoot, the insults they thought up for the people of the Circle.

At first, they hadn't gone into any gardens but walked on the tarmac, kept in view of one another, waited for the ambush, the flushing out of the first of the druggies, knotty-locks and loonies to come crashing out of a house or hedge like a zombie. ready to be smashed over the head, like they do in the films.

John called them back and told Ray there was no one around.

'Have you had a look in the houses? Is it a trap?'

'Not sure, just wasn't what we thought it was gonna be. There's obviously something going on if they put up a fence an' that,' said John.

'Yeah. Let's take a look inside some of the houses. Get some kit to break down the doors. I'm just fuckin' hopin' we find some rats, I tell yer.'

Ray and John are shouting at them all now to come over the fences. All of them with all the kit: the shillelaghs, crowbars, hammers, battering rams. Some of it ex-military. They headed for the first houses on the right, disciplined they were, worked as a team. John had them drilled, from his army days, before PTSD and Iraq. They walked up the path to the house we call the House of Flowers. Two round the back, four at the front, four at the gate and the rest with John onto the next house. Ray was just behind the one who broke the door down. It took fifteen minutes. He was sweating.

The rain was just falling, aimlessly from the very grey heavens. The house was empty.

John wanted to do next door, but Ray directed them to another house. Same procedure, but this time they split up into smaller groups, two groups to break in and two others to scout around further afield, into the streets that were not visible from the main entrance road.

I'm watching, as were eyes from every lived-in house. If they carried on like this, they'd eventually hit a house with people, and that would be the moment. I wince in expectation.

I whispered to Chow Mein.

We got an hour, he signed.

I sent a message to Heather, *Yes, they've come, they've started breaking in.*

Good, she replied. *The wait is over.*

I sent a message to Jalapeña. *Tell Taco to get ready as we agreed, and Kebaby. OK? But wait until I tell you.*

Ray was getting annoyed, and told John to get them all opening up every house. From the opposite side of the Sacred Grove, messages were coming through that there were men at the front and back of the house. Inside this house were six people, Picnic and his crew. *They're at the front door*, he said, let *me know what to do.*

Go, Taco, go. Go Kebaby, go. I sent the message to Jalapeña.

If only we had Smoothie, I thought, and all his wizardry, we could have some fun. Picnic is texting, describing the sounds of the hammers and crowbars and men telling one another what to do. *Hurry up, hurry up*...I'm urging Taco to hurry up, hoping I haven't left it too late.

Then, the first toot. Big long, drawn out toots. Shouts from down at the estate entrance. I can hear Taco and Kebaby raising hell down by Ray's mates' vans. All the crowbarring, hammering and shouting stops. Ray and John and some of the others go to see what's happening. What Ray and John see are two young lads messing with their vans. Laughing, shouting at them. Winding them up.

'For fuck's sake,' says Ray. 'John, take some lads and sort them out, will you.'

Then, Taco starts one of the vans, and Kebaby gets in the other side. One's enough, they think. They wait for Ray's mates to reach the fences and then slowly, slowly they edge the van forward and slowly slowly pick up speed and head off up the hill to where the cops are sleeping. But slowly.

Quickly, John packs four of the guys into the other van with exhortations to give them a fuckin' good hidin' but not to kill them, and off they go quickly quickly, following Taco in the other van. Taco, by now, has disappeared over the hill towards town.

In the Circle, the men have regrouped around Picnic's house. There are three of them pressed against the big, nailed-on boards across the whole of the front, when, from underneath the door, through some discreetly drilled holes, comes some white smoke. One of them shouts 'Fire, fire, fire' and for a moment, everyone steps back.

John takes command. 'Fall back,' he says, 'fall back.'

At first, they do fall back a few paces, wafting the smoke away from their eyes to get a better view of the fire. Then, one of them falls to his knees clutching his chest, like he's having a heart attack. Within a minute, they're all running from the house, the garden, covering their eyes and their mouths in whatever way they can. The coughing and spluttering are akin to the retching of vomiting. John gets them, with difficulty, over the fence to the space where their vans were. It's here that they rest.

'Tear gas,' he says. 'Where the fuck did that come from?' He bends over Ray who is breathing with difficulty. 'Shall I get an ambulance?' he says.

Ray shakes his head, like a dog on all fours that's been winded and beaten.

Inside Picnic's house, they open the vents to get rid of the smoke. They don't speak in the gas masks, just sign. Then, they wait for it to go away.

Everything good? I message Picnic.

All good, he says. With lots of smiley faces in what look like gas masks.

'I think we call it a day,' says John. 'Come back tomorrow. I'll try to get some more kit.'

Ray is still coughing and spluttering. 'Don't know who these fuckers are but get some fuckin' machine guns, will yer?'

John pretends to understand, but what Ray is saying isn't making sense.

Half an hour later, two blue Transits appear on the brow of the hill. The doors slide open and Ray and his mates climb inside.

Still not a living thing has appeared from anywhere in the Circle.

27

In Yrechwydd

We arrived at the exact spot Heather wanted us. We've followed her written notes to the letter. A small village, in which all the houses are set back a hundred yards from the main road. We parked in the pub car park and walked over to the bus stop, hidden in the overhanging trees of the village church. We waited and a car pulled up, exactly as Heather had explained. There is even a coded question.

'Hi,' he said, 'going far?

'To the Gatehouse.'

'Great, get in.'

We get in. We are to keep it simple. No exchange of information, no names, nothing personal. We stared out of the window as we slowly did a large arc through the hills, almost coming back on ourselves, but not quite. The sky was a dazzling pink, as the sun took its time to set, the rain had stopped, and an evening calm had settled on everything we drove through.

Then, we slowed down to ascend some curves and the view below was delicious: the shades of green, the pattern of fields and clumps of trees in a creamy light. The driver took a right, half-hidden and pulled up. Out of the hedge, he pulled some triangular diversion signs and set them up across the road, blocking it off, before driving quickly down the lane of high hedges and pulling up at the grand entrance to a country house.

I signed to ask Chow Mein if he knew where we were.

Only roughly.

And if he knew this place?

No. Somewhere in North Yorkshire.

Just a little further down the lane a van is parked, and a young couple get out. They have the lean, unspoilt look of Heather. They greet the driver and wave at us. We sit in the back of the car. Our driver nods to us, so we follow him. From the back of the truck, they quickly pull out the false panels and start unloading the gear. We're told to put ithe gear on the ground near the gates.

For the first time, I look at the gates properly. Black wrought iron, graceful patterns and a large sweep, cresting upwards, where both gates meet in the middle. They're hung on large columns. Each column is topped off by a large, plaster sculpture of a *Green Man* motif with the aspect of a roaring lion. I want to take a photo of the face because he's such an unusual version, but I don't. I go back to my task: taking the equipment out of the van. Through the gates, I can see well-maintained parkland and the road disappearing out of view. I wonder what's behind that last little ridge. And who lives there.

The team works at lightning speed, and mostly in silence. Within minutes, they cut through the locks and they've scaled the gates and have angle grinders spinning away at the gate hooks, cemented into the pillars. The woman is up the left-hand ladder and the man is on the right one that I'm holding onto, so it doesn't crash into him or anyone else when he cuts through. Chow Mein is on the other one.

They finish at the same time and skip down the ladders, and we let go on three. The right-hand one judders and tilts inwards and then stops, still attached by the lower post. The left hand one falls down completely, taking the lower post with it. I'm set to work, to chop the right-hand gate into as many pieces as I can in fifteen minutes. Chow Mein does the same with the other half. We're told to take out the key pieces: the coat of arms, the main struts, the hooks and throw them in the back of the van.

Moments later, down the lane comes a small JCB driven by another guy. They ask me to come and help, grab the rope, make a loop. She's up the ladder again, the column on the right first. I'm amazed by how quickly the top part half-slides away and is half-wrenched. They're not happy because the full height of the wall on that side is still intact, so they start to nudge it with the shovel of the JCB. It's an ancient wall, mossy and covered in plaster and after five minutes of more and more aggressive nudging, the thing starts to crack. The driver is sweating with concentration. There's a feeling that we're running out of time, that we're under pressure. The driver decides it's time to take a risk and reverses the JCB fifteen yards, then gets the angle of the shovel just right and charges at the wall. It cracks at the bottom, with the sound of ripping and the plaster crumbles and about twelve feet of it breaks away to fall inwards. He reverses and finishes the job. Within moments, he's signalling he's going to do the same with the left-hand side. We're told to tidy up. Leave nothing behind. When the left-hand side is reduced to a stump, he scrapes the covering of the road, and within five minutes, he's dug a small trench in the space where the two pillars once stood and piled up the dirt on either side. The house is cut off. The gates are down.

The light is fading.

'Hurry,' says our driver and we jump into his car. 'One more.'

He drives ten minutes down the single-track road in the opposite direction to where we'd come earlier, and pulls up outside Mrs. Morrison's house.

Now, I know where and why, signed Chow Mein.

Whose was the other one? I signed back. He shrugged.

With the same efficiency, we do the same to Mrs. Morrison's

and Viscount Tristan Clones-Dyke's wrought iron front gates.

When we've removed the gates, pulled down the pillars, dug the trench, the young woman nods at us and says, sweetly, to everyone, 'We could do twenty of these a day at this rate. Imagine...' and they laugh.

They've got all the metal packed in the back. Could be worth a fortune down the scrapyard, I think. Just don't go to Ray's, he might recognise them.

The night has drawn in by the time we say goodbye to our driver in the village where we'd parked.

'Take a long, slow route going home,' he says. 'We'll meet again, I'm sure.'

We went for a coffee on the way back into town. A little Kurdish place in Headingley, full of guys on their own sat at the plastic tables, reading a Kurdish paper or flicking away at mobile phones.

I waited for our coffee, which was creamy and thick and strong and waited for our waiter to leave, and for us to have some time. We didn't sign because that would be more noticeable than speaking.

'What was that, then?'

'I dunno,' he said.

'It was a series of criminal acts, brother.'

'Yeah. Same as what they doing to us,' he said.

'That's not the point, really is it? We aren't businessmen employing psychos or Viscounts with connections. We have...' I actually couldn't speak or find the absolute level of my thoughts.

'You could've said no,' he said.

'Well, yeah. That's not really going to hold up with our friends in blue or the hordes of people whose job it is to keep us in our place? 'I wanted to say no, but I didn't, Sir, sorry, will do next time. Or, they made me do it. I didn't know what I was doing."

For some reason he laughed. He looked at me.

'Brother, do you exist? No. So, they gotta find you first. Then, they gotta prove you were there. You wore gloves. Now, put your invisible cloak on. Get real, this seems to me like, fair do's, was the next option. Some piece of shit stepping in and taking our homes, our lives being dismantled overnight, not paying a penny for the land or the houses or anything and using thugs and clubs to hurt us. This feels good. In a very limited way, it feels good, that he going to wake up tomorrow morning and find he ain't got a front door,' and he starts laughing again., 'then when he rings his friend, he can tell him his front gate's gone, too.'

And who will we ring? I sign, forgetting myself.

Rules of Looting

Hi there, we're here to help you make looting easier and more user-friendly than you imagined. We're going to show you some of the basic rules that all new serious looters need to know to 'join the club'. Enjoy making new friends Looting!

What you wear
This is the key thing. Looking good is the main weapon in any looter's armoury: suit TICK pastel silk tie TICK big hair, angular, not too presidential TICK real tan TICK

Your equipment
Business cards, Directorships, lawyer friends, nice-looking woman/man, several computers, insiders, corrupt officials, a handful of metal pens, offical headed paper, with appendices.

Your club
Londonclubs, Golfclubs, Hostess Bars, Yachtclubs, Banker's Clubs, Gangster's Nighclubs, no dodgy Boxing clubs or British Legions.

Teeing Off
We use this term to mean where you tee off with your fellow looters, on your exciting journey to asset strip productive companies, enslave workforces, rob good-hearted innocents, break up small and large companies, bribe national governments and separate sovereign nations from their wealth, savings, minerals, land & more!

Watch out for the Haters!
Customary International Law, Unions, Hague Convention of 1899 and 1907, Statute of the International Criminal Court, doo-gooders, NGO's, workers rights, blah bollux blah. Be aware of something called the FSA or FCA or FUCAL which is rumoured to have an office or something but has no known employees or ever answered the phone.

28

About the beck, the river and the weir

Bad things happen in such an inevitable way. Good things are so much more effort. Bad seems so natural and obvious that we seem to have grown blind to it. I once read an article that argued all famines in history have been caused by humans, from the beginning of our knowledge of our own existence all the way through time to the evidence of our own eyes. Hard to imagine that much cruelty, and even worse, that much continuing cruelty. Hunger, homelessness, injustice, inequality, violence, intimidation, lies, racism, prejudice. Have you ever met anyone who proposes these as principles of our society? Puts them in their election manifestos? Says them out loud and is applauded? How many times have we hung our heads, and wrung our hands, over the inevitability of it all, like watching your mother die from cancer, and not knowing what to do with the rage of the unfairness of it all? Unfairness is at the heart of rage. At the heart of the mob beats this rage, at the heart of cruelty is this rage, at the heart of the rage is the human heart, broken and lost.

By the light of a candle on the floor of Smoothie's room, I sign my thoughts to Chow Mein. He has to help me with the more abstract vocab.

The first light of day comes through the gaps in the boards.

How many times have we sat and talked like this? I ask him. *I have stared at your hands like you might stare at a favourite painting or read a favourite poem. You taught me to sign. Alwena taught me, but you taught me again.*

He laughs.

When you started, he signed, *you used to make me laugh my head off, because your hands were going ten to the dozen, bang bang bang bang, but it was just gobbledygook, but so funny, then, I started to try to make the sounds you were signing, try to jump the gap, make sense of it, 'cos it meant something to you...I love the sounds of the old language, I would like to learn it one day.*

'Thank you.'

Pause.

'I think we should tell 'em all to leave. It isn't gonna end well.'

'You're right,' he says, and stands up.

I hug him. 'There is only now.'

'There is no tomorrow.' He finishes my thought.

After an hour, we have persuaded half of them to leave.

They leave in the early light. Molly stays with Picnic, but we move her into the house with CJD and his team. Molly's friends, the Duke, Harry, Marshamalla, Chip and their dog say goodbye. Jalapeña, Kebaby and Taco stay. Raymondo, Hamburg, Tats and Doner, Giblet and Feefee leave. I promise them that this is not the end.

Uncle Kevin won't leave.

When I arrive with Molly, he won't open the door to us. He's boarded up his house so securely, not only can we not see him, we can hardly hear him.

'Please, Kevin, let's talk. Even if it's just to say goodbye,' I shout through his boarded up front door. From somewhere he's got some metal bars and fixed them across as well.

'Tara, OK? Now leave me alone. Fuck off, if tha' helps.'

'No, Kev, it doesn't. If they find you here they won't be knocking nicely and talking to you.' I'm shouting now.

'Don't give a shit. I've had enough of bein' pushed aroun'.'

'Kevin, let us in, it's Molly,' she wanted to find a gap or space to be able to make eye contact, but there was none.

'You can fuck off, as well, you mad old bag.'

'Kevin!! Please, not like this!' I shouted.

Molly burst out laughing. 'That's why we love you, you old wanker.'

'I wonder how he got back in after he boarded the place up?' I ask her. 'Let's try the back,' I said to her..

We shuffled off around the back. He'd put barbed wire along the top of his fence and cemented the back gate in place with bricks.

On the boards at the back of his house, he'd written in red paint 'This House is EMPTY.' Capitals for the last word.

I shook my head.

'The finest irony imaginable, Molly. We ain't going to get him out of here. They might struggle as well.'

We had to leave him.

They come earlier than I'd imagined. Just after dawn.

Jalapeña texts us they're coming. Just before the transits pull up, Taco, Picnic, Chow Mein and Molly ignite the smoke grenades and the whole of the entrance road to the Circle is enveloped within seconds in low, dense clouds of white smoke. The transits pull up where they did yesterday, but they're soon lost to view. Behind them, coming over the low hill is a low-loader with a large JCB on it. And four cop cars.

As soon as the cover is enough, Picnic signals that he has arrived at the outlet valve and is about to release the backed-up sewage from the last two days from the whole estate. After a minute, he emerges in yellow waterproofs out of the white cloud on our side of the smoke wall and runs back to his position.

Jalapeña says that, from her position in the most fortified

of the houses overlooking the entrance road, there seem to be fewer than a dozen of Ray's mates this time. *Getting into riot gear,* she adds. After a couple of minutes, *A bunch of coppers have just arrived and are hanging about, but not getting kitted up.* She also reports that she can hear shouting and swearing and some of the guys, half-dressed in riot gear, are hopping and skipping out of the smoke to drier ground. She can see the foul water gathering in a huge puddle just across the entrance road, where they've parked the cars. Just out of sight, they're unloading the digger. Then, they move the transits. The coppers walk off back to their cop cars a few hundred yards away. Jalapeña counts nine thugs and John and Ray. And the digger driver. Ray is furious and shouting at them that it's just a bit of shit and that's what he's paying them to do – deal with the shit.

'Three hundred quid each one of yer,' he keeps shouting.

Ignoring all the humans fussing in the foul water, the digger starts up and aims straight for the fence and pulls it down in almost an instant. Same with the cars, moved easily. John directs the men to pull it out the way, but most are in trainers that are now covered in dirty water up to their ankles and show no willingness to help. He's got boots on and steps in and three minutes later they are through the fence. The men are still reluctant to walk their way through the foul-smelling water and hold back, or pick their way gingerly, avoiding the worst of it.

As I'm watching through the binoculars, the JCB is pushing the burnt-out cars out of the way and Ray's men are gearing up and following the digger as it advances slowly up the main road. Then, from my position overlooking the Sacred Grove, I hear the sound of an engine coming down the road from my left. It's a figure on a motorbike. The bike stops in front of the house, and the person pulls off the helmet. It's Smoothie. He raises his hand in salute and signs, *I will find you* and laughs and puts the helmet back on, revs the bike and turns to spin around.

Down where the entrance road meets the Grove, he drops a couple of canisters that burst into violet life and does a turn. Out of his panniers he pulls a control box. A moment later a drone arises from behind him and flies over the trees and hovers over the violet smoke. As the first figure emerges from the smoke, Smoothie steers the drone to hover just above his head and releases something. The bright red liquid splatters all over the figure so he looks like he's covered in blood. Then, he releases another three bags that splatter all over the road. Immediately after, he throws down another couple of canisters that fill the place with smoke, and I lose sight of him, but the drone rises overhead and sails down to where the transits are parked.

Jalapeña is furiously asking what is going on and who is controlling the drone? *We didn't plan a drone, did we? Anyway, it's on our side,* she says, *it's just dropped a bag of red paint over each van. All over the windscreens.*

The JCB doesn't stop for anyone's smoke but its tracks pick up the paint off the road. The drone reappears just outside the driver's cab, and a voice bellows out from inside its systems: 'We are recording everything you do, we are recording everything you do, we are recording everything you do, we are recording everything you do, we are recording everything you do, we are recording everything you do...' Incessantly, loudly, insistently.

Smoothie is going to follow them with the camera on his drone.

I wonder where he's been hiding? signs Chow Mein.

'I hope he gets away and doesn't do anything too daring.'

'When they realise that he's controlling the drone, they'll aim for him, then he'll have to run,' he replies.

The JCB is facing the house next to us, very near where Smoothie did his grand salute. The driver grinds his gears and moves slowly forwards. Behind him, the guys in balaclavas have gathered. When he gets to within striking distance, the arm is extended, and the teeth of the bucket are raised, ready to scrape down the front wall and rip off the boarding. They have planned this well. Take out the middle of each of the rows and the others will follow. It also cuts off our ways out. I hear some text messages arrive, but I don't have time to read them.

Down the drainpipe that we have cut away, we send yellow smoke. The final signal. Out of the pipes comes the smoke, whirling in the disturbed air and covering our escape. Out of all of the houses that we occupy comes the yellow smoke. I can see gusts of it drifting across our Sacred Groves, I can see the fires that have been set rising up all around the Circle. I can see tomorrow's scene of flattened rubble and burning embers and hear the loggers and the machinery and the trucks coming, carrying away the lives we made here. I can imagine it in a single flickering book of images done in a second. The hearth that was ours will be dark tonight, without fire, without light, without roof, the rain will fall, the fire will die, the hearth that was ours will die tonight, the fire will not be lit, the blest ones all departed, alas, I wonder why death spared me.

I pick up my bags as I hear the splinters of the boarding crack and feel the building move. How weird to feel the fabric of a house move, but it does, just a shudder, then shifts back to its place. How odd to hear the drone of the digger and the quietness of humans. We know how to live without sound and move without being seen, and outside the thugs cling to the digger for safety, waiting for the rats to emerge from the broken cages.

And so, we do, as planned, all leave at once. There aren't enough of them, we reason, to run us all down. Chow Mein is ahead of me as we rush down the stairs into the kitchen and out of the back door. We just check the garden to see if there's anyone there. They must still be gathered by the JCB, which I can hear tearing into next door. I bend down to light the fire that we have laid to stop them getting through the ginnels between the houses. The flames rise and I can hear shouting from the other side.

We run, and further up, I can hear some of the other groups running for their lives as well. I get to the garages that are grouped behind the houses. I see that everyone who should be there is there. We hug one last time. We have a number each. Some have nowhere to go. Some are tearful and raging and we agree. *Save the rage. Save the energy. Stay out of sight.* I wish them well. Molly, Picnic, Peachy, Full English and the rest. I ask Picnic to check on the other groups that were on the other side of the Grove. If you go the long way round, you should be fine. Take Chow Mein. 'Please', I said. Then they are gone. All running into the woods.

Picnic says, 'Uncle Kevin?'

I cannot speak or answer that. 'Go. Travel safe. See you on the other side.'

He runs off to catch up others up.

I check my texts. Three from Jalapeña. One: *Range Rover's turned up + two men.* Two: *Who's driving this bloody drone? It's going mental.* Three: *A guy in a motorbike helmet slashing transit tyres. Who he????*

I read them in horror. Oh, God, Smoothie's doing more damage. I wish he'd told us what he was going to do, we could have worked this out. I tell her and the boys to stay tight, don't move. *It's probably Smoothie. He'll be fine.* Our messages cross in mid-air. Four: *FFS, it's Smoothie, they've got him and beating him. What shall we do?*

Nothing, I write, *DO 0.*

I'm running through the gardens, past Alwena's grave, down the gaps between houses, past the Big Yew. I can't leave him. Not with those bastards. They'll beat him up and then hand him over to the Police, and then he'll get another beating, and they'll hand him over to the Army and then...

I ring Chow Mein. No answer. I'm running as I ring.

'Jalapeña, I am on my way. Have Taco on standby. You and Kebaby need to leave now. It's all over. Most of the thugs are up with the JCB, so get going.'

'OK, she says, OK.'

'Take care, Jalopeña. Let me know you good.'

When I get to her house, I see her leave by the back door and cross the road into the trees opposite her house. Kebaby is with her. She'll be OK. Taco's waiting for me at the back door, he looks nervous. I hug him because he looks so young and scared. He's probably looked like that all his life.

'Listen, Taco, you have been a very good lad, thank you. But now you need to do exactly as I tell you. The most important thing is you don't do anything stupid. In two minutes, you'll be gone, you'll catch up Jalapeña and find somewhere safe, but now I need you to help Smoothie. Good man.' I gave him my knife. *Look after it,* I signed.

He nodded.

When we got a view of Smoothie, he was face down on the ground, and Mr. Nosey was kneeling on his back. Ray was stood above him, crushing his hands under his feet and was on the phone, facing the guys in the Circle. Probably calling in reinforcements. The Police were nowhere to be seen.

We didn't have long.

I strode out from behind the hedge, when both of them were looking away. I walked slowly and with the limp, walking stick in hand and my hood up, towards them. They both ignored me. Ray's still on his phone, Nosey still kneeling on Smoothie. As I get closer, I can see Smoothie's bike lying on the floor and I can see where he's lost control and skidded into the Transits.

I walk up to Nosey, and with a cracked voice, I say to him, 'Bloody hooligans, been like this for years. Glad you got one o' em. Gi'm a kickin' for me, will yer?' and give him a big thumbs up and a smile. I stand and gawp at him and the situation.

Nosey looks up and stares at me as if I'm not there. Smoothie squirms. Ray ignores me, still on the phone.

'Yus doin' a grand job clearin' them bloody rats out o' there, Mister.'

'Will ye fuck right off?' he says, with a strong Scottish accent.

'My hearin's not reet good, pal. Wha' yer sayin'?'

He looks up at me and shakes his head, then points with his finger indicating down the road. 'Ye – Fuck – right – off. Old codger.'

At that moment, there's a hiss from the far side of the other transit. Then, another one. Ray moves away from Nosey and Smoothie to see what's happening. He sees that one of the Transit tyres has been slashed.

'What the fuck?' he shouts. Then, he walks towards the slashed tyres and hissing air that Taco has caused.

I take my cue and lift my walking stick and whack Nosey across the side of his head. He wasn't expecting it. He has to loosen his grip on Smoothie. I jab Nosey's face as hard as I can with the end. He screams out and clutches his eye and recoils, leaving Smoothie free. Smoothie stands up and kicks Nosey in the back of the leg bring him down to the floor. Ray reappears around the near side of the vans. Behind him is Taco, still holding the knife. Ray turns around and sees he is caught between us.

'Come on, you pieces of shit,' he says and turns with his back to the van. 'Be a pleasure.'

I tell Smoothie to stand on Nosey and Taco to do a couple more of the tyres. I smile at Ray. I hear the hissing of the tyres and call Taco to me.

'Go, go, go...' He wants to stay, but I tell him to go and look after our people. 'And thank you.'

He sets off running across the fields.

'Ray,' I say, 'you shouldn't work for these people. Why you doing it? Working against your own people?'

'You ain't my people. You're fuckin' wasters, scroungers, druggies, whatever you are, you're scum. I wouldn't be seen dead with twats like you.'

Now there are only two of us, he gains confidence and walks towards me.

'Come on, you old nonce, have a fuckin' go if you want to...'

He's a big guy with a big gut. Once upon a time, he was probably terrifyingly good at street fighting, but he was breathing heavily already, and his fists were up like a pugilist.

Nosey made a noise as he tried to sit up and Smoothie kicked him back down. That was enough for Ray to be distracted and he turned to my left and looked to see what was happening, and in that split second, I stepped forward, bent my knees so I was half my size and swept his left leg away from under him with my stick, and he was down. As he turned on all fours, I jabbed him in the ribs twice to wind him, and he clutched his side. Then, I hooked his right arm with my stick and forced it behind his back and then knelt on him with my full force, so his face hit the tarmac.

'My quarrel is not with you, Ray. But you shouldn't be doing the bidding of people who're just using you. Think about it, Ray. Work out who the enemy are, just like everyone else, you have to choose sides.'

'Fuck off,' he said, through a mouth that appeared to be bleeding.

I reached into his pocket and pulled out his phone. 'In one minute, I'm going to be gone, with my friend here. But it's not over for you just yet, because by the end of today, we will have started to destroy your house. OK?'

I looked around at Smoothie. 'Is your bike working?' I said.

Smoothie stood up above Nosey and peered around the front of the Transits. Then he shouted to me, loudly, 'B-man, they're coming, the fuckers are coming back. There's two of them coming down the hill.'

'Go, Smoothie, just go, go – leave the bike – go. I'll be OK. Please, go...'

And he ran off in the same direction as Taco. When I saw him disappear down the slope out of view, I turned back to Ray. 'I'm taking your phone, Ray, I want to speak to your friends.'

In an instant, I removed my stick from in his arm and ran back in the direction I'd come. No one knows the Circle like me.

By the time the two guys have worked out what was happening and found Ray and Nosey, and Ray had barked out some orders, I had gone into the snicket next to Jalapeña's house and worked my way as quietly as I could back to where I'd left my big bag of stories in that canvas rucksack I'd grown so fond of. I could hear the digger working its way through the houses and then it stopped. I heard voices and shouting and commands roared out. I needed to think, but didn't have time.

I decide to run down the garden and take a right upwards and along the little lane where the garages where. I guessed that Ray would have sent two of them after me, into the same gap between the houses he had seen me dive into. If it were me, I would send two of them to cut me off, in a diagonal heading for the top left-hand corner of the Circle, then, I'd send two to the top of the Circle to watch if I emerged there, and then another two to the middle, around the Sacred Grove. That is what I would have done if I had been Ray. Ray wasn't stupid. But he was very angry.

I thought I would put as much distance between me and the immediate pursuers as possible and ran up the hill with the bag swinging on my back. I was already beginning to sweat. I stopped when I heard a strange sound in the air above the

Sacred Grove and immediately shrank into a hedge at the end of a garden. I waited for it to pass, but it didn't pass, it got nearer and nearer and was hovering over one of the houses just near where I was lying. It was the drone, hovering. Smoothie's drone, that they had obviously made work, the one that had a camera attached. If it moved, it meant they hadn't seen me. It hovers, then went slowly down one side of the row, and I breathed a sigh of relief, then it turned back up the row and seemed to dangle in the air over all of the gardens then turned to look into the woods behind the garages. I stop breathing, don't move an eyelid, just wait, terrified, while I sense it drop a few metres to get a closer look. If they see me here...then, it rises very slowly and moves up, swinging back and forth over each garden. I count to twenty. I can't hear any voices or any steps, and the drone is drifting away up the row and crossing over the houses to search the other side.

I stand up slowly, look around. The lane is quiet, upwards and downwards. I make a dash. I can't risk the Circle, not with the drone watching every open space, so I run at the fence between the garages and the woods and I try to pole vault without a pole. The bag swings over but I'm caught, not having made quite enough height and I can't move. For several awful seconds, I'm hanging halfway over the fence, the bag is on my back but is on the far side while most of me is still hanging on the inside of the fence.

From down the lane, I hear voices and look across at two of the thugs in riot gear and carrying shillelaghs, flinging themselves up the lane towards me. I desperately try to free myself and roll backwards over the fence and land in a big heap on the other side. Just at that moment, one of them makes a lunge for me through the fence but he can't get his hand through it. The other one is shouting for help. I pull my stick out of its case inside my coat and thwack his hand and jab him in the chest to wind him but he just manages to deflect it with is hand and makes a lunge after the stick, but I twist it so violently he has to let go. I can see he's already sweating and breathing heavily.

I turn and rush down the steep side of the woods and skid, fall and tumble down the steep, pathless undergrowth getting scratched and bruised, until I hit the little ravine with the dirty stream in it, and climb up the opposite side. Below me is a main road, which I cannot go to, but on the other side of the woods is a private housing estate. I aim for that.

Behind me, I can still hear one of them shouting to the other to send more of them after me. He's over the fence and running down the woods towards me. I zig-zag up the slope, knowing exactly which point of entrance I am going to use to get into the estate. If they're clever, they might send a car round, but then I realise, they might not have any cars or transport, so I pray I can get across and reach it, with just this one following me.

I stop, have to catch my breath. I can hear the guy following me shouting out to the others where I am, but I can't hear anyone answering him. I squat down out of sight. Above me, I can hear the drone. It won't be able to see me when I'm in the wood, but there's an open field that is sometime filled with cows, between the edge of the woods and the gardens with the drystone walls. I listen, and raise myself slowly to see where he is, but I can't see him because of the trees and the undergrowth, so I set off again, as quickly as I can and reach the fence at the edge of the wood. I throw the bag over the fence and fall over it myself.

I can't hear the drone now, so I make a dash for it through the field. The cows are way over in the far corner, and I run as fast as I can on the uneven grass. When I reach the drystone wall, I check that there is no one in the garden and I'm over in a second but dislodge a stone that slides off and sets off next door's dog. I go down the passage and over the wooden gate and land next to a very surprised woman lopping the Russian vine with a very long pair of shears. I apologise profusely. She holds the garden tool across her like a weapon. I tell her I'm just passing through. Down her drive to a neat little road and I turn right to the cul-de-sac at the end. The drone has found me again. This time I have nowhere to hide if I want to keep going.

I go down the snicket at the side of the last house in the road and into their back garden, which is terraced upwards. I leap up all of the terraces and have to fight through a wall of box hedge, the drone just ten metres above. I keep going across the open ground behind the gardens and in the distance below I can see the safety of Leeds, the familiar skyscape, Bridgewater Place, Sky Plaza and the distinctive red, round tower of Candle House.

I'm sure that if I can get over this strange bit of ancient heath just above the Otley Road, I can lose the drone. The guy following me seems to have given up, and I take a breather in the shadow of an old stone ruin that was once a shepherd's shelter. I can hear the drone still following me, but now I don't care. I have the advantage of being able to see for a few hundred metres here clearly in every direction. No one near.

I breathe deeply, curse this bag on my back, but can't let it go yet. I think about Smoothie, Taco, Jalapeña, Picnic and Chow Mein and hope they are ok. I can't think about what's happened.

What would I do if I were Ray? Will he guess where I'm aiming for? What is he going to do about it? Has he passed my description to Brian, the DCI? Do I have to beware of them all? I have always been wary of them all.

I stand up and pull my hood over my face. The less they know the better and I begin the run across and down this open heath as fast as I can. I leap a spiked fence, cross the road and over another stone wall past a boarded-up farmhouse and then out onto some grassland. I can run now at a steady pace, this is easy, leading gently downhill and into the woods.

Meanwood Beck. Safe, for a while.

There are people now, walking their dogs and pushing prams, not many, but enough to stare at me, running, sweating, carrying a big rucksack, swaying from side to side. I look like I'm being pursued. I don't have a choice. Some of them even seem to be looking up at the drone that's flitting up and around, and then at me, trying to work out if there is a connection. I keep my hood up, move as fast as I can. After ten minutes I hit the section that follows the road that's hidden below. It's cobbled and easy.

I pull up again to take a ten second breather. I can't believe it, but the sun has come out and it's starting to get warm. I start running again, knowing I've got to hit those tunnels as soon as possible. A minute later, I can see them just ahead. It's going to be dark in there and I don't have a torch. I've got Ray's phone, if I can make the light work. Two hundred yards further back, the drone has stopped in mid-air, like it's being guided to land on the road above the beck. Seconds later, a couple of faces peer down over the parapet. Ray's and John's. *Shit, how did they get here?* I switch Ray's phone on and jump into the water. No lights, just tunnels. I don't wait to see if I'm being followed.

It's cold and the bed of the river is a concrete culvert but stony, limiting the pace, not wanting to trip or turn my ankle. I start to wonder how well they know Leeds. Ahead of me is the end of the culvert, and I take no chances but run at full pelt and leap onto the walkway accompanying the beck. In my mind, there is no road that follows the beck into town, but they might have worked out where it ends. I can't stop to think about that now, just have to keep going.

I run as fast as I've ever run, along the narrow parapet above the water, which is walled in on both sides by huge stone walls, now bathed in sunlight. I'm desperate for the protection of cover and run round the long bend till I see the next covered section. Jumping down from the parapet about five feet and am lucky that I don't crack my ankle, and head straight into the tunnel, conscious now that I'm starting to panic, running on instinct and adrenaline. This section is roofed by very low timbers and it's quicker to stay in the narrow water channel rather than risk knocking myself unconscious on a beam, so I splash and wade through the thigh-high water, carried along by the beck itself.

When I reach the beach at Cross Stamford Street, I can feel the anxiety and panic rise. It's not long now. In a mile or so I'm at the river. Ten more minutes of this. Being a kid and playing with my mates on this place with a bit of dirty sand was the closest we got to a beach, and the memories of the characters rise up in a distracting way. I can picture the path ahead and the course of the beck and how it felt when I was ten years old. Huge three or four-storey redbrick buildings rise up on each side, towering over me in my young imagination and now they seem just as large, not diminished in size at all, as they follow the soft curves of the watercourse, intimately.

After minutes of running, the parapet leads under a very low bridge, and I have to jump into the water again where the water widens out and it's deeper and I'm in a culvert again that's full of builder's rubbish and piles of refuse swirling about in the flow. I'm wading now, pushing through the brown, scummy water where the path at the side has crumbled away, to Skinner Lane where the beck is channelled into a series of S-shapes and intersected with bridges and joined by other streams, and where the noise of the traffic from above is louder and more insistent.

I'm nearly there, nearly there, I tell myself, exhausted, wet and terrified thinking about what's coming. If Ray has a brain he'll know where I'm going. If he's going to be anywhere, he could be waiting somewhere in the next quarter of a mile.

Mabgate. And under the A64. Huge girders holding up the traffic above. Thunderous noise and the sound of water amplified by the strange, underground architecture housing this little stream that brought down its silt all the way along its journey from Otley Chevin to deposit it in the River Aire, busy, strong-willed river that it was. Meanwood Beck deposited so much silt in the River Aire that it made a fording place and Leeds was born. And now, just me and the crayfish are lodged in the silt, for very different reasons.

I take one last breather in the dark. Plan out the options. Then, I'm off, jumping the culvert at Hope Place, back into the water and bending down under the red brickwork arch into the darkness that swallows me. I stop for a moment, think I hear splashing behind me, straining to hear any sound coming from the darkness behind or ahead. Maybe, maybe...maybe a man fumbling in the dark.

This is the longest part in complete darkness. It's wide, but the arch comes right down to the floor, so I have to walk on the edge of the water as it flows along its cobble bed. I'm still amazed at what our forefathers could do and would do, to make our cities livable. The darkness and the silence are overwhelming. For a moment I freeze, not because I hear a noise, but because I hear and see nothing. All of a sudden, I bang my head against a much lower span and feel the bruise rise in seconds. I have to be very careful.

I rub my head and then almost slip over the edge because the water has been channelled into a course some four or five feet below the parapet. I try to remember if I ever came down here as a kid. Surely, I did, but I can't find it in my memory.

Here, in this darkness, inches from the edge of a deep drop, in the terrifying darkness, I can't run, I can barely go at walking pace. I shuffle, almost feeling for the edge with the toe of my shoes, inch-by-inch. I find Ray's phone again, I might not get out of here without some light. In the dark, I can't find the right button for the torch. I keep walking, shuffling, feeling my way. I can't stop. That would be the worse thing to do.

Out of nowhere, comes the sound of voices, and I freeze. Where are they coming from? I stop and look around. Ahead slightly and upwards, there's a vertical airshaft going twenty feet or more up to a cover at street level. I breathe out, relieved. I'm almost there. *Keep going,* I tell myself, *keep walking.*

The path starts to descend without warning. It's like a slope. I keep going, feel the wetness around my feet, then sloshing into the freezing cold water, waist high, pushing against the water. Where's the light at the end of the tunnel? Trying to keep my breathing deep, planning the next move, but walking, pushing through the foul water.

I keep going. It's so much longer than I thought, I'm thinking that I've made a mistake. Round one last corner, I smell fresh air, see the light, run towards the opening. The river. Never has it looked so beautiful to me. The *Yr*, the *Isara*, the Aire of *Loidis*. The beautiful river. I go left. Up on the bank by the new flats, I can see The Armouries across the river. The city is bathed in a dry light. I'm almost blinded, breathing like a drowning man.

Up to the new footbridge. This is pedestrian land, Ray can't get to me here, only on foot. I cross the river. Loads of couples and shoppers and people enjoying the weather, time off for a coffee or a beer. They stop and stare at me, soaked to my waist and still splashing water off my clothes and shoes. I keep my head down. Take a right off the bridge, follow the south bank of the river. I don't look up at any cameras or people.

Under the red and cream ironwork of Crown Point Bridge. Follow the narrow path along the river and between the chic new developments. People moving out of the way of the madman smelling of rank water, shuffling along like a water-bagman on speed. Back across the river to The Calls, take a left. Traffic. People. Cars. Ray and his men. I can't see them. I run all the way down the road, cross the lights and dodge between cars. Hear people tooting and shouting, maybe at me, maybe not. Bear right. Can see it above me. Nearly there. Nearly there.

One last massive effort to bounce up the stairs. Across the taxi rank. The concourse. I'm there. The railway station. Get a train, anywhere. Safe, for a while. I haven't got a ticket. I haven't got any money.

I go to the toilets, go to a cubicle. Sit down. If I were Ray, I would be watching this place. The longer I stay here the more time he'll have to figure that out. I wash my face. Take out his phone. Consider what to do with it. Sell it. It's an iPhone. No one is going to buy anything from me. I can't cause a scene or do anything to attract attention. I could get a taxi. I'm going to blag a taxi and then do a runner.

I go outside. Walk towards the taxi rank. Hood up. I'm almost at the doors of the concourse when I see John with one of the thugs. They don't see me. I glide behind a pillar. Two British Transport Police walk past, chatting about something and nothing. They don't see me, I'm invisible. I look round the corner to see where John and his mate are. They're still there at the door, checking everyone coming in. I move away and drift towards the far entrance. Just as I get there, I see Ray on his own, on another phone. He sees me almost before I see him.

Shit, shit shit. FUCK.

I turn, run, knock people. The bag is swinging wildly, I pull the shoulder straps tightly to me. I'm blindly heading away from him, anywhere. I take a right into the concourse, coming to the ticket barriers, I join a big surge and flash Ray's phone at the guard, who doesn't give a shit. I'm on the platforms. Ray is thirty yards away. He's going to leap the barriers, but two guards warn him. He's talking to them.

I don't wait. I run off. Down to the furthest platform. I go through a door that is signed ***DO NOT ENTER.*** I'm in a long corridor. There are some iron stairs immediately on the left. I almost slide down them, don't touch the floor. At the bottom, I burst through a door into a familiar place. The Dark Arches. A place of ill-repute that sits like the meat in a sandwich of railway station on top and the weir of the River Aire below. The strange product of Victorian building madness.

Which way now? On my right is the exit to the main road a few hundred yards away. I take the other option. I run. The redbrick arches are huge and cavernous on each side, some bricked up and some are intricate car parks that keep going into the earth, in never-ending burrows, and some house the echoing waters of the river, angry and deep and fast-flowing in long straight sweeps of white water hurtling past.

I stop dead. Ahead of me, there's two figures crashing through the new glass doors taking people up to the station platforms above. It's John. I turn around and behind me, Ray. And behind him, one of his mates. Ray's two hundred yards away. His voice echoes down the nave of this monstrous dark palace.

'He's fuckin' mine. Don't fuckin' let him past.'

Ray starts jogging, I can hear him shouting things, but I can't make out the words. John and the other one block my way out.

He's getting nearer and shouting to make sure I get every word. 'I'm gonna fuckin' pull your eyes out, you piece of shit, for what you did to Jim.'

Ray's not jogging, he's enjoying the build-up. He swaggers down the concourse, all our sounds disfigured in the roaring Aire, as loud as Reichenbach.

The thought makes me laugh. Ray stops walking, watching the sodden figure in front of him laugh out loud.

I walk a few more paces towards John. John can't move because he has to let Ray be the one to bring me down.

The lights suddenly strike me as ridiculous. The purple, violet, pink and lemon all shifting in such an unpredictable way, like something from a 70s disco at the entrance to hell.

I turn to face, Ray. I want to see his face.

'You still think I'm working for the wrong people, fuckface?'

'Wait,' I say, with my hand up to him.

He stops, instinctively.

'Ray, I still have your phone, remember.'

I take three steps backwards, without looking, and feel the metal parapet against my back. Ray moves towards me, knowing he's going to grab me. But I spin over the rusty metal fence, without looking. When I land, I'm on a parapet about six feet below him, and about eight or ten feet above the river.

He looks down at me, surprised to see me still standing, still looking at him. John's head appears next to Ray's.

Five or six yards behind me, on the walkway above the river is a large metal gate, locked and adorned with barbed wire, to stop people walking further up the river. I've always wondered why it was there. It looks so symbolic, as if it is guarding something important. I stand with my back against it.

'Ray, come on, come down to my world... Come down here... Come on, jump down. I've always wondered why that gate was there. Always wondered why these arches were here... Come on, Ray, I'll show you...And your phone, Ray, I've got your phone,' and it gleams in my hand, in the phosphorescence of the violet light.

I dial Heather's number. 'Hi, Heather, it's me. Ray Forrester's house. Do to him what he's done to us. Ray, I can't stop them now. You're like me now, homeless...' and start laughing.

He stares down at me. Then, he does what I knew he'd do and climbs over the fence above me.

John is holding him back.

'Don't do it, Ray, he's just winding you up, don't fuckin' do it...'

Too late. Ray jumps down. Before his feet touch the ground, I run full tilt at him and launch us both into the dreadful cauldron of swirling waters and seething dirty foam.

Epilogue

Exactly three days after Burgerman recorded a sound file on her phone, Heather sits down in a quiet corner of her room to listen to the message. It's late afternoon, and the memory of saying goodbye to everyone at the Circle still sits with her, uncomfortably. She has tried to call him several times a day in the last three days, but no response. *This number is not available.*

The rain was drifting in big gusts and he'd stood looking at her, as mad as Van Gogh in the rain, she remembered.

She pressed play. 'Heather, if you don't hear from me within three days then I want you to relay this message in its entirety to –' and she stopped it at the point he 'd stopped it and wondered why he didn't want to hear any more. She thought she might need to make a note of something important and picked up a pencil and paper.

His voice had sent that strange shiver through her again and she found herself shaking and disturbed. For days now, faces and images and scenes that she couldn't believe she would ever have imagined had been coming to her in endlessly reconnecting sequences that had made her shout out, reach for something solid around her, made whoever was around her stare, and ask her if she was all right. People drowning, being beaten, staring up in grim death agonies, voices in strange languages, colours she'd never noticed and shadows surrounding everything, horrors waiting close by that in her visions were making her gasp and scream without sound. When she heard his voice again, she could recall the scene that really had happened. It brought her back to safety. The fear disappeared and she could breathe again, stop the choking sensation.

I'm haunted, she said to herself, oh, God, how can this be? It's not possible, is it? To become the things you hear? She breathed deeply. It will pass. It will pass.

She pressed play. The real Heather pressed play, pencil and paper in hand. The efficient Heather who made things happen. She listened to his words as if she were listening to the news on the radio and made notes. She would do as he had asked. At the end, were some instructions how to reach Rowena. She was just the messenger. She breathed deeply. She pressed play again and listened for anything she might have missed. There was a bit she'd missed where he'd said she was wonderful and a big kiss and a thank you. She considered not passing the message on. She considered doing what he had asked herself. She felt that disturbed feeling again. The disappointment.

Finding Rowena was not that difficult. She'd tried to imagine her and found it more and more difficult to picture a woman who would deserve those words, as she walked through the market lanes. She'd had to ask someone where Rowena's shop was, because the shop she was standing outside of was closed.

'Press the bell, luv,' said a man carrying a box of fruit.

So, she did. There was no bell noise, so she pressed again. The door opened a little and a face appeared in the crack.

'Hello,' said Heather, and smiled.

The face nodded.

'Can I come in?'

The face turned, quizzically.

'Can I come in? I need to speak to you.' Heather was mesmerised by the pale face and the blood falling from the corner of her mouth. The face said no, the voice said nothing.

Heather carried on. 'It's really important, please.'

The woman pointed at the sign. *Back in half an hour*, and smiled. Heather hadn't noticed it.

'OK, are you Rowena?'

Of course, you're her, thought Heather, you're extraordinary.

Then, Rowena spoke her name, 'Rowena' and nodded.

'Oh, ok, sorry, you're deaf, aren't you? Oh, sorry, sorry, that sounds so bad, Rowena, I am so sorry. He didn't tell me, sorry. He should have told me.' Heather blushed.

Rowena shook her head. *Slow down, too fast*, she signed.

Heather got that. *Heather, you dimwit*, she said to herself.

She mouthed slowly and felt patronising. 'I have a message for you,' doing simplistic signing as she went. Then, pointed at her phone, 'Message from Burgerman for you. Very important.'

Rowena looked at her again, quizzically, and said 'Burgerman?' in that deep, resonant way that muted the consonants.

Heather felt Rowena's eyes speaking and let her eyes speak back. Made herself relax. Rowena opened the door and signed for her to come in.

Inside, Heathers eyes widened even more. Costumes, furs, feathers, shoes, lipsticks, wigs, boots, make-up, jewellery, knick-knacks, corsets. Everything in piles and stacks and groups. Mirrors and cameras on tripods. Clothes, every shade of red, purple and black on hangers, in piles and strewn after use.

Heather smiled, 'Oh, I see, you model this stuff as well?'

Rowena nodded. And sent Heather's eyes to the clock.

'Sorry, sorry. Ok, I have a message from Burgerman, he wanted me to deliver it to you, personally. He didn't tell me that you were deaf, so sorry. Sorry...for saying sorry.'

Rowena let her talk and stared at her lips intently.

Heather stared at hers, even though they didn't move. Rowena was the most striking woman she had ever seen in the flesh and had a presence that was not of this world, that made her wonder and smile. She felt something change in her as she felt the presence. It all made sense to her and she didn't know how she could have doubted it. Burgerman was right, Rowena was the perfect person to stop the destruction of the Circle.

But first, Rowena was on a deadline and had to take these photos of the jewellery and the outfits and upload them.

Heather rang the bell that flashed at 5 o'clock, as agreed.

Rowena opened the door to a transformed space. No clutter, no mess, no blood dripping from the mouth.

In the intervening couple of hours, Heather had realised she now had more questions than before. Where was Burgerman? Why wasn't he answering his phone? None of the people from the Circle had been in touch with her in the last three days. Why not? Were Burgerman and Rowena lovers? How did he communicate with her? Who was Burgerman really? What was his real name? How on earth could Rowena do what he was asking her to do? And how could *she* communicate what he was asking Rowena to do? What if Rowena said no? Heather felt lost again. She thought of how often he had suggested the sea as her real home. She felt so foreign.

She'd thought about finding someone who could sign and paying them to translate for them, but then thought that she should try first and if she failed, then the translator would be a last resort. So, she'd prepared some pictures and some words to show to Rowena. She wished so much that Rowena could hear his words. They were so full of love. She'd decided to tell her the main parts of it now, then write down the rest, later. Afterwards.

They sat down behind her sales counter.

'Stop me if you don't understand,' she mouthed.

Rowena nodded.

'This is the gist of what he's saying.'

'Gist?' mouthed Rowena.

'The most important things.'

OK.

'This is a message from Burgerman.'

Burgerman? Who's Burgerman? wrote Rowena.

Jesus Christ, she doesn't know who I'm talking about. What does he call himself to her? Everything that man did is so hidden and difficult. Heather wanted to scream with frustration.

She drew a picture of him, as best she could. Then, she drew a harp next to him. He had told her, but she'd ignored it.

She nodded and said out loud, 'Haaarp' and giggled.

Rowena turned her face to the right and held her earring in her two middle fingers, as if to show it off.

It was a small figurine, without a face, holding a large amber bead. It was so strange. It wasn't anything Heather would have ever noticed in a shop or ever thought a woman like Rowena would ever wear. Rowena pointed to the words on the paper. And the man with the harp.

'Oh, a gift from him,' she mouthed, 'beautiful.'

Rowena instinctively signed in response, but it was too difficult for Heather to decipher. After more misunderstandings, Heather moved her back to the message.

'Remember the coffin in the Circle?' and she showed her the picture she'd drawn of a coffin with a body of a woman lying in it. It was like a child would draw, because Heather was no artist.

Rowena nodded and took the pencil out of Heather's hand. *Many coffins,* she wrote. Heather stared at the words on the page. Rowena had written something else:

My coffin. And giggled.

Oh, God, thought Heather. *What the hell is this?*

Rowena pointed at the sign and then at herself, and spoke the letters out loud, beginning at the bottom and going upwards, 'A - l - w - e - n - a,' and smiled.

She thinks she is Alwena. He thinks he is Ceadd.

Heather is not expecting this. She can't think. She is looking at this strange woman sitting next to her and all the things she has heard Burgerman, or whoever he is, say, and the icy shiver and the fluttering, churning feeling roll through her in that reel of sound and images that won't leave her alone.

She wrote the next words down, and they look so out of place, so wrong, so unspeakably dull:

COUNCIL.

'He wants you to go to the Council and tell them everything about the Circle being a valuable burial site. You can name the people in the graves. That is unique.'

She looks quizzical again. *Me*?

NEWSPAPER.

'He wants you to go to the papers and tell them what you know. They will love you.'

POLICE.

'There is criminal damage of Alwena's grave. You can stop them, Alwena. If you don't do this now, they will destroy everything.'